'A constantly engaging and witty novel from a tremendously clever writer' *Telegraph*

'This perfectly constructed drama explores the moralities around unconditional love and self-preservation. And it also weaves an intricate story of redemption starting in the trenches at Passchendaele and continuing till Britain's current terror threat . . . storytelling at its best' *News of the World*

'Farndale's evocation of trench warfare surpasses Sebastian Faulks's *Birdsong* . . . Exquisite and luminous . . . gives a master class in the power of literature to illuminate the physical world and the human soul' *Australian*

'Love, cowardice and redemption are the themes that stalk Farndale's beautifully intelligent tale' *Daily Mirror*

'Profound, moving and compelling' Emily Maitlis

'Philosophically ambitious and deftly crafted, Nigel Farndale's novel has one leg planted in the trenches of the First World War and the other placed sure-footedly in the present . . . beautiful' *Country Life*

THE ROAD BETWEEN US

NIGEL FARNDALE

BLACK SWAN

TRANSWORLD PUBLISHERS
61–63 Uxbridge Road, London W5 5SA
A Random House Group Company
www.transworldbooks.co.uk

THE ROAD BETWEEN US
A BLACK SWAN BOOK: 9780552776981

First published in Great Britain
in 2013 by Doubleday
an imprint of Transworld Publishers
Black Swan edition published 2014

Addresses for Random House Group Ltd companies outside the UK
can be found at: www.randomhouse.co.uk
The Random House Group Ltd Reg. No. 954009

The Random House Group Limited supports the Forest Stewardship
Council® (FSC®), the leading international forest-certification organisation.
Our books carrying the FSC label are printed on FSC®-certified paper.
FSC is the only forest-certification scheme supported by the leading
environmental organisations, including Greenpeace. Our paper procurement
policy can be found at www.randomhouse.co.uk/environment

Typeset in 11/14.25pt Giovanni Book by Falcon Oast Graphic Art Ltd.
Printed and bound by CPI Group (UK) Ltd, Croydon, CR0 4YY.

2 4 6 8 10 9 7 5 3 1

To Alfie, Sam and Joe

'The heart wants what it wants, or else it does not care.'
Emily Dickinson

PART ONE

I

FROM HIS ELEVATED VIEWPOINT, A HOTEL WINDOW THAT also serves as a balcony door, Charles Northcote cannot see the foot on which Eros is balanced. It is obscured by the statue's outstretched wings, the feathers of which appear to be moving. The illusion may be caused by a haze of heat, or the shifting golds, reds and pinks of the surrounding neon billboards. Either way, it makes the god of love look as if he is afloat, shimmering, about his business in the night air.

With the same flickering lights reflecting their colours up on to his own hands and face – Bisto, Brylcreem, Ty-phoo tea – Charles wonders what his silhouette looks like to the eyes studying him from the bed. As his bare shoulder is resting against the top of the window frame on one side, and his feet are crossed at the bottom on the other, he must form a clean diagonal. A Nazi salute, perhaps. Thinking this inappropriate, given their situation, he stands upright and girds himself for the conversation he must have, the one he has been trying to avoid.

'Like Piccadilly Circus down there,' he says.

The man on the bed yawns. The muscled contours of his pale body are barely covered by a tangle of sheets. His name is Anselm and he is twenty years old and six foot three inches tall, two years younger and three inches taller than Charles. His sandy hair is parted to the right, floppily shading his eye. As he flicks it back he says: 'Did you bring me here just so that you could use that joke?'

'No,' Charles says. 'I . . .'

'I what?'

The hum of the traffic below dims as Charles closes the balcony door, and the discrete smells of the room become more noticeable: carbolic soap clouding a basin of water; human hair damp with sweat; whiskey fumes and cheap red wine. He brushes imaginary dust off the shoulder of his blue-grey RAF tunic, which is hanging over the back of a chair, a single row of braid visible above the cuff. Draped neatly over this is a pair of silk briefs. They are maroon.

'They're going to pack Eros off to the countryside, I hear,' Charles continues. 'When the war starts.'

'There's a war about to start? No one tells me anything.'

Charles stares at the crumpled jacket on the floor. Double-breasted. Frayed cuffs. The trousers that go with it are lying by the bed. They have a shiny seat. Between the jacket and trousers there is a trail of discarded civilian clothes: a still-knotted college tie, a single sock, a shirt half buttoned up and inside out, a snag of braces and a starched collar sprung wide, like the mouth of a man-trap.

His eyes are now on the sketchbook propped against the bed. It is open at a charcoal life drawing, a male torso without arms or head, foreshortened, viewed from below. Alongside this, as if arranged on a gallery wall, is a second drawing, this one pinned to a corkboard. Again, the model is naked, but the style is different, looser, almost abstract.

Charles crosses the room, picks them up and holds them at arm's length, one in each hand, before sliding them under the bed. He is kneeling now, as if in childish prayer. 'Anselm . . .'

'Yes?'

Their faces are close. Though Charles's hair is dark brown and cropped short at the back and sides, they could be brothers. Both have the lean bodies of athletes. Their mouths are sulky and full. And their jaws could have been carved from the same block of marble.

When Anselm turns away, Charles turns as well and rests the back of his head on the mattress so that he can stare at the ghosts of cigarette smoke above him. 'Will they let you finish your degree?' he says in a voice he had hoped would come out warm and nonchalant, but which makes him sound as stiff as an announcer on the Empire Service.

Anselm drags on his cigarette before answering, making the tobacco crackle into the silence. 'How would that work exactly? Do you suppose they say, "Here are your call-up papers. Report for duty immediately, or in a year's time, if that is more convenient"?' There is more than a trace of German in his sarcasm.

Dancing languidly on the cracked ceiling are colours

from the electric hoardings outside. No one is sure when, but it is expected they will be turned off soon, until further notice. When the blackout comes into force. When the billboards finally declare war on behalf of an ungrateful nation.

'You could just stay,' Charles says.

'And spend the war in an internment camp on the Isle of Man? No thank you.' He pronounces the 'th' of 'thank' as a 'z'.

Charles, for reasons he cannot explain, finds this pronunciation erotic. He stands, crosses the room to the sink and pulls the plug. As the soap-clouded water gurgles away, he wets a flannel under the cold tap. The night air is close and sticky, as if the heat stored in the tarmacadam roads outside is creeping up through the foundations of the building, melting it from the inside out. Had he been hoping that by closing the balcony door he would make the room feel cooler? It has had the opposite effect. He drapes the cold flannel across the back of his neck and cups his hands under the still-running tap. He splashes his face, takes several gulps of water and squeezes the material so that cold water trickles down his back.

Should they have the conversation now?

More Dutch courage is needed. Well, Irish. Single grain is his preference, with an equal measure of room-temperature water. He pours, takes a slug and swirls the amber liquid around in the tumbler. For a dead man, he reflects, he drinks an impressive amount. Some might say too much . . . But what the hell. *Prost!* He empties the glass and lets the alcohol burn for a moment on the back of his tongue before swallowing. Now?

Charles tilts his head back. As well as smoke there is condensation on the ceiling. On the mirror, too. He wipes it, stares at his reflection for a moment then returns to his position by the unmade bed. 'Come and work for us,' he says, holding the flannel to his forehead. 'My father was a diplomat. I know some people in the Foreign Office.'

'You're assuming I'm on your side,' Anselm says.

'You're no Nazi.'

'I'm a German. I believe in holy Germany. I believe in the *Volk*, in their *Weltanschauung*.'

'You like the uniforms, that's not the same thing.'

Anselm flicks Charles's ear. 'Someone is jealous.'

'Well, it's true, isn't it?'

'There is more to the Wehrmacht than fine tailoring.' A grin. 'There's also the choreography. Haven't you seen *Triumph of the Will*?' Anselm places four fingers vertically across his mouth.

The Englishman is laughing now. Two aesthetes together. Knowing. Ironic. When his laughter subsides he stubs out his cigarette, turns once more and, with a thumb, traces the arc of his friend's mouth as he wipes away some tiny beads of sweat.

'This heat,' Charles says.

'I know. Can you open again the window? It's like all the fucking air has been sucked out of the room.'

Again Charles hears eroticism in the pronunciation – *fakink* – something to do with the way Anselm curls his tongue around the hard consonant in the middle, the

17

way he comes to a stop at the end, blocking the vocal tract but continuing the airflow through his nose. His own tongue runs over his lower lip. He can still taste Anselm's heavy, ruttish cologne on it.

Don't go, he thinks.

As his thumb follows the line of that Teutonic chin and the tendons on that strong Teutonic neck, the words are repeated in his head.

Don't go.

Instead of opening the window, Charles continues his journey over the barrel of Anselm's ribs, over the ridged iron of his belly. It is as if he is measuring his friend for a coffin.

'Don't go,' he says, almost as a breath.

'Can't stay.'

Charles swings himself around fully now, so that he is sitting on the side of the bed, his feet on the floor. He stands, returns to the window and looks down at the lights and the circling traffic. 'They're going to find a safe place for him, somewhere in the Welsh countryside. That's what I've heard anyway.'

'Who?'

'Eros.' He turns his head towards the bed, his feet remaining where they are. 'Such a depressing thought.'

'What is?'

'Eros leaving. London losing its libido. A sexless capital.'

'Don't be so fucking dramatic, Charles.'

'We can go back to the Chelsea Arts Club soon. I just don't think we should push our luck there.'

'We are artists. They are artists. They understand.'

18

'That's as maybe, but there are limits to their tolerance.' Charles turns his back to his friend again. It is easier this way. 'In the new Germany they have already reached their limit.'

'What do you mean?'

'They don't understand our sort.'

Anselm stiffens. 'Says who?'

'We are not welcome there.'

'Speak for yourself.'

'Anselm. Don't be naïve.'

'I'll be careful. They need never know. And when the war is over I will come back here, get on the first bus to Gower Street, march into the Slade and ask if I can finish my degree. That is a promise. I will then wait for you in the Student Union bar.'

The rush of tenderness Charles feels at this moment makes him want to hold Anselm with such force that the two of them melt into one. But he remains standing by the window, still looking down, addressing his words to the road below. 'As you did that first time.'

'On Good Friday.' The German must be feeling the same because he rises from the bed, crosses the room and rests a hand on Charles's shoulder. 'And we will meet there again on Good Friday next year, once the war is over. We will have oysters and champagne. Until then we can keep in touch via the Swedish Embassy in Berlin.' With a fingertip he reads the vertebrae down Charles's back. 'You're not the only one who knows people in the diplomatic service, Grumpy.'

Charles shivers and smiles. Feels for his friend's hand. 'Or we could meet halfway. In Paris.' He is drunk now, intoxicated by the sinking, delicious helplessness of one who yearns to possess. 'Don't go, Dopey. Please.'

'It won't be for ever.'

'There is an alternative. We can go away together. Start a new life in Ireland.'

'I don't understand.'

'We could leave this week. Take the ferry from Fishguard.'

Anselm considers this before answering. 'You will be asking for a posting there?'

'No.' Charles exhales slowly, guiltily. Once the words have left him there will be no taking them back. 'Ireland is going to stay neutral. The south, I mean. We can start a new life there. New identities. I have some money.'

'You will become a deserter?'

It is time for his announcement, yet still he hesitates. 'No, I . . .' Now, Charles. Say it now. 'I will fake my own death. I've worked it out. A sailing trip. They know I like to sail on my own. The abandoned boat will be reported. My body never found. Assumed washed overboard.'

Anselm tries to take this in. 'You would fake your own death for me?'

'Without you I'm a dead man anyway.'

Charles stares at a notice pasted on the peeling wall, one that stands out because it has had time neither to fade nor to gather dust. It informs hotel guests what to do 'in the event of an emergency', by order of the Home Office, and is dated 5 June 1939. Two weeks ago.

The sound of a key chattering in a lock makes him flinch. He turns his face to the door; reaches for Anselm's hand.

Another key is tried and the door yawns open. Dimpled fingers feel for the light switch. When the hotel manageress, a short woman with badly dyed hair, sees the two naked men by the window, the fingers rise to her mouth in shock. She steps to one side to allow two RAF police officers to enter.

'Northcote?' the taller of the two says. 'Pilot Officer Charles Northcote?'

'You might have knocked.'

'Get dressed please, there's a good gentleman.'

'Are you arresting me?'

'We're arresting you both.'

II

Kandahar Province. Late spring. Present day

FOR THE FIRST TIME IN ELEVEN YEARS, ONE WEEK AND FOUR days, Edward Northcote opens his eyes and sees daylight. Recoiling in pain, he closes them again and, at the same time, tries to cover his face, only to realize his hands are tied behind his back.

He opens them again, two narrow slits this time. There is a blur of watery light, but no hard edges. After a succession of blinks, he is able to open his eyes a little wider and, by ignoring the stabs of light, look out on to a world that is strange and cold. A landscape in black and white.

He is lying on his side on what appears to be a dirt track. There are small rocks scattered around him. He stares at one of them, trying to find his focus.

What has woken him? A noise is dimming in his memory. It sounds like wood tapping against wood. He remembers now: it had been this noise that had been tapping its way into the depths, like sonar signals hundreds of leagues below the surface of conscious thought. He had been trying to climb towards them, against a weight of water, up a mile-high ladder.

He blinks again. There are blotches before his eyes now, floating like petals in a slow current, and, in his peripheral vision, a shape. It is a boy, about eleven years old, wearing a hooded sweatshirt over a white cotton *thoub* and holding a cricket bat in one hand and a mallet in the other. The boy studies him for a moment then carries on 'knocking in' his bat. *Tap. Tap. Tap.*

Edward tries to move his head but a dense gravity prevents him.

The boy stops knocking. *'Salaam alaikum,'* he says with an uncertain smile.

Edward tries to speak but his vocal cords have no energy. Instead his narrowed eyes track from the boy to the cluster of concrete-grey, flat-roofed shapes at the end of the road. The boy follows his gaze, then turns and runs towards the shapes. Edward's lids droop, the muscles unused to the heaviness.

Time becomes fragmented now as he drifts in and out of consciousness. Men wearing helmets and flak jackets are lifting him into the back of a truck. They are asking him questions, in English. One of them is wearing sunglasses and Edward manages to signal to him that he needs some, that the light is hurting his eyes. The soldier understands, takes them off and places them gently on Edward's face. He can now see he is in a jeep. It has a long, whippy aerial that dances in the wind as they bump over potholes and swerve around corners. He recalls seeing an aerial like this years ago, on the day he was kidnapped, moments before his convoy was attacked.

I've survived, he now thinks, with sudden, shocking clarity.

It is over.

Now he is being dragged along on a gurney with a squeaky wheel. Drips are attached to his arms. Over his mouth there is an oxygen mask.

And now there are plumes of dust spiralling upwards and the *thump, thump, thump* of helicopter blades beating the air. After so many years of near silence, this noise seems impossibly loud, as if it is tearing at the very molecular structure of the universe.

Now there are flashbulbs and Edward is being dragged along on a gurney again. The flashes are creating a stroboscopic effect. Voices are calling his name.

'What was it like, Edward?'

'Was there a deal done for your release, Edward?'

'What did you think when you heard about your wife, Edward?'

His next realization is that he is on a military plane of some sort – as cavernous as a hangar, as empty as space – and he is being strapped to a bed. A screen is being put up around him. There are more drips on stands. More electrical equipment. More lights. Webbing is clattering against the metal sides of the cabin. His stomach is lurching. They are taking off.

Level now. He can hear the steady throb of an engine. Stars are visible out of the small porthole but, having forgotten what they look like, he takes a while to register what they are. Needles are being stuck in his arms. He soon finds himself submitting to the spin of sleep.

Edward's longest period of consciousness comes when he is in a hospital bed with a cage above it – a chrome contraption with pulleys. To his left is a machine with lights that are grey – *grey?* – a monitor of some sort. It is making a humming noise. There are electrodes taped to his chest.

Am I hurt? He says this wordlessly; a thought that does not carry to his mouth. He doesn't feel ill. There is no pain. A rhythm is pulsing in his head. *I need a little time to wake up, wake up . . .*

Sensation is returning in a flood now, a surge of warmth. He notices the oxygen mask by his bed and the drip taped to his arm. There is another tube taped to his stomach.

I'm being fed through a tube?

A woman appears in the doorway. She has pale, tumbling hair. Her grey eyes are flecked with grains of sugar. The eyes of a snow leopard. To Edward she is unmistakable. He has called out her name many times over the missing years, to himself, to the walls of the cave, to the darkness, but now the word comes as the sort of soft, gummy, slack-mouthed noise that dental patients make before the anaesthetic has worn off.

'Frejya!'

The woman's face contorts. She holds a hand to her mouth, then turns and leaves.

A tall doctor with hairy wrists and unnaturally white teeth arrives. He is wearing a grey, hospital-issue gown.

Why am I seeing everything in black and white?

'Mr Northcote,' he says. 'Edward . . . You are in a

25

hospital. The Cromwell Hospital in London. You are safe now.'

'*Frejya!*'

'I'm afraid . . . A lot has happened.' Pause. 'How are you feeling?'

'*Frejya!*'

'That wasn't your wife you saw. That was . . .'. The tall doctor puts his hand to his mouth, as the woman had done. 'Let me call . . . There's someone waiting outside to see you. He's from the Foreign Office. He will explain everything.'

With his well-pressed, navy-blue suit and cream-coloured, open-necked shirt, Sir Niall Campbell looks like what he is, a formal man who has removed his tie to try to make himself look informal. The tie is rolled up in his hand and he stares at it for a moment before stuffing it in his pocket.

In his other hand he is carrying a laminated TRiM card. It lists the standard Trauma Risk Management questions he is supposed to ask on behalf of Human Resources, so that an assessment can be made as to whether, or rather when, Edward will need to see a 'psych'. Niall knows that the questions will be irrelevant in Edward's case – Have you had any flashbacks? Any recurring dreams? Are you drinking more than normal? – but he finds it reassuring that he won't be entering the ward empty-handed.

He breathes in, buttons up his jacket, the middle of three, then unbuttons it again and breathes out. Why is he stalling? Why doesn't he simply march in like the busy man he is? He knows why. Northy might not recognize him. Niall has put on weight in the past decade. About two and a half stone. His once-thick and dark hair, meanwhile, has gone thin and grey.

When he enters, his personal vanities evaporate. The skeletal figure on the bed bears only a passing resemblance to the tall, dark-haired, heavy-shouldered young man he had first met on the rugby field as a student. Edward had been a flanker, Niall a fullback. A bitingly cold wind had been blowing in over the Fens and they had grinned at one another as they shivered. Niall had felt slightly in awe of Edward as a student, not least because he had been an all-round sportsman – as useful with a tennis racquet and a cricket bat as he was with a rugby ball – as well as a witty and persuasive speaker at the Union. Yet he had also been a man of quiet modesty and decency, all substance and no show, liked and known. And because Niall was part of his circle, he found himself becoming liked and known, too.

It was after they graduated and sat their civil service exams together that their friendship deepened. For eighteen months, they had shared a desk at the Foreign and Commonwealth Office, in a room with a fireplace. The fire was no longer used by the time they arrived, a tradition that had disappeared along with women having to resign when they got married. But on mornings when they had hangovers they would rest their heads on their desks, knowing that FCO custom meant they would not be disturbed (it being assumed that they had worked through the night).

It had been Edward, with his urbane manner and

27

starred First, who was the one everyone tipped to go all the way. Then, with his posting to Norway, something changed. He fell in love. Had a child. Got married. And the price for his contentment was a loss of ambition. Edward had once confided to Niall that he sometimes thought of giving up the diplomatic service entirely to live off the land: growing his own vegetables, fishing, chopping wood. His wife's family had a log cabin they rarely used, up near the fjords where the summers are short and the winters long. It was theirs for the asking. He could write a book there. A novel perhaps.

And Niall encouraged him. But instead Edward and Frejya moved to London, with plans to settle there and perhaps have a second child, and that book was never written.

Now, according to the chart on the end of his bed, Edward weighs just under seven stone. Niall has heard that they decided to test his DNA to be sure it matched that of the Edward Northcote they had on record. He has also been told that, in the five days since Edward first opened his eyes in daylight, he has not managed to keep them open for longer than a few minutes.

Whether he is still aware of what is being said to him when his eyes are shut is debatable. Apparently there is not much sign of recognition, and scant evidence of memory.

But however prepared Niall thought he was for this encounter, the reality of it is shocking. Seeing a pedal bin in the corner of the room, he walks over to it, opens the lid and drops in the TRiM card.

Edward's eyes have closed again now, and there is a clear fluid dribbling down his chin. His right arm flails, then goes limp. The bones are pushing against his skin, smoothing it out and leaving baggy creases where it falls away. His eyes appear to be sinking deep into his skull, as if his face is melting. The membrane inside his mouth is protruding so that it looks like part of his lips. Behind them, his teeth look too big for his mouth, brown and decayed with pus oozing out from the gum line. His hair is silvery and long, hanging below his shoulder blades. He has a beard that reaches his barrelled ribs, and his skin is yellow and leathery, almost translucent. The plastic hospital ID band around his wrist is loose on him. He looks a hundred years old.

'Northy? Can you hear me?'

Niall wonders if his friend will remember the circumstances that led to his kidnapping, how he had been the one who persuaded him to go. The assignment had made sense, at the time. Because Edward had once worked as a cultural attaché in the Middle East – and spoke some Arabic – he had been asked to join a multinational UNESCO team being sent into the remote mountain region of Hazarajat in central Afghanistan. There had been reports that the Buddhas of Bamiyan, two sixth-century monumental statues carved into the side of a cliff, had been dynamited and destroyed by the Taliban. That was in March 2001, six months before the jihadists hijacked two passenger planes and flew them into the Twin Towers.

When Edward's convoy had driven into an ambush, he had been in the third of four Land-Cruisers. A rocket-propelled grenade attack. Officially, there had been no survivors. But when eleven out of thirteen bodies were recovered and identified, Edward's was not among them. In the weeks that followed, Niall had awaited the inevitable ransom or demand for the release of political prisoners, but neither came. Although the possibility that he had been taken hostage was never ruled out, the unofficial presumption was that he must be dead – and dead was what he was officially declared after he had been missing for ten years.

But what he seems to be going through back home in London is not so much a resurrection as a regression. His reflexes are those of a baby, especially his hand-grasping, sucking and asymmetrical neck reflexes.

'Northy. It's me, Niall. Niall Campbell. Do you remember me?' He holds his hand. 'We worked together at the Foreign Office. I was best man at your wedding. You were best man at mine. Can you speak?'

Niall has drawn the short straw. It was decided that, because of his involvement with the Friends of Edward Northcote campaign, the bad news Edward would have to hear at some point would be best coming from him, someone he knew rather than an anonymous civil servant. But the doctors have advised that the patient may be too fragile. Niall should wait until Edward has built up his strength. The shock could kill him.

'Northy? Can you tell us anything about what happened?'

Edward raises his chin and opens his eyes. They are dilated with panic. He makes a heavy-tongued noise.

'*Frejya?*'

III

WHEN EDWARD'S FIRST REASONABLY CLEAR SENTENCE COMES, two and a half weeks after returning to London, it is directed at Niall. 'Where am I?' he says in a slurring voice.

'You're at the Cromwell Hospital in London. It's good to have you back, Northy.'

'I know you.'

'Yes, it's me, Niall. Niall Campbell.'

Edward's beard has gone now and his hair has been cropped close to his skull. He looks around the room and raises his hand towards the mirror.

'You want to see a mirror?'

Edward shakes his head stiffly.

'You think *I* should look in a mirror, is that it?' Niall is speaking in the kind of loud, laughter-edged voice adults use with children. 'You think I've changed?' He pats his stomach. 'I have changed, Northy, and so have you. It's been a long time.' He pulls up a chair and takes his friend's hand. 'Can you talk about what happened?'

Edward blinks but says nothing. Niall knows better than to try to fill the silence. There is emptiness in

31

Edward's eyes. They are red-rimmed and unfocused, like a sleepwalker's. Is this, he wonders, what is meant by the thousand-yard stare?

A minute passes before Edward finally speaks. 'The Cromwell? Not St Thomas's?'

Niall gives a snort of laughter, his friend's memory for Foreign Office protocol taking him by surprise.

'We've made special arrangements for you . . . Can you remember anything? Do you know who was holding you hostage?'

'There was a boy with a cricket bat.'

'He was the one who found you.'

'My hands were tied.'

'Who tied them?'

'I never . . .' Edward's mouth dries up mid sentence.

Niall is struck by the absence of emotion in his friend's voice. It is a whispery monotone devoid of strength and expression, like a guitar without tension in its strings.

The tall doctor who has been hovering by the door now enters, pulls down the bed cover and jabs a pin in the patient's foot.

Edward jumps.

'You can feel that?' the doctor asks. 'That's great. Can you clench your fists?'

Edward manages a half-clench.

Next the doctor sits on the bed, holds up a pencil and moves it from left to right and up and down to see if Edward's eyes can track it. They can. A small torch is now being shone in his eyes.

'Don't do that, please.'

32

'Sorry.'

'They shone torches in my face.'

'They?' Niall leans forward.

Edward does not elaborate.

'How is your vision?' the doctor asks. 'Is it OK?'

Edward thinks for a moment. Blinks. 'Everything is black and white . . . Why is everything black and white?'

'You can't see any colours?'

'Only grey . . . Like Niall's hair.'

Niall grins.

Edward blinks again. 'Where's Frejya? Where did she go?'

Niall looks down. 'That wasn't Frejya you saw.'

'But she was in here a minute ago.'

Niall exhales slowly. 'That was a couple of weeks ago. You're going to have a problem with time gaps for a while, until your brain recalibrates itself . . . And it wasn't Frejya you saw. It was Hannah.' He sighs again, more heavily this time. 'I'm not going to lie to you, Northy. This is all going to seem really fucked up, for a while at least. You're just . . .'

Edward has fallen asleep.

The doctor flips over a sheet on a clipboard and gives Niall a sidelong glance. 'You family? I recognize you.'

'A friend. I've been interviewed on the news a bit lately, talking about Edward's release.'

'That's it; you're the guy from the Foreign Office. Sir Niall . . .'

'Campbell. And it's pronounced Neil. It's Scottish.'

'You don't sound Scottish.'

'It's not compulsory. Can I have a word with you

outside?' The two men walk out into the corridor and speak in lowered voices. 'So what's the situation here?'

The doctor looks over his shoulder before making eye contact. 'He should make a reasonable recovery but we are going to have to monitor his food intake carefully. One of the mistakes they made after the liberation of Belsen was to feed the prisoners too quickly. Thousands died because their bodies couldn't cope. Cardiac failure mostly. We'll keep him in intensive care for a few weeks, on a controlled diet and a glucose drip, then we'll start giving him some physio to try and rebuild his muscles.'

'But no lasting medical problems?'

'I didn't say that. It's too early to tell whether some of the conditions he is suffering from will be permanent, but so far we have detected . . . Well, do you want the whole list?' He begins counting them off with his fingers. 'Early evidence of renal failure, cirrhosis, possible diabetes, anaemia, dehydration, calcium deficiency and impaired vision which we think will leave him with a permanent sensitivity to light.' The doctor shakes his head. 'He also has fungi growing under his oesophagus, which makes swallowing painful for him. And our tests are showing he may have scurvy and rickets, which we haven't really seen in this country for decades. But we think all these things will prove temporary. His long-term problems are going to be psychological.'

'We've got a good therapist lined up for when he's ready . . . Poor old Northy.'

'Yes, poor old Northy,' the doctor echoes.

When they step back into the ward, Edward's eyes are

open but they are unfocused. They seem to be looking through Niall – the thousand-yard stare again. 'It *was* Frejya,' Edward says through closed teeth. 'She was here.'

'Well, I'll leave you two to it,' the doctor says.

'You've been away for just over eleven years,' Niall says, once the doctor has closed the door. 'That was Hannah you saw. She's twenty now.'

Niall can see the blood pulsing in Edward's face. Sense his dizziness and feeling of time dislocation. He now knows that his friend has been unable to take in any of the information fed into his brain on an aural drip as he drifted in and out of consciousness these past couple of weeks. This is not the first time Niall has explained to Edward that his daughter is now an adult.

For a full minute, Edward is silent. Then he says softly: 'Hannah is nine . . . She was nine.'

'This is going to take some time to . . . to get used to.'

'Can I see my wife? Where is she?'

Niall hesitates. 'One thing at a time, Northy . . .'

Edward eyes him, as if recognizing him for the first time. 'Did you say you were still at the Foreign Office?'

'Yep. And you can come back to work for us whenever you feel ready, in whatever capacity.'

'Says who?'

Niall looks embarrassed. 'Says me.'

'I don't understand.'

'I'll explain later.'

'Tell me now. What grade are you?'

Niall looks away. 'I'm the Permanent Undersecretary.'

Edward tries to sit up. 'You?'

'For the moment. There's a general election expected

soon and the new lot will probably want their own man in.'

'Sir?'

Niall studies the floor and nods. 'But I don't use it. Tell me about the people who kidnapped you.'

Something happens to Edward's eyes, as though a shadow is passing over them. 'They . . .'

'Do you remember anything about when you were captured?'

'Everything went black.'

'You were in a convoy. There was an ambush. Your Land Cruiser was hit by an RPG.'

Edward frowns. 'Who were they?'

'We figured it would be local opportunists who didn't know they'd got a high-value target. We had a press blackout and notified the Met's Hostage and Crisis Negotiation Unit. But nothing. No demands. No video posted on the web. We had no idea where you were.'

'I was underground. In a cave. It was dark.' Edward grimaces, as if a bubble of pain has entered his blood. 'Do we have to do this now?'

'No. Whenever you are ready. I understand.'

'Can I see Frejya?'

'You've lost a lot of weight.'

'I want to see my wife.'

'I've brought a mirror.'

Niall hands over a mirror, but Edward does not look in it. Instead he places it face down on the bed. His eyes look distant and cloudy again; the eyes of a dead man.

'How old am I?'

'Forty-seven.'

A beat.

'Forty-seven?'

'Yeah.'

Another beat.

'I'm forty-seven?'

'Yeah, you're forty-seven, Northy. Same age as me.'

'How old was I when I was taken?'

'Thirty-six.'

Niall feels for his friend's hand. 'It's going to take time.'

'Why won't you talk about Frejya?'

'Northy . . . There's no easy way to say this . . .'

Fear suddenly registers on Edward's face. His hands try to cover his ears but the muscles in his arms are too atrophied. He shakes his head. Closes his eyes. Mouths the word 'no'.

Niall's eyes are wet now. He puts a hand on his friend's shoulder. 'I'm sorry. She died.'

'Can I speak to her?'

'Listen to me. You've got to listen.' There is a crack in Niall's voice now. 'Frejya is dead.'

IV

Berlin. Early autumn, 1939

ANSELM HAS NEVER SEEN THE PEOPLE'S COURT BEFORE, BUT HE has heard of it. Everyone in Germany has heard of it. The Volksgerichtshof. A place of fear. A place without memories. Today its nineteenth-century façade is draped with three red, white and black swastika banners. They are thirty feet long and make the building look as if it is bleeding.

He is brought in via a side entrance off Potsdamer Platz and taken down stone stairs to a holding cell. There is no window. No bed. No chair. Noticing that it smells of urine, Anselm realizes that there is no lavatory either. His belt and shoelaces are taken from him. The policeman from the *Ordnungspolizei* with kind eyes and a brass gorget around his neck looks him up and down thoughtfully, then takes his tie as well.

Once the iron door has clanged shut and heavy keys have been turned in the lock, Anselm leans his shoulder against the wall, closes his eyes and tries, for reassurance, to summon Charles's smiling face. He

38

wonders what has happened to him. Is he in prison, too? When he opens his eyes again he notices some words scratched at eye height. They are messages from the damned.

'My name is Josef Mann. I have a wife and two children in Hamburg. Please let them know where I am.'

And in another hand: 'Please God, why?'

But the one at which he stares the most is the simplest: 'Help me.' This one chills Anselm's blood. *Help me.* A man can be forgotten in this place, he thinks. *Help me.* All traces of his life can be erased. *Help me.* He can be reduced to a single pitiful plea.

While under *Hausarrest* in Berlin, Anselm had written to Charles in London. He had also written to his parents in Aachen, giving them his temporary address, but he had not told them about his deportation from England, or the reason for it. As the weeks went by, he had allowed himself to think that he had fallen through the Reich's bureaucratic net. Then, as August drew to a close, a *Blockleiter* arrived to apply crosses of tape to his windows to prevent shattering. In the gaps between them, Anselm had been able to watch trenches being dug near the bandstand in the Tiergarten. The Berliners who walked with urgent steps over the cobbles below had started carrying gas masks. But he could still hear a barrel organ being played somewhere nearby and, occasionally, the heavy flapping of wings as a swan took flight. One day, on the cusp of autumn, war was declared through the loudspeakers. Soon afterwards an air-raid siren was tested. Then they came for him.

Now, as he hears the rattle of the heavy keys again, he looks towards the cell door. The lock turns with a solid clunk as before and the door yawns open with a squeak of unoiled hinges. While the man with the kind eyes remains outside the cell, another policeman stoops to enter, even though he is not especially tall, certainly not as tall as Anselm.

'Arms out,' he barks.

Anselm raises his arms, bent at the elbows. The policeman's touch is icy, his skin forged from the same steel as the handcuffs. Once outside the cell, Anselm stands between the two guards. He is half a foot taller than both of them and, with the prisoner wearing a white shirt buttoned to the throat as if he is a priest, the three of them look like a scene from a stained glass window, an unholy triptych. As Anselm follows the first policeman up a spiralling metal staircase, he has to grip the waistband of his trousers to stop them falling down.

The iron-barred gate at the top of the stairs opens into a narrow white corridor that smells of fresh paint. At the end of this another prisoner, about Anselm's age, is sitting head down, leaning forward, on a bench. His handcuffed wrists are resting on his knees. He has his own escorts. Anselm is about to walk towards them when he feels a restraining hand on his shoulder.

The prisoner is breathing quickly and, as Anselm tunes in to the sounds coming from the other side of the black wooden door he is facing, he appreciates why. Shouting can be heard. He cannot make out the exact words, but it is clear that someone is being cursed in there. Anselm feels a chill in his stomach. His scrotum tightens.

After a minute, the ranting stops. A minute after this, the black door opens, the policemen stand and the prisoner is escorted inside. The door closes and Anselm is nudged forward to sit on the bench. It is still warm. His police escort remains standing either side of him, as the others had done, and, after two minutes of silence, the ranting starts again. This time Anselm tries to block the words out. He searches for a song to sing in his head instead, but all he can think of is the *Horst-Wessel-Lied*. His bowels are turning to water.

After ten minutes the shouting stops. As if operating by clockwork, the black door opens a minute later. Anselm's guards stand up and steer him through the door. He has a dozen yards to walk to where there are two chairs. His shoes echo hollowly on the waxed parquet floor, then comes a silence that is so deep it terrifies him.

The policemen sit in the chairs and Anselm remains standing between them. He looks up. Above him is a high, vaulted ceiling. To his right there is a table around which sit five clerks of the court wearing black gowns and white wing collars. Some of them are writing, others consulting notes. Behind him there is a public gallery of some sort, but it is empty. The side of the room he entered from has a raised seating area, presumably where the jury sits. This too is empty. Ahead there is a witness stand. Again, empty. No jury. No witnesses. The courtroom smells of disinfectant.

Only now does he look at that which he has been

avoiding since entering the court. The wall behind the bench is dominated by three blood-red swastikas. The two at each side reach from the ceiling to the floor. The one in the middle is slightly lower, fitting into the frame of a double doorway with an ornate frieze on top. Above this is a Nazi eagle. Gilt, or possibly gold. Its wingspan must be ten feet. In front of the central flag is a marble plinth on which is displayed a bronze bust of the Führer. And directly in front of this is a carved black chair that looks like a throne. Chair, bust and flag are all in perfect alignment with the prisoner.

A door opens to the right. A clerk of the court shouts: 'All rise.' Three Reich-judges enter.

The first and the third are wearing black gowns and white collars, like the clerks to Anselm's right, but these men are also wearing what look like floppy velvet mortar boards on their heads. The judge in the middle is wearing a sumptuous red robe. On his head is what looks like a fez. On his gown there is a brooch, the eagle insignia again. Before they sit down, they give the Nazi salute and, for a brief moment, Anselm thinks they are saluting him – then he looks over his shoulder and sees a giant portrait of Hitler high on the wall behind him.

All three judges remove their hats as they sit down. The one in the middle is bald apart from some hair at the sides of his head. This he smooths down with fussy dabs of his hand. With his feathery eyebrows and hooded eyes he looks like an eagle.

He twirls the deep sleeves of his robe like a wizard about to cast a spell, then he studies the papers in front of him. Finally he looks up and, according to his widened eyes, he seems surprised to see that the defendant is a fine specimen of Aryan manhood. Then his lean features stiffen. His eyes turn cold and dark.

The prisoner is asked to identify himself and, after he is sworn in, a clerk with a hog-bristle moustache grinds back his chair, stands and reads from a piece of paper: 'Under Paragraph 175 of the criminal code, as defined by the Reich Central Office for the Combating of Homosexuality and Abortion, you are hereby charged with being a degenerate. How do you plead?'

Anselm is confused. What does this word 'degenerate' mean? He is guilty of being a homosexual. Indeed he feels that if he were to plead not guilty to that he would be betraying himself, and Charles. But in truth he is not sure of what he is being accused. He does not know how to answer the question. A lock of sand-coloured hair has fallen over his eye. He flicks it away with a backwards tilt of his head.

The judge in the red robe signals impatiently to the clerk: 'Enter a plea of guilty.'

The judge looks down at the piece of paper in his hand. 'What were you doing in London?' he asks.

'I was a student,' Anselm says. 'At the Slade.'

'And you committed your vile acts with an enemy of the Reich?'

'We weren't at war then.'

'*Silence!*' The judge's voice cracks the air like a whip, before returning to ominous normality. 'In times of war,' he continues, 'baseness cannot find any leniency and must be met with the full force of the law. Your degenerate acts threaten the disciplined masculinity of

43

the German people. You are an antisocial parasite and an enemy of the state . . .'

As the judge's voice begins to rise in pitch again, Anselm looks down at his own handcuffed hands holding up his trousers and recalls how he and Charles dressed in silence that night in London. The hotel manageress sat on the bed fanning her stupid fat face in shock, denying them their last moments of privacy. As a precaution, or so one of the military policemen had said, the two prisoners were handcuffed together. Perhaps out of misplaced respect for Charles's uniform, the other MP draped a mac over the iron bracelet that bound their wrists together. Anselm didn't mind. It meant they could entwine their fingers as they descended the stairs. With these handcuffs I thee wed.

The judge is shouting now, but Anselm can register only random words . . . '*Deutschland* . . . traitor . . . repulsive . . . sodomical . . . corruption . . . *Schweinehund.*' Each word is accompanied by a thump of the table.

There were two additional policemen waiting for them in the lobby that night in London and, when he saw them, Anselm fought a pointless impulse to run for it, to keep Charles's hand in his and disappear into the night. They could lose themselves in the crowds of Piccadilly. What sweet anonymity that would have been. He had often dreamed of them doing that since. Running down narrow streets, over lush meadows, to the bare, rugged safety of the mountains.

Instead they were taken outside into the street. There, to the curiosity of a newspaper vendor who had piled sandbags up against his stall, the handcuffs were unlocked and Charles was led to a waiting Black Maria, without even being permitted a backward glance over his shoulder. Moments later, Anselm was led away to a nearby police station. Neither had had a chance to say goodbye.

The Judge-President is banging the table furiously now. 'Why?' he is demanding, his voice hoarse from shouting. *'WHY?'*

'Love,' Anselm answers. 'Because of love.'

'Silence!' the judge screams. He seems like a rabid dog, flecks of spittle appearing at the corners of his mouth.

Anselm feels his eyes welling, but wills himself not to cry. He also feels an insane urge to reach for the hand of the kind-eyed policeman and hold it.

'I hereby sentence you to five years' hard labour,' the judge says, with a bang of his gavel. 'Take him away.'

Anselm is led to a door at the back of the court. His trial has lasted seven minutes, three fewer than the previous case.

V

London. Present day. Five weeks after Edward's release

UPON RETURNING TO THE HOSPITAL, HANNAH FINDS HER FATHER on the floor and rushes to help him up. 'Did you fall out?' she asks. 'Why haven't the nurses been in?'

'I was more comfortable here,' Edward says, getting to his feet. 'Still not used to this mattress.'

Supporting him as he goes to sit on the bed, she asks: 'Would you rather I slept on the bed and you slept on the pull-down?' For the past few weeks she has been sleeping in the small pull-down bed next to her father's. Her routine has been to rise early and slip away before he wakes up. Sometimes she heads back to the house to wash and change, sometimes she finds a café for breakfast and to catch up with her friends online. But the truth is, she would rather not be sleeping by his side at all. She is scared by her inability to read his needs. Perhaps, she tells herself, things will improve once he talks about his time in captivity. Niall says that he still hasn't said a word on the subject, not to him, not to anyone.

She pours him a glass of milk. It seems to be his favourite drink.

'Thank you,' Edward says as he takes a sip. 'You really don't need to sleep here, you know. I'm much better.'

'I want to,' she says.

'Well, I appreciate the company.' Edward looks as if he is going to say something more but checks himself.

'What?' Hannah prompts.

'Nothing.'

'What?' Hannah insists. She is smiling a smile she hopes will look reassuring rather than nervous. Is he going to start telling her terrible things about what happened in Afghanistan? Oh God. She doesn't feel ready. If he was tortured, or chained to a radiator, or was sharing a windowless cell with dozens of others, she would rather not know. She wishes Niall was here.

'I thought you were Frejya just now.'

He seems to find it hard to say the word 'Mummy'. She understands. She is finding it hard to call him Daddy. The word doesn't seem to fit her mouth. It is the wrong shape. The wrong weight. Dad might be better. 'I know,' she says. And I also know I am going to have to tell you about what happened to her, she thinks. If I can summon the courage. If I can do it without crying.

Edward reaches for her hand. He does this in the night sometimes, in the silence when she thinks she can hear him screaming inside.

This morning he looks different. His hair has been cropped close to his skull again. Malnutrition oedema, meanwhile, has bloated his face and the skin around his shaved jaw is the colour of bone. Though he is no longer being fed through a tube, he looks twice his age. An old man. A concentration camp victim.

'How is your band going?' he asks. 'What's the name of it again?'

He has remembered, she thinks. This is progress. She has told him two or three times now about how she is the bass player and backing vocalist in a pub band that plays covers. 'The Sextuplets, though there are only five of us at the moment. We've played a few gigs. All girls. You should come and hear us.' She wonders if he will also remember about her one-year art foundation course, the one she has had to drop out of in order to look after him.

'And how is school?'

'I'm not at school any more. Remember? I started a foundation course. I'm hoping to get a place at the Slade.'

'Where your grandfather went . . . When can I see him?'

'I'll take you to see him as soon as you're out of hospital.'

'Can't he come here?'

'He's aged a lot since you last saw him.' She doesn't elaborate. One thing at a time. The two are not so different, she reflects. Father and son. Tomorrow Edward will ask again about his father, and her life, and forget that they have had this conversation. The difference is Edward's memory is improving. With each day he is becoming less confused.

'I've asked about him before, haven't I?'

Hannah nods.

'You must think I'm mad.'

Hannah plumps up his pillow, so that she doesn't have to look him in the eyes. 'No, I don't. You're fine. You're going through a period of readjustment, that's all.'

She begins tidying away her things and wants to open the curtain but sees her own Post-it note, the one she has stuck above the switch for the benefit of the nurses: 'Please keep closed.' Also in her handwriting is a note stuck above the light switch: 'Please keep dimmed.' Her father's eyes are too sensitive to stand bright light, but, equally, he cannot bear being in the dark. A low-wattage nightlight is the compromise.

She turns and studies him. He is staring at the ceiling now, lost in contemplation. How far this seems from the fairytale reunion she had imagined. While he may now be taking in certain things about her life, he doesn't know her, and doesn't seem to want to know her. She keeps telling herself that this is going to be a long haul, that gradually he will become less insular and less frightening, that he will become the friendly man into whose arms she pictured herself skipping. But there are times when she doesn't believe that will ever happen now. She looks out of the window and sees a couple of photographers waiting in the ambulance bay. She recognizes one of them. Why won't they leave her alone? In this moment she realizes that what she wants more than anything is to have her old life back, to go back to a time before . . . She feels guilty for even thinking of it. Tears are rising to the surface again, beading her lashes.

'Everything OK?' her father asks.

Hannah checks the time on her mobile as a way of averting her eyes. 'Actually I've got a band practice to get to. Will you be all right till I get back?'

Downstairs she gathers her long pale hair into the baseball cap she uses as a disguise to get past the photographers. She then heads outside and walks quickly towards the tube. Before she reaches it she slows down and changes direction. There is no band practice to go to. She will sit on a park bench for an hour or two instead.

A week later, Hannah arrives at the hospital wearing her black-framed glasses rather than her contacts. It seems to help remind her father who she is, or rather who she isn't.

She finds him on the far side of the hospital garden, partially veiled by the sprawling fronds of a yucca plant. He is sitting in a wheelchair, staring at an empty bird table from behind sunglasses. Across his knees is a blue hospital-issue blanket. By his side is a small portable oxygen tank.

After a month in intensive care and a fortnight in a private room, his doctors had recommended he be moved to a clinic for a further month's rehabilitation. But Edward had insisted that he was now fit enough to return home, threatening to walk there by himself if he had to. Realizing he was being serious, the doctors had agreed reluctantly. But when they told him arrangements were being made for an ambulance to take him there, he became angry again. He wanted to drive himself home, he said, in his own car, like a normal human being, 'not some freak'. A compromise was reached. Hannah would drive him and Niall would follow them in his car. So as not to alert any reporters who might be waiting for them at the front of the hospital, they would be allowed to park in the ambulance bay around the back.

As she studies her father, Hannah rubs her arms and regrets wearing a sleeveless top. He might see the Sanskrit tattoo that runs from the base of her neck to her shoulder, the one she has been trying to conceal from him on her visits to the hospital. She worries at the strands of silk and leather about her wrist, tugging them around in full circles before moving to the chunky ring on her thumb and turning that instead. When she looks up, her father is staring at her.

'Hi,' she says with a small self-conscious wave from waist height when she is a few feet away from him. 'You all set?'

Edward smiles unconvincingly when he recognizes her, a stretching of his lips that does not expose his teeth.

'Got any bags?'

He shakes his head.

'No. I guess you wouldn't have. Stupid of me.' Hannah gives a single clap and rubs her hands. 'They've let me park in the ambulance bay, so we'd better not hang about. Do you want me to push you?'

'You can drive?'

'Passed first time,' Hannah says. 'You OK for me to push you?'

'Thank you. I can walk OK but they like you to use

these things.' He taps the armrests of the wheelchair. 'In case you fall on the premises, I suppose. Liability.'

Spits of rain are falling on the dusty paving stones. As Hannah pushes her father along a path and around the corner of the building, she hums to herself, out of nervousness rather than contentment. When she realizes she is doing it, she stops. 'OK,' she says. 'Now close your eyes.' She brings the chair to a halt in front of his old Volvo estate. 'OK, you can open them . . . It's been sitting in the garage. Mum hardly ever used it.'

Edward nods. 'She kept it all these years . . . Maybe I should go in the back. It'll be easier with the oxygen tank. I don't really need it but . . .'

Hannah thinks she would prefer it if he was in the back too, that way they can talk without facing each other. There is an awkwardness to their conversations which she does not know how to avoid. Though she has rarely left her father's side since his return, they are still strangers. Their discomfort with each other lies between them like a wall of glass.

A few minutes later, as she waits for a Royal Mail van to let her out on to the Cromwell Road, Hannah drums her fingers on the steering wheel. The Saturday afternoon traffic is thickening, she thinks. Conscious that the Volvo smells of rust and damp carpet, she says: 'I guess she still smells the same.'

'My sense of smell hasn't returned yet.'

Hannah angles her rear-view mirror. Her father is staring straight ahead, motionless, as if he's clicked out the light.

Chelsea are playing at home, she now realizes, so the

traffic will be worse the nearer they get to Parsons Green, a couple of miles away. To her house. To their house. Their. Again the word doesn't seem to fit. At least there is an occupational therapist waiting for them there, one who has been making all the rehabilitative arrangements, preparing his medication, sorting out the beds and chairs. And Niall has briefed the hospital staff about the need for discretion: it would be in everyone's interests if the press didn't hear about this homecoming.

'What was it like in the cave?' Hannah asks abruptly, surprising herself with the bluntness of her question. She has avoided asking it and the avoidance has built up a pressure in her mind. 'It must have been . . .' She can't think of a way to finish the sentence. It must have been what? She has no frame of reference.

When Edward's voice eventually drifts over from the back seat it is distant, as though through a mist. 'Can we talk about it later? I don't mean to be rude, it's just I need to . . .'

Hannah adjusts her rear-view mirror again so that she has a better view of her father's face. He is staring out of a window braided with rain, nodding as if in mental preparation for a difficult conversation. Bracing himself.

'What was Niall like while I was away?'

She considers this. 'He was like our protector. Kept promising he would get you back for us. He was devastated when Mum died.'

'Why won't anyone tell me how it happened?'

Hannah answers too brightly, unable to find the right tone. 'She was found floating in the sea off the Cornish coast. Near Doyden Point. The coastguard said she could have drifted in the current.' She thinks: if I stick to facts, that will be OK, won't it?

'She drowned?'

'She'd been in the water a couple of days. The coroner's report mentioned "injuries consistent with an impact".'

'Hit by a boat?'

'They think it's more likely she fell on to . . . She fell from a considerable height.'

Hannah has a sudden, unambiguous sense that her father is angry with her, something to do with the way his eyes in the mirror narrow and harden. He seems angry that his daughter is here and his wife isn't.

'What was she doing up there?' There is accusation in his question.

'Doyden Point was her favourite place. We used to have picnics up there. You remember?'

'I know all that.' Impatience in his voice now. 'How did she seem when you saw her last?'

'Fine. She'd rented the cottage for a week.'

'On her own?'

'She did that sometimes, when she needed a break from the campaign. It was a full-time job for her. The vigils. The TV and radio appearances. Fundraising . . .' She knows he has heard about the Friends of Edward Northcote campaign already, but she doubts he has taken much of it in. Perhaps, she thinks, if I raise the subject again now it will deflect the fear I am feeling, fear of this stranger who used to be my father.

But she knows it is also guilt she is feeling: in an effort to escape the relentless campaigning at home, she

54

had sometimes gone to stay with friends, leaving her mother alone and vulnerable. She had been asked on that Cornish trip and had said no. 'I spoke to her on the phone that day,' Hannah says in a rush, her voice cracking. 'She told me she was going for a walk.' There are tears on her cheeks now. 'She sounded fine. I didn't know. It wasn't my fault.'

For the first time Hannah catches her father's eyes and sees something approaching paternal warmth in them. It is as if the biological fact of her tears has made him see her as his daughter at last, reminding him that his role is to protect her.

'She loved walking along those coastal paths,' Edward says in a gentler voice. 'Especially in bad weather, when she was wrapped up warm underneath a raincoat. She said it made her feel cosy. More alive.'

'They found one of her hiking boots up there,' Hannah says, feeling stronger. 'At the Point. She might have taken it off to rub her foot.' She sees her father draw a clenched fist to his mouth. 'What do you want to ask me, Dad?' She wants to get this over with.

But he meets her question with silence.

'Go ahead,' she prompts.

'Do you think it was an accident?'

'Mum didn't leave a note, if that's what you mean. The coroner had to record an open verdict. But if you really want to know . . .' Hannah looks at her father, who now has his hands over his face. 'I don't think it was an accident.'

*   *   *

By the time they reach Parsons Green, Edward's eyes are closed. After they have circled the house twice, a parking space comes up a few yards from it. Hannah turns the engine off and jogs up the steps to open the front door. 'Hello?' she calls out. When the occupational therapist does not reply she repeats her question, scans the street to see where Niall has got to and then returns to the car. After insinuating an arm behind his upper back and another under the crook of his knees, she lifts her father out. His lightness is shocking, as if he is a Chinese lantern that might blow away.

He does not wake up as she ascends the stone steps, crosses the threshold and carries on up past the 'welcome home' helium balloons she has tethered to the banister. She has helped make up the bed in his old room, the bedroom he had shared with his wife for three happy years after they returned to England from Norway. They had met, fallen in love, had a child and married in Oslo, her mother's home town. Hannah had been a bridesmaid, a three-year-old wearing a lily-of-the-valley hair garland. When her father's diplomatic posting came to an end, this was the house they had bought together. When her mother died, it had passed to her.

Hannah lowers her father on to the bed and sees her fingers have left an impression on his skin as if it were warm wax. As she draws a coat up around his neck like a blanket, he asks drowsily: 'Frejya? Is that you?'

Hannah lays the back of her hand on her father's brow. 'I wish it was,' she says.

VI

London. Early summer, 1940

THE CHELSEA ARTS CLUB HAS ONLY ONE TELEPHONE, A 1920s brass candlestick set with a separate earpiece on a cord. As the porter hands it to Charles, he moves along the reception desk to afford him some privacy, a futile gesture given that the entrance is silent save for the *tock-tock* of an early Victorian longcase. Every word of both sides of the conversation can be overheard.

'Charlie? This is Funf speaking.'

'Hello, Funf.'

Charles covers the earpiece and says in a stage whisper: 'It's Funf, the German spy.'

Creases appear at the sides of the porter's eyes, and these tunnel to the corners of his mouth in matching bands. Like everyone else, he listens to *It's That Man Again* on the wireless. He knows all the catchphrases. Is in on the joke.

In fact the caller is Charles's friend and sailing companion Eric Secrest, a GP with a practice in north Kent and a fifty-seven-foot motor yacht moored at the Isle of

Dogs. Eric is the only one of Charles's friends who knows about his court martial, and the dishonourable discharge from the RAF that resulted from it.

Charles suspects that some members of the club may know the truth, but none has raised it with him yet. As for his other friends, most seem to have accepted that the reason Charles is not protecting the retreating British Expeditionary Force in the skies over France is that he has been taken off front-line RAF duty for 'medical reasons' (kept vague), and has been given a desk job somewhere at the War Office instead.

And at least Charles's parents never heard about his disgrace. They had died in a plane crash when he was seventeen, old enough to ignore his father's ambition that he should follow him into the diplomatic service. He is sure they would have been upset by the language used at his trial – 'You have been found guilty as charged of gross indecency and conduct unbecoming an officer.' The formality and Englishness of those words – and the polite restraint with which they were delivered – would have eaten into their souls like acid.

'Well?' Eric prompts. 'I'm returning your call.'

Charles lowers his voice: 'You heard that announcement on the wireless about everyone with a small vessel having to register it with the Admiralty?'

'Yes. Why?'

'You know what it's about, don't you?'

'I can guess.'

'So what do you think? You and me. We could sail *The Painted Lady* over to France like in the old days. Do our bit . . .' He hears a click as the connection is lost. 'Hello?

Funf?' He shakes his head at the porter. 'German spies,' he says. 'So rude.' He jiggles the grip up and down a couple of times and stares at the earpiece. The line is dead. While he waits for it to ring again he does a thumbnail sketch of Anselm on the blotter. Eventually he looks up and says: 'I'll be in the bar if . . .'

He orders a whiskey and sits on a high stool a few feet away from a man he hasn't seen in the club before, a drinker judging by his cratered and purplish nose. As he waits, Charles plucks grapes from a bowl on the bar and takes in, with sidelong glances, the man's thinning dirty-blond hair. It is threaded with grey and frosting at the temples. The man half turns his back towards him, as if worried his drink might be stolen. Charles stares at the empty grape stalks. They look sinister now, like birds' claws.

He puts a cigarette in his mouth and pats his pockets. But instead of a box of matches he takes from his pocket the letter he received from Anselm four months ago. He rubs it between his finger and thumb, as if the friction will bring it to life. It was sent via the Swedish Embassy in Berlin. Though he knows every word by heart, every endearing misspelling, grammatical mistake and unneeded Gothic capital, he re-reads it.

My dear Grumpy,

If you have receive this letter it means my friend at the Ambassy has been true to his word. I hope it is finding you in a better state than me.

I have been on trial at the Volksgerichtshof, the People's Court in Berlin, and sentenced to five years in

*an Erziehungslager, or 'education camp'. I am not told
yet where they take me but I will write and tell you
when I am knowing. Do not worry for me.*

*I hope you are well. What happen to you after
Picaddilly? Remember our Deal to meet at the Union
Bar at the Slade. Remember? I think of you.*

Yours, Dopey

Yours. When he had first read that ending to the letter,
he had wondered why his friend had not been warmer
in tone. Was it simply a matter of Anselm's written
English being less impressive than his spoken? Did he
think it would be incriminating? But then Charles had
decided he couldn't have asked for more. Anselm meant:
'I am yours.'

Since that communication, Charles has heard nothing
from his friend, his own letters back via the diplomatic
pouch at the Swedish Embassy in London having gone
unanswered. He has even written to Anselm's parents in
Aachen but this letter, too, has not received a reply, as he
knew it wouldn't. All post from Germany is routinely
intercepted.

If only he knew where this 'education camp' was.
Anselm had mentioned the name of the court in Berlin
and he did wonder if there might be some way of gain-
ing access to its records. He had weathered the
suspicious glances of the staff at the London Library in
order to go through the German newspapers held there.
But if Anselm's trial had been reported, he hadn't been
able to find any references.

His whiskey arrives and he drinks it in one gulp before

nodding at the barman for a refill. The drinker seated two stools away now turns and looks him down and up. He has a frayed collar and food stains on the tie that is resting on his bloated belly. 'What's your excuse, then?' he says. His tone is not friendly.

'I'm sorry?'

'Why haven't you joined up?'

Charles stares at the grape stalks. 'I'm an air-raid warden.'

The man gives a dismissive grunt and half turns his back again.

Charles stares at the letter. An 'education camp' doesn't sound as if it would be a particularly difficult place from which to escape. A few guards perhaps, but if the inmates are expected to work as well as attend classes, presumably they will be going in and out all the time.

In moments of desperation, Charles has considered volunteering for the Red Cross, in the vain hope that he might be able to join one of their concentration camp inspection teams. But he knows this is unrealistic. Of course they won't use an ex-RAF officer, not when the country is at war and the Red Cross is supposed to be neutral.

But anything would be better than the monotonous routine of his life here at the club these past nine months, waiting every day for word from Anselm. He keeps himself busy painting at night while doing his Air Raid Precautions training during the day, a course that has mostly involved simulated fire-fighting, blackout patrols and stretcher-bearing. But this is more pretence. More phoniness for this phoney war.

Feeling emboldened by the whiskey now, Charles mulls over the new idea he has had for getting himself to France: persuading Eric to sail over there with him as part of the rumoured evacuation of the BEF. It seems a long shot, but . . .

The drinker on the stool is studying him again. 'You're that queer, aren't you?'

Charles folds the letter and slips it back into his pocket. He does not make eye contact.

'I've heard about you,' the man continues. 'Bloody queers. Shouldn't be allowed in here.'

The porter has appeared and is clearing his throat. 'Your caller is on the line again.'

Charles reaches the front desk before the porter. 'Funf? We were cut off.'

'Yes, yes. I know. Look, Charlie. I can't just drop everything . . .'

Charles doesn't fill the silence.

'Hello? Are you still there, Charlie?'

'Yes.'

'What have you heard?'

'That they, the Admiralty, need shallow-draught boats to help with the evacuation, to act as a shuttle. The navy can't get close enough to the shoreline with their destroyers.'

'Where?'

'No one is saying. Calais, I should imagine.'

It is Eric's turn to be silent for a moment. Then he clears his throat and says: 'The Painted Lady isn't really seaworthy. I was planning on giving her a proper overhaul this summer.'

'I could get over there this afternoon. Make a start. Is she still at the Isle of Dogs?'

'My patients will need . . .' Eric's protestations are sounding weaker.

'It would only be for a day, two at most.'

There is a longer pause while Eric weighs this. 'I couldn't get there until at least seven tonight.'

'Great. I'll see you there. You won't regret this, Funf.'

'I already am.'

By the time Charles steps on to the deck of *The Painted Lady*, wearing gumboots, an off-white submariner's roll-neck and a duffel coat, Eric is already on board whistling to himself as he repairs a bilge pump. 'Ah, there you are, Charlie,' he says. 'Merry Syphilis!'

Charles gives a wide grin as he remembers their crosstalk routine. 'And a Happy Gonorrhoea!'

Inside, *The Painted Lady* seems more ornate than the last time he saw it, with a mahogany drop-leaf table and a scattering of oriental rugs. It smells different too: mildewy, sour. Eric, however, is exactly the same; still a short, barrel-chested man with smooth skin that looks like freshly scrubbed teak. Though he is only a few years older than Charles, his fair hair is already going silvery. And with his blustering, distracted manner, this transforms him momentarily into the hopelessly late but time-obsessed White Rabbit.

'Good to see you again, Funf.' Charles extends his hand. 'I've missed you.'

Eric has no volume control, emphasizing words erratically and punctuating his monologues every so often with a friendly, snuffling laugh. 'No time for all that bollocks,' he says, wiping his oily hands on a rag before ignoring Charles's extended hand and putting his arm around his shoulder instead. 'Let's get cracking or they'll be finished before we get there. You can start by checking the lights and the lifebelts.'

As Eric supervises the provision of food and fuel, other volunteers arrive and climb aboard the neighbouring tugs and barges. A dockyard commodore, a big man with a high whispery voice and eyes like bags of cement, comes aboard with a clipboard to take their names. He asks Eric to sign a T124 form that declares his boat is now officially a Merchant Navy vessel serving under Royal Navy command. He then informs them that they are to collect steel helmets and charts from the dockyard office and set sail for Ramsgate. There they will meet the rest of the evacuation flotilla and be told their ultimate destination. They are to watch out for mines.

With the falling caw of gulls overhead and the lusty blow of klaxons, *The Painted Lady* sets off with three other vessels. Being towed behind her is a six-seater rowing boat, and, as it bobs in the wake, it looks as if it is trying to overtake them.

Having made their way out of the Sheerness basin, they realize they will not be able to reach Ramsgate before dark and so decide to stop for the night. This they soon regret. The sea is choppy and, feeling nauseous, they get little sleep. Eventually they give up and open a bottle of Irish that Charles has brought for the journey.

Eric has a habit of stubbing cigarettes out after a

couple of puffs. He lights one up now. 'How you been keeping?' he says before inhaling.

'So-so. Bored mostly.'

'Anyone said anything about your court martial?'

'Nope. It would almost be better if they did. I've become a non-person.'

'Well, maybe this . . .' Eric takes another drag then flicks the cigarette out of the window. He doesn't need to finish the thought. Both men know that this trip could be an opportunity for Charles to redeem himself.

'How is your friend, anyway?' Eric asks gently. 'Heard from him?'

'A letter. From prison in Berlin. Nothing since his trial.' Charles closes his eyes for a few beats then opens them and slaps the table. 'So. Where do *you* find love these days, Funf?'

'The usual old haunts. Buggers can't be choosers.'

'Have you considered joining the Medical Corps?'

'To be honest, I think my services are going to be needed more on the Home Front in the coming days. They're already clearing beds in the south-east.'

Charles raises his glass. 'Here's to finding love, assuming we both survive the war.'

They clink, drain and refill.

They reach the assembly point at Ramsgate a couple of hours after the sun has risen. Here they find themselves part of a strange flotilla of more than three hundred small boats: trawlers, tugs towing dinghies, motor launches like theirs, drifters, Dutch scoots, Thames barges, paddle steamers and cockleboats. As he contemplates them, Charles feels as if he has wandered into someone else's dream. The little vessels look like exotic misshapen seabirds gathering behind a trawler. He takes out his sketchbook to record the chaotic scene.

Via the radio they are now told their destination is Dunkirk, and they must take Route Y, which will amount to 175 sea miles. In theory this will mean avoiding mines and coastal guns, but it will also add the best part of another day to their journey time. After studying their charts, they follow the serrated coastline of north Kent for a few more miles before heading out to sea.

They encounter neither mines nor U-boats on the crossing but no sooner has Charles made out the coast of France under a chill, lowering sky than his mouth goes dry. Two Messerschmitts are approaching, flying in low from the east. He ducks for cover as they strafe the convoy but none of the bullets hits *The Painted Lady*. Instead they send up jets of water along her starboard side, making it look as if a family of whales below the surface is spouting in sequence. Eric and Charles exchange a look, trying to hide their shock behind a mask of British insouciance. None of the other boats seems to have been hit. As the ME 109s circle around for another pass, Charles's shock turns to gnawing, guttish fear.

Again, the bullets send up water, but none hits the boat.

He smells Dunkirk before he sees it: burning bricks, wood and plaster. The town itself has been veiled in a pall of black smoke, churning from a bombed oil tank. But in patches where the smoke breaks, he can see the glow of a hundred fires, tangled telephone wires, abandoned trucks. It looks like the end of the world.

If the ME 109s had rattled him, their strafing was as nothing compared to the disorientation he feels now. Until this moment the war has been an abstraction, something that was happening in another country, to be discussed soberly over a pot of tea rather than actively engaged with. As they await orders from the Royal Navy via the radio, Eric and Charles do not talk. Cannot. They are speechless.

Charles looks around for the rest of the flotilla but because of the oily smoke all he can see is a minesweeper, dark and silent as it lies at anchor, and the vast hull of a destroyer that has been sunk near the East Mole, the sea wall protecting the harbour entrance.

The tide goes out and a mile of shallow, sloping bay is revealed along a seafront ten miles across. The radio crackles into life. 'Because of the obstacle in the harbour,' a disembodied naval officer orders, 'the embarkation will proceed at Bray-Dunes.'

Bray-Dunes turns out to be an undulating area tufted with long, reedy grass, a couple of miles due east of the harbour. When they reach it, Charles raises his binoculars.

At first he thinks the thousands of men on the beach there are shrubs that have spread down from the dunes. Then they all start moving into long lines. Without waiting to be asked, he begins pulling the rope to which the rowing boat is attached. When it is as tight to *The Painted Lady* as he can make it, he climbs unsteadily down the stepladder and unties the rope before sitting down and reaching for the oars. He can feel his heart stuttering in his chest. A rush of blood is making a roaring noise in his ears, louder than the boom of the surf. He doesn't think he has felt more fear-frozen in all his life.

'Maximum of six,' Eric shouts. 'You included.'

Because the tide is still going out, the rowing is harder than Charles imagined it would be, but after twenty minutes he feels the nudge of sand against the hull. The seawater laps his rubber boots as he jumps out with a splash and then drags the boat ashore. A corporal from the Welsh Guards helps him.

'I can take five this trip,' Charles says.

The corporal holds up five fingers and the men at the head of the queue trudge over, their boots silent in the sand. Two of them, their faces smeared with oil, have half-empty bottles of wine in their hands and are clearly drunk. Another with his arm in a sling has abandoned his rifle and helmet, while a fourth soldier, in dis-obedience of an order, is refusing to abandon his haversack. He is also clinging on to a large suitcase held together with a belt. When the corporal snatches this from him it spills open, scattering souvenirs looted from the town: bottles of wine, a porcelain chamber pot, a pickelhaube helmet, and a brass dolphin holding on the end of its tail a small, broken clock. When the corporal points his gun at him, the soldier looks at the boat, shrugs and wades into the surf. Charles helps him in and then gets in himself, using the oar to steady the boat. The corporal helps them push off. A private takes the other oar.

It is easier rowing this way, though the weight of the men has lowered the boat so much that water is now splashing in. Once the rescued soldiers have been pushed on board *The Painted Lady*, Charles returns to the shore and sees there is now an ambulance on the beach where he has just been and that it has sunk up to its axles. The whole town behind it seems to be burning.

This time when he calls the next five men over he says to the corporal, "And you."

'You not getting in, sir?'

For a moment Charles wonders to whom the man is talking. He hasn't been called 'sir' for nine months. 'No,' he says. 'I'll go in a later one.' He taps the helmets of the two soldiers in the stern. Points. 'You're heading for that boat there. *The Painted Lady*.'

Once he has pushed the boat a few yards into the water, he looks up and sees Eric on the deck of *The Painted Lady*, holding his shoulders up questioningly. Charles holds up six fingers. He knows there is no going back now and this knowledge makes him excited and fearful at the same time. Guilty too, for not sharing his plan with Eric, or even saying goodbye.

As he turns and strides up the beach past the line of waiting soldiers, he isn't even sure if he can explain his plan to himself. Some ignore him but most look at him as if he is insane. He continues on up past a group of engineers who are setting up a makeshift jetty: lorries parked side by side on the hard sand exposed by the low tide. Some are stripping off the canvas covers and puncturing the tyres by firing bullets into them, while others are weighing them down with sand and lashing them together with ropes.

As Charles reaches the bandstand at the end of the

beach, someone shouts: 'Dover's that way, chum.' The scene here is more chaotic. No one seems to be in charge. The air is acrid with smoke and brick dust and there is broken glass underfoot; he makes a crunching noise as he walks along the esplanade. Soldiers carrying rolled-up blankets under their arms have not formed up in lines but are instead milling, not sure what to do, and thousands more are arriving down every road, swelling their number. From somewhere a goat has appeared, trotting back and forth bleating. Charles looks back and sees Eric is helping the last of the soldiers on to the boat, all the while darting looks across the beach. When he then gets in the boat himself and starts rowing to shore, Charles finds his resolve weakening. What the hell is he doing? Eric is supposed to head back to England without him . . .

He carries on down an alley that brings him out on to a wide boulevard. More columns of men are arriving, weary from marching. Down the road the hulks of abandoned trucks, Bren-carriers and staff cars can be seen. Some are on their sides and men are trying to keep in step as they negotiate them, like water flowing around a boulder in a stream. Fires mark the treeline. The crackle of sporadic gunfire and mortars can be heard in the distance. And the skirl of bagpipes. Bagpipes? Here? Yes, the sound is unmistakable and dreamlike.

Some of the marching soldiers are too exhausted to notice him walking the opposite way, but others follow him with curious eyes, their heads turning like a wave. Their fatigue is palpable. There are abandoned greatcoats littering the road and a couple of times Charles trips up on them, seeing them too late. As he continues against the flow, he thinks of his reason for being here, for not getting back in the rowing boat, and a cold charge of fear runs through him. He reminds himself again of his purpose: he is here in this foreign land to find his friend. Wearing the clothes of a fisherman he will probably be ignored by the advancing German troops. He will sleep in barns. Steal food. Survive.

Before he sees the Stuka he hears its scream as it goes into a nosedive. The two files of soldiers scatter like a parting of the sea, taking cover where they can: on road-side verges, in shop doorways. A 25-pounder field gun and limber being towed by a Quad takes a direct hit. A soldier who had been standing near it has been almost sliced in half by shrapnel and, as he lies on the ground, he tries to put his own entrails back into his stomach. Charles hears high-pitched screaming and turns to see a child running across the road with half her clothes missing. Her hair is alight. He takes his duffel coat off and, running after the child, wraps it around her to douse the flames. When he looks under the coat he sees the child's skin has fallen away, and she is dead.

The groans of the wounded can be heard for a moment before another explosion leaves Charles briefly blinded by plaster dust. Someone is shouting for a stretcher-bearer. He turns and sees a French soldier lying on the ground drumming his heels. His jaw is missing. Charles is distracted by the sensation of rock fragments stinging the back of his neck. As he brushes them away with jittery hands, he hears bullets silence a whinnying horse.

71

A soldier now staggers into his path rubbing his belly and looking confused as his hand comes away wet with blood. He takes his helmet off and doesn't seem to realize that his ear and a flap of skin from his neck are still attached to it. When a medic arrives dragging a stretcher, he gently persuades the man to lie down on it. Charles gets hold of the other end. Suddenly he has no choice. He has to go back to the beach.

On the promenade, the choking dust and smoke is dispersed by a damp and salty breeze blowing in from the sea. He sees decking panels from bridging trucks are now being laid across the backs of the line of lorries, along with planks that have appeared from somewhere. These serve as a walkway along which soldiers can head to the launches. Charles and the medic break into a jog, their boots squishing in the wet sand. A riderless cavalry horse canters past. The boarding is disordered and noisy now. Nerves are frayed. The jostling soldiers, some holding their rifles above their heads to keep them dry, have grown impatient of waiting. Those who have now realized they won't be rescued unless they reach the front barge past others who are standing still. German shells are reaching the outskirts of the town. Two ME 109s are strafing the beach. In desperation some soldiers fire their rifles into the air where they have passed over. Charles hears someone shout: 'Where's the bastard RAF?'

Eric is running up the beach. 'What the fuck are you playing at?'

Charles does not answer. He has no answer. Blood is roaring in his ears. The shifting sand at his feet seems nebulous and blurred, like cloud vapours. From somewhere on the beach comes the incongruous sound of a mouth organ.

'Jesus!' Eric's voice brings him back to consciousness. He sees his friend examining the man on the stretcher. It is clear now that a section of his skull has been sheared off. 'Dead,' Eric pronounces. 'Leave him here.'

Charles and the medic lower the stretcher and transfer the body on to the sand. The medic rolls up the stretcher and runs back to the town, knocking over a tripod of rifles as he passes it. Three soldiers are sitting waiting in the rowing boat. When they reach the tide line, Eric signals across to the queue of waiting troops. 'We can take one more of the wounded.'

A man with a bloody bandage around his head pushes forward and strips off his webbing and bayonet.

German guns are now ranged on the beach, sending up irregular storms of sand and bodies as the barrage creeps from east to west.

As they row, a soldier appears alongside and they drag him on board. He lies down flat across the others, to keep the boat balanced. Charles sees another uniformed figure about seventy yards away, more boy than man, being held afloat in the inky water by his life jacket. He has had both his arms blown off at the elbow but is still alive. His screams seem to carry along the entire coast.

Before they can change course to attempt a rescue, the man's life vest slips off and he is silenced as he disappears under the waves. There is another man bobbing nearer to them, coated in thick oil. His brains are hanging out. Mercifully, this one is already dead. Geysers of water rise turbulently in the air as shells fall nearby.

Everyone in the rowing boat is drenched as the water showers back down.

There are seventeen rescued soldiers now on *The Painted Lady*, shivering on the deck and in the cabin. Some of them must have fallen back in as they were scrambling on board: they are barely able to move because of the weight of their saturated uniforms.

While Eric tends to the wounded, Charles hands out blankets. Remembering his bottle of Irish he goes around giving each of them a tot. Their faces, staring out from under their helmets, look gaunt. Their skin is black from the oil and smoke, emphasizing the whiteness of their eyes. There are no smiles of relief, only blank expressions of resignation and exhaustion. Some strip off their wet clothes and wring them out.

A nautical mile out, the noise of battle subsides and they become more aware of the chug-chug of the motor. They look back to Bray-Dunes and see another destroyer has been hit amidships and is listing. As he considers this spectacle, Eric says to Charles: 'Would you mind telling me what the bloody hell you thought you were doing back there?'

'Attempting a rescue,' Charles says, unable to disguise the defeat in his voice. He watches a parachute descending in the distance like a strange blossom. In another quarter of the sky he sees white figures of eight scratched like skate marks on ice, evidence of a recent dogfight. Then he hears a wailing siren and, in a moment of choking horror, turns to see a black, hump-winged Stuka coming towards them in a series of jinking dives.

PART TWO

I

London. Summer. Present day. Two and a half
months after Edward's release

EDWARD IS CLIMBING UP THE WALL OF THE CAVE, FINDING
footholds, breaking his nails on the rocks as he clings
and inches higher and higher. He is near the entrance
now. He can almost taste the daylight . . .

He opens his eyes and tries to establish where he is.
The inner man has woken with a jolt. He stretches, testing the walls, nudging himself to consciousness. There
is something touching his head, but what? The envelop-
ing darkness makes it difficult to determine. He brushes
it with the back of his hand. Apart from a slightly raised
pattern, it has a flat surface. Wallpaper. It is the ceiling.

His eyes have adjusted to the gloom now and, when
he looks down, he can see he is standing on a bedroom
chest, the drawers of which have been pulled out to
make a tier of steps. He has been sleep-climbing again.
It is the third or fourth night he has awoken to find
himself here.

He touches his brow and finds it mantled with sweat.

The T-shirt he has slept in is damp, too. As lightly as he can, he lowers himself down. The digital clock on the bedside table reads 3.23. He turns on the light and, though it is only a forty-watt bulb, has to shield his eyes. He looks around. There are tones of grey in the bedroom, but they do not run to the spectrum of colour. He is still inhabiting the shadow world between black and white.

Now he feels a floating sensation in his groin and belly, as if he is in a lift that has come to an abrupt stop. The room seems to be spinning slowly. Sitting on the bed, he tries to focus on a stationary object, a bowl on the dressing table. Why has he never noticed it before? A hand snakes out towards it. The bowl contains hairpins, a disposable contact lens in a blister pack, euro coins, earrings, an AA battery, mascara, tweezers, an Oyster card, a ski pass, a packet of Rennies, three rings.

The traces of Frejya.

He examines them with jittery fingers, as if each contains a part of her. And then his heart dilates. Curled up at the bottom of the bowl he sees a photograph: a scarf, a towel, some socks and a bra on top of the duvet, fashioned into the letters 'LYA'. It is the 'Love You Always' sign he made for her on the day he left for Afghanistan. She must have photographed it. LYA. The last words she had said to him as he wound down the taxi window to wave goodbye. The shorthand that spoke the immeasurable words of their love.

His fingers loosen. The photo drops to the floor. He reaches out to steady himself and his hand falls on a

78

brush. There are long, balled-up hairs caught on its teeth. Pale blonde. It must have been Frejya's brush. These must be Frejya's hairs. He tugs them out, holds them to his nose and, for the first time in years, thinks he can smell something. It is sweet and musty, the smell of flour. As he detects it, a faint blur of colour swims before his eyes like a shoal of tropical fish, and then is gone. He picks up a bottle of scent. Frejya's scent. Again the brief suffusion before he returns to his world of black and white.

He closes his eyes and pictures her slow blink. Hears her loose laughter as he tips her on the bed and kisses her bare feet before tugging off her jeans. Feels the warmth of her soft belly against his.

Her absence is like a presence now, as tangible as an indentation, as if she has just risen from the bed and the sheets are still warm from where she had been lying. He walks over to the fitted cupboard and, opening the door, contemplates the dresses queuing up on the rack. As he runs his hands along them, setting them in motion, he remembers Frejya trying them on, smoothing them out over her hips.

He pulls out a cocktail dress of oriental brocade. It looks grey, though he remembers it as red and gold. As he holds it to his nose there is a shimmer of colours, a brief sensation of softness in his hands and a prickly awareness of someone else in the room. He looks up.

Frejya is standing in the bedroom doorway in her dressing gown, watching him.

'They told me you were dead,' Edward says.

Hannah covers her mouth with her hand. Shakes her head slowly.

Edward holds up the dress and smiles. 'Your clothes still smell of you.'

II

AS HE APPROACHES THE HOUSE, NIALL ACKNOWLEDGES WITH A half-salute the lone photographer waiting under an umbrella across the street. When he reaches the doorstep, he pumps his own up and down a couple of times and pats his pockets for the housekeys. The lock turns with a familiar *clack-clack* and he stamps his shoes on the mat before bending down to scoop up the post scattered across it. He shivers as the prickles brush against the backs of his fingers. More familiarity.

'Hello,' he says at the foot of the stairs as he drops the free newspapers, fliers and magazines in a bin. The bills and letters addressed to Frejya he puts on the radiator cover. 'Anyone home?'

The house smells of two-week-old flowers. It is gloomy, but no one has turned on the lights. He listens. Hearing Hannah playing an acoustic guitar upstairs, plucking the strings with her fingertips in the Spanish style, he remembers how alive it made him feel when he used to call round here and check on her after her mother died. She had turned the house into student digs, renting out bedrooms to two nineteen-year-olds on her foundation course. They seemed to spend all their time texting, experimenting with eyelash extensions and listening to hip-hop. There would be unwashed plates around the sink, labels on food in the fridge, the stale smell of marijuana in the air.

Niall hesitates before entering the sitting room. Edward will be in there, staring out of the window as usual. It will smell like an infirmary: overheated and chemical. But he hopes his old friend will be more communicative this time, hopes that the thin layer of ice in which he is encased will have thawed a little.

He skitters his fingernails against the door panel before entering. 'Hello? Northy?'

Edward looks up, sees who it is and looks down again. He is wearing a tracksuit with a hood. His feet are bare. He hasn't shaved.

'Shall I put the kettle on?'

Edward forces a smile. 'Just had one.'

'There was a snapper outside,' Niall says. 'I'm assuming he's a freelance because, as far as I know, all the editors on the nationals have agreed to call their boys off in return for . . .'

'Don't think the neighbours were too happy about them being camped out there.'

'No.'

'At least they've stopped shouting through the letterbox.'

Good, Niall thinks. He seems quite talkative today. 'That must have been horrible. I've told the editors that all requests for interviews have to come through me from now on. Not sure how much good it will do

82

though, to be honest. Your best bet might be to give one interview, and then the others will lose interest. Go for one of the broadsheets. I know the editor of the *Guardian* pretty well. You might need to pose for some snaps too.'

'I'll think about it.'

Niall looks at the ceiling as he hears Hannah turn up the volume on the music she has started listening to. Coldplay, if he is not mistaken. 'I gather it's not going that well with your therapist,' he says. 'Han says you won't talk to him.'

'Waste of time.'

'But you're looking much better. You've gained weight.'

'So you keep saying.'

Niall hears these thin words as a reproach. On his last few visits he has felt increasingly self-conscious about his own weight. Edward's attenuated frame seems to be a criticism of him, a confirmation of his moral inferiority.

He looks for a distraction, sensing that his old friend is going to prove hard work today after all. Still chilly and absent. As he looks around the room he realizes, with a stab of guilt, that he probably knows its layout better than its owner does. Though most of the objects are relics from Edward's years in the diplomatic service, their locations have changed. Niall had helped Frejya rearrange them after they decorated this room together and he put up the new shelf. He tests this now with his thumb to check its rawlplugs are holding. It is fine, easily standing the weight of the African mask and fly switch, the statue of Buddha, the paperknife in the style of a Florentine dagger, the Russian doll and the pair of Spanish candlesticks shaped like entwined serpents.

The lacquered Chinese screen that Edward would have remembered as being against the window is now in the corner, concealing the television. The Turkish scimitar that used to lie on top of the bookcase is now displayed on the wall. Only the old French rifle is in its original place, mounted above the fireplace, its spiked bayonet still pointing at the rocking chair in the corner. Edward's father had brought it home from the war as a souvenir.

Niall picks up a framed photograph of himself with Edward. They are wearing the same college scarf as they punt together on the Cam. He checks his watch. Almost six. 'Oh, sod tea; let's open a bottle of wine. Fancy a glass?'

Edward shrugs.

Niall puts a hand to his stomach as if trying to flatten it as he goes through the doorway. In the kitchen he selects a bottle of red from the rack, and blows dust from its label before pulling its cork, pouring two glasses and swirling one of them around. He sips. Its thickness takes him by surprise, like meat on his tongue.

When he returns to the room he hands a glass to Edward then he points at the old Staunton chessboard with his index finger and cocks his thumb like a pistol. 'Fancy a game?'

'Only if you've improved.'

Niall laughs, grateful for the change of mood. 'You know me, I am to chess what Wayne Rooney is . . . to chess.' This is better, he thinks. In the past few weeks, the chessboard has proved a useful no man's land between them. A game that does not require conversation. He sets up the pieces before taking a black pawn in one hand and a white in the other and holding them behind his back. Edward taps his right arm and, seeing he has picked white, makes the first move, developing a knight. Niall moves his queen pawn two spaces. Edward mirrors it.

'Got some good news,' Niall says without taking his eyes off the board. 'I don't know whether your solicitor has been through the details yet but when you . . .' he curves the air with his fingers, ' "died" your half of the mortgage was written off and Frejya's half . . .' Pause. He has realized what he is about to say. 'The building society have now said that they are satisfied that Frejya's death wasn't, you know, that she didn't . . . Anyway, you don't have a mortgage now.'

A black cat pokes its head around the door, like a nervous publicist checking on a client.

'Didn't know you'd got a cat,' Niall says.

'Not ours. Belongs to a neighbour. Hannah has been feeding it scraps . . . Whose decision was it to declare me dead?'

Niall crosses his arms. Pretends to be weighing up his next chess move. 'It was a departmental decision, really. Standard procedure.'

'How did Frejya take it when you told her?'

'She was upset, obviously.'

'She had her accident soon afterwards, didn't she?'

Niall moves his head in agreement. 'Anyway, in

addition to the death-in-service payment we made to Frejya, which I will make sure doesn't have to be paid back, I gather that you both had private life insurance. Frejya got half a million when you "died" and Hannah got a further half-million when Frejya died. So financially . . . I don't know what becomes of that, but I'll make sure we cover you for it if the insurance company want your half back.'

'Thanks. Again.' Edward moves a bishop from one side of the board to the other but ends up on the wrong diagonal. A frown. 'Have I moved that properly?' he asks.

'Perhaps we shouldn't rush things.'

'In the cave I used to try and replay games in my head,' Edward says, placing the piece on the correct square.

Niall leans forward.

'There was one I'd memorized when I was at school, Bobby Fischer versus Donald Byrne, the one where Fischer made a queen sacrifice on move 17, getting a rook, two bishops and a pawn in return. He then went on to force a checkmate while Byrne's queen sat helpless at the other end of the board. I kept trying to picture the notation but I couldn't do it. It's hard to . . .'. He trails off.

'Concentrate when you're light-headed from lack of food?' Niall nods encouragingly. Keep it light, he thinks. Keep him talking. A conversation between friends rather than a debrief. 'What did you miss most?'

Edward closes his eyes, his usual signal to change the subject.

'Do you want to see your obituary?' Niall pats his pockets and then shakes his head, making the flesh under his chin double up and crease. 'I must have left it in my case. They rang me for a quote when they were writing it. I told them you were lazy and feckless.' He grins to show he is joking.

'My guards showed it to me in the cave. It was in the edition of the *Telegraph* they filmed me holding up.'

'Yes, of course it was. I'd forgotten that.'

'Is that why you had me declared dead? To make them show some proof of life?'

Niall looks away. 'There were a number of options we were considering.'

Colour is rising to Edward's face. 'Did anyone think to tell Frejya that was why you were doing it?' He says this loudly, almost shouting.

Niall puffs out his cheeks. 'We thought it would be kinder not to. We thought declaring you dead would give her some closure.'

'It gave her closure all right.' There is heat in Edward's words now.

Niall castles, moving his king first with an emphatic click of wood against wood. The silence flows back into the space between them heavily, like oil.

But Edward hasn't finished yet. 'Why did they let me go?'

'We don't know . . . Did they talk to you at all?'

Without taking his eyes off Niall, Edward bites his lip and moves his head from left to right, right to left.

'There were no other hostages?'

'None. Why did they release me?'

Niall shrugs clownishly. 'Perhaps they found you too annoying.'

No smile from Edward. There is an urgency to his next question. 'Was my liberty bought? Did I endanger other people? I need . . . I can't seem to . . .'

'Sorry, Northy. I'm not very good at this. What advice did your therapist give?'

'I told you, he's a waste of space . . . He kept asking me how I felt about the people who held me hostage.'

'And how do you feel?'

'Don't feel anything.'

Niall purses his lips as he nods. 'Well, I hate them. Fucking animals.' Realizing he is breathing rapidly, he holds up his hands and laughs. 'Sorry. It's just I felt terrible about persuading you to go. I had to live with that for years.'

'Poor you.' Edward runs his hands through his hair. 'Sorry. That sounded . . . It must have been hard for you, too, Niall. I'm grateful that you put your own life on hold to look after Frejya and Hannah.'

'You were telling me about your captors. How many were there?'

'Actually, would you mind if we talk about this another time?' Edward is studying his friend's fleshy face and looking puzzled.

'I know what you're thinking,' Niall says with a smile he hopes will lighten the mood once more. 'You're thinking the features are more or less the same, but he's aged into his own father. Right?' He becomes aware of the ache in his jaw as he holds his smile.

'What was Frejya like when I disappeared?'

Niall understands now that Edward is not going to let things go today. 'Amazing. She was amazing. She lobbied constantly to keep your story in the news, keep the pressure up on the FCO to find you. She organized petitions and did things like sponsored bike rides to raise campaign funds. And she would do these vigils outside the gates of Number Ten, holding a photograph of you. There's some video footage of her giving a press conference if you'd like to see it.'

'Not right now.'

The cat enters again, pads around the room and leaves. Niall nods at four cardboard boxes stacked against the wall. 'You had a chance to look through them?' He stands up, opens one and takes out a mug and removes its bubble wrap. Written on its side are the words 'Friends of Edward Northcote'. He hands it to Edward and opens a second box. From this he takes out a T-shirt wrapped in cellophane, some pens and balloons and a mouse mat. He holds them up in turn to show they all have the same words printed on them. 'And have you read any of these?' He unties the neck of a bulging bin liner, reaches inside and pulls out a hand-ful of letters. 'There are three or four more of these around here somewhere. Letters of support from the public. Cards from well-wishers.'

Edward holds the mug up to the light from the window. 'When I was declared dead . . .' he says. 'How did Frejya react?'

'She sort of lost the will to, um . . .'

'Do you think she killed herself?'

'No. Definitely not.'

'Was there a ransom paid for me?'

'I don't mean to be evasive, Northy, but we're having an internal inquiry about what happened and once—'

'What I don't understand is why there was no intelligence about who was holding me. Why was . . . We were occupying their country, for God's sake.'

'We didn't know you were alive.'

'But you didn't try and find out whether I was or I wasn't? What about that French academic who was taken at the same time as me? His government got him released quickly enough.'

'The French always pay ransoms, that's why their citizens are always the preferred targets for kidnappings . . . Has Hannah shown you the cuttings file about the campaign? Let me see if I can find it.' Niall opens a drawer, searches around it for a moment then tries the one next to it. From this he takes out a ring binder. 'Here.' He opens it and taps with his finger at a newspaper cutting. It shows Frejya holding a lit candle in one hand and a photograph of Edward in the other. There is tape over her mouth. As Edward studies it, Niall hears in his memory the loud crackle as she pulls out a strip of duct tape and cuts it with scissors before sealing her lips.

Edward turns the page and sees a photograph of himself, the one taken in the cave with him holding up a copy of the *Daily Telegraph*. 'So the ransom demand came after this was taken?'

Niall hesitates again. 'Yes.'

'And was it paid?'

'The British government cannot pay ransoms.'

'Was it paid?'

A beat. 'Yes.'

'Who paid it?'

Another beat. 'I did.'

Edward's eyes widen. '*You* did?' He rubs his brow. 'Why didn't you say? How much was it?'

'Three million dollars.'

Edward stands up. Begins pacing. 'Where did you get . . . ?'

'I found a way to channel it from our overseas development fund . . . There's nothing on paper about it, but if it comes out I'll take full responsibility.'

Edward shakes his head. Cups the back of his neck with his hand. 'Fuck!' He shakes his head again. 'I mean, I don't know what to say, Niall. Thank you. You saved my life.'

Niall gets to his feet. The two embrace.

'Thank you,' Edward repeats in a whisper, kissing Niall's neck. 'Thank you so much.' When he sits down again he adds: 'And thank you for levelling with me. It puts my mind at rest.' He folds his arms and looks up at the ceiling. Hannah has turned the music off and is practising her guitar again, her bass this time. 'She showed me a clip of herself playing in her band. They were pretty good. She holds her bass low, like Sid Vicious.'

'Did you tell her you thought they were good?'

'I don't recall.'

'Well, you should. She needs your approval.' Niall looks away, his lower lip drawing back. He is thinking about how much he had enjoyed being a surrogate father to Hannah when Frejya was busy campaigning.

She had become the child he and his wife Sally had been unable to have. 'She's grown up to be beautiful, hasn't she? Smart too. And confident. You must be very proud.'

'It didn't exactly have a lot to do with me.' Edward draws his fingers down his face until they are resting against his chin. 'She reminds me too much of Frejya . . . And I can't deal with it.'

'Can't or won't?'

'What do you mean?'

'I mean . . .' Niall isn't sure what he means. He has seen the way Edward sometimes looks at Hannah and it worries him in ways he can't quite articulate, as if even to give a shape to his thoughts would be taboo.

Edward sighs. His hands are shaking slightly. 'I think I know what you mean. She's like . . . like Frejya's ghost haunting the house, this stranger impersonating my wife. It's unbearable.'

The tips of Niall's fingers grow cold as he realizes what it is that bothers him about the way Edward's eyes sometimes fix on his daughter: he used to look at his wife in the same way. The same fervent stare. He is sure Edward hasn't realized this himself. Not yet. But now he finds himself wondering whether, when he does, it will be too late. 'Actually, I don't think they are all that similar,' he lies.

'Really?'

'And even if she does look a bit like Frejya, it's not her fault.'

'Fault? What are you talking about?'

'Perhaps being cooped up in the house together all

92

day doesn't help. Too many memories. Why don't you get away somewhere? A long holiday.'

'Now you mention it, I had a letter from someone offering me the use of his holiday home in Alsace. Acres of garden. Very private.'

'Who?'

'Some investment banker. His driver delivered the invitation by hand.'

Niall shifts in his seat. 'I'd say no to that one, if I were you. Too risky.'

'Risky?'

'He hasn't been vetted. Besides, the FCO has lots of quiet retreats dotted around the world. Just tell me where you want to go and I'll arrange something. Somewhere hot with palm trees and a pool.'

'Thanks, I'll think about it.'

'You OK?'

Edward is staring at his thumb as he rubs the handle of his walking stick. He looks as if he is about to cry.

'Perhaps it would help if you wrote about what happened,' Niall says. 'It might be easier than talking about it. I've had a few calls from publishers and agents wanting to get in touch with you. A book about your time in captivity. There would be a sizeable advance in it, and they've offered to ghost it for you . . .' There is a pinging noise and Niall holds up his hand in a 'halt' gesture before reaching into his pocket for his mobile. He looks at the screen then over his shoulder before texting a reply. 'Sorry. What?'

'What?'

'A memoir. You always used to love writing.'

'That was poetry, and it wasn't very good.'

'But you used to talk about writing a book as well. Now's your chance.'

'I don't know, Niall. There isn't much to say. Nothing happened. It was eleven years of nothing happening.' Edward raises his head stiffly. Stares at the ceiling. 'Did I tell you the *Daily Mail* offered to buy me a new car in return for an exclusive interview?'

Niall raises his eyebrows questioningly.

'I said no.' Edward takes a sip of wine. 'You mentioned a video of Frejya . . . ?'

'It's a DVD actually, but yes. Shall I put it on?' He searches the shelf above the television, finds the disc he is looking for and feeds it into the player.

III

THE SCREEN IS FUZZY FOR A MOMENT THEN REPORTERS AND photographers can be seen gathered outside Edward's house. They are checking their watches, talking into mobiles and stamping their feet against the cold as they form a semicircle around a microphone stand. Niall, looking slimmer and younger, emerges from the house first, followed by Frejya who is wearing sunglasses and, pinned to her lapel, one of the black ribbons that the Friends of Edward Northcote wear.

'She lost weight,' Edward says in an undertone. 'She looks . . .'

In the film Niall is now clearing his throat and tapping the microphone. 'Mrs Northcote would like to read out a statement and then she will answer a few questions.' He stands to one side as Frejya moves up to the microphone.

'On the fifth anniversary of Ed's abduction I appeal to his kidnappers to show mercy and compassion and end his, and our, ordeal,' she begins, her voice faltering for a moment and then finding strength. 'My family has suffered terrible uncertainty and distress over the past five years. We have worried about Ed every single minute of every single day. Please give us some indication that he is still alive.'

There are traces of Norway in her intonation and lack of pauses. She looks directly into the lens of the camera before continuing. 'I would like to thank all those who have stood with us during these most difficult of times. Without their support we would not have made it through these dark days. Thank you.'

Niall steps forward again and says: 'I would like to add that the British government remains firmly committed to finding Edward Northcote. Our latest initiative is the distribution of a hundred thousand leaflets around Kabul and Islamabad asking for information on his whereabouts. We continue to do everything we can to secure his safe release and we remain in close contact with his family. Now, if any of you have questions for Mrs Northcote . . .' When no hands are raised he adds: 'I'm afraid she won't be able to do any one-to-ones afterwards.' Four hands go up. 'Yes?'

'Dan Simpson, Sky News. If Edward *has* been kidnapped, how do you think he will be coping?'

Frejya leans in close to the microphone. 'I think if anyone can get through it, he can. He has a great memory for poems and films and books. And I think he can handle stress. He is fit. He used to run marathons.'

'And how are you coping?'

In the sitting room as they watch the footage, Niall looks across at Edward. He knows what the truthful answer to this question would have been, because Frejya had told him. She hadn't been able to sleep properly for five years. She could not stand the sympathy in strangers' eyes when she was stopped in the street. She couldn't bear to be away from her phone in case it brought news. She felt exhausted and weepy most of the time and, every now and then, when she realized she had forgotten what her husband's voice sounded like, when she couldn't even summon his face or find his smell in her memory, she had wanted to kill herself.

'I'm fine,' she says to the reporter. 'Thank you. Though my friends say I should find a hobby to distract myself.' She adds this with a quick yet withholding smile, giving the journalist permission to smile back. 'But the trouble is, I can't think of anything that does not remind me of him.' When she sees the smiles drop, she shrugs. 'What can I say? I just want him back.'

'Janet Conroy, Radio 4. Do you think your publicity campaign has prolonged Edward's captivity?'

'I hope not,' Frejya says. 'If he is able to hear any news where he is being held, I think it will give him strength to know that he is not forgotten.'

'In his press conference, the French hostage Dominique Chapelle said he never saw Edward or heard whether or not he was alive. Is that what he told you in private?'

Frejya nods.

Someone at the back shouts: 'Speak up!'

'Yes,' Frejya says.

'He also said in his press conference that he didn't give up hope because he knew the French government would do anything to get him out.'

Niall steps forward to the microphone. 'And now

every terrorist in the Middle East knows, too, that the French government will do anything to get their citizens out. Anything. Pay any price. Compromise any principle. The British government prefers to take a more moral line. No deals with terrorists, plain and simple.'

'Peter Bligh, *Washington Post*: Has a ransom been demanded for Mr Northcote and has the Foreign Office refused to pay it?'

'Tireless efforts have been made to determine Edward's whereabouts and to establish whether or not he has been taken hostage,' Niall says. 'Rest assured, we will do everything in our power to secure his release, as and when we are contacted by his kidnappers. Any other questions?'

'You haven't answered my question,' the man from the *Washington Post* says.

'Our position is that we do not pay ransoms and we do not facilitate concessions to hostage-takers,' Niall says.

'Have you advised the family not to pay a ransom?' the reporter presses.

'All I can say is that we have been in close contact throughout.'

'Martin Cullen, the *Irish Independent*. Five years have passed without proof that Edward is alive. Why do you think he is?'

Frejya hesitates before answering. 'Because I feel it in my heart.'

Niall makes a chopping mime across his neck. Seeing that Frejya is blinking back tears, he leads her back indoors. Questions are shouted at her retreating back.

As he sits in his own house now, in front of his own television, Edward takes rapid, shallow breaths. 'Dammit, Niall!' he shouts suddenly, slamming the chessboard with the flat of his hand. 'Why did you have to declare me dead? Why? You took away her hope!'

Niall gets to his feet. 'I'm sorry, Northy,' he whispers, 'I'm really, really sorry.'

At the door, he turns back to see his friend crouched on the floor shielding his eyes with a hand. His mouth is open wide in a soundless howl.

IV

Four months after Edward's release

WHENEVER HANNAH GOOGLES HER FATHER'S NAME, HUNDREDS of links to websites appear, and they are rarely the same ones from day to day. But the three images that come up first are always alike, the ones that all the papers continue to use whenever the subject of Edward Northcote is in the ether.

The first shows him on the gurney being transferred to the helicopter ambulance, his gaunt features barely discernible under a tangle of hair and beard. The second was taken when he was in hospital in a room darkened by closed curtains. A tabloid reporter had impersonated a hospital orderly to gain access to him and the resulting photograph showed Edward raising his hand to protect his eyes against the flash. The Press Complaints Commission had censured the papers that used this image, but no legal action had been taken.

The next photograph of him to appear, several weeks later, had been taken on a mobile by a passing member of the public. It showed him being carried up the steps of his house by Hannah. That one had revived interest in the story, partly because it signalled to Fleet Street that Edward had finally returned home.

After this last one was taken there was a small encampment outside the house. As well as vans with darkened windows and a TV film unit with a satellite dish, there had been a semi-permanent huddle of reporters and photographers with long lenses and tripods. From time to time, film lights would go on, illuminating a man with a microphone talking into a camera. Occasionally one would knock at the door and shout through the letterbox: 'How did you feel when you heard your wife was dead?' Inside, the phone would ring at regular intervals, only to go straight through to the answering machine. Edward had effectively become a prisoner again.

The press assumed that the curtains were drawn permanently to avoid the long lenses, but the truth was that sunlight was still painful for him. Either way, it had the desired effect. After a few days, the press ranks were reduced to a couple of freelancers. The papers more or less lost interest, having become distracted by the latest infidelity of a golf champion and the grounding of flights because of volcanic clouds emanating from the Norwegian island of Jan Mayen.

And now Edward has gone out on his own for the first time since returning from hospital. Hannah is not sure where – nearby, walking distance – but the important thing is that he is out, and she is preparing a meal for when he gets back: her mother's version of *bidos*, a traditional Norwegian stew.

On the board already, heaped into tidy piles, are chopped carrots, garlic, celery and rosemary. She takes a sip from a bottle of lager as she checks the recipe written in her mother's hand and, without looking, simultaneously points the remote to turn Lana Del Rey up louder on the sound dock.

The onions come next and, once she has peeled off the outer skin of one and sliced it in half, tears quickly follow – onion tears and not, for once, tears for her parents. This is something to savour, she thinks, something from which she must derive strength. Her pale eyebrows pointing down, she nods her determination not to cry in front of her father again, however frustrated she might feel, however desperate she has become for his attention and acceptance.

She chops up a chilli next, drizzles olive oil in the casserole dish and tips in the cubes of venison she has coated in flour. It is supposed to be reindeer, but the butcher assured her that this farmed deer from Wiltshire will taste the same. They sizzle and, as she stirs, she rubs her eyes and then runs cursing to the sink. Here she splashes her face with water. Stares at her hands. They are shaking.

Taking the stairs at a jog, she heads for the bathroom and looks in the mirror. Her eyes are red now. Fuck. She opens the medicine chest and feels around for her eyedrops. Before applying them, she takes out her contact lenses and flicks them into the wastebasket. Now she heads to her bedroom for her glasses. Once she has put them on, she returns to the bathroom and stares at her reflection.

Growing up, Hannah was often told how like her mother she looked. Apparently children rarely look like a cross between both parents, because one set of chromosomes always dominates – they don't simply merge – and as she studies her face now she sees nothing of her father in her features.

But she knows she is only a pale imitation of her mother. The set of her mouth is similar but her eyes do not have the same upsweep at the outer corners nor are her cheekbones as defined. Frejya had been un-ambiguously beautiful. From her teens onwards, she had once confided to Hannah, people had told her that she should be a model, a suggestion she had always laughed off. But then, when she was nineteen and studying languages at university, she was approached by an agency and, as much out of politeness as ambition, found herself modelling clothes for a catalogue.

Certainly her mother had had none of Hannah's little imperfections: the hint of a list in her left eye, the skin-coloured mole on her jawline, the slight gaps between her too prominent teeth – teeth that make her top lip bulge out and emphasize the weakness of her chin. Her mother had been slimmer: no cellulite, no fluid retention around the ankles, no suggestion of a double chin at certain unflattering angles.

And in truth it wasn't just the surface beauty for which she envied her mother. Hannah also wishes she possessed her passion and single-mindedness, as exhibited by her dedication to the cause of getting her husband back . . .

She checks the time. Fuck, fuck, fuck. The venison.

She jogs back downstairs and takes the pan off the stove. The chunks are on the cusp of burning, but are probably OK. She piles the vegetables in the dish and then pours in the stock and half a pint of red wine. After stirring for a few minutes she pops the lid on and checks the time again. Perfect.

She prepares the starter next, another traditional Norwegian dish – *gravat laks* and *kaviar*, salmon marinated in sugar, salt, brandy and dill, with sugar-cured and smoked cod roe cream – but as she is putting them on a plate she finds herself doubting that her father will like them. He seems to find rich food repulsive, preferring bread, anything without much taste.

Although he has been out of the house with her, this is his first time on his own, and she has had to cajole him into it. Now she worries that he will have lost track of time, an inability to read his watch being another of his peculiarities. Should she drive down the road to check he is OK? She feels anxious now that he is out of her sight, as if he is the child and she the parent. This reversal of their roles has happened so insidiously neither has acknowledged it. But Hannah has bought him a nightlight, so that he doesn't have to wake up in the dark – the dark he seems to be afraid of.

Sometimes when he has night terrors she will come through to his room and cool his brow with a compress, a damp flannel chilled in the fridge. Because he seems afraid of the silence, too, she will sometimes lie down on the floor beside him and whisper. She knows that what she says matters less than that he hears a human voice.

Sometimes she even sings him lullabies. It calms him.

On certain occasions he will still think, in his confusion, that she is Frejya. When this happens he will not look anxious, for a change, but instead relieved. To play along with his delusion seems the kindest thing for her to do. There is no need to correct him. Not yet. She stirs the pot faster as she thinks about this.

Part of his disconnection from the world seems to arise from an inability to express himself. He hardly ever speaks; just gives tense half-smiles, and even these seem more like a remembered reflex than a genuine expression of happiness. It is as if someone has told him that when you want to be polite, you smile, so he smiles. But his smiles cannot disguise his indifference to her.

If only he would let her help him. But she has come to suspect that she is part of the problem. Because of her constant presence, and her resemblance to her mother, he is retreating into himself, becoming more silent and withdrawn.

She contemplates the usual difficult evening ahead and finds herself longing for some of her old life back. She misses her friends, or rather she misses being able to meet them in the pub at short notice, without first having to arrange for Niall to come and 'father-sit'. And though none of the other band members have said anything to her face, she can tell they are growing tired of her skipping practice sessions. Even when her old housemates, Aisha and Kate, come to visit, the atmosphere feels strained. They sit upstairs in her bedroom, skinning up and listening to music. When they talk it is in hushed voices.

As she thinks about them now, Hannah wonders whether it might help to lighten her father's mood if she were to smoke a spliff with him. Might it help them bond? Perhaps she should roll one for him in readiness. As she opens the drawer where she keeps her Rizlas, she sees a photograph of her mother walking on Polzeath beach, back-lit, kicking up water. It has been placed in there face down. He must have done it because he can't bear that she isn't here, but Hannah is almost relieved. She has grown tired of being reminded of how far she falls short of her mother's ideal.

Edward's pace is slow as he walks down the King's Road, his stick making clicking noises as it contacts the pavement. He realizes that there are more people around than the last time he did this. As they nudge, and edge, and sidestep, he finds himself having to weave constantly to avoid collisions.

London seems too big, too loud, too crowded – more crowded than it used to be, and, something else that's different, everyone seems to be talking into mobile phones as they walk. He feels lost, navigating a strange and hostile land without a map and a compass. By the time he reaches Sloane Square, he feels exhausted too. He rests on his stick and looks up. Starlings are balling and massing overhead in a white-clouded sky being wiped blue by a gathering breeze.

Where am I, he thinks? What is this place? The shops here seem impossibly bright and vivid. A blur of expensive sensation. As he is taking it all in he notices someone staring at him with cold eyes. A stranger. An old man with angular features. Only gradually does he realize it is his own reflection in a shop window. Unrecognized. Unrecognizable. As he stares back at the stranger, he becomes aware of the hidden universe of machinery beneath his skin, the scaffold of interlocking bones, fibres and muscles. This makes him feel dizzy, so he looks around for a café in which to sit down.

There are two young mothers with children in pushchairs at the next table. They are not talking to one another but texting on their phones. Seeing a queue of people, he realizes that he is supposed to get up and order from the bar. He looks at the coffee options on a board – latte, mocha, cappuccino – but cannot recall what they mean. When his turn comes, he asks for a glass of milk and looks around. Most of the customers are either talking into their mobiles or reading compact news-papers. Several are working on their laptops.

When a bearded man in a djellaba enters, his heart starts pounding and his palms begin to sweat. Thinking the man will not want to be looked at directly, for fear he will be identified, Edward averts his eyes and stares at the laptop screens around him instead.

He feels confused again. There had been email before he was kidnapped but no Twitter, no Facebook, no YouTube, and these inventions seem alien and hostile, reminders that his home country has moved on, and left him behind.

Hannah has given him a smartphone and shown him the new applications on the computer, but he finds it hard to take in what any of them can do. Something about high-speed broadband. Leaning forward to see better, he studies a nearby screen: the home page of the BBC news website. Since he was a schoolboy he had followed British and American elections assiduously. His equivalent of soap operas. But the cast of characters on the screen are unfamiliar to him now, and his lack of political knowledge seems to emphasize his alienation. Apparently there is a black president in the White House.

Some of the other customers are staring at him now. Do they recognize him? A young man strides over and holds his phone up in both hands, at arm's length, as if showing it to him. A woman nearby starts doing the same. When the young man looks down and touches his screen, Edward realizes that he has been filming him. The young man looks up, smiles and says: 'Can I buy you a coffee?'

Edward shakes his head, no. He wants to say something in reply – maybe these people mean well – but without his senses working as they should, he feels incomplete, disengaged, a halfway man. He can understand what people are saying to him, yet he cannot always hear them, as if he is lip-reading.

His doctors have him on a course of serotonin and antihistamines and this has helped with his disequilibrium and mild agoraphobia. And the Prozac and Xanax he is being prescribed are supposed to subdue his emotions – leave him incapable of anger, love, anything. But for some reason the medication doesn't seem to be working. Today he feels anxious and tired.

He stares at his hand as if unsure it is his own. In his fingertips there is still numbness, but in other ways he feels as if he is recovering his health. The colour is returning to his skin. The doctors have told him they are pleased with his weight gain: a stone a month. He has also been getting some of his muscle tone back, thanks to regular visits from a physiotherapist.

It helps that Niall has arranged to have some gym equipment installed in the garage: a treadmill and an exercise bike to go with Frejya's cross trainer and his old dumb-bells. If he gets himself back in shape physically, it will help him regain his mental composure; that's what the doctors say, anyway.

He trusts them, but not the therapist, who has told him that the past eleven years were effectively a living death for him and that it was no wonder that now, in this 'afterlife', he is confused, detached and exhausted. If he still doesn't feel as if he has reconnected to the world, if he feels he is in limbo, then this is hardly surprising. His ordeal has taken him back to zero, the therapist said. Taken him 'off-grid' emotionally. He is having to learn to speak again, and walk again, have feelings again, as if he has never done any of these things before. And if he is seeing things, the therapist added, these are only the hallucinations of a mind disturbed by grief.

And all of this has confirmed for Edward that the therapist doesn't know what he is talking about. Is he hallucinating when he looks at his daughter and sees his wife? No. He sometimes sees a double exposure, as if the outline of one face has been superimposed on the other. And the illusion of familiarity combined with strangeness is unnerving him, leaving him feeling as if he is being haunted in his own home.

The therapist had come three or four times but has now put his visits on hold. Unless Edward is prepared to co-operate, he said, there seems little point. He even had the nerve to take Hannah aside and explain to her that her father had barely spoken in their last session, and had then fallen asleep. It wasn't quite true. He had only been pretending to be asleep.

There is nothing to say. Nothing to be done. Frejya is dead and, at least once a day, Edward catches himself wishing that he was, too.

A man parks his scooter on the pavement outside the café. A second man arrives on one. While the first talks into a mobile, the second takes out a camera with a bulky lens. The man on the phone jabs with his finger in Edward's direction, turns to the other man and mouths the words 'got him'. The photographer starts taking photographs through the window.

The young man who offered to buy the coffee looks concerned as Edward passes his chair on his way out. Another two photographers have arrived outside the café. As Edward heads back towards the King's Road, a corona of electric light forms around him. The photographers walk backwards in his path, their flash units tripping rapidly.

V

HEARING HER FATHER BEFORE SHE SEES HIM, HANNAH RUSHES to the window and watches his approach. Being forced to sleep on a hard surface for so many years has left him with a slightly sideways gait. She can see how hard he has to concentrate just to keep his balance, even with his stick, as if walking on an uneven surface.

The front door closes. 'I've got a surprise for you,' Hannah says, holding out her hand. When he takes it, she leads him into the kitchen. 'I've cooked reindeer stew.' She gestures at the flickering candles on the table she has set for two. 'Guess whose recipe?'

Edward drops her hand and says: 'Excuse me a moment.' He seems agitated as he heads upstairs.

A minute later, Hannah steps out into the hall and listens to the thumping noises that come from one of the bedrooms. It sounds like boxes being dragged. She runs up the stairs and stands in the doorway to the master bedroom. Her father has pulled out a couple of suitcases and is packing clothes into them on the bed. 'What are you doing?' she asks.

He looks up with dry eyes. Out of breath. One of Frejya's dresses is in his hand. 'I think we need to get rid of these,' he says. 'Give them to a charity shop.'

Hannah ruts her brow. 'Right now? Why can't they stay in here?'

'It's not healthy. I don't think it's doing either of us any favours. We need to clear her desk out, too. Put all that stuff in storage.'

When Hannah places a hand on his shoulder, he recoils.

'Sorry,' he says. 'I just think it will help. And we need to take her message off the answering machine.'

'Yes, I've been meaning to do that. Do you want to do it now?'

She follows him downstairs. When she presses play on the machine, an electronic voice says: 'Your outgoing message is . . .' then Frejya's voice is heard, that hint of a Scandinavian glottal stop. 'If you'd like to leave a message for either Frejya or Hannah, please do so after the tone.' Hannah presses it again and the message is repeated. 'Are you sure you want to delete it, Dad?'

Edward is calmer now. 'Let's take the tape out and put it with her things.'

'Sure. You know we have her speaking on some videos, don't you? Do you want to watch them?'

'Later maybe.'

They return to the kitchen and eat without speaking, forced to listen to the cruel scrape of cutlery. He leaves his plate mostly untouched. When she has finished, she picks up her guitar. 'Do you want to hear this song I've learned? See if you recognize it.' She strums the guitar and sings 'So Long, Frank Lloyd Wright'. Halfway through she trails off, as if interrupted by a broken A string.

'It's Simon and Garfunkel,' she says.

'Yes.'

'I love that line about how architects may come and go and never change your point of view. That has to be the most improbable line in . . .' She looks down. 'You haven't heard a word I've been saying, have you?'

'Sorry. I'm . . .'

'Don't push me away, Dad. Tell me what happened.'

'Not now.'

'How was my stew?'

'OK.'

'OK?'

'Yes. Fine.'

'That's it? That's all you're going to say? OK this? Fine that?' This is better, she thinks; her frustration is pushing her into anger. She feels strengthened by it. 'Why are you being like this?'

'Like what?'

'Is it me? Do you hate me?'

'No, of course not . . . I'm sorry.'

'And stop apologizing all the time . . .' She strums the guitar, a single chord that lingers. 'We had a funeral for you, you know. There was a coffin. We filled it with things of yours. Clothes, CDs, books . . . You did die in that cave, didn't you? In a way?'

Edward raises and drops his shoulders.

'It's quite a procedure, you know, declaring someone dead. There are all sorts of, like, legal implications. People can turn up again many years after being presumed dead. They might have been in a coma, or they might have faked their own death as an insurance scam.' Feeling she has gone too far she puts her arm around him.

He dips his shoulders away from her.

'Do you ever cry about Mummy?' It is the first time she has used the word in front of him. He stares at her mouth. He does this, she has noticed, as if unable to hear her unless he is looking at her, and he always seems to want to avoid looking at her.

'Look at me,' she says.

He looks. Afghanistan is still scratched on the backs of his eyes.

'I think I should move out,' he says. 'I'll move into the Travellers Club.'

'Why?'

'You need to get on with your life.'

Hannah folds her arms. 'I should be the one moving out then. This is your house. There's a girlfriend I can stay with.'

Edward scrapes back his chair and takes a step towards the door. 'No, this house is yours now. You can have it. I don't want it any more.'

'This isn't just about you, you know,' Hannah says, bringing her voice down by three notes. 'When I was nine I was told that my father had disappeared and might be dead. The father I loved and played with and had always assumed would be there in my life for ever. Throughout my teens I had to live with a mother who dedicated her every waking moment to campaigning for her missing husband.' An intake of breath. 'And when I was nineteen I had to watch as they buried you in an empty box, and a few days later I opened the door to a policeman and a policewoman who had come to tell me my mother had died. A nineteen-year-old orphan.' The edge of a laugh. 'Poor Orphan Hannie. Then you come back and now I have decided that I'm never going to let you out of my sight again. Never going to leave your side.' She is breathing quickly; her mounting indignation is making her words come in a steady, unstoppable stream. An unfamiliar hardness enters her eyes as she puts one hand on her hip and, with her other hand, holds the corner of the table, as if preparing for an impact. 'I never left your side in the hospital, you know. For the first three weeks you didn't even know who I was. And now, now when I've got you home, it's like . . .'

'I'm sorry, Han.'

Hannah puts out her arms and lowers herself on to the floor. She crawls forward and prostrates herself at her father's feet, circling her hands around his ankles as she had done as a child, a game in which he dragged her around as she clung on.

'Hannah! What are you doing?'

'Don't go again.' She doesn't look up as she says this. 'Please don't leave me.'

His hand hovers over her hair. 'Get up off the floor.'

Hannah doesn't move for half a minute, and then

when she slowly rises to her knees, she holds his appalled gaze. She is at the height she had been on the day he left for Afghanistan.

He cups her face in his hands and brushes her wet cheeks with his thumbs. 'I have to go,' he says.

Hannah sniffs. 'Why?'

Edward hesitates before he speaks. 'You remind me too much of her.'

VI

WITH A WATCH ON EACH WRIST, MIKE BARKER COULD BE mistaken for a trader in derivatives or equities, especially as the one on his right is set to the Eastern Standard Time of Wall Street, the one on the left the British Summer Time of the Square Mile. That he is also sitting behind one of the finest German engines money can buy – on hand-stitched nubuck leather that still smells of the showroom – adds depth to this illusion. But the dragon tattoos creeping out from under the watchstraps give him away, these and his thick moustache, the sort only a six-foot-two-inch ex-paratrooper with gym-hardened muscles can carry off without looking ridiculous. No one ever laughs at Mike Barker's moustache.

He checks the left watch now and presses in the ignition key. He has been enjoying listening to the dawn chorus, as he always does at this time of day, and the discreet hum of the V-12 engine does not bring it to an end. The car, a four-wheel-drive Mercedes, is a turbocharged model, so thoroughly black, from the bodywork to the dashboard, it seems to absorb light, giving the impression that it is all part of the same fluid surface.

It has armour-plated doors, run-flat tyres and black-tinted bulletproof windows that do not open. It also has a separate oxygen supply and an emergency medical unit built into the boot space, including blood plasma and morphine. For a six-seater that has been customized to four, it handles well, despite its extra weight. Indeed, as Mike has discovered when he has taken it to a race-track to practise his high-speed turns and reverse getaways, it is so well balanced it would take a side impact from a juggernaut to roll it over. Inside there is an electric glass panel dividing the front from the back and, behind the driver's seat, twin Bloomberg screens showing the FTSE and Dow Jones in red and green zigzags, the only colours permitted in the interior.

Mike puts in the earpiece linked by a transparent coil that disappears behind his collar to a radio receiver attached to his belt. This pack, which is connected to a monitor at Scotland Yard, is to be turned on only in emergencies, but he likes to wear it anyway, feeling it gives his boss some added value. He checks the rear-view mirror, takes in the white-stuccoed house with its bulletproof windows and turns the screens on in readiness. The front door is opening and Friedrich Walser is stepping out into Belgrave Square, a briefcase in one hand, a Nike sports bag in the other.

A sinewy and laconic 56-year-old with a German accent, manicured nails, all-year skiing tan and silver hair that hangs down below his collar, Walser looks more like a Milanese art dealer than a master of the universe. As is his custom, when he reaches the car he gets to his knees as if in Muslim prayer. It is to check for explosives under the 4×4. He knows Mike will already have checked with his mirror device, but for Walser the double check has, as he once explained, become a superstition. Mike doesn't take it personally. He understands. If anything, it makes him admire his boss even more.

Walser opens the door, acknowledges Mike with a nod, says nothing.

He is known for his silence. According to a profile Mike has read about him in the *Financial Times*, he wears it defensively, like a layer of body armour, but he can also use it offensively, crushing his opponents under its weight, or obliging them to fill it with one-way chatter that puts them at a psychological disadvantage. From what Mike can determine, Walser has been married three times but is single now. And he has few friends at work. While his more clubbable colleagues in the banking world will cultivate a certain urbanity and wit as tools of their trade, Walser won't even start a phone conversation with 'hello'. And he will always be the first through a door that is being held open for two people.

Smiling does not come easily to him either – and when people approach his desk he will wave them away. He protects his privacy fiercely and has for the most part managed to avoid giving interviews to the financial press, despite being the most senior executive in the London division of Rheinisch-Westfälische, the provincial German investment bank he has, over the past four years – and almost single-handedly – turned into a bulge-bracket, mainly through a series of mergers and hostile takeovers. Walser weathered the financial crisis of 2008–9 better than most.

Into the vacuum of Walser's silence has been sucked a blizzard of rumours, as blinding as it is white. In the 1970s he had been a member of the Baader-Meinhof gang, that is one. He has had death threats, hence his obsession with security, that's another. The most persistent is that his father had been in the SS – the commandant of a concentration camp, no less. Mike has checked the records but hasn't been able to find any SS members with the surname Walser. Then again, the commandant of a concentration camp would have changed his name after the war, presumably, perhaps when escaping to Argentina with the likes of Mengele and Eichmann.

When the infamous 'Arbeit Macht Frei' sign disappeared from above the gates of Auschwitz in 2009 there was a rumour that it had been stolen to order, for a collection – Walser's order, Walser's collection. Mike has no idea whether that was the truth, but he does know that his boss collects Nazi memorabilia. The usual items: SS ceremonial daggers, Iron Crosses, documents signed by Hitler. Mike has seen them. But he also knows that rumours of this sort are not uncommon about German bankers of a certain age, especially in recent years after it emerged that German banks had loaned the money for the building of the concentration camps. Deutsche Bank had funded Auschwitz-Birkenau; Rheinisch-Westfälische, Bergen-Belsen.

Another rumour doing the rounds at RWB is that Walser's driver is also a bodyguard, one who is licensed to carry a handgun.

When he started, Mike was approached by one of Walser's colleagues and asked about this alleged gun. He had merely said that his working arrangements were private; Walser, not the bank, employed him. The colleague said that Walser had a strange habit, that twice a day he would close and lock his office door for five minutes or so. His blinds were always shut anyway. The man had speculated that Walser was having a 'power nap' in there – either that or a 'power wank'. Mike said nothing but took satisfaction from knowing that the man would never have dared say that to Walser's face. Besides, Mike knows what his boss is doing when his door is locked, and there is another odd habit only he knows about, something Walser does at the same time every day. Mike isn't about to share that with anyone either, because he respects Walser. More than that, he feels a keen loyalty to him, something approaching devotion.

At 6.30, the car begins its glide towards the City, taking, as usual, a slightly different route from the one taken the day before. Mike turns on Radio 4 so that Walser can hear the news headlines. More phone hacking, more crises for the euro, more about the disruption to flights being caused by the eruption of Norway's Beerenberg volcano. When the sports news comes on, Mike turns the radio off so that his boss can read the *Financial Times*. He knows his routines. It is one of the reasons Mike likes working for him. Another is the uniform: he is not required to wear one. An open-neck shirt and jacket is fine. The jacket is needed anyway, to cover the shoulder holster in which he keeps his Browning 9mm pistol, the one with the clip filed down and the safety on.

After dropping Walser off at the main entrance of RWB, Mike drives round the side of the building and parks in the underground car park there. He then sips black coffee as he waits in the bank's refectory, located in the corner of a second-floor atrium. He likes it in here because he can watch the stressed-looking bankers come and go, trying to imagine what it is they do exactly, apart from worry.

He also likes to use the time to catch up on some military history. Today he is reading a critically acclaimed new hardback about the atrocities committed by the Red Army in the final months of the Second World War.

He is so engrossed in the book he forgets the time and when, six hours after sitting down, a text comes through from Walser's secretary, he feels momentarily disorientated. Can he be ready with the car in five minutes? Walser wants to go to the Imperial War Museum. Mike has driven him there before.

They cross town in their customary silence and, after he has dropped Walser off at the entrance gate to the museum, Mike goes to the Library Street car park, an eight-minute walk away. There, he removes his jacket, unstraps his holster and locks his handgun away in the glove compartment. He had been searched last time they went to the museum and, even though he had been able to produce his small-arms licence and show his security ID card, the police had been called, the gun had been confiscated and the red tape involved in getting it back had been irritating.

Mike doesn't mind the trips to the museum. Quite enjoys them, in fact. He is obsessed with the Second World War himself and will sometimes plan his whole evening's viewing around the Führer. The Hitler Channel, as he calls the History Channel, usually has back-to-back Nazi porn, even if, as a fig leaf, they will sometimes squeeze in a documentary about Mary Queen of Scots, or the invention of the steam engine.

Mike takes the stairs rather than waiting for the lift to the Holocaust Exhibition on the third floor. At the top he takes in the sign warning visitors to turn off their mobile phones, as if they are entering a church. In a way they are – a shrine to human suffering.

As he reaches the dimly lit room showing photographs of living skeletons staring mutely into the camera from behind barbed wire, Mike feels the usual gravity descend upon him, a stealthy saturation. He studies an image of a man in civilian clothes kneeling on the lip of a mass grave, an SS soldier holding a gun to his head. How had they allowed these photographs to be taken? For their records, no doubt – that Germanic craving for bureaucracy always damned them. Another image shows a pyramid of naked female bodies in a mass grave. The caption reveals it is the work of the Einsatzgruppe C, the SS paramilitary death squads in the Ukraine. Mike wonders what it is with the Nazis and nudity. There was something fetishistic about this need to strip people before they killed them. But there was probably a practical reason. Flesh decomposes more quickly than fabric.

Mike sees Walser across the room contemplating a painting. He is folding his arms and putting his hand to his chin. He then takes a couple of steps back and cocks his head. It is an oil painting about three feet by five which shows an SS officer on a black horse. The officer is wearing a black leather jacket, the tails of which are spread out over the back of his saddle. His boots, jodhpurs, gloves and cap are also black. Were it not for the stillness of the painting, its lack of emotion and movement, this SS man might have been one of the Four Horsemen of the Apocalypse. As it is, he is looking at the gallows to his left, as if contemplating his own fate. The signature and date appear to have been painted over, but a caption on the frame reads: 'An SS officer believed to be the commandant of a con-centration camp, painted during the war by a prisoner.'

Mike gives Walser a sidelong glance and wonders if this is his father. Probably. It would make sense. But he knows better than to ask. Don't mention the war. He is sure Walser has loaned this painting. Mike hasn't seen it in his private collection, but a week earlier he had delivered a painting to the museum that was about this size, handing it over to the curator in a packing crate.

He doesn't know whether it is true or not about Walser's father being in the SS but even if it is, Mike feels that the sins of the father should not be visited upon the son. He reckons he isn't a bad judge of character. He finds his boss to be a decent and sensitive man. Those who are suspicious of him do not know how his eyes have a wet film on them whenever he listens to Bach.

As they drive back to the City, Mike puts on a CD of the Brandenburg concertos, without needing to be asked. After dropping Walser at the bank, he goes for some lunch and then reads his book again, this time in the car. He will not be needed now until after the markets close.

At 5pm he is waiting in the bank's underground car park. This is the strangest part of his daily routine – the 'odd habit' Walser's colleagues would love to know about. He will drive his boss a couple of miles and then drop him off at Mile End tube. What Walser does then, Mike knows, is none of his business. He will wait there for him, outside the station, and Walser will return in an hour, get in the car and clip on his seat belt without saying a word.

The Nike bag suggests he is going to the gym, but Mike suspects it is something to do with a charity, his boss doing an hour's voluntary work in a homeless shelter, perhaps. Because that is something else people don't know about Walser. He makes substantial charitable donations, always anonymously. Mike usually acts as the go-between.

Walser's latest act of unsung generosity has been to offer Edward Northcote and his daughter, either together, separately or with friends, the use of his château in Alsace, for as long as they like, any time they feel in need of a holiday. Mike had driven round to their house in Parsons Green to deliver the letter personally, and as it wasn't sealed he had taken the liberty of reading it. Walser explained in it that he had heard about their story in the news and had been moved by it. Northcote's daughter had opened the door. Mike had liked the way she smiled when she read the invitation; the way dimples had appeared in the corners of her mouth. He left her his card.

VII

Four and a half months after Edward's release

AS HANNAH DRIVES, EDWARD TAKES IN THE COUNTRYSIDE – sunlit heaths and open farmland punctuated by round bales and thick hedgerows, each blurring into the other. This is his first visit to see his father at the nursing home, and he hopes that Hannah doesn't sense his apprehension about it.

'I used to go and see him after school,' she says, keeping her eyes on the road. 'Before his memory went. He taught me to use oil paint.'

'Did he? Wish he'd taught me, but then I never had any talent for painting.'

'He had a very unorthodox way of holding his brush, because of his missing thumb. It made his style, like, much more bold. Visible strokes of the palette knife, too. Mixing paint right on the canvas. Thick layers of it . . .We're almost there.' A gear change down into second. 'Just over this hill. You get a great view from the top.'

'Would you mind if I get out here and walk the rest?'

Edward asks. 'I could do with some fresh air, before we go in.'

'Course not.' Hannah brings the car to a halt once they have crested the hill. 'I'll go on ahead and park. Just follow the road down. It's a couple of hundred yards.'

Edward watches the Volvo disappear around a corner and then walks over to a dry-stone wall. Below him are the bosomy folds of a deep, wooded valley bisected by meadows feral with dandelions and buttercups. Only the bleating of unseen sheep and the song of skylarks disturbs the silence.

He inhales slowly and, on his out breath, realizes that he is home at last, that this is deep England, the remembered country. But where there should be joy in his heart he feels only resentment and melancholy. Frejya should be here with him. They should be savouring this view together.

He takes in another sound. A peal has started up, rung on eight bells, summoning Christians to church. It must be Sunday. He turns in their direction and sees a spire rising above a distant sun-dappled coppice. The change-ringing, as old as the Norman invasion, and as evocative in its way as the minarets of Arabia, weaves with memories of church from his childhood: of fits of giggles at moments of solemnity, of the smell of mown grass around the gravestones, of wood polish, of mildew, of tattered regimental flags . . . of a handkerchief licked by his father to clean his face.

The bells have re-ordered now, changing their sequence with mathematical precision. As he listens to their descending scale he turns and follows the road around the slope of the hill.

He sees the lawns first, ripples of heat-mist dancing across their even surface. A few yards farther on he sees a Palladian hall. With its mellow stone-flagged terraces and its strutting peacocks it could be the home of a duke.

Hannah is striding with unbearable youth towards him. She waves. They enter through the main door and, once inside, the building's function becomes un-ambiguous. Though his sense of smell has yet to return fully, Edward recognizes the stagnant air immediately from his stay in hospital: cloyingly warm, stifled by self-closing fire doors, pricked with disinfectant, urine and flowers.

The linoleum on the floors renders a passing wheel-chair silent. Its occupant waves a friendly stick to greet an old man with amputated legs who is descending on a stairlift. Hannah leads the way through a communal room where a dozen elderly residents are watching *SpongeBob SquarePants* on a wide-screen television. Their faces seem frozen, old men looking gormless without their teeth in, women with hairy chins. Their features seem exaggerated: big noses, big ears, big, arthritically crooked hands. Some have overbite, others yellow eyes, one has glasses too large for his head. They look like aliens.

Once through this area, Hannah points in the direction of an open door.

'That's his room.'

'Does he know I'm back?'

Hannah shakes her head. 'He's been told, several times, but . . . I think I'll leave you to it. He gets agitated when he has more than one visitor. I should warn you, the only thing he says is "answer". Don't know why. There's an empty pond in the garden with some chairs around it. I'll wait for you there.'

Edward hesitates before entering. At first he does not recognize the old man sitting in a wheelchair by the window. Age has shrunk him and the old kimono he is wearing looks the wrong size, as if he is a child trying on his parents' clothes. His eyebrows are wiry, there are dark pouches under his eyes and his chalky hair looks weightless and soft against his small, birdlike skull. The bones in his shaking hands look too big, the skin on them loose, except for the stump where his thumb was, before it was amputated during the war. There the skin is tight.

Apart from a few liver spots, the hands are almost transparent. The only patch of skin that still looks young and smooth is on the side of the old man's face, where he has been burned – another war injury. It is a different colour, yellow and taut. Stray silver bristles make it look like an unripened nectarine. He is recognizable to his son, just about, but his edges are softer, as if someone has placed a veil over him. There is a whistling sound coming from him, as elusive as steam from a boiled kettle. He is taking little sips of air.

Edward raises the sunglasses he has to wear even indoors. 'It's me, Dad. Eddie.'

When his father fails to look up, Edward puts out his hand to shake. The old man stares at it with watery curiosity.

'I've brought you this.' He hands over a bottle of Irish whiskey.

His father transfers his stare to the bottle.

'Would you like a glass?'

The old man looks at his son with pale, cloudy eyes.

'It's me, Dad.' He reaches over and touches his father's mottled hand. 'I came back . . . Dad?'

'You OK there?'

Edward turns towards the female voice. There is a nurse in the doorway holding a tray with two cups and saucers, a jug, sugar bowl and a teapot. 'Come along now, Charlie,' she says. 'You've got a visitor.'

Edward chews his cheek. 'I think he would prefer to be called Mr Northcote.'

The nurse looks embarrassed. 'Sorry. We tend not to use titles and surnames here.'

'His generation are quite formal. They like strangers to address them by their surnames.'

'Sorry.'

Edward sighs. 'No, I'm the one who should say sorry. It's fine to call him Charles, or Charlie. I'm sure Charlie no longer cares what he's called. I'm just a little shocked at seeing him like this, that's all. It's been a while.'

'You're his son, aren't you?'

'Yes, I've . . . been away.'

'I saw that on the news. I'm pleased you're back safely. Mr Northcote watched you on the news as well, though I don't think . . .' The nurse smooths the old man's hair. 'He's no trouble, you know. He just sits here. Listens to music sometimes. The Beatles are his favourites. And he paints.' The nurse points at some

131

childish paintings of trees and houses Blu-Tacked to the wall. In one the sky is green, the grass blue. There are pots of poster paint and thick, numb brushes. 'He's quite the Picasso, isn't he?'

Edward stiffens. 'He used to be a Royal Academician.'

It strikes Edward as odd to be talking about his father as if he isn't here, yet in a way he isn't. He is a husk. How old must he be? He was born in 1917 so that would make him ninety-five. His dentures are in a mug and his face looks like it has collapsed in on itself without them. Edward reaches over, rinses them in the sink and holds them up to his father's mouth, which opens obligingly. When he then straightens his father's tie and takes a comb from his pocket and runs it through his fine, white fringe, Charles looks up in surprise and says in a small, high-pitched voice: 'Answer.'

Edward recalls how deep his father's voice had always been. 'Answer what, Dad? What's the question?'

'Answer,' the old man repeats. Alzheimer's is thickening his tongue like some strange accent.

'How have you been, Dad?'

'Answer.'

Edward pours two cups of tea. 'Are they treating you well in here?'

'Answer.'

'I'm sorry I never got a chance to say goodbye properly. I thought I was only going to be in Afghanistan for a couple of weeks. I was always heading off somewhere, wasn't I? All those postings . . . We never did get to spend much time together, did we? . . . But it's what you wanted for me, right, Dad?'

'Answer.'

'I always knew how proud you were of me. University. Foreign Office. You didn't have to say it.'

Edward is finding it oddly reassuring and easy to be here with his father having this one-way conversation. There is no comeback. No attempt to understand or empathize. It is like talking to himself, a monologue for two voices. 'Did you hear what happened to me in Afghanistan? They took me hostage. Held me for eleven years in a cave . . .' He shakes his head and smiles grimly. 'I did some painting in there, Dad. You would have appreciated it. You were always trying to get me to paint but I didn't have the confidence, do you remember?'

'Answer?'

'I didn't have any paint so I used my own faeces. Daubed it on the walls like Jackson Pollock.'

'Answer.' An urgency has crept into his tone. 'Answer.'

Charles is now staring at a wooden information board on the wall, like the ones in church that tell you the hymn numbers. On one side are painted the questions that residents must frequently ask, and alongside these are slots for the handwritten answers.

Today is . . . Sunday.
The month is . . . August.
The weather is . . . warm.
Dinner is . . . lamb.
The season is . . . spring.

'The winters were the worst,' Edward continues,

133

changing the piece of wood with the word 'spring' written on it for one with 'summer'. His breathing has quickened, shallow breaths through his nose. His jaw muscles are tensed. 'There was one especially cold one where they threw down some extra blankets for me. I was even allowed a fire sometimes. Sticks and matches, when it got really cold . . . I sang to myself. Talked to myself often. Sometimes I would hear screaming and then realize it was me.'

Edward stirs his cup but still doesn't take a sip. 'Am I still in the cave? Am I imagining this?' He stops stirring, distracted by the white noise of his scudding thoughts, then starts again.

There is a packet of nappies in the corner. 'Nappies to nappies,' Edward says when he sees them. Wrapped in his kimono, with his bald head sticking out, his father looks like an outsized baby in a swaddling blanket. In this moment he thinks he loves him more than he has ever done in his life. Unlike the Foreign Office therapist, his father isn't trying to cure him. He isn't judging him. He has never judged him.

'Daddy,' he says. There are tears in his voice, but not in his eyes. He takes hold of his hand again and, when he notices his father staring at it and realizes he is squeezing too hard, he lets it go. He straightens his shoulders. 'Know what I used for a loo? A corner of the cave. After a while I no longer noticed the stench.' He rubs the back of his head. His eyes are glassy now. His lips are trembling. Running his hands through his hair, he stands up and begins pacing the room. 'I almost came to admire their genuine contempt for me. No, not contempt, their indifference. They didn't care if I lived or died . . . Just didn't care. Being ignored is nearly as bad as being abused. It's the lack of human contact . . . But I guess you know about that in here, Dad. No one to talk to. I guess it hasn't been much of a decade for you either, has it.' He kisses his father's head. 'I missed you. I'm sorry I haven't been here for you. They said I shouldn't come and visit. That it wouldn't be good for either of us. But I'm going to see if I can get you out. You can come back and live with us. We can get a full-time carer.'

'Answer.'

'When I got home they told me Frejya was dead . . . She had been my reason for staying alive. And then that's it, she's gone, replaced with this exact replica. This, this . . . mockery.'

'Answer,' Charles says.

Edward hears someone behind him and turns to see Hannah at the door. She is staring at him with wolf-grey eyes that are molten and unblinking.

VIII

EDWARD CONTEMPLATES THE BLANK WORD DOCUMENT ON HIS laptop. He thought after his visit to his father he might be capable of writing down some notes for a memoir about his time in captivity, but the empty screen seems to represent the future to him, a future that is fogged and inarticulate, like an invisible barrier. Besides, he doesn't want Hannah to read it when . . .

He can't even give shape to the words in his head.

When . . .

He closes the laptop, walks out into the hall and, opening the cupboard under the stairs, drags out two of the boxes of merchandising from the Free Edward Northcote campaign: more mugs, more T-shirts, more bumper stickers. They represent the scale of Frejya's campaign, as well as his guilt at having gone and been captured. She would still be alive if he had done as she asked and turned the assignment down. Every time he sees these boxes he feels sick.

Behind them there is a bin liner full of the ephemera of Frejya's life. He knows what it contains, all the things which Hannah collected together and intended to throw out but never did: the circled takeaway menus, the used Jiffy bags ready for recycling, the pages ripped from catalogues, old birthday cards, bank statements, a shopping list on the back of an envelope – 'kitchen towels, bread source, olive oil, HP, tomatoes, milk'.

And behind this is the clear plastic crate he is looking for. It contains the edited records of Frejya's life. He drags it into the hall and sits down cross-legged as he goes through it. The answering machine tape with her voice on it is sitting on the top. Hannah must have put it here. Underneath it are Frejya's diaries, her photograph albums, her school certificates written in Norwegian: a second place in the 100 metres, a prize at a swimming gala, a commendation for chemistry. Her passports are also here, several of them, dating all the way back to her first one, the photographs inside them showing how she aged every ten years. Her credit cards are here too, along with a copy of her will, her birth certificate, their marriage certificate and her death certificate. Birth, marriage, death – all neatly filed by Hannah in a clear folder.

Edward is picturing Frejya's face again now, an inexorable habit of thought that sucks him down into the quicksand. He sees her slow, languid blink, the one that he has noticed Hannah also does. It always made Frejya look composed. It makes Hannah look as if she is doing an impersonation. Now he feels, for the first time, a sense of shame that he robbed his wife of her composure. Ruined her life. He killed her by breaching her heart.

And worst of all, he hadn't been there to look after

her when she needed him, when she was most under stress – stress he caused her by his absence.

A memory of her half-smile comes to him. Their few years together had been happy, especially their time in Oslo where he had been deputy head of mission at the British Embassy and she had been his interpreter.

They had been introduced to each other on his first day, at a small reception held for his benefit. He had just emerged from the Embassy's secure room, where the ambassador, a thin-lipped veteran of the Cold War, had been giving him a briefing on sexual liaisons. The essence of it was, 'You're a young chap and you're bound to have flings, but remember the golden rules: keep it female, keep it single, keep it white, and keep it in Nato. Any questions?'

When she had introduced herself – 'Hello. My name is Frejya Ødegaard. Do you speak any Norwegian?' – her voice had seemed so weightless it was like hearing a warm spring breeze folding over itself to form shapes that resembled words. She held out her hand and, when he took it, it felt as smooth and cold as flour. He was transfixed. Beguiled. He simply stared at her, smiling. When she repeated her question he pulled himself together and told her he had just completed an intensive two-month course in the language. She then asked him something in Norwegian and, when he looked blank, she laughed.

Their first project together had been the shipping of the Christmas tree to Trafalgar Square, the annual gift from the Norwegian people to the British. They had accompanied it to London and taken adjoining rooms at Brown's Hotel. That had been the first time they kissed. They slept together upon their return to Oslo. Oslo, where they met. Oslo, where they married. Oslo, where they had been happy.

But had their happiness back then been enough to compensate his wife for the years of frayed loneliness that followed his disappearance? The grief when she was told, after ten years of waiting for him to return, that he had been declared officially dead? As he looks at the crate now, he thinks he knows the answer. No.

He realizes he has been so absorbed with self-pity at his own suffering he has rarely thought of hers. In agreeing to go on the UNESCO mission he had been selfish. He knows that now. He could have pleaded other commitments, but he had been too eager to please the head of his department. Too ambitious. His wife had been sacrificed on the altar of his ambition.

She had been so young when they married. Four years his junior. Still a girl. And he had taken her youth and her happiness and left her with nothing but grief and the ache of separation. Shame on him for that.

As he places the plastic folder carefully back in the box he realizes that it also contains his own archives. His A level certificate. His degree. A copy of his diplomatic credentials, stamped with a Foreign Office watermark. And then something he hasn't seen before, his death certificate. He stares at it in appalled fascination, holding it by the edge, as if it is doused with poison.

As he has done many times before, he wonders whether he did indeed somehow die in that cave, as

Hannah said; that the passage of time since his release has been some telescoped dying moment, a lingering death throe. Or is he now the wandering ghost of a man not yet dead, looking for his home? He is sure that this is where the word 'haunt' comes from. To haunt: to search for your home.

Seeing some tissue paper wrapped around something at the side of the box, he reaches for it. There is a small glass stem and a bowl. Removing a layer he sees it is a wine glass. There is a lipstick print on its rim. Hannah must have preserved this. He puts his own lips to the mark and closes his eyes for a couple of seconds before wrapping up the glass again.

Now it reaches him, a thought he has been avoiding. He will never see his darling wife again. Never. Those non-negotiable syllables. She is only a photograph and his only connection with her is to read letters she has written, hold paper she has breathed upon, touch a wine glass that she has touched.

'We only missed each other by a year,' he says in a clenched whisper. 'If only you had waited.'

He runs a bath and lies in it, staring at the tap, listening to the echoey drip-drip.

After half an hour, perhaps an hour, he pulls the plug by wrapping the chain between his toes. He remains in the bath as the water runs out, feeling the gravity return to his body, waiting for his skin to cool.

Can he really go through with this?

He gets dressed, walks stiff-legged back downstairs and looks intently at the letter he has written to Hannah, folded into an envelope yet to be stuck down.

He opens it and, as he re-reads, feels ashamed that he hadn't even had the strength to write it out in longhand. It is a printout from his laptop.

I'm sorry, Han. I know this will be as hard for you to read as it is for me to write. The truth is, I cannot live without Frejya. I've tried. I've failed. Please forgive me. I love you.
Dad

He knows it is too perfunctory, too selfish and cowardly, but what else can he write? How else can he phrase it? He has considered writing 'your mother' instead of 'Frejya', but the words make him wince. 'Frejya' seems less personal. Somehow less hurtful.

He unscrews the top of his fountain pen, writes 'Hannah' on the envelope, licks it down and places it in the middle of the sitting-room table. No. He props it up on the chimneypiece instead. No again. It will be better to leave it in Hannah's bedroom. She will find it when she gets home. Before then he has a few hours alone, enough time for the sedatives to do their work. He has already emptied what he thinks will be a sufficient number of benzodiazepine capsules into an envelope and now he pours himself a large Scotch and adds ice cubes that crackle in the tumbler. The powder turns the liquid cloudy when he stirs it with his finger. After drinking it he should have time to walk to Brompton Cemetery and lie down unseen behind a tombstone and wait, so that Hannah doesn't have to be the one to find him.

He walks upstairs and stands for a moment in the

doorway of her bedroom. The bed is unmade and there are clothes and shoes scattered all around the floor. A bass guitar with a rosewood fingerboard is propped against an amp. There are framed posters of Steve McQueen and a female singer he doesn't recognize, and on another wall prints of paintings by Lucian Freud and Mark Rothko. On a shelf sit school photographs and badly stacked books, and a doll with one eye missing and biro scrawled over its face. On the desk lies a blister pack of pills, half used, the rips of tinfoil indicating which have been taken. He crosses the room and examines them. The Pill. There is also an opened packet of Tampax, a bottle of shampoo and a laptop with a screensaver running. It is forming patterns that look like the aurora borealis. He sits down and touches the mouse. It is open on Hannah's Facebook page. There are photographs of her drinking in bars with friends, at parties dancing, pulling faces and blowing kisses at the camera. She will be OK, he tells himself. She has friends. He closes the laptop with a snick and heads back downstairs.

Feeling a familiar tightness around his heart, the ache that means his thoughts are spiralling back towards Frejya, he collects the tumbler, opens a cupboard door in the sitting room and sits cross-legged again as he stares at the black pewter urn that contains her ashes. His hands reach out for it but hover in mid-air. He clenches them. He can't bear to feel the coldness of the metal.

Tilting his head, he can see there are fingerprints on it. Hannah must have been holding it. She has told him two or three times that she wants to scatter the ashes off Doyden Point, but every time she raises the subject he changes it. The thought of scattering Frejya anywhere is agonizing.

He downs the adulterated Scotch in four gulps, gags and wipes his mouth.

The heat from his fingertips now creates pools of condensation on the surface of the urn. Once they have shrunk his hand returns and this time he unscrews the lid. The ashes are paler than he imagined. Almost eggshell. He feels a sensation in his stomach of rising and falling, as if driving over a hill at speed, then he dips his fingers in and finds the heavy, fine texture as soft and cool as her hands had been.

He wants to get as close as he can to the ashes, rub them into his hair, consume them. If only he can shed tears into the urn, and have some contact that way. But he has not been able to cry for years.

Feeling hot and dizzy, on the blotchy edges of hallucination, he rubs his temples, smearing them with grey powder. He then puts the urn back in the cupboard.

'No!'

He turns to see Hannah making a hard chopping motion, one hand against the other as she stands in the doorway. He hadn't heard her come home. Why is she back early? His letter is open in her hand.

'Don't you *dare* do that to me! Don't you *fucking* dare!' She marches over and slaps his face. When he rolls with the impact, she makes a fist and punches the side of his head. As he cowers, she brings the fist down on his crown. When he looks up, his hands covering his face, he sees her eyes are wild with energy.

'I screwed up my A levels because . . .' She draws a ragged breath. 'Because of her, and I had to drop out of my foundation course to look after you, and now . . .'

They hold each other's gaze as they try to regulate their breathing. Then, as he tries to get to his feet, she launches herself at him, knocking him off balance again. She is lying on top of him now, her fingers circling his wrists and tightening, her hair dangling in his face. 'I can't,' she says breathlessly. 'I can't lose you again.'

After half a minute she loosens her grip and, turning her head, raises his wrist to her lips. 'I can help you,' she says in a whisper. 'I can make you happy.' She raises his other wrist and kisses that too. 'I will do whatever it takes to make you happy again.' She lets go of his hands and sits up, her knees astride his waist. 'I can make you happy like she made you happy.'

PART THREE

I

Alsace-Lorraine. Summer, 1941

FOR A FEW NUMB SECONDS, AS THE WHISTLE PENETRATES HIS sleep, Anselm is confused. He blinks repeatedly. Where is he? Whose stinking feet are these in his face? Why can he smell shit?

It is the same every morning.

Reveille comes at exactly 4.30. At least he thinks it does. He has a vague memory of being told once that reveille came at exactly 4.30, but perhaps he dreamed it. Not that he has dreams any more. His sleep is too deep for that, the dreamless sleep of the exhausted, of the still-breathing dead, of the dead who do not know they are dead.

A second whistle slashes through the nothingness like a machete through powdery snow and the frantic activity begins: the vibrating of the hut as the men who are half-men half-ghosts make their beds, shake out their blankets, raise clouds of fetid dust. Anselm has to wait for the occupants of the two beds that lead to the aisle to move first before he can get out. The narrow

147

wooden bunks have three tiers and are pushed tightly together. He sleeps on a middle bunk, three in. Shares it with a Frenchman whose name he does not know. Nor does he know what age the man is – his hair is white and thin and he could be twice as old as Anselm. All he knows is that they sleep head to feet, and the Frenchman's feet smell ripe. Under the same blanket, the strangers exchange their flatulence and their sweat; the flat and sour odours of their bodies. Bony hips meet in the middle and fight for space, applying a progressive pressure at the base of the spine.

Anselm gathers his bundle: a bowl and clogs wrapped in his jacket. He uses this as a pillow, for fear the possessions will otherwise be stolen in his sleep. After performing his ablutions, he endures the agony of putting his sore feet into the clogs. While still only half dressed, he limps outside into the dirty dawn and, as he joins the procession of the damned, breaks into a run. Some urinate as they move, to save time, because time can be a matter of life and death here. To be late means a beating, and the more beatings you receive the more likely you are to die. Each beating makes you slower, which makes you more likely to receive another beating.

There has been rain in the night and the dust has turned to orange mud. Anselm stands with shoulders dropped, his hands dangling by his side, his neck rigid. He is shivering. The straw he has used to pad out his jacket is no protection from the cold this morning. The rags he has wrapped around his feet are not preventing them from aching either. They are too calloused, too raw, too swollen from chafing. He is as rotten as the rags and, with his emaciated limbs and distended belly he looks like he belongs to another species, something inhuman, something bestial.

Under a sky pregnant with rain, he checks his wide collar is not raised and that his buttons – big ones, like a child's – are properly done up. There must be five. Even one less will mean a beating. And now the *Appell*, roll call, begins. It will last for an hour, an hour of standing to attention that will seem like a day. Anselm has no watch. It was taken from him when he arrived and, with it, his last vestige of human identity. For the first few days he still looked at his bare wrist to check the time. Phantom watch. Phantom time.

The guards, he has worked out, belong to the Totenkopf or Death's Head division of the SS. The rankers wear a skull insignia on their caps, jackets and olive-green uniforms. The officers tend to wear the more traditional black uniforms of the SS: the long leather overcoats in winter, the black jodhpurs, the jackboots. They, too, have been stripped of their identity. It may explain why they are so efficient in the way they strip the prisoners of theirs.

From the shaving of heads to the replacing of names with a tattooed number, the guards have been methodical. Ingenious even. Anselm recognizes this. As a German himself he ought to be able to relate to the *Ordnungsliebe*, the passion for order. Yet he is Dionysian chaos. He could never keep things tidy. Could never remember his appointments. Charles was Apollonian order. They used to joke about it. About being the wrong way round. He was Nijinsky performing en pointe for the lumbering benefit of Charles's Diaghilev. Dear, uptight, English Charles. His Charles. His fire. His soul . . .

No.

He must not think of Charles. Such thoughts will sap his strength, his will. Yet his mind cannot help but picture Charles's face, forming it feature by feature, like two or three ascending notes that build into a familiar symphony.

As he shifts his weight from leg to leg, Anselm wonders what Charles would make of this place. Perhaps in his cerebral way he would compare it to a painting by Hieronymus Bosch. Perhaps he would talk of Dante and the circles of hell. Perhaps he would say the sign over the gate should read 'abandon hope, all ye who enter here'.

Anselm accepts that God has no dominion in the camp, yet he still has hope and he still prays, not to God but to Charles. Charles will come and save him one day soon. Charles will descend into this underworld, this manmade hell. Charles will rescue him from his tormentors with their whips.

When he had written to Charles to tell him about his sentence he had not known what an education camp was. That must have been a year and a half ago now. Did the letter ever reach him? And what could Charles do to help him now, even if it did? Anselm closes his eyes, draws air deep into his lungs and thinks: If you come for me, Charles, will you even recognize me any more?

He tries to recall the song they had sung on the way

home from seeing *Snow White and the Seven Dwarfs* at the picture house, but it won't come back to him.

According to the strip on the chest of his striped jacket, Anselm is '*Häftling* 15567', prisoner 15567. This number is also tattooed in bluish characters on the underside of his wrist, where his watch used to be. He has no name. No watch. No hair.

But losing your identity can have its advantages. He is a *Reichsdeutscher*, an Aryan German, but he has no wish to advertise this here. Without his blond hair, Anselm looks less Germanic. If it weren't for his height, he wouldn't stand out at all. And it pays to be anonymous in this place. Anselm, indeed, has learned well the art of anonymity, of deflecting attention away from himself, of never making eye contact, of always keeping his posture unthreatening. He removes his cap whenever a guard is near. He never asks questions but instead replies '*jawohl*', the one cold, hard German word he allows himself. Even the French prisoners must use it.

Every now and then a guard will ask '*Wer kann Deutsch?*' but Anselm never steps forward. He knows the guard will speak in German anyway and the French prisoners will have to work out what he is saying for themselves, or suffer the consequences. There have been occasions when he has been tempted to help them, translating for those who speak no German. But he doesn't want to draw attention to himself. You have to be selfish to survive here.

If the guards know he is German they don't care. He never speaks. All he does is listen. And he runs when he is expected to run. He shows his masters utter subservience. They are the *Übermenschen*, after all, he the ape. And what is the ape to man? A joke. A painful embarrassment. Anselm has read his Nietzsche, he used to read him with Charles, but the guards and the other prisoners do not need to know that. His secrets are his own. He knows he is an *Übermensch*, too. Part of this Nietzschean master race. Indeed he is more Aryan-looking than the strange little dark-haired, short-sighted, club-footed men who strut around the Reichstag. Better educated, too. What was Himmler? A farmer. Hitler? A corporal. Upon reflection, he thinks Goebbels might have a doctorate from somewhere. But still.

As well as making himself invisible to the guards, Anselm has made himself so to his fellow prisoners. The first lesson in survival he learned in this place was not to make friends. If the guards notice you making friends, that makes you vulnerable. You can be killed with your friend, beaten with your friend, punished with your friend. If they suspect you of something, they will torture your friend until you confess.

Besides, most of the prisoners are French, and if they knew he was German he would not last long.

There are perhaps a dozen *Untermenschen* in the camp, distinguished by a red triangle over a yellow to form a Jewish star. But no more than that. Most of the five thousand or so inmates here have plain red triangles which signify that they are *Nacht und Nebel*, political prisoners who are made to disappear in the night and the fog. The F that comes before their prison number indicates they are French. Partisans. The Resistance.

But some at this camp have pink triangles, three hundred or so. The SS are known to use these triangles for target practice. This is what Anselm has – what he is – a walking target with a pink triangle, a human being reduced to a single proclivity.

He is also a survivor and part of his survival strategy is to tune out the barks of the Alsatians, the metallic whistles, even the wet noises made by the whips as they slap the air. He has also trained himself to avoid thinking of happier times, because with those thoughts come tender feelings, and they are dangerous. They make you vulnerable.

But even when he empties his mind, what he cannot ignore is his hunger. It is so chronic it leaves him delirious, imagining he is gnawing at himself from the inside out. He thinks about food at least once a minute and when, at dawn and dusk, the bread and the watery soup arrive, he tries to eat and drink slowly to savour them. But he cannot. Without pausing for breath, he holds the bread to his chin as he eats it, so as not to drop any crumbs, and he crams his mouth like a hog. Afterwards, he feels neither sated nor drowsy but more keenly aware of his hunger. Forget my sexual persuasion, he sometimes thinks, this is my essence here. A man reduced to an empty intestine.

He has learned to time his arrival in the soup queue carefully. Those at the head get the most watery soup. Those towards the end get the soup that has chunks in it, potatoes or turnip, settled on the bottom of the vat. Once his bowl is drained, he scrapes the bottom of it repeatedly with his spoon, as if willing more to appear.

His only relief from these obsessive thoughts of food is sleep, and this is disrupted by a soup-weakened bladder. His kidneys are no longer capable of filtering his blood efficiently and, without the relief of the bladder, his ankles swell with fluid. It means at least three visits every night to the piss bucket, and this in turn means having to climb over five prisoners – the Frenchman he shares his bunk with and the two pairs in the bunks on the way – and to run the gauntlet of their fists and curses. Last night he mistimed his visit and had to take the bucket outside into the cold air to empty it in the latrines. For that is the rule. He normally listens to hear how full the bucket is and makes sure he goes before it has filled to the top. Such are his little victories in this place of cruelty.

II

London

AS CHARLES STRIDES DOWN THE STRAND, HE LOOKS LIKE A MAN who doesn't spend much time in front of the mirror. The collar of his checked shirt is frayed and his tie is carelessly knotted. His trilby looks as if it has been lifted too many times by oily fingers, his flannel trousers are shapeless and his hairy jacket has patches on the elbows.

Whistling as he hastens across Trafalgar Square – 'Hi-Ho! Hi-Ho! It's Off To Work We Go!' – Charles swings his heavy black portfolio of drawings by his side. When a woman approaches with short, urgent steps he raises his hat in greeting. It has taken a year – a year in which he has been working as a volunteer air-raid warden by day and painting by night – but the *Picture Post* has finally accepted and now published his paintings of Dunkirk, and it has given him an idea of how he might find Anselm.

His positive mood is dampened when he passes two Royal Navy officers with medals on their greatcoats and white cotton covers on their peaked caps. He cannot be sure, but he thinks he hears one of them say to the other: 'queer', or 'dear', or possibly 'fear'. Whatever the word, the look of contempt that accompanies it makes him shiver. Had they taken him to be a conscientious objector? Was his court martial for gross indecency somehow written on his face?

He is still feeling rattled by the encounter as he climbs the steps to the National Gallery. The receptionist has sandbags piled up around her desk and Charles notices with curiosity that she is in uniform. She is also wearing make-up, which surely must be against Auxiliary Territorial Service regulations. They are about the same age. If he were that way inclined, he would say she is attractive. White teeth. Good bone structure. Glossy chestnut hair worn in a neat roll around the nape and over the ears. She looks bored.

'Do you know what I miss most?' she says in a crisp, Ascot voice.

Charles points to himself as if to ask if she is addressing him, then says: 'What?'

'Church bells.'

'They can only be used as an alarm, in the event of an invasion.'

'I know.' The receptionist is trying to suppress a smile as she taps some papers on her desk. 'I'm just saying I miss them, that's all. What do you miss?'

Charles thinks for a moment, amused by the receptionist's peremptory manner and relieved to find a friendly face. If she is wondering why he isn't in uniform, she isn't showing it. 'Love,' he says.

156

'Oh yes, love. That's much better than mine.' She cocks her head to one side and gives him an appraising look. 'Can I change mine to love, too?'

'I'll see if it can be arranged. Meanwhile, I'm here to see the director. I have an appointment. Charles Northcote.'

'Follow me,' the receptionist says, her brown leather shoes creaking as she walks. Charles notices how the tightness of her uniform shows off her curves and he suspects she has taken it in at the back to make it do just that. She turns and, catching him staring, gives a smile he is clearly supposed to feel in his hip pocket. (Since coming across that phrase in a Chandler novel, he had been wondering what it meant.) He has, and knows he has, always been attractive to women. It is the great irony of his life.

The gallery is bare. Rectangular shapes of unfaded wallpaper show where paintings have been hung. The high windows are taped with crosses. 'Looks like you've been burgled,' Charles says.

The smile again. 'They've been sent to Bangor,' she says. 'I suppose they think Nelson's Column makes a good aiming point for German bombers. But I can't believe that they would bomb the centre of London. Even Hitler wouldn't be that beastly. The docks perhaps. But not these beautiful old buildings. Have you met the director before?'

'No, what's he like?'

She thinks for a moment. 'Mercurial. No one ever sees him arrive or leave. Although the caretaker claims he once saw him flash through the wall of the

Renaissance gallery leaving a strong smell of brimstone behind him.'

Charles grins. 'I see.'

'And you, I take it, are an artist?'

Charles pats his jacket self-consciously. 'Do I look like one?'

'You have paint on your hands.'

He inspects them. 'Ah.'

'My last boyfriend was an artist. That's how I ended up here.'

Her choice of words strikes Charles as being loaded with ulterior meaning. She is not a novice in the ways of the heart, he thinks, and something about the way she said 'last boyfriend' makes Charles suspect that she is sizing him up to be her next.

She has reached the door to the director's office and, with her fingers on the handle, she turns smartly on her heel, so that one arm is behind her back in a submissive gesture that simultaneously manages to make her bust look more prominent. 'I used to model for him,' she says. She then leans in closer to Charles's ear and whispers: 'In the nude.'

With this, she turns again, taps on the door and opens it. 'Mr Northcote here to see you, sir.'

From inside, a clipped patrician voice. 'Come in, come in.'

Sir Kenneth Clark is a short, compact man with a large forehead and a beaky nose. His handshake is firm and dry.

Feeling buoyed by his encounter with the receptionist, Charles finds himself raising his chin and making eye contact for the first time in a while. 'Like what you've done with the place,' he says.

'I know, I know. I'm a gallery director without any paintings. We were considering sending them to Canada, but Winnie doesn't want a single picture to leave the country. Bad for morale. If the royal family can stay, he reckons, the paintings should, too.'

Charles notices that on the director's desk is the copy of the *Picture Post* that has reproduced two of his paintings. They are dramatic compositions with swirling smoke, staring eyes and blackened faces that contrast with the oranges and yellows of the explosions in the background, illuminating the night skies. The evacuated soldiers look as if they are being eaten away by the shadows.

Clark follows his gaze. 'You have a good eye, Mr Northcote. A fluid style. Is this your first publication?'

'It is, yes.'

'The Prime Minister dabbles, you know. Says he prefers painting landscape to portraits because trees don't complain that you haven't done them justice. Anyway, he fancies himself as an artist.'

'Like Hitler.'

'Indeed, like Hitler.' Sir Kenneth claps. 'From your letter I take it you know all about the War Artists Advisory Committee.'

'A little.'

'Well, you're in luck. We have three hundred active official war artists at the moment and we've just been given the budget to recruit a further hundred. You trained at the Slade, did you not?'

'I did, yes.'

'Who was your professor there?'

'Matthew Waterhouse.'

'I know him. Good man. When were you commissioned?'

'To be honest I've never really had a commission.'

'I meant in the navy.'

'Oh, I see. I'm not an officer.' In his mind he finished the sentence with the words 'any more'.

Sir Kenneth looks confused. 'But weren't you part of the evacuation?'

'As a civilian. I went over to Dunkirk on my own initiative.'

'And you haven't been called up yet?'

'I've been working for the ARP, but I'm keen to see some action.'

Sir Kenneth seems satisfied with this. 'You know war artists are not permitted to carry weapons?'

'I know, I meant . . .'

'We can pay you a salary. You would be, if you like, part of the Ministry of Information.'

'Thank you. You won't be disappointed.'

'Do you have any languages?'

'French. Some German.'

'That might be useful.'

'And I can go anywhere? Any theatre, I mean.'

'Up to a point. But you have to be assigned. We need to know where you are. Would you consider the Atlantic convoys? North Africa, perhaps?'

'I was wondering if I could do something with the RAF.'

Sir Kenneth scratches an itch on the back of his hand as he ponders this. 'Actually, Winnie has asked if we can paint some of the pilots at the RAF bases. Middle Wallop. Biggin Hill. Tangmere. Might you be interested in that?'

Charles wonders whether he will be recognized on those bases. The young men he had gone through training with will be considered veterans by now, those who are still alive. Perhaps they will recognize him, perhaps they won't. And perhaps it won't matter either way because once he has got himself established on a base and chosen his moment he is going to 'borrow' a plane to get over to France – something small, something they won't miss, like one of the Tiger Moths he did his training in. 'Absolutely,' he says. 'What did you have in mind?'

'We're not after caricatures. Studies, really. Pretty much what you did at Dunkirk.' Clark impersonates Churchill's voice. ' "Something *inspiwational*." You might also pop into Fighter Command up at Stanmore. Give people a sense of what they do. I'll draw up some bona fides for you to show at the checkpoint. Officially, at least, the purpose of the committee is propaganda. I can't pretend otherwise. Exhibitions will be organized here to raise morale. We also want to hold some in America. Get them involved.'

'And unofficially?'

Clark taps the opened copy of the *Picture Post*. 'Do you want to know why I really started all this? Far too many of our best artists were killed in the last war. I'm hoping with this scheme that we can avoid the same thing happening with your generation.'

'Well, I've always thought being killed was overrated.'

Sir Kenneth guffaws and pats him on the back. 'Excellent! Excellent! I can't guarantee that you won't find yourself in harm's way. The whole idea is that you will be in the thick of it.'

'I studied the war paintings of Nash and Spencer at the Slade.'

'Yes, I see something of their style in your work, a certain gritty integrity. Did you work from photographs at Dunkirk?'

'Sketches. Then I worked them up in watercolours. Then completed them in oil.'

'We've already signed up Spencer, you'll be pleased to hear. Henry Moore, John Piper, Graham Sutherland, too. You will be in distinguished company.' He touches Charles's forearm. 'You have a talent you must use. Do a good job and you will be doing more for the war effort with your paintbrushes than you ever could with your rifle. Now, Maggie will make all the arrangements.'

'Maggie?'

'The girl on reception. She'll sort you out with a uniform. You're a captain now. That's the honorary rank that goes with being an official war artist.' He salutes.

Charles grins and, with a click of his heels, salutes back.

III

WITH HIS FLY-SPATTERED GOGGLES ATTACHED TO A BROWN-leather motorcycle helmet, Charles looks more like the RAF pilot he used to be than the honorary army captain he is now, or at least he assumes he does, based on the reaction he is getting from pedestrians as he rides through the tree-lined suburb of Stanmore, north-west London, on his sidecar motorcycle. He acknowledges their waves with a half-salute of his leather gauntlet but, as he nears the entrance to RAF Bentley Priory, he realizes they are pointing, not waving. He follows their gaze and sees a ceiling of grey aluminium. Are the planes German? Their high altitude would suggest they are on their way north. Certainly the bystanders don't seem unduly concerned.

And he isn't too concerned either. Not since his court martial has he felt so positive about his future. The more he has thought about being a war artist, the more the idea has appealed to him. Not only does it represent an opportunity to redeem himself and get involved in the war properly, it might also offer him a chance to find Anselm.

The entrance to Fighter Command, when he reaches it five minutes later, is camouflaged under green netting. It hasn't changed much since he came here back in 1938, during his training. The only signs that this might now be the place from which the RAF runs its entire south coast operation are straggling coils of razor wire around the perimeter, the barrel of an ack-ack gun poking out from a semicircular pile of sandbags and an Alsatian dog tethered to a long chain outside the guardhouse.

The sleeveless leather jerkin Charles is wearing adds to the illusion that he is an RAF pilot who belongs here and, were it not for the wooden contraption sticking out of his sidecar, he wonders whether the sentry on duty might have raised the barrier and let him through unchallenged. As it is, Charles follows an emphatic signal to close down his throttle and switch off his engine. Once he has removed his gauntlets and reached into his pocket for his ID papers, he brushes dust from his jacket. His fingertips feel tender and tingling from the vibration of the motorbike, a not unpleasant sensation.

The guard studies his papers then looks at the sidecar. 'What's that then?'

'An easel,' Charles replies. 'I've come to paint the Ops Room.'

'You're a decorator?'

'No, I am an official war artist.' Charles enjoys the novelty of saying this. 'I've come to do some preliminary studies. This is my easel.' He points to the sidecar. 'My paints and brushes are in that bag.'

The look of confusion on the guard's face does not change as he opens the bag and peers inside.

For a moment the guard looks as if he is about to repeat his question then he shakes his head, disappears into the guardroom and reappears half a minute later with a clipboard. 'Thank you, sir. I have you down on my list. The Operations Room is under that building on the end, beneath the barrage balloon. I think you'll find they are busy down there at the moment. We had the siren go off twenty minutes ago.'

Charles parks and checks his reflection in the motor-bike's mirror. When he raises his goggles up on to his leather helmet he can see the skin around his eyes is pink, in contrast to the tan of dust on the rest of his face. His brow and nose are beaded with sweat and, as he wipes them, he smears himself with oil.

Once inside, he is directed towards a metal staircase that winds several flights down to about the depth of an Underground station. When he reaches the bottom he follows big yellow arrows along dimly lit passages lined with metal pipes. They smell of oil and fresh paint. The walls have large numbers written on them in red, count-ing down from eighteen to one. Upon reaching '1' he finds himself in front of a heavy iron door marked 'Control Room'.

He knocks and enters. A guard puts a tick on a clip-board and nods towards some metal stairs. Charles has to go up this time, one flight. At the top he finds him-self on a vast, circular gallery above Fighter Command's Operations Room. From here he watches in silence for a few minutes before taking out a sketchpad. In the gloom below he can see the white faces of the WAAF as they chart a raid on an enormous map of southern England, plying their long-handled magnetic plotting rods as deftly as croupiers. On the wall behind them are identification charts showing dozens of silhouettes of Heinkels, Messerschmitts, Junkers, Stukas and Dorniers. Alongside these are blackboards with names of airfields and numbers chalked on them and, along the base of this wall, a display panel which has glowing red bulbs showing the squadrons that are currently engaged or out of action. They all appear to be lit. Another electric panel is flashing the words 'Enemy Sighted'.

Charles hears the approach of shoes on the metal gantry and feels a vibration underneath his own feet. Then he hears a voice he thinks he recognizes. It is more like a bark. 'I don't care how you do it, just bloody well do it.' It belongs to an officer and, when Charles registers the gold braid on his cap as he appears around a corner, he realizes he is a senior one, a group captain. His face is flushed. By his side is a junior officer who wears a wounded expression.

'What the hell are *you* doing here?' The group captain is now standing in front of Charles. 'I know you, don't I?'

Charles feels the heat drain from his cheeks as he realizes that the group captain was one of three judges presiding at his court martial two years ago. 'I'm an official war artist,' he says, 'come to paint the Ops Room.'

The group captain slaps the metal handrail. 'Is this some kind of joke?'

'I've got clearance from Sir Kenneth Clark at the National Gallery.'

'You could have clearance from God for all I care; I'm not having you standing around my bloody Ops Room gawping at my bloody staff. I know the sort of picture you would paint. Fuck off.'

The junior officer hangs back while the senior marches on. 'Sorry,' he says. 'He hasn't slept for three days. Try Biggin Hill. It's more scenic anyway.'

As Charles rides away he stills the shaking in his arms by gripping the handlebars tightly. The group captain's hatred of him had been shocking, and he tries to justify it to himself as a consequence of the strain of being braced for invasion for a year – everyone he meets these days seems to be jumpy.

At the entrance to Biggin Hill he is confronted by rows of white bell tents. The hangars are better camouflaged, covered in netting and branches that blend with the thick hedgerows. Beyond them is the shimmering gold of a wheat field. Charles pulls on the elasticized armband he has been given. On it are written the words 'Official War Artist'. He had forgotten to wear it earlier at Stanmore, and now regrets his negligence.

Hearing the tap of metal on metal he turns and sees a Spitfire close up for the first time since his abrupt departure from the RAF. An eighteen-inch gash in its wing is being repaired with a slice of metal cut from what looks like a petrol can and tacked into place with rivets. Incongruously there is a grey Fordson tractor next to it.

'Can you direct me to the mess?'

The engineer pushes his cap back on his head. 'See that windsock?'

'Yes.'

'It's near there. An ugly block. You can't miss it.'

The mess is a prefabricated hut with taped windows. There is a blackboard outside it with the previous week's losses chalked on it as if they were cricket scores: 'RAF v Luftwaffe, 61 for 26 – close of play, 12 for 0.' From somewhere inside he can hear a fragment of a Flanagan and Allen song drifting out of a wireless: 'We're gonna hang out the washing on the . . .'

A group of pilots, no more than a dozen, are lolling in deckchairs outside the mess hut, enjoying the sunshine. Some are smoking, some reading the papers, others playing backgammon. One, wearing a cricket jersey piped with what look like school colours, is sleeping, using a parachute for a pillow. Their faces are smeared with oil and smoke. Clearly they haven't been back long and are now trying to recharge before the next telephone call from Wing Command. With their sunglasses, rollneck sweaters and 'Mae West' life vests slung casually over their jackets, they look, to Charles, different from mere mortals, even from their fellow servicemen. They are like young gods, golden and invincible. Most seem too young to have fought in the Battle of Britain the previous summer.

While some haven't even taken off their fleece-lined flying jackets, despite the heat, one, he notices, is wearing a powder-blue RAF uniform that has been customized with scarlet lining. He is also wearing a blue cravat rather than the standard black RAF tie and, on the ground next to his stockinged feet, there is a plate with a half-eaten jam sandwich on it. This is attracting wasps. He doesn't appear to notice them as he concentrates on riffling a deck of cards. Apart from two smears of oil, his skin is like ivory, his wavy hair is the colour of vanilla ice cream and, caught in a rhombus of sunlight, it resembles a halo.

The squeaking wheels of a tea trolley make the young man look up. His movements are slow and languid. With his long eyelashes and clear skin, he looks about eighteen. 'Pick one,' he says when he sees Charles staring at him. He has the long vowels and easy confidence of a public-school boy.

Charles strides up to him and selects a card.

'Don't show it to me. Just remember it and put it back in the pack.'

This done, the young pilot shuffles the pack several times then holds up a seven of diamonds. 'This it?'

It isn't. 'Very good,' Charles says. 'How did you do it?'

'Ah,' the young man says. 'Trade secret . . . You look lost.'

'Not any more,' he says, turning sideways to reveal his armband. 'Been asked to come and paint you chaps.'

'Hear that?' the pilot says, turning to the others. 'We're going to be models.'

'Can I just set up and get started?'

'Be my guest. Make sure you get my good side. My name is Hardy, by the way.'

'As in "Kiss me, Hardy"?'

'No. Hardy is my first name. Pilot Officer Hardy Richmond.'

As Charles sets up his easel and takes out some water-colours, the young pilot puts on his flying boots, picks up some flight charts and, after a moment's thought, stuffs them down the side of the boots. Bathed as it now is in a patina of gold, his hair reminds Charles of Anselm's. He must say this out loud because Hardy says: 'What?'

'Nothing. Can I paint you in front of a plane?'

'OK, but if we're scrambled you'll have to leg it. We're having a bit of a busy day for some reason. Been up twice already.'

As they walk towards the planes, Charles says: 'How long have you been a pilot?'

'A year. Joined up straight from school.'

Hardy's Spitfire is the third along a row covered in grass and matting camouflage. He taps the tip of its wing, a perfect ellipse. 'Beautiful, isn't she? The most romantic plane ever built. She reads your mind. You only have to think of a move and she responds.' He runs his hand over the aircraft's skin. 'It's like having wings yourself.'

Charles stares at the machine and nods. He never got to fly one – the closest he came during his training was a Harvard – but he would have loved to have had the chance. Victory rolls. One of the Few. Perhaps . . . No, if he is going to borrow a plane it must be one that is not needed.

There is a cartoon painted on the fuselage, Doc from *Snow White*. It triggers a memory of Anselm. He tries to remember why they had gone to see *Snow White and the Seven Dwarfs* together that day in Leicester Square.

Afterwards, as they strode home singing 'Some Day My Prince Will Come', Anselm had linked arms with him but, fearing this a risk too far, Charles had pulled his arm free. They had called each other Dopey and Grumpy after that.

There are also three miniature swastikas on the fuselage, marking Hardy's kills. On the tail fin is a parachute, ready to be grabbed. When the red, white, blue and yellow target marking on the side of the Spitfire reflects in the young man's round sunglasses it gives Charles an idea. 'Could you stand in front of the target,' he says, 'use it as a sort of frame?'

He begins sketching, a series of circles and cubes. The yellow outer band of the target looks like another halo around the young man's head. 'I like the cravat,' Charles says. 'Is it silk?'

'You have to wear them,' Hardy says. 'Because of the constant twisting left and right as you search for bandits. It chafes the neck . . . Some of the boys borrow their girlfriends' stockings to keep them cosy at high altitudes.'

Charles hesitates. 'I bet those blue uniforms are an aphrodisiac.'

'You bet right. But you can't do so badly with the girls. Don't they all want you to paint their portraits?'

Charles laughs the question away, feeling strangely exhilarated by his own imposture, as if he is a spy operating behind enemy lines. Hardy has mistaken him for one of his own, a red-blooded ladies' man. Wholesome. Normal. And he likes how it feels. How much easier his life would have been if he was one.

The outline done, he begins experimenting with his watercolours, holding one brush between his teeth as he dips another in a jar of water. 'Do you hate the Germans?'

'The Luftwaffe pilots? No, not really. Sometimes. There's a mutual respect, I suppose. I heard of one pilot in a duel with an ME 109 who ran out of ammunition at the same time as the Hun did. Our boy spread his hands philosophically. Jerry did the same and they both banked away from each other, laughing.'

'We have more in common with them than we do with the French, or even the Americans,' Charles says, rolling the paintbrush to one corner of his mouth so that he can talk out of the other. 'We're Anglo-Saxons, after all. The Germanic tribes were here before the Normans. And we were on the same side in the Napoleonic wars . . . Well, I mean the Prussians were on our side, and we couldn't have won at Waterloo without them.' He holds up his brush in line with his thumb to judge the scale of his subject. 'We enjoy the same things. Prefer beer to wine. Love the forests. Sausages. Brass bands. We have the same temperament. Phlegmatic. Even our royal family is German.'

'You seem to know a lot about them.'

'I knew one once. Before the war. He was studying art in London.'

Hardy flicks his hair like Anselm used to. 'Can I have a look?'

'Not yet.'

'They're a funny lot, the Hun. When the rescue boats pick them out of the water they salute and stand to attention. And when they are taken prisoner, the first thing they ask for is boot polish . . . Do you have a girl?'

Charles flattens the bow of his lips as he thinks. He then pictures Maggie at the National Gallery. Well, she had seemed friendly. He blinks his assent.

'Does she have a friend?'

'Why?'

'*Gone with the Wind* is showing at the Plaza in Croydon. We could take them there. Do you fancy it?'

Charles laughs, partly out of surprise, partly embarrassment. Hardy seems so guileless, so keen. 'Why not? Is there a telephone I could use?'

'We're not supposed to use the one here. There's one in the village. Leave a message for me at the mess if . . . What's her name?'

'Maggie.'

'If Maggie clears us for take-off.'

When Charles arrives at the picture house at 6.30, still wearing his battledress, he buys four tickets. He is having to fight down his breathlessness, as if his deception might be exposed at any moment. Seeing an old and partly ripped Ministry of War Transport poster pasted to the cinema wall, he wanders over to it and starts reading. Its message, hastily written the previous summer, no longer seems relevant.

IMMOBILIZATION OF VEHICLES IN THE EVENT OF INVASION. Every owner of a motor vehicle should be ready in the event of an invasion to immobilize his car the moment the order is given. Owners of petrol vehicles should

173

remove distributor head and leads, and empty the tank or remove the carburettor. HIDE THE PARTS REMOVED WELL AWAY FROM THE VEHICLE.

The words seem to take on a personal meaning. Am I the invader here? Will Maggie be immobilizing her vehicle? He scratches his head as if to clear it, checks his watch and wishes he hadn't agreed to this strange double date.

'Charles!'

He looks up to see Maggie stepping off the back of a still-moving bus. She is wearing her ATS uniform and it becomes her. She is followed by a voluptuous young woman whose breasts jounce against her cotton frock as she jumps down. Even with the white wimple she is wearing over her bunched-up auburn hair, she cannot be mistaken for a nun. The nurse's cape covering her shoulders confirms her true vocation.

Maggie gives a little wave as she gets closer and then, to his surprise, she kisses him on the cheek. She smells of strawberries and sunshine.

'This is my friend Gloria,' she says. 'Gloria, this is Charles, our latest recruit to the WAAC.'

'Charmed,' Gloria says with a West Country lilt, holding out her hand.

'Thank you for coming all the way out here,' Charles says. 'Hardy should be here soon.'

'Is he really a Spitfire pilot?' Gloria asks, her eyes widening.

'Really.'

174

Maggie brushes dust off Charles's jacket with flicks of her hand, a motherly gesture. 'Do you live around here?' she asks.

'No, but Biggin Hill isn't far away. That's where I was working today. Where Hardy is based.'

'Did you tell him I was your girl?' Maggie says with a playful punch.

Charles can feel the colour rising in his cheeks.

She laughs. 'I'm just teasing. You look very dashing in your new uniform, by the way, Captain.'

'Thank you. So do you. Pretty, I mean.' His smile dims momentarily.

Hardy announces his arrival with a honk of his car horn. He is driving a small, red two-seater Alvis. 'I borrowed it!' he shouts over the noise of the engine. He parks to the side of the cinema and vaults out of the seat as if dismounting from his plane. Charles looks at Gloria. Her mouth has gone slack. She swallows audibly.

When the film starts and Maggie's hand feels for his, Charles imagines for a moment that it is Anselm's hand. But the illusion does not last because this hand feels softer and smaller. His thoughts now on Anselm, he suddenly remembers why they had gone to see *Snow White and the Seven Dwarfs* that day in the spring of '39. They had heard about *Gone with the Wind* and wanted to see it, without realizing it hadn't been released. *Snow White* had been considered an ironic compromise. Each had dared the other to go in.

Maggie gives his hand a squeeze. As he realizes he has never held a woman's hand before, apart from his mother's, he also realizes how much he has been missing physical contact. He likes Maggie, she has a certain warmth and a sense of fun. But what he likes most about her is how she makes him feel. Wanted.

It strikes him now that in the two years since he last saw Anselm, he has not thought of another. He has been thinking of himself as 'the man who waits'. But what if his friend isn't coming back? What if he is dead? They will meet at the Student Union bar on Good Friday, he said. How naïve and empty that promise seems now.

Forty minutes into the film, the screen goes blank and a notice appears announcing that an air raid is in progress. The audience boos. Some get up to leave but others wait to see if the projectionist will put the film back on. When the lights come on instead, there are more boos, less emphatic this time, and patrons start making their way to the exit.

Outside, the four of them can hear the distant sound of air-raid sirens, fire engine bells and ack-ack guns pounding the night sky. Maggie makes Charles laugh with her imitation of Scarlett O'Hara: 'Fiddle-dee-dee! War, war, war; this war talk's spoiling all the fun at every party this spring.'

Instead of making their way to the shelters, they enter a pub which has sawdust on the floor and woodworm in its low beams. When Hardy goes to the bar, a man in a patched and rumpled suit registers his uniform and, drunkenly slapping him on the back, offers to buy him a drink. Charles looks around: there are a few other servicemen in, but mostly the regulars are civilians who look tired and lean, their teeth gappy and crooked, their hair greasy. The women are wearing boxy dresses and laddered stockings. One, with horn-rimmed spectacles, is wearing a scarf. Rubbing hair with dry towels has become a substitute for shampoo, he has heard, just as sponging with lukewarm water in the sink has replaced regular baths. Certainly the close, smoke-filled fug of the pub seems to bear this out. Hardy returns with a tray bearing two halves of foaming bitter and two sherries. 'Now,' he says. 'Who wants to hear my story about being rescued by a fisherman from Weymouth who thought I was a Jerry?'

As Charles listens to Hardy entertain his small audience, he takes out his pad and begins sketching the scene. He wonders if it might be possible to have an ordinary relationship with Hardy. A proper friendship with a man. Would that wash away the taint of Anselm, of his court martial? Instead of stealing a plane, he could begin a new, manly life of drinking and gambling and football and chasing girls and telling stories. A life free from rumour, innuendo and blackmail. Free from dirty words shouted by strangers, from conversations that stop when he enters a room.

Even as he is thinking these things he finds himself investing Hardy with Anselm's beauty. Projecting Anselm's face and voice on to him. Trying to feel for him what he felt for Anselm. The beast that Anselm has awoken in him, it seems, will never go to sleep again.

No, he tells himself with a nod of determination. He must find his friend. There can be no substitutes.

At 10.20pm, when the barman rings a bell, Charles

realizes two things: first, that he has been having so much fun listening to Hardy's stories he has lost track of time; second, that he is drunk.

Ten minutes later they hear a bicycle bell being rung outside. A policeman wearing a cloak attached around the neck by a chain appears in the doorway and, catching the barman's eye, taps his watch. The barman gives a thumbs-up signal. Charles finishes his bitter and thumps it down as a signal for the others to do the same. Policemen make him nervous.

As they stumble out past the sandbags into the night air, they gasp with laughter and hold on to each other for support. Hardy has his arm around Gloria's waist and only when he reaches his borrowed sports car does he recall it is a two-seater.

'Don't worry,' Charles says, 'we'll walk.' When he sees Hardy getting into the passenger seat by mistake, he adds with an indulgent laugh: 'Might be safer anyway!'

Because of the blackout, the headlights have been all but covered, leaving only two slits of light showing. Hardy revs loudly for a few seconds before putting the car in gear and dropping the clutch. 'Good to meet you, Maggie!' he shouts over the noise of the engine. 'See you tomorrow, Charles!' The car swerves to avoid a litter bin. Gloria waves goodbye. They disappear into the night.

With Hardy gone, Charles suddenly feels self-conscious. Left alone with Maggie he wonders again why he is here, why he has agreed to this double date. Was he trying to impress Hardy? Was he using Maggie to get closer to him? To befriend him? He tries to put these thoughts from his head as they walk arm in arm, following a kerbstone that has been painted black and white to help pedestrians navigate the darkness.

In the distance, over the London docks, they can make out the shapes of barrage balloons silhouetted against the glow of burning buildings. 'Looks like the East End caught it again,' Charles says. 'Poor devils.'

Maggie tilts her head so that it is resting on his shoulder. '*Carpe diem*, Captain,' she says. '*Carpe diem*.'

In the absence of street lighting, other pedestrians are reduced to dark shapes. They listen to footsteps recede. The moon emerges from behind clouds to reflect on the canal. There is a small iron bridge across it and, leading down, stone steps. Maggie goes first and then, when they are under the bridge, she turns. She is breathing rapidly. As their fingertips touch, she tilts back her head. When he withdraws his lips from hers, he sees her eyes are closed.

Without releasing her hold of him, Maggie takes a couple of steps backwards so that her shoulders are against the wall of the bridge. She unbuttons her coat, hitches up her skirt and wriggles her hips as she tugs down her camiknickers and steps out of them one leg at a time before stuffing them in her pocket.

When she starts to unbutton the flies on his trousers and reaches her hand inside, he stops her. 'Not here,' he whispers. 'How far is your place?'

'A taxi ride.'

IV

OPENING HIS EYES WITH A SUCCESSION OF BLINKS, CHARLES tries to work out through the blurred morning light where he is. There is a smell of cigarette ash and damp carpet. The blackout curtains haven't been closed properly and are framing a shaft of sunlight. On the floor is a trail of clothes, their shapes and texture unfamiliar to him because of their femininity: a bra, a satin camisole, a khaki shirt with buttons on the wrong side.

With hungover eyes, he follows them backwards to an old and opened Advent calendar and a drawing pad propped against a chair. On the pad there is a female nude with crescent breasts, one slightly bigger than the other, standing with one hand on her hip in a coquettish pose. She is wearing an officer's cap and her hair is loose underneath it. She is blowing a kiss. She looks like one of the pin-ups he recalls from his RAF days.

He remembers drawing it now and, without turning round, feels under the sheets with the back of his hand. The shin he encounters is hairless. Half roused from

180

sleep by his touch, Maggie rolls over, taking the sheets with her. They are in two single beds that have been pushed together and, as this movement disturbs the air, Charles smells her flowery scent and is reminded of the night before. His first time with a woman.

True, he had seen them naked in life classes before, and had appreciated their form, their curving lines, their aesthetic qualities, but back then he had thought there was something a little off-putting about the join of their legs, as if they were incomplete down there, deformed. He doesn't any more.

But when he tries to recall what the act itself felt like, he struggles. He thinks it probably felt . . . different. He had felt tenderness towards her, but her softness, the pliancy of her flesh, had seemed wrong. It was something to do with the lack of muscle fibre, with her being more yielding.

The memory of their lovemaking induces a stab of guilt. Yet it wasn't betrayal. Not really. In the darkness, as she lay on her front, he had imagined she was Anselm. He remembers this now. He hadn't felt guilty during the sweaty abandon of coitus, only afterwards.

Maggie yawns and gathers the sheet around her as she sits up in bed. 'Morning, handsome,' she says sleepily. 'What time is it?'

Charles checks his watch. 'Almost seven.'

She swings her legs out of the bed, reaches for a dressing gown and, as she walks to the bathroom, reveals the seam of her drawn-on stocking. It has smudged.

When Maggie emerges from the bathroom she is brushing her hair. 'I had a jolly time last night,' she says, crawling on to the bed and nibbling his ear. 'I'd never tried that position before. Where did you learn to do it that way?'

Charles does not answer. Smiles. Again he's thinking how much easier things would be if he could find it in his heart to fall in love with this woman. He tries to imagine his life with her. A pipe and a newspaper. Sunday roast. Perhaps even children. Would that be so bad?

'There's someone else, isn't there?'

Charles remains silent. Closes his eyes. He feels the warmth of her honeyed breath on his face a fraction before the gentle brush of her lips against his closed eyelids.

'Do you love her?'

He thinks about this for a moment before he finds himself nodding.

'Then what are you doing here with me? Captain? Mm?'

He opens his eyes, strokes her hair and says: '*Carpe*-ing the *diem*.'

Maggie laughs and, adopting her southern belle accent, says: 'Well, fiddle-dee-dee!'

By the time Charles arrives at Biggin Hill and sets up, Hardy has already been up for a sortie over Dover. When the young pilot sees him he ambles over, pulls a silver hip flask from his flying jacket, takes a swig and offers it. 'Hair of the dog,' he says.

'Thank you.' Charles takes a sip. Wipes his mouth. Brandy.

182

'How's Maggie?'

'Fine. Gloria?'

'More than fine. She's the cat's meow. Where did you find her?'

'I didn't. Maggie did.'

'Well thank you. I tell you, Charlie, it's love. Chocks away!'

Charles feels a sudden urge to share his news with Hardy: he is like him now. He too knows the feel of a woman's belly and hips, the soft wetness of her mouth, the heft of her buttocks. He imagines himself stroking Hardy's hair as he explains to him that his conduct is no longer unbecoming a gentleman, an RAF officer . . .

A siren sounds and the airfield becomes alive with mechanics in pale blue overalls – sceneshifters running to remove the camouflage netting from the planes. Hardy grabs his parachute off the tail and shouts: 'We'll have to finish this conversation later. I wouldn't stand too close if I were you.'

Charles fights down an adrenaline-wrought urge to join in. Instead, with a flush of disappointment, he gathers his easel, runs back to a safe distance and turns to watch Hardy, now in his cockpit and wearing his leather helmet, giving a thumbs-up signal to an engineer. Small flames shoot from the engine as it starts and the still afternoon air reverberates with the sound of harnessed energy. The grass behind the aircraft dances in the slipstream. The engineer pulls the chocks clear and the Spitfire quivers for a moment before its plump tyres prowl forward.

Then Charles hears a noise like hailstones on a tin

roof and, as he looks up, sees a blue-bellied Junkers 88 dive-bomber, its twin engines bulking enormously, barely a few thousand feet above the hangar, gliding like a giant bat. It seems suspended in space and, for a surreal moment, benign. Then its bomb doors open and half a dozen small dark tubes tumble out, a point at one end, a fin at the other. He watches transfixed as gravity tugs their noses down first. They don't fall vertically, but on a trajectory, towards him.

Abruptly it feels personal. These small dark objects are filled not with curiosity but with death and hate.

He dives headlong towards some sandbags as the bombs explode behind him, sucking up the air and lifting him from the ground. Time seems to slow down, allowing his brain to shift gears for a few postponed seconds and perceive the world at half speed. Then, realizing his face is pressed against broken glass, he looks up to see the Junkers curving steeply away. A moment later he is shrouded in white dust.

He is on his knees now and, looking up again, sees another Junkers on a course towards the airfield, its bomb doors open. As the black objects tumble from it his eyes dilate and he dives for cover again. There is a screech of tearing metal then smoke plumes from the gutted hangars to his right. The entrance, a spawning cloud of rubble, is more like an abattoir – a foot blown off an airman, an arm torn from a shoulder. Three men lie dead, their torsos a tangle of white tripe rapidly turning red.

Coughing and retching through a fine rain of chalk dust, Charles runs for cover again, this time to a slit trench, but another explosion knocks him off balance before he can reach it. He staggers to his feet, one hand clapped to his head, and gropes his way through the writhing smoke. Once he is clear of it, he sees a Dornier that is trailing a thin ribbon of black from its cowling. For a moment it hangs like a torch in the air before tearing into a tree a few miles away.

His attention is now caught by a Spitfire taxi-ing blindly through the smoke. The cartoon of Doc on the side reveals it is Hardy's. His wheels are skidding and scarring the soft turf. The plane takes off briefly then cartwheels across the airfield before slewing round into a hedge. The Spitfire's back now broken, it catches fire almost as an afterthought. Lazily. Hypnotically. As Hardy struggles to open the canopy, Charles limps over as quickly as he can to help him, levering himself up on to the wing. The flames are licking the cockpit now and, as Charles tries to break the glass with frantic blows from his elbow, he sees the skin melting off Hardy's face. It looks like molten wax. Hardy's mouth is open but Charles cannot hear his screams.

Hosing towards him now are heavy jets of liquid. His face feels wet and hot, as if he is being scalded, and when he looks at his hands he sees flames dancing on them. Realizing he is being doused in aviation fuel, he jumps down off the wing and staggers clear of the wreckage.

The next thing he knows he has been knocked to the ground – a rugby tackle – and a blanket is smothering him.

He doesn't know for how long he is unconscious,

perhaps only a few seconds, but when he emerges from under the rug he is on his own. Through his one good eye he sees that heat has cracked the glass of his wrist-watch. The strap hangs by a charred thread. On the ground next to him is Hardy's hip flask, now blackened with soot. All around him are grey-white mounds of chalk and concrete. In his nostrils is the pungent reek of gas and plaster dust. Shadows are gathering over the hayricks. His face is numb. The Spitfire is now a charred skeleton.

When, three weeks later, the gauze and bandages are removed from Charles's face, he is given an intimation of the extent of his disfigurement by the reaction of the nurse. She hides her horror well, clenching her jaw as she smiles, but her eyes give her away as they widen. The coolness of the air on his skin is a relief and his first instinct is to scratch it, but the nurse gently holds down his hands.

'Can I have a mirror?'

'All in good time.'

'A mirror. Please.'

'There's one above the sink.'

The nurse supports him under the armpit as he levers himself out of the bed and shuffles three paces. When he looks in the mirror he is immediately sick into the basin, a reflex prompted not so much by vanity as shock. The skin on one side of his face, from his brow to his jaw, is tarry black and swollen. The act of vomiting hurts because it stretches the skin further, but he is unable to weep in pain, his tear ducts having been cauterized. Where once he had eyelashes, eyebrows and hair, he now has only charcoal.

The nurse helps him back to the bed and he lies down and closes his eyes. When he opens them again it is dark. He turns towards the wall so that he can retreat once more into sleep. When next he opens them it is daylight and the nurse is sitting beside his bed.

'Mr Northcote, there's a visitor to see you.'

Charles turns his head awkwardly and sees Maggie standing in the doorway. She is holding a bunch of flowers. 'Hello, Captain,' she says too lightly, keeping intense contact with his eyes for fear of straying to his cheek and neck. 'How are you feeling?'

Charles blocks her sightline with his hand. 'Don't look at me,' he says. 'Please.' He turns his face to the wall. 'Go away.'

Three weeks later when a letter arrives from Buckingham Palace informing him he is to be awarded the George Cross 'for conspicuous courage in circumstances of extreme danger', he lets it fall from his grip to the floor.

The day after that another letter arrives. When Charles sees Maggie's signature at the bottom of it, he stops reading. She has written almost every day. He wants to weep, but cannot. It will be kinder this way, kinder to her. She need not feel guilty about abandoning him if he abandons her first.

V

Alsace. Autumn 1943

ANSELM'S ONLY DISTRACTION DURING THE DAY IS WORK, THE SS are right about that. *Arbeit Macht Frei*. Work does set you free – the freedom of the emptied mind. But it also kills you. It had not taken him long to determine the true purpose of this maze of compounds and sub-compounds divided by high fences and watchtowers. It has not been built to provide slave labour for the Reich – that is a moderately useful by-product – but to work prisoners to death.

As this is an *Arbeitslager*, a work camp, the prisoners must march every day to one of three destinations: the granite quarry, the forest or the construction site. All are within a mile radius but even this distance is enough to leave a starving man exhausted. The work at the quarry involves breaking rocks and carrying them to boxcars mounted on rails and is considered the hardest, leaving men crippled in pain. Those sent to clear the forest must transport sleepers and this is considered easier, because a single man cannot lift one on his own – it takes four

even voice, *'Hier ist kein warum,'* there is no why here. But Anselm thinks he knows why. He has overheard the doctors talking, assuming the prisoners cannot understand German, or not caring if they suspect they can. By injecting synthetic hormones into the gonads, testosterone, they believe they can cure Aryan children of the future who might be afflicted with 'the homosexuality gene'. He looks at his groin now. It is swollen. Already there is bruising where the needle has entered.

VI

London. Spring 1944

FOR ROUGHLY TWO YEARS OUT OF THE PAST THREE, CHARLES HAS
been a visiting member of the Guinea Pig Club, in East
Grinstead. Though it is mostly made up of RAF pilots
with burn injuries, membership is open to anyone who
has undergone experimental reconstructive plastic
surgery at the Queen Victoria Hospital. Anyone, that is,
who likes a drink. And few like drinking more than
Charles.

He feels at home whenever he is there. The Guinea
Pigs are allowed to wear their service uniforms, or
civilian clothes, instead of 'convalescent blues' and may
come and go from the hospital at will. Local families,
meanwhile, are encouraged to treat them as normally as
they can. East Grinstead has become 'the town that does
not stare'.

Part of Charles's treatment has included the 'walking-
stalk skin graft', a new reconstructive surgical procedure
that involves taking skin from one part of the body and
grafting it on to another. He has also had belladonna

laid over his eyes and endured a complete immersion of his skin in saline solution. The treatments have certainly improved his appearance. In half profile, left or right, it is no longer obvious at first that he has any scar tissue at all. But in full profile, it is soon noticeable that one side of his face, extending from his hairline to his neck, looks papery: more smooth, dry and sallow than the other weathered, greasier, pinker side. In the three years that have passed since his injury, his eyebrows, lashes and hair have mostly grown back, at least in the areas where there is no scar tissue.

Good though the Guinea Pig Club has been for his self-esteem, it hasn't prepared him for his return to the world beyond East Grinstead. Londoners, he finds, do stare. Children point. Outdoors, he tends to wear a wide-brimmed fedora, regardless of the weather, because it casts a shadow over his face. Around his neck he wears a cravat. He finds the silk is soothing against his burns.

Lately he has taken up permanent residence at his old club, the Chelsea Arts, and in the privacy of his room here he tends to wear a kimono. In other ways he has developed a certain perverse vanity, spending hours staring at his reflection while sitting at his triple-mirrored dressing table. Sometimes he plucks nasal hairs with a pair of tweezers, or dabs at his skin with cold cream, or parts his hair with a comb so that it better covers the mottled side of his brow. But most of the time, unlike the people of East Grinstead, he stares. During his three years of surgery and convalescence he has been unable to contribute to the war effort, other than a few light duties as an ARP warden, doing black-out checks. All he has really been able to do is paint.

As he sits here now with a cigarette in the corner of his mouth, pouring himself his second glass of whiskey in ten minutes, he shakes his head. A bottle of Irish rarely seems to last more than a couple of days, but it is medicinal. His doctors told him if he didn't come off morphine his kidneys and liver would fail, so they started giving him a 'Brompton cocktail', invented in the Royal Brompton Hospital for tuberculosis patients. A combination of morphine, cocaine and highly pure ethyl alcohol, the body absorbs it quickly and it doesn't kill the patient.

When it became clear he was becoming addicted to this, too, the doctors started supplying him with the whiskey he requested. Alcohol is as good a substitute for pain relief as any, they said, perhaps recognizing that this particular patient has few pleasures left and, with his disfigurement, cannot now expect a pretty girl to marry him.

Perhaps they have sensed that Charles drinks to numb a pining heart, the attempted drowning of private sorrows that have learned to swim. Perhaps they have even sensed he is not the marrying kind. Who knows? Doctors are contrary. But they are right about the alcohol. And when he is away from the club bar, he likes to drink from the silver hip flask.

He had telephoned Hardy's mother to ask for her address, so he could send it on to her, but she had insisted he keep it. She had heard about the George Cross and asked him if her son had suffered. Charles couldn't help but hesitate for a second before answering. No. She said she understood.

While he still thinks of Hardy from time to time, he thinks of Anselm every hour of every day. When the air-raid siren sounds, Anselm. When the tiled walls of the Underground shudder and the sheltering families draw their loved ones close, Anselm. When he picks his way past the rubble of bombed houses in Chelsea, Anselm.

It doesn't help that the Chelsea Arts Club is one of Anselm's old haunts. And as a place of convalescence, it is not without its faults either. The rooms are cramped and gloomy and it has a number of steps that are difficult to negotiate on a crutch. But it is cheap, there is a good supply of Irish whiskey and in truth Charles no longer needs the crutch, he has grown used to it and he likes to keep it as a talking point, a way of deflecting attention from his face.

The club also enjoys a steady supply of venison, rabbit, salmon, woodcock and grouse, none of which is rationed, and all of which are generously supplied by the club's country members. These delicacies are a welcome antidote to the dreary blandness of wartime London. This week alone Charles has had saddle of rabbit braised in wine and truffled goose livers.

Above all, he feels at home here. His room smells of white spirit and oil paint, and it is scattered with evidence of his semi-bohemian life – a canvas primed in readiness for inspiration, an easel set up but empty, unwashed plates, his crutch, unopened bills, empty whiskey bottles, a half-eaten slice of Kipling cake, over-flowing ashtrays, a hurricane lamp, dirty underwear, half-empty cups of tea, a palette upon which colours have been squeezed only to be left to dry, and a bowl containing a ping-pong ball, a collar stud and some cufflinks.

Of his old friends, only one has been to visit him: Dr Eric Secrest, also known as Funf. Now with the Royal Army Medical Corps, he has been awarded a DSO for his work in Burma. As he delighted in explaining to Charles, his regiment is nicknamed the Handbags, 'which is the main reason I wanted to join it'.

Eric has now returned to England as part of the preparations for D-Day. On his visit he had looked more like the White Rabbit than ever and, in his usual loud, distracted and impatient way, he had told Charles that he needed to stop feeling sorry for himself, stop drinking so much and get himself back into the action. 'Paint a few battle scenes or whatever it is you do.'

Though still painterly, Charles's work has become more abstract lately. His injuries have even changed his technique for the better, making it bolder – the burns on his fingers having forced him to hold his brushes in a looser way. When he showed his 'Biggin Hill' series of paintings to a director of the Royal Academy, they were well received and exhibited.

But he knows he is struggling to find his own style. Most of his work, stacked facing the wall, has featured injured pilots recovering at the Queen Victoria Hospital – not only burns victims but also amputees whose remaining limbs he twists and distorts in gruesome abstractions. Not quite the propaganda Sir Kenneth

Clark had in mind. He needs his muse, and every day he checks his pigeonhole in the hope that there might be a letter from him.

He sighs now as he angles one of the side mirrors so that he can see the scarred side of his face and begins to sketch it in charcoal. Distracted, his eyes fall on the air-raid warning sign on the back of his door. It never fails to make him smile. 'ARRIVAL OF AN IMPENDING AIR RAID WILL BE GIVEN BY A FLUCTUATING OR "WARBLING" SIGNAL OF VARYING PITCH,' it reads. For some reason it amuses him that 'warbling' is in inverted commas, as if whichever civil servant wrote it was aware that the word didn't sound very warlike.

When he closes his eyes the same two images always come to him, one after the other. The first is of his own eyes reflected in those of Anselm as they held hands for the last time by the balcony window over Piccadilly Circus, the moment they heard the hotel door being opened, fearing what might be on the other side.

The second is of Hardy's face melting like wax, his mouth open in a silent scream as he perishes in the flames. Love, sex and death. The only three subjects that matter, especially when the world is at war. But what personal vision can he bring to them?

As he sits at his dressing table, he tries once more to sketch a self-portrait but sees only the stranger in his life, himself. He then pulls in the two smaller mirrors hinged to the sides of the larger central mirror, so that his profile is reflected back an infinite number of times, to a vanishing point. He frowns for a moment then opens his mouth as wide as it will go, stretching the skin on his cheeks painfully. He looks like a taut rubber mask. Munch's infinite scream.

In one side mirror, his face is still handsome, in the other it is disfigured and ugly. The middle panel shows his divided self in full. In disgust, he slams his hand flat against the top of it, causing it to spin around 180 degrees and nearly catch him under the chin. He is now staring at an empty expanse of unvarnished wood, the back of the central mirror. He tilts his head to one side, his eyes looking unseeing at the corner of the room, and then he spins the mirror around again so that he is looking once more at his reflection. He spins it again so that he is looking at the blank wood . . . It is like a blank canvas . . . He rummages in a drawer for a softer 2B pencil and finds one under the presentation box that contains his George Cross. He then sketches the outline of an elongated face, giving it a mouth that is gaping wide in a mute scream. He adds a flying helmet and, without taking his eyes off the sketch, he reaches for his oil paints and begins dabbing.

Half an hour later he lowers his paintbrush and realizes how tightly he must have been gripping it. His hand is aching. The pilot's face looks distorted and fore-shortened because of how close up it is, the same intimate and intrusive distance one has to one's own face in a mirror. With the paint still wet, Charles sits back and spins the panel. The paint runs, making the face look as if it is melting and, as it alternates with his own open-mouthed reflection, the two faces appear to blur into one. He lights the stubs of two candles and places them in front of the two angled side mirrors, just out of reach of the spinning arc of the larger central mirror.

He spins the mirror again. As it passes over the imaginary axis connecting the two subjects, he sees his own reflected face melting in the flames of the candles.

VII

Alsace

SEVERAL MONTHS HAVE PASSED SINCE THE EXPERIMENTS BEGAN – Anselm is not sure how many – and thanks to the light work and the extra rations he and his fellow human guinea pigs are looking healthier. Whatever is in the injections they receive once a month, the side effects all appear to be positive, for now. Anselm's eyes are no longer jaundiced, a pinkness has returned to his skin and he feels stronger, so much so he can even get through the hour-long roll call without black spots dancing before his eyes.

Today he feels uneasy. Something is wrong. Are there prisoners missing? This will mean more hours standing in the square. Or worse. For every *Häftling* absent for the roll call, ten will be shot. That is the rule. Not that this is a deterrent to escape attempts. The fate of one prisoner is of little concern to another. They are all condemned here, after all, and empathy is a luxury none of them can afford.

But something is definitely wrong today. Something

is different. Something is . . . protean. The camp even has a new smell. It is more than the usual acid combination of disinfectant, human sweat, damp straw and excrement. It is something chemical in the atmosphere. Sulphurous. Today the camp smells like the cauldron of hell.

An hour after it begins, the roll call comes to an end, and a corpulent *Unterfeldwebel* carrying a clipboard marches up to the officer on duty and salutes. He is known as the Ukrainian. Known and loathed.

'*Wieviele Stücke?*' the officer barks.

'*2,632 Stücke,*' the Ukrainian answers.

There are 2,632 pieces. Pieces, not people. The numbers are correct. Yet the electricity of violence is still in the air.

Anselm looks around. Two fences of barbed wire, the inner one carrying a high-tension current, surround the camp. Positioned at regular intervals along this perimeter are watchtowers, fourteen of them, and under each is a pole bearing a speaker, like that of a gramophone. These are used as air-raid sirens, an ugly shrill tested from time to time, but so far never needed. They are also used for announcements, made in German to the mostly uncomprehending ears of the French. Before these are made, the microphones are switched on for a few seconds and a crackling noise fills the air. The sound, more àn amplified absence of sound, is heard now and it fills Anselm with dread.

The other prisoners now sense that something worse than usual is to happen today. There seems to have been a change in the atmospheric pressure that has increased gravity, made the air heavier.

Then Anselm hears it. The sound of a needle scratching rhythmically on a gramophone. The music is almost inaudible at first. A repeated rolling of the upper strings followed by a slow, dissonant wailing of oboes and flutes and a deep sustain of bass instruments that anchor the harmony. Then, as the choral voices come in, the volume increases so that it is distorted and raw and the emphatic chords take up the rolling violin sounds. Its mood is one of despair, of impeding tragedy. Anselm recognizes it. The St John Passion. He cannot remember the last time he heard Bach, but this is beautiful, like rainwater easing over his parched soul. Yet it is also, in this context, sinister and theatrical. There is a movement to his left. A wooden contraption is being dragged out: a cross of two planks of wood, the size of a man. It is being placed below the gallows in front of the assembled prisoners.

Feeling overwhelmed, Anselm closes his eyes and savours the music while he can, clinging to its beauty as to a lifebuoy. As well as losing himself, he loses track of time. When the emotional climax comes – Jesus's last sung words, '*Es ist vollbracht*', it is finished – he feels confused. It cannot be over yet. Just one more passage of music, please. The long, flowing, downward phrases seem unbearably heavy now. He opens his eyes and stares emptily at the cross.

There is another movement, to his right this time. A dozen SS officers in full dress uniform file out and, with their boots clattering on the stone and their heads snapping in unison, goosestep towards the gate. Here they form a guard of honour, six down each side. As two sentries open the gate, the SS officers come to attention as one, with a synchronized clicking of heels. They now draw their ceremonial swords and hold them out to form an arch.

Two minutes pass before a horseman appears, riding at a steady walking pace from the direction of the Commandant's house, a white château that is all but hidden from the camp by a row of trees. By his side is a dog, an Alsatian, walking at the same measured pace. It looks different from the other camp dogs, longer in the leg, its thick, greying coat better groomed. It could be crossed with a wolf. No, Anselm now realizes what the main difference is: it is not barking, not baring its teeth. Unlike the others it has no need of a leash.

His gaze returns to the horseman, who is wearing the black silver-braided cap of a senior SS officer. His riding boots glint with polish. Though it is warm today, he is wearing black leather gloves and a long leather trench-coat, the tails of which are spread out over the horse's flanks. Its blackness merges with the black coat of the horse, a chiaroscuro that makes it hard to see where the rider ends and the horse begins. It is as if their very blackness is absorbing all light. Then a sunbeam catches the metal of his death's head, as well as the Knight's Cross with oak leaves around his neck, and the bit in his horse's velvety mouth.

This must be the new commandant, the fourth since Anselm's arrival here. His predecessors all made their entrance in Mercedes staff cars with small swastikas flapping on the bonnet. They all quickly demonstrated they meant business with an execution, a show of cruelty, to remind prisoners and guards alike what they are all here for, the task that must be done, the business in hand.

The silver-piped collar tabs on this commandant reveal he is a *Hauptsturmführer*. According to the rumours circulating around the camp in the past few days, he has served in an SS cavalry division in Poland. He is of tall stature and agile build and is about forty years old, at a guess. His eyes are shielded by the peak of his cap, which rests on the bridge of his long and straight nose, a nose that seems to exaggerate the length of his lupine face. The vertical of this nose ends dramatically with the wide, thick horizontal of his mouth, as though he were a line drawing. It is a visage of terrible beauty. If Death had a human form, Anselm thinks, it would be like this.

The Commandant comes to a halt in front of the cross. The Alsatian sits on its haunches without being asked. A *Häftling* is marched out from the compound near the infirmary. He has a pink triangle over a yellow star with a green bar. A Jewish, homosexual thief. This will be bad.

'The man before you has stolen food from an officer,' the Commandant drawls in a slow, educated voice. 'He knows the penalty for stealing food . . . You all know the penalty for stealing food.'

Food. The word triggers a convulsion in Anselm's gut. Since taking part in the medical experiments he has been fed better, but hunger is still a habit. Perhaps this execution will distract him for a time. They know the drill. If they avert their eyes from what is to come they will be punished – in all likelihood they will be obliged to join the poor bastard on the gallows. They watch as the *Häftling* is stripped, his thin arms and legs shivering violently. He is to receive lashes on his back, for sure.

But no. When he is tied upside down on the cross, facing outwards, the air thickens further. Anselm has studied images such as this in Renaissance art. But wasn't it St Peter who was crucified upside down? No, he thinks, it must have been St John. In this senseless place, that would make sense. Bach's passion of St John. That piece of choral music.

The Commandant is speaking again, Anselm under-stands his German. 'This man is hungry. He is going to be fed. He will not be hungry again.' He unbuttons his leather overcoat, removes his ceremonial dagger from its scabbard and points with it at a prisoner in the front row. 'You. Come here.' The prisoner doubles forward, removes his cap and stands to attention with his eyes downcast. The Commandant flips the dagger up in the air so that he is holding it by the tip of its blade. He presents it handle first to the prisoner. 'Feed him. Feed him his own *Fleischklösschen*.'

The prisoner looks at the dagger out of the corner of his eyes but he does not move.

'Slice off some meat and feed it to him.'

Anselm understands now what the prisoner is being asked to do. He has heard from the Slav inmates that the Waffen-SS do this on the Eastern Front. They cut the genitals off dead and dying Red Army soldiers and stuff them in their mouths as calling cards. The Russians do it back to the Germans. Meatballs, they are called. *Fleischklösschen*.

The naked prisoner upside down on the cross also seems to understand what fate awaits him. He gives a pitiful scream. More a whimper. A guard silences him with a jackboot to his face.

The standing prisoner gives a single, almost imperceptible shake of his head.

Anselm cannot believe his eyes. What is this? Defiance? Not a good idea, my friend. Surely he must know an act of defiance will result in his own death?

The Commandant nods and his mouth turns down at the edges, as if he is weighing this action up and is, despite himself, a little impressed. He slips his dagger back in its sheath, removes his Luger from its holster and digs his spurs into the horse's ribs. Once the horse has turned and he is sideways on to the standing prisoner, he lifts the safety lock on the pistol, takes aim and, without anger, shoots him through the top of his head. The horse flinches but stands its ground. The prisoner buckles at the knees and falls forward, steam rising from his wound. There is a delay of a few seconds before the blood seeps out into the dust, as if it had been too surprised to leave his skull any earlier.

The Commandant now rides along the ranks of prisoners, like a visiting dignitary inspecting troops, and the leather of his coat makes a squeaking sound against the leather of his saddle. Please God, Anselm prays, make him pick someone else. Anyone else.

But his height draws the Commandant's eye.

'You.'

Anselm will later try to convince himself that he hesitates at this moment, yet he knows in his heart that this is not true. There is nothing with which his conscience has to wrestle. The skin and bone on the cross is a corpse already, his continued breathing an affront to nature, a cruelty that should not be prolonged. He cannot be saved. Unlike Anselm. Maybe. This will be a mechanical act from which he is distanced, about which he has been spared the agony of choice. With this action Anselm will be buying himself another hour of life, another day, another week.

'Hast du verstanden?'

Has he understood?

Anselm removes his cap and stands to attention. When the Commandant leans forward in his saddle once more to proffer the handle of the dagger, Anselm takes it, marches to the front and, without hesitation, without even a whispered apology to the man whimpering below him, takes the fear-shrivelled testes in one hand, pulls them out at an angle to stretch the scrotum, and begins sawing with the other. The blade is sharp. This time the blood does not hesitate, and if it cannot be easily staunched, the screaming can. When Anselm places the *Fleischklösschen* in the upside-down man's open mouth, he tries to spit them out but chokes on them instead. His nostrils are filling with the blood cascading down his torso and neck.

Anselm steps back, his breathing now rapid and audible. He picks up the man's clothes and wipes the dagger on them before handing it back to the

Commandant, holding it by the tip. He must not look up. To look this devil in the eye will be to turn to stone. The Commandant positions his horse between the prisoner and Anselm and studies the pink triangle on his jacket. '*Vous êtes français?*'

Anselm knows the truth must out now. Lying to the Commandant would be like lying to God.

'*Nein, mein Kommandant.*'

'*Reichsdeutscher?*'

Anselm hesitates. '*Jawohl, mein Kommandant. Reichsdeutscher.*'

The German words sound foreign on Anselm's tongue at first, then he tunes in to them.

'Where are you from?'

'Aachen, Commandant.'

'You have a fine cathedral there.'

Anselm looks up. From this angle the Commandant's eyes are visible below the cap. They are narrow and a fraction too close together. 'Yes,' he says in bewilderment. 'It is very fine.'

There is a gurgling sound as the crucified man continues to drown in his own blood.

'How old are you?'

Anselm has to think for a moment. He must be twenty-five by now. 'I am twenty-five, Commandant.'

'Why are you not serving the Fatherland?'

'I was going to.' It is not a lie. 'I was studying in England before the war when I got my call-up papers. I was about to return to Germany when . . .' He hesitates.

'You were arrested?'

'Yes, Commandant.'

Instead of the expected blow, there is another question. 'What were you studying in England?'

Anselm feels as if he is in a dream. He has not had a civilized conversation in almost five years, and after the violence he has just perpetrated it seems illusory that he should be having one now. He is no longer aware of the guards, of the dying man, of the thousands of prisoners behind him, accusing ghosts whose eyes must be boring into his head as they listen. 'Fine art.'

'You are an artist?'

'Yes. I trained at the Slade.'

The Commandant thinks about this. 'Our Führer is an artist.'

Anselm has to fight an urge to laugh. He feels hysteria bubbling up inside him like a spring of cool water. Looking down, he fixes his gaze on the horse's hooves.

'And Reichsmarschall Goering is a keen collector of art,' the Commandant adds. With this he gives a smart tug on his rein and, with a touch of his spur, rides towards the administration block. The Alsatian follows him with a loping stride, without being called. Only now does Anselm realize that throughout the entire performance the animal has not moved from its position. It has not barked in excitement. Nor even snarled.

The Commandant has reached his destination now. When he dismounts in one easy movement, the horse does not move. A guard runs over, takes hold of its bridle and leads it away. The Commandant enters the block, the dog at his heel, and the other officers march back across the square and follow him inside.

Anselm passes into a trance in which everything is being enacted before him in slow motion, without sound. Perhaps it is another change in the atmosphere causing a pressure on his inner ear. Perhaps he is becoming deaf.

The rhythm of the camp soon returns to normal. *Ausrücken und Einrücken.* Go out and come in. The workers march out of the camp gate now in step, heads lolling, arms rigid, and their gait is hard, boneless and unnatural, like puppets made without joints.

Since he was 'volunteered' for the medical experiment, the doctors have ordered that Anselm should perform only light duties, repairing prisoners' uniforms. He has become deft with a needle and thread and today, as he has every day since the injections began, he soon manages to slip into a self-induced trance: it spares him from thoughts of the upside-down man he has martyred. By the time the sun is setting in a tumult of angry crimson, he has almost forgotten about his deed altogether.

But the crucified man is there to remind him as he trudges back into the square for the evening roll call. The skin is leathery, the body white, drained of blood like a slaughtered bullock. It is moving with flies, alive with them. Anselm has encountered scenes like this in art books: Goya's series of prints 'The Disasters of War', in which naked, mutilated torsos are mounted on trees. Had the Commandant seen them? Is that where this idea for random butchery came from? Is he a man of culture?

As Anselm considers this, one of the other prisoners walks past him and spits in his face.

*　*　*

Three days later, Anselm is summoned by the Ukrainian to see the Commandant in his office at the end of the administration block. His muscles freeze at this order, not in fear necessarily but in something closer to relief. The long, empty, friendless days are over, it seems. This is his time. He will surely die now, and he feels vaguely honoured that his death will be at the hands of a commandant rather than the vicious little Ukrainian. But when he knocks on the Commandant's door and hears that dark brown voice say 'enter', it is not the barrel of a Luger that greets him but a large sheet of thick white paper attached to a board by two clips. The Commandant is eating a peach noisily. He finishes it, throws the stone in a bin and wipes his hands before signalling for Anselm to take the paper. He then hands him a slim stick of charcoal. Anselm has seen shards like this in the crematorium. Is that where this comes from?

The Commandant removes his cap to reveal blond, swept-back hair, shaved at the sides. 'Draw me,' he says.

Only now does Anselm notice the Alsatian at the Commandant's feet. It is studying him with cold eyes.

Seeing a movement, he realizes his hand is shaking. As he steadies it by pressing the charcoal against the paper, an unfamiliar calm descends upon him. As his hand sweeps back and forth across the picture plane without making a mark, he begins to lose himself. He knows he should be nervous – that he is drawing for his life – but the thrill of having clean paper to draw upon outweighs his fear. He studies the Commandant for a moment, mentally reducing him to spheroids, ellipses and quadratic surfaces. The only sound is the scratching and slurring of the drawing point against the paper.

After ten minutes he is finished. He holds it at arm's length, feeling slightly out of breath. It is a good likeness. He turns it around so the sitter can see himself.

As the Commandant purses his lips, cocks his head to one side and contemplates the sketch, there is a silence so thick Anselm can hear it humming in his ears. He now regrets not making his drawing more flattering, the eyes wider apart, the face less elongated. But it seems to meet with approval.

'Not bad . . .' The Commandant takes it from him and places it on the desk. 'I want some drawings of life in the camp,' he says. 'Roll call. Prisoners marching to work, lining up for food, sleeping. Some studies. Try and be as accurate as you can. Don't idealize. I shall notify the guards that you are not to be disturbed. Take the board with you. And take those.'

Anselm notices for the first time that there are more white sheets in a roll tied with string, as well as more sticks of charcoal, also neatly tied. With this the Commandant wafts his hand to indicate the prisoner is dismissed.

Anselm had known better than to ask questions, but as he shuffles out of the office, with the board and the sheaves of paper in one hand and the sticks of charcoal in the other, his head is crowding with them. How many studies does the Commandant want? By when does he want them completed? What are they for? He

214

blocks out the thoughts. Thinking gets you killed. He determines to start immediately and keep going until he runs out of paper. He counts the sheets. There are ten. He should be systematic. The Commandant has requested a drawing of the roll call: the next one is not until the evening; that gives him the afternoon to produce a landscape of the camp from a high viewpoint, as well as some individual studies of prisoners. But it is lunchtime. He will start with the food queue. It will mean missing out on his own food but since he became part of the experiment, nutrition is no longer the urgent priority it has been. He no longer fears he might die of starvation between meals.

There is a raised terrace outside the kitchen. This will give him a vantage point. And there is a chair here. He looks around self-consciously then sits on it with caution, as if it might be an electric chair. Positioning his board on his lap, he holds the piece of charcoal over it, poised.

'What the hell is going on here?'

Anselm recognizes the sharp voice as belonging to the Valkyrie, the most feared of the *Aufseherinnen*, or female guards. In the same movement he stands up, removes his cap and speaks in a tumble of words. 'The Commandant has asked me to draw some pictures.' He holds out the board as proof and waits for the inevitable lash of her whip. When it does not come, he risks a look. The Valkyrie, a narrow-hipped woman with pock-marked skin, seems unsure what to do next. The clean white paper and the board are an incongruous sight, evidence that this prisoner must be telling the truth.

'Stay here.' She disappears into the administration block and returns a couple of minutes later. 'Then get on with it!' she shouts.

Anselm begins sketching as the prisoners form a line. There is the usual minor jostling for position but the queue is orderly, each man staring blankly ahead, his thoughts only on the food. The idea for this composition comes to him now. He will sketch the first prisoner in detail and the faces of those behind him will become progressively less detailed, until, as their heights diminish with perspective, they merge and disappear into a vanishing point.

Feeling braver now, he turns to the Valkyrie and says: 'I need to do a sketch from the top of the camp, looking down.'

'Follow me,' she says.

At the top of the camp the Valkyrie signals to the guard in the watchtower that the prisoner has her permission to be here and then looks around before she lights a cigarette. Anselm begins sketching his landscape, conveying a sense of the symmetry of the camp, the line punctuated by watchtowers. He has realized for the first time that it is arranged in the shape of a noose. This is deliberate, he presumes. The SS never does anything by accident.

But something is missing from the composition. He contemplates the Valkyrie now sitting with her back to him about ten yards away, a little down the slope, slightly to his left. He sketches her as a hunched figure, small under her SS-Gefolge cape. Her forage cap is covering a neat coil of braided brown hair held by pins. As she concentrates on smoking, she draws in her shoulders. She is wearing high boots that reach to the hem of her grey field uniform. Every now and then she turns and watches him sternly, and Anselm feels as if he cannot move out of the target of her glare.

Although days have no name for the prisoners in the camp, Anselm knows this is an *Arbeitssonntag*, a working Sunday. The previous evening he had to visit the *Blockfrisör*, the official barber who shaves heads and chins on a Saturday, and the interval between visits is always a week. The other prisoners don't look at him as he heads up the hill to the top of the camp and sets up his board. Under the Valkyrie's protection, he is invisible again.

He has been sketching for perhaps fifteen minutes when he notices that a group of new arrivals is being herded into the camp below, about fifty of them, men and women, old and young. All have yellow stars on their striped uniforms and hair cropped close to their skulls. The blisters, pustules and welts on their skin are familiar, but the sight of so many Jews in this camp of mostly French political prisoners is not. Even more unusual is the presence of so many women. All look malnourished and their movements are slow and list-less to the point that even the barking of the dogs does not seem to register with them.

Instead of being taken to the barracks, as usually happens when inmates arrive from the station, they are made to stand in the square for about a quarter of an hour before two doctors, recognizable from their white coats and SS peaked caps, emerge from the infirmary and order the prisoners to remove their clothes. They do as instructed without complaint, like sharp-boned robots, and then they follow instructions to throw the clothes into one big pile in the middle of the square.

One of the doctors counts off fifteen prisoners and leads them out, back towards the village. They follow him, arms raised, still in single file, with three female and two male guards bringing up the rear with their dogs on leashes. As they leave the camp, the men drop their hands to cover their genitals. The women do the same, with some covering their breasts, too. This modesty strikes Anselm as peculiar. Surely they are used to this by now?

He has to get to his feet to see where they are being taken: a white building. With a tiled roof and a metal chimney, it looks like a small hotel. To reach it they have to pass an *estaminet* and the locals drinking in it have brought their chairs and their glasses outside to watch the strange procession. Some of them are laughing and pointing. The prisoners file into the building and, when the last has gone through, the guards follow them in, only to emerge again a minute later and stand outside, leaning against the wall, smoking and talking.

Anselm sketches what he is witnessing. After a while the guards check their watches and go back into the building. A further ten minutes or so pass before they emerge again and march back to the camp and count off fifteen more of the naked, waiting prisoners. As the others did, they cover their genitals as they leave the camp. Anselm realizes now what the scene has brought to mind: Masaccio's fresco of Adam and Eve being cast out of the garden.

The following day, Anselm is sketching a former kapo, one of the prisoners with the green triangles who administer most of the beatings to the other prisoners. This one has become too sick and weak to carry out his duties and so has been left behind from the daily work details. He looks old and his death is a matter of weeks, perhaps days away. When a kapo is of no more use to the SS he dies.

Anselm does not resent the kapos as much as others do. In this place you do what you have to do to survive for another day. The kapos have chosen their way to survive. He has now chosen his. And the opportunity to draw is giving him back his sanity. He feels nourished by it. A man again.

The Commandant rides across, followed by his dog, and without dismounting studies the picture of the kapo over Anselm's shoulder. He looks at the model, an emaciated man, with head dropped and shoulders curved, on whose face and in whose eyes not a trace of a thought can be seen. 'I wouldn't even know where to start,' the Commandant says, drawing out the words. 'How do you start? Do you start with the form? The composition?'

'I always start by thinking of the figure as a series of solid volumes which can move in relation to one another,' Anselm says, holding up a piece of charcoal at arm's length to form a vertical line down the centre of the subject.

The Commandant cocks his head. 'It doesn't look

right.' He taps his chin with his riding crop. 'Let us see what he looks like on the gallows.' He signals with a click of his finger for the kapo to mount the scaffold. With a look of confusion, the old man obeys.

'Now remove your clothes.'

Without lifting his sad, opaque eyes, the kapo obeys again. He looks like a human skeleton.

The Commandant clicks his fingers. 'Come on, come on. Your head in the noose.'

The kapo steps on to a stool and slips the rope around his neck. It hangs loosely.

Anselm looks at the Commandant.

The Commandant makes an impatient signal for him to start sketching. Then, after watching Anselm at work for five minutes, he tuts. 'It was better how you had it before.'

Anselm watches as the Commandant rides away, his Alsatian breaking into a trot to keep pace with him. He then signals for the kapo to come down. Without a word the old man removes the rope, steps off the stool and puts his clothes back on.

The following day Anselm is again summoned to the Commandant's office, this time by the Valkyrie. He removes his cap and presents his sketches rolled up.

The Commandant studies them without comment. 'Can you use oils?'

As Anselm nods he notices that the sketch he did of the Commandant the other day is now propped against a shelf, on display.

'Then I have another commission for you. Come to my residence at one tomorrow.'

Anselm considers explaining that he does not have a watch, that it was taken from him, but he thinks better of it. Besides, he knows the noon roll call begins when the sun is overhead. It is shorter than the morning and evening roll calls because most of the inmates are at work. He will use the flagpole as a sundial after that.

The Commandant seems to read his mind. 'The *Erstaufseherin* will collect you at one and escort you over.'

The residence, a white, ivy-mantled château with a turret, is a short walk from the camp gate and is partially hidden by a screen of beech trees. There are square-shouldered eagles guarding the entrance – made from granite – and, inside, crystal chandeliers, silk hangings and Persian rugs. The Valkyrie leads the way into a drawing room and looks around. This is clearly her first visit here too.

Stacked on the floor are cases of French wine and champagne, while leaning against the wall, evenly spaced out but not yet hung, are half a dozen paintings by French Impressionists. Anselm recognizes one as being by Renoir, a voluptuous young woman bathing in a lake. The spoils of war. Anselm also notices an easel set up in one corner and a canvas stretched on a board. Beside it are a selection of sable brushes and bone-handled knives with rounded blades, a palette and dozens of unopened tubes of oil paint. The smell is intoxicating.

The Valkyrie has picked up two framed photographs of Fräuleins on the desk and is contemplating them. Both have plaited blonde hair and are wearing folk costumes which show off their ample bosoms and broad hips. Both are smiling and holding babies.

The Commandant enters in full dress uniform, his medal around his neck. He is cleaning his nails with the point of his ceremonial dagger. 'You may wait outside,' he says to the Valkyrie.

She puts the photographs down and crosses the room without looking up.

'Can you paint horses?' The Commandant asks once the guard has closed the door behind her.

Anselm has never painted a horse in his life. 'Yes,' he says.

'I was thinking of posing on mine.'

'If you have a wooden horse we could put a saddle on that for now and add the real horse later. I could paint it separately.'

The Commandant slips his dagger back into its sheath and disappears from the room for a few minutes before returning with a saddle, followed by two prisoners carrying a vaulting horse. He has them position it by the window, places his saddle on it then mounts it, putting his boots in the stirrups.

Anselm wants to work with as little preparatory drawing as possible and so tries to cover the canvas quickly with a big brush. He will dispense with the usual primer because he knows if he wants to relate his colours accurately any white on the canvas will have to disappear anyway, and carefully filling in a tightly drawn outline will inhibit his response to the different tones.

'What is it?' the Commandant asks.

Anselm has seen a swastika armband on the desk. 'I need some colour. Could you put your armband on?'

The Commandant does as asked. 'And could you remove your gloves? You could be holding them in your hand. Hands are always a good counterpoint to faces and the skin tones will complement the black of your uniform.'

After almost an hour of intense painting, the Commandant checks his watch. 'We must stop for today,' he says. 'We shall resume at the same time tomorrow.'

Anselm glances at the two photographs of the Fräuleins on the desk. The Commandant catches him staring and says: 'I have two children from two different mothers. It is an SS officer's duty to father Aryan stock for the Fatherland.'

'I hope to have a child one day.' Anselm does not know why he has said this. He has never thought it in his life. He scratches under his left armpit to cover the pink triangle on his chest with his right forearm. Is he trying to impress the Commandant? Ingratiate himself? Pretend he is something he is not?

The Commandant looks thoughtful. 'What is your name?'

Anselm is so surprised he forgets for a moment.

'You must have a name.'

'Anselm.'

'Anselm,' the Commandant repeats, as if trying it out on his tongue. 'You have heard of Ernst Röhm?'

'The SA commander?'

Anselm had been aware of the scandal surrounding Röhm's open homosexuality in 1934. Everyone in Germany had heard the rumour. It was the unofficial reason Röhm had had to die in the 'night of the long knives'. The story was that Hitler had wanted to give his friend an opportunity to shoot himself and so had arranged for a gun to be left in his cell. When the guards returned, they found Röhm bare-chested and demanding that Hitler should come and shoot him himself. A theatrical end.

'Exactly. Röhm was the only one allowed to address the Führer by his first name.'

Anselm rubs his neck as he tries to read between the Commandant's enigmatic lines.

'My name is Manfred,' the Commandant says, reaching the door and holding it open.

As he walks through it, Anselm says: 'Thank you, Manfred.'

The door closes behind him. Anselm ignores the glare of the Valkyrie who is waiting for him on a chair by the front door.

When the Valkyrie collects Anselm at the same time the following day she presents him with a new prison uniform neatly folded, along with a bar of soap, a toothbush and a towel. He takes them without asking what they are for and then follows her as she leads the way out of the camp entrance gate towards the château. 'The Commandant will see you in half an hour,' she says when they enter. 'You are to use his shower. The first door at the top of the stairs. He finds your smell objectionable.'

When Anselm comes back downstairs feeling clean and enjoying the itchiness of his new clothes, the

Valkyrie is not in her usual chair. As he waits for her in the entrance hall, he notices a tray of letters ready to be posted on a desk. He hears a flushing sound and a door opens. The Valkyrie emerges, tugging down the hem of her skirt.

'What should I do with these?' Anselm says, holding up his dirty old clothes.

The Valkyrie turns up her nose and points to a bin in the corner. Once he has deposited the clothes there he is led through to the drawing room and told to wait. The Valkyrie checks her watch and then leaves. He sees the wooden horse in the same place, still with the saddle on it. He also sees his easel set up where he left it. On the Commandant's desk are sheets of writing paper and a wad of envelopes.

His heart hammers as he sits down and reaches for a pen with fumbling fingers that seem too thick and numb. 'My dear Grumpy,' he writes, trying to steady his shaking hand. The pen feels awkward, almost too thin to hold. He looks over his shoulder as he thinks he hears the door handle turn, but it remains closed. Writing comes back to him quickly but the pen is soon out of ink. He looks around for an inkwell, opens it, refills and starts scribbling again. As he is signing his name he loses control of the pen and it falls to the floor. Reaching for it too quickly he knocks over the inkwell. Half of the ink spills out on to the desk before he can set it upright again and seal its lid. By using several sheets of blotting paper he is able to absorb most of the spilled ink on the desk, but not before it has dripped on to the wooden floor. He tries to blot it there too but it leaves a splashy stain. The desk leg, when moved a few inches, casts a shadow over it, making it less obvious.

With his teeth clenched in concentration, he licks the envelope with a dry tongue and hesitates before writing the name and address. He snatches a second sheet of paper. On this he writes a covering note to his friend at the Swedish Embassy in Berlin. He folds this in half, slips the folded envelope inside it then places both in another envelope which he also addresses. As he crosses the room, he wafts the envelope to dry the ink. He opens the door a crack and sees the Valkyrie is sitting in her chair, her back to him.

He rests his head against the doorframe, trying to control his breathing, wondering what to do. Hearing the rattle of a chair being drawn back he looks through the crack again. The Valkyrie has stood up and is opening the drawer of a filing cabinet. A moment later she walks past the door down a corridor that leads deeper into the house. Anselm takes his clogs off and pads barefoot to the desk and slips the envelope behind others in the tray.

VIII

London

AS IS HIS HABIT, CHARLES CHECKS HIS PIGEONHOLE MORE IN hope than expectation. The letter he longs for is not here, but there is one from the War Artists Advisory Committee inviting him to submit work for a Royal Academy Summer Exhibition. The letter also notifies him that he has been appointed an Associate of the Royal Academy, an honour that will provide him with a modest stipend, enough to pay his bar bill at the club.

Two men in brown smocks and bowler hats arrive the next day to collect the triple-mirrored dressing table and Charles, wearing a three-piece suit and bow tie that feels uncomfortable against his neck, travels with it, and them, in a cream-and-red van to Piccadilly. Here he watches protectively as they lift the artwork from the back of the van into the courtyard before carrying it through the main entrance and up the stairs.

There are three galleries being used for the exhibition and as Charles accompanies the table up through the first two to reach the third he feels like an imposter. Here, being hung on the wall by two more brown-smocked men, is a complex study of Clydeside's shipyards by Stanley Spencer. Further along are Henry Moore's claustrophobic charcoal sketches of Londoners taking refuge from the bombs in the Underground. And in the second room, as a curator removes a dust cover from it like a magician flicking back his cape, is a cinematically striking painting of a sea of mangled German planes glinting mutely in the moonlight. It is by Paul Nash.

Once he has removed his own dust cover and angled the side mirrors that frame the central painting, Charles stands back and has an idea. Five minutes later he is in Regent Street, searching for two candles and a mirror the same rectangular shape and size as the wooden top of the dressing table. He finds them in an antique shop and, when he returns with the mirror under his arm and the candles in his pocket, he sees Sir Kenneth Clark contemplating the dressing table, his arms crossed, his head to one side.

'Ah, Charles,' he says. 'Very interesting. Very interesting. The use of scorching orange, the twisted and contorted features, the way the face looks as if it is melting. I like it. It's unflinching. Apocalyptic. Do you have a title?'

'I was thinking of calling it "Crossing the Line".'

'Yes, I like that. Good. Good. An RAF pilot, I take it?'

'A young man who died in 1941. Burned to death in his Spitfire. I saw it happen. But it's also a self-portrait of sorts.'

'How so?'

'It's a portrait of anyone who sits in front of the dressing table. Try it.'

When Sir Kenneth sits down, Charles spins the central panel so that the painting is alternating with the mirror.

'Oh I see! Ingenious! Ingenious!'

'The effect will be better with this.' Charles slides the mirror he has just bought over the top of the table and then lights the candles one at a time, dripping wax to hold them in place either side of the central panel. 'There. Now try spinning it again.'

Sir Kenneth does as asked. 'Yes. Very good. Very good.'

'I had the idea that the spinning mirror might be like the spinning propellers of the plane. Convey movement in the aeropainting style of the Italian Futurists.'

'Yes, yes. Excellent.'

Both men contemplate the artwork in silence for a moment, then Charles clears his throat. 'Sir Kenneth, may I ask you something? Is Maggie still working for you?'

'Maggie? No, she's long gone. I believe she joined ENTS, entertaining the Eighth Army out in Africa. Why?'

'Oh, no reason.'

A short, square-set man in a black leather coat and poloneck approaches. He has quizzically raised eyebrows and his wiry hair, arranged in a quiff, looks dyed. His face appears flushed with alcohol, which he has clearly tried to disguise with make-up. He is smoking a cigarette.

'Hello, Francis,' Sir Kenneth says. 'Charles, have you met Francis Bacon?'

'No.' Charles holds out his hand to shake. 'Hello. Charles Northcote.'

Bacon ignores the proffered hand. He sways slightly. Smells of alcohol. 'You a war artist?' he asks flatly.

'Yes. Was. Before this.' Charles touches his cheek. 'I've seen your work. You exhibited with Sutherland and Pasmore, didn't you?'

'Before the war, yes. Then I gave up messing around with paint to fight for my king and country.' He is slurring his words. 'Unlike some.'

'Weren't you in the ARP, Francis?' Sir Kenneth interrupts, perhaps sensing the older artist bullying the younger.

'We had it harder than any front-line soldiers,' Bacon says, drawing on the cigarette. 'During the Blitz.'

Sir Kenneth's smile is dangerous now. 'Didn't I hear that you went to live in the country during the Blitz? Somewhere near Petersfield, wasn't it?'

'I was medically discharged.' Smoke curls from Bacon's mouth. 'The dust from the bomb damage aggravated my asthma.'

'Well, as I mentioned on the phone, Francis, it's still not too late if you want to exhibit something. Now, if you will excuse me, gentlemen, I have to try and persuade the man printing the catalogue to reduce his fee. Has this been photographed yet, Charles?'

'Not yet.'

'I'll get someone on to it.' Sir Kenneth nods at both artists in turn then marches off.

'You've just copied "The Scream",' Bacon says, flicking ash on the new mirror.

'I suppose Munch might have been a point of reference,' Charles concedes. 'Subconsciously.'

'What do you call this thing you've done with the mirrors?'

'It hasn't really got a name.'

'It reminds me of one of those triptychs you get in medieval churches.' Bacon draws on his cigarette. 'I don't like it.'

Charles stares at him. 'Have I done something to offend you?'

'You tell me, darling.'

Charles pats his pockets. 'Well, if you will excuse me, I need to be heading along, too. Good day.' He walks off in the same direction as Sir Kenneth, leaving Bacon contemplating the dressing table. Once he is back out in the courtyard he takes several long breaths and feels calmer. He takes a slug from the hip flask and, as the alcohol warms his belly, he sets off to walk along Piccadilly to Hyde Park Corner. By the time he reaches the Chelsea Arts Club he has almost managed to put his encounter with Francis Bacon out of his head. The club porter tells him there is a telegram waiting for him in his pigeonhole. It is from Sir Kenneth Clark and reads simply: 'Please call soonest.' It takes two attempts for the operator to connect him with the National Gallery.

'Bad news, I'm afraid,' Sir Kenneth says. 'Your painting has been damaged. One of the candles must have fallen over and . . . you know how inflammable paint is. I'm so sorry.'

'Damaged? How badly?'

'I'm afraid it was a few minutes before anyone noticed and we were able to get to it with a fire extinguisher. I'm so sorry. For what it's worth, I thought it was a wonderfully original work of art and I'm sure the public would have agreed.'

231

'Did your photographer manage to . . .'

A long pause.

'I'm so sorry, Charles.'

As he sits at the bar, lost in his thoughts, Charles watches a couple of the younger members playing snooker and doesn't notice for a moment the porter approaching with a letter in his hand.

He recognizes the Gothic handwriting immediately.

Five minutes later he is back on the telephone to Sir Kenneth. 'It's Charles Northcote again. Forget the painting, I need your help with something. You've heard the rumours about an Allied invasion of southern France?'

'I try not to listen to rumours.'

'But you've heard there is going to be one?'

'Yes.'

'I want to volunteer for it.'

The Commandant is late for his sitting again. When he arrives, followed by his dog, he is wearing cream-coloured broadfall breeches that are buttoned up the side, and a matching cream sports vest. Over his shoulder is draped a coat trimmed with ermine and mink. There is a foil in his hand. 'I have been practising,' he says, holding the weapon up and slicing the air.

He shrugs and, as the coat falls from his shoulders to the floor, the sinewy curves of his upper arms and broad shoulders are revealed. 'My blood group,' he says when he notices Anselm staring at the tattoo under his arm. He parries into the air with circular motions of his foil. 'All SS men have it tattooed on.'

On his desk there is a plate of fresh raspberries. The

Commandant reaches for one and tosses it to the dog, who opens and closes its long jaw with a gummy snap. It doesn't beg for more. Next to the plate is a kidney-shaped enamel tin on which a full syringe has been placed. When Anselm sees three ampoules of morphine next to it, he speculates that he might be in the presence of an addict. When the Commandant follows Anselm's eye he says: 'I nearly competed in the '36 Olympics, but an ankle injury meant I had to drop out. Fencing was very fashionable at my university. Some of the students used to give themselves duelling scars deliberately.' He holds out the foil by the tip of its blade. 'Go on, take it. Feel its weight and balance in your hand.'

As if in a dream again, Anselm does as he is told.

'It is the duty of every good German to fence. The most noble of the Germanic sports. That moment of anticipation when guards are taken and the swords touch. Exquisite.'

Anselm gets the feeling that whatever it is the Commandant is talking about, it is not fighting with swords. 'Your university?' he says as he places the foil on the desk.

The Commandant lights a cigar and sits astride the saddle. 'Before the war I was an academic. Taught philosophy at Freiburg. Does that surprise you?'

Anselm is not sure what the right answer should be. He nods his head, then shakes it.

'A fine university,' the Commandant continues. 'We had Martin Heidegger as our rector there for a while. A true National Socialist. I believe he is still a member of the faculty. A great man.' A funnelling of the lips at this

233

memory. 'And a great philosopher. His phenomeno-logical explorations of the "question of being" are still highly influential.'

Anselm begins painting.

'And he was very thorough when it came to flushing out the Jewish professors. Though he wasn't so keen on the book-burning. We did it anyway. Books by Jews and Bolsheviks, they all went on the bonfire. We would burn them at night to make more of a spectacle. Half the library was emptied in the end.' The Commandant draws on his cigar and blows out a tumbling shaft of smoke. 'My students adored me. Adored me. You think I am making this up, don't you?'

Anselm shakes his head again.

'Well, I might be. Everything I say is a lie. Have you heard that one? I like to think of it as Goebbels's Paradox. If everything I say is a lie then the statement "everything I say is a lie" must also be a lie.'

Anselm nods uncertainly.

'Except that it could also be a false dichotomy, because it is possible that I occasionally lie and I occasionally tell the truth.' It is as if the Commandant is talking to himself. He stares at Anselm and then gives a twitch of a smile. 'As it happens, I am telling the truth. Do you know what truth is?'

Anselm thinks for a moment. 'Beauty?'

'Ah, a man who knows his Keats. Not as great a poet as Goethe but interesting nonetheless.'

Anselm has only heard the word 'man'. He hasn't thought of himself as one since his trial. He stares at the floor, trying not to smile, feeling as if a crushing weight is being lifted from his soul. Unless he concentrates hard, he might float away.

'My students looked on me as a father figure. Often they would share their news with me first, before telling their parents . . . You remind me of one of my students, Anselm. He was about your age.' The Commandant blows out smoke and studies Anselm with his small eyes. They are hazel. 'Did you study aesthetics at the Slade?'

'A little. Immanuel Kant. Hegel.'

The Commandant picks a tobacco flake from his tongue. 'I hope to return to teaching after the war. When the world is cleansed. I miss the conversation. Alas, not many of my colleagues here share my interest in Socratic dialogue. They are suspicious of intellectuals . . .' The Commandant gets to his feet and circles the easel so that he can see how the painting is progressing. 'Excellent.' He rubs Anselm's shoulders. 'You have talent. That is because you are German . . . Tell me, Anselm, what do Kant, Hegel, Schopenhauer, Nietzsche and Heidegger have in common?'

'All philosophers?'

'Yes, and they are also German. The greatest philosophers the world has ever known have been German . . . And Mozart, Bach, Beethoven, Schubert, Brahms, Schumann, Strauss, Haydn? What is it that they have in common?'

'German?'

'German. Exactly. The greatest philosophers and the greatest composers have been German. Well, Austrian and German. Why is that, do you suppose?'

'Because we are the master race?' Anselm shocks

himself with his use of the personal plural pronoun. If he hasn't thought of himself as a man for years he certainly hasn't thought of himself as a German.

'Exactly. Because we are the master race.'

Anselm nods thoughtfully. 'What about Wittgenstein?'

The Commandant slams his fist down on the wooden horse. *'Fuck Wittgenstein! That fucking Jewish whore!'*

Anselm is stunned by the ferocity of this reaction.

'Do you want to know a secret, Anselm?' The Commandant is calm again.

'What?'

'I can't abide Wagner either.'

Anselm splutters. He was not expecting that. It is the first time he has laughed in four years and the sensation leaves him light-headed.

The Commandant is also trying to suppress a smile. 'He is so fucking melodramatic, don't you think?'

Anselm nods again. 'And he never knows when to stop.'

'I know! Hour after fucking hour. It's torture . . . I could tell you were a man of taste, Anselm. Did you enjoy the Bach the other day?'

Anselm has a paintbrush between his lips. He nods again.

'I think I shall play some Bach every morning. That way we will civilize them. The French are not an un-civilized people, but they are savages when it comes to music, like the British. Some of the French prisoners here may survive this war and, when they return to their homes, it will be important they understand German music. My favourite is the Goldberg Variations. Shall I play it now?' He dismounts, reaches for a record and places it on a turntable.

Using his finger as a baton, the Commandant points out how the variations do not follow the melody of the aria, but rather use its bass line and chord progression. He closes his eyes. Lost in his thoughts. When it is ended he blinks as if coming out of a trance. 'Perfect,' he says. 'Would you like some wine, Anselm? We are in a famous wine region here. But I am not fussy what I drink, so long as it is not schnapps.' Without waiting for an answer the Commandant pours two glasses of Riesling.

Anselm coughs after he takes a sip. When the warmth of the alcohol hits his belly the unreality of his situation is complete. A prisoner drinking wine with a commandant. It feels like he is riding a thermal.

'Come with me, Anselm, there is something I want to show you. Bring your glass.'

The Commandant strides across the floor and holds the door open. As he follows him out, Anselm avoids looking at the chair by the entrance where he knows the Valkyrie will be sitting. Instead he eyes the display box of butterflies in the hall as he heads up the stairs. The shuffle of his clogs against the stone seems intrusively loud. In between his steps he can hear the dog breathing behind him. At the top of the stairs, the Commandant holds a door open again; the Alsatian enters and jumps up on a dark mahogany four-poster bed, swagged with faded dark-red velvet, and tasselled grips.

'Lord Byron once slept in it.' He directs his voice at the bed. 'Go on, try it.'

Anselm takes a couple of steps towards the bed but,

seeing the Alsatian staring at him as impassively as a statue, he stops. The beast has hooded eyes, like those of the lions guarding Nelson's Column.

'Don't worry about Hilde, she won't bite.'

This hellhound has a name, Anselm thinks as he reaches the bed and extends a tentative hand to pat her head. When the Alsatian does not react, Anselm crawls up on to the bed beside her, as if crawling across a minefield.

'She is my only true friend,' the Commandant adds, talking over his shoulder as he locks the door and walks over to a chair by the window. 'She never leaves my side.' As he sits down, the leather of his boots creaks.

The room has an odour that Anselm finds hard to identify. Incense? A stirred cocktail? No, more elusive even than that. It evokes an image of heavy-hanging fruit, ripe and forbidden. A grape losing its elasticity, perhaps. And a taste: not the acid of an orange exactly, nor the sweet obviousness of a pear, but something more restrained, more decorous. 'I think Lord Byron was not very tall,' he says, rotating his feet as they hang over the end of the bed. He eyes the bowl of chocolates on the bedside table. Hunger makes his stomach clench.

'Have some,' the Commandant says.

Anselm takes one and tries not to eat it too quickly.

'I think Hilde would like some, too.'

Anselm takes another and, when he holds out his hand, the Alsatian swallows it in one efficient gulp, leaving only saliva.

As he chews, Anselm looks around the room. On a plinth is a marble bust. He suspects it might be by Rodin. More spoils of war.

'Do you know who carved that?'

'Rodin?'

'Very good. You know your art . . . Look under the bed.'

Anselm steps off the bed and gets to his knees. He sees a wooden panel, unframed. Thin glazes of oil over a tempera underpainting. He holds it up to the light and sees it depicts a one-legged woman in a man's suit. Though she is wearing heavy make-up, her hair is cut in the style of a man. She is smoking a cigarette and drinking a cocktail. Anselm looks at the signature. Otto Dix.

'It was going to be destroyed but I managed to rescue it. The artist is a degenerate. Do you like it?'

Anselm shakes his head.

'You can be honest.'

Anselm nods. The room seems to be melting and shimmering, like the horizon in a desert. He leans his back against the bed, happy to find a tactile connection with reality there.

'I like it, too. I also like to listen to swing and jazz. Negro music. Does that surprise you? Both banned, of course, but you can still hear it on the wireless if you know where to tune the dial. Dr Goebbels plays it for the Doughboys. Gets them feeling sentimental, then he slips in his propaganda about what a useless, wheezing, bandy-legged dolt Roosevelt is. Quite ingenious, really.' The Commandant puts his cigar to his lips and inhales. 'There is a place in Berlin where you can still hear jazz. Along with Latin music. Have you ever danced the tango, Anselm?'

Anselm shakes his head and wonders if this is what

madness feels like, having a sane conversation in an insane context.

'It was originally a dance for two men, a way for them to practise.' The Commandant sips from his glass. 'Have you ever been to Berlin?'

'Yes.'

'When?'

'On the eve of the war, when I was . . .' Anselm has noticed the SS uniform draped over a chair by the bed. It is a terrifying sight, like a giant, red-eyed spider staring at him from the corner of the room.

'Would you like to try it on? We are about the same size, I think.'

Anselm places the painting back under the bed and with the slow movements of one who suspects he is trapped in a dream, gets to his feet, pulls his striped jacket over his head and, with his bare back to the Commandant, slips on the black breeches and tunic. He catches his reflection in the mottled glass of a convex mirror. The Commandant comes over and does up his top button. He then places the cap on his head, tugs the sleeves to straighten the shoulder pads and stands back. 'Turn around.'

Anselm turns and the Commandant tugs the tails of the jacket to remove a crease and make the fit around the shoulders better. 'It is tight on you. You have broad shoulders.'

'It is more comfortable than that,' Anselm says, pointing at the striped jacket and trousers on the bed.

'Really? I always think they must be comfortable. May I?'

As Anselm watches the Commandant slip the striped jacket over his fencing vest, he feels the world tilt sideways, as if it is no longer pivoting on the correct axis.

'Yes, I see what you mean. The cloth is inferior. Itchy. We could be like the Pauper and the Prince. What do you think?' The Commandant smiles an inscrutable smile then takes the jacket off and throws it on the bed. 'Perhaps not. How long have you been here?' He asks this as a crude seducer might ask a woman in a bar if she goes there often.

'Since 1941, I think.'

'Yet you look healthier than the others.'

'The doctors have been feeding me. I am taking part in an experiment.'

'Ah.' The Commandant draws on his cigar. 'May I see?'

Anselm blinks. He cannot remember the last time he has been asked something so politely, rather than ordered. He drops the SS jodhpurs.

The Commandant signals him closer with small circles of his wrist. 'Come.' Anselm takes two shuffling steps forward. The Commandant sits on his haunches, takes Anselm's penis between his finger and thumb and, with unexpected delicacy, lifts it out of the way. He then cups Anselm's testicles in his hand, as if weighing them. They shrivel at his cold touch. The Commandant gets to his knees and studies them at eye level. Anselm can feel the cool tickle of the cigar smoke as the Commandant exhales.

'It is said that our Führer has only one. Do you believe that?'

Is this a trick? 'I don't know.'

'I have heard it on good authority. A shell exploded near him in the last war.' He draws on his cigar and blows the smoke out at Anselm's groin again, a soothing plume of blue-grey. 'Did you know that every SS officer has to have both his balls cut off, so as not to outdo the Führer?'

Anselm's eyes bulge. He becomes aware of the dog on the bed. A sideways glance confirms that he is being stared at.

'I am joking!' The Commandant lets out a roar of laughter as he pats Anselm on the leg. 'Look. I still have both of mine.' He stands up and unbuttons his fencing breeches. 'Come closer. Check them properly. Take them in your hand.' Anselm's hand rises tentatively, as if about to test an electric fence. There is no shock. As he does this he hears the Commandant's breathing become shallower.

This has already gone too far, Anselm hears himself thinking. Perhaps this cannot now end other than in my own destruction.

Yet he is too absorbed in the unreality of the moment to stop himself, to run away, to run for his life. He feels as he imagines a struggling fly must feel, caught on the tension wire of a web, sealing his own fate with every shuddering attempt to escape.

He knows what he is expected to do. He has done it before.

PART FOUR

I

London. Spring. Present day. One year after Edward's release

WHILE HIS MISSING YEARS, ALL ELEVEN OF THEM, HAVE congealed in his imagination, this past calendar year has had texture, a clean arc and recognizable seasons. It represents a coherent passage of time for Edward. Three hundred and sixty-five days. Fifty-two weeks. Twelve months. The time it takes for the Earth to orbit the Sun.

He looks very different now from how he did when he first came back. The shape has returned to his face, though it is leaner and more handsomely angular than it was before he disappeared. His hair and nails seem healthier and the tone has returned to his muscles, even if the vigour has not quite yet. As for his damaged teeth, they have been repaired with veneers that he is in the habit of grinding, but they look natural enough. The colour has returned to his skin, moreover, and it seems to be fitting him once more.

He spends his days reading news reports and watching documentaries about the years he missed. He also keeps trying, and failing, to start writing a memoir about his time in captivity. Niall, with the help of a literary agent, has negotiated a substantial advance for him to write one. But he can waste hours staring at the blank screen of his laptop, his fingers hovering over the keyboard.

Niall keeps pressing him about his progress, tells him he will find it therapeutic, insists he must be the first to read it. But the truth is he still hasn't even been able to talk about his experience, not in any detail anyway, let alone write about it. Every time he tries to think about his missing years, a heavy curtain comes down. And the fog left by the Prozac and Xanax he takes for his anxiety hasn't helped, flattening him out, taking the life from his eyes.

Nothing more had been said about the possibility of Edward returning to work, and he cannot blame Niall for that. He himself is beginning to doubt whether he will ever be employable again. Once a week he goes to visit his father.

He has now progressed from sleeping on the floor to sleeping on a bed. But comfort does not assuage the night terrors. Hannah, he knows, is often woken by them and sometimes rushes into his room to find him sitting up in bed, his eyes open and wild, yet still asleep. He only knows this because she tells him about it in the morning. She says the reassurance of her hand on his shoulder seems to help.

Sometimes, she returns to her own bed at dawn, before he wakes. On the one occasion when he did see her rising from his bed, he felt confused and assumed at first it was she who had come to him for comfort, she who had been afraid of the dark.

Though neither talks about it, he knows that she sleeps in his bed partly to keep an eye on him. Had she not returned home early and called an ambulance that day seven months ago he would not be here now. The doctors said that if his stomach had been pumped even half an hour later it would have been too late.

At least she is now going out at night with her friends more and, during the day, she has resumed the art foundation course she put on hold when he came back into her life. He no longer needs to feel guilty about that.

To mark the anniversary of his return, the BBC is planning to screen an hour-long documentary. The feedback from the previews of *The Forgotten Diplomat* has been positive and already it is being tipped for a Bafta.

It opens with a re-enactment of the UN convoy coming under attack, scenes filmed in the deserts of Morocco. The cave they used to represent Edward's is in Wales. The moments of light each day, when the hole in the roof of the cave opened so that scraps of food could be thrown down to him, make for dramatic images of the actor playing Edward shielding his eyes in a shaft of buzzing light.

The re-enactments are combined with interviews: Niall explaining the Foreign Office position on not paying ransoms; a doctor from the Cromwell Hospital charting Edward's medical history; and a former SAS officer sharing his expertise on hostage psychology.

Edward himself has declined to be interviewed for the programme, but he did not object when the film-makers asked Hannah if she would speak on his behalf.

Having promised that they would not be unduly disruptive, the film crew spent three hours setting up lighting and sound equipment in the house. Edward watched from the back of the room as a make-up artist dabbed Hannah's brow with powder to prevent the heat from the lights making her skin shine. Her eyes glistened as she talked about what it was like at home waiting for news.

When father and daughter watched a preview of the documentary together, in a Soho screening room, her eyes had repeatedly flicked over to his face to gauge his reaction, but there had been none.

In giving his blessing to the documentary project, a line will be drawn under the story as far as the media is concerned – or so Niall has assured him. It has the opposite effect. Once bloggers report that a documentary is being made, it starts trending on Twitter and the BBC publicity department is inundated with requests for interviews, from radio, television and the print media. Edward passes on them all, but is eventually persuaded to do an interview with the *Guardian Weekend* magazine 'at some future date', partly because Niall knows the editor, partly because they have offered to make a donation to Amnesty International in return for an exclusive.

Edward doesn't know how he would have coped without Niall, who has had more quiet words with the editors of the nationals. They were individual calls reminding them of their agreement that there will be no doorstepping, in return for access at a later date, as well as exclusives on other Foreign Office stories.

Hannah is wearing an old-fashioned England rugby shirt, her face painted in readiness for the rugby match – white with a red cross running down from her brow to her chin, and across her cheeks to her ears. Edward looks at her. Smiles. Today's trip to Twickenham to see England play Scotland will be the first time he has been out of the house since the documentary was aired.

He has been expecting Niall to cancel, caught up as he is in the latest stage of the Arab Spring, the violent suppression of another rebellion in a Middle Eastern country. The FCO is considering imposing a no-fly zone on humanitarian grounds, without full UN backing.

International relations may be reaching critical mass, and Niall may be at their centre, but when he comes to collect Edward and Hannah from their house, in his chauffeur-driven government Jaguar, the PUS is a model of insouciance. He is wearing a Scotland scarf and when he sees the St George cross on Hannah's face he takes it off and waves it above his head.

'Hello, Uncle Niall,' she says, kissing him on each cheek.

'Careful!' he says. 'Don't get any of your filthy English paint on me!'

'They'll know you've been fraternizing with the enemy.'

'Know why Scotland's going to win today?'

'Why?'

'Because for you it's just a game of rugby, for us it's about . . .'

'Mel Gibson?'

'Exactly!'

Hannah makes a fist salute. *'Freee-dom!'*

Niall copies the salute and echoes her. *'Freee-dom!'*

Edward, who is trying to manage without his sunglasses and walking stick today, sits in the front and twists himself round so that he can talk to Hannah and Niall in the back.

As they cross Putney Bridge, Niall answers his mobile. He looks grave and ends the conversation: 'Call me if the situation gets worse.'

'Trouble?' Hannah asks.

'Oh, you know,' Niall says. 'Elections in the Middle East have a nasty habit of producing results that are not congenial to Western interests.'

'Thanks for this,' Edward says. 'The rugby, I mean. We appreciate it.'

'Don't thank me. They're Foreign Office debentures.'

'I'll write to the Foreign Secretary to thank him.'

'Best not. You are supposed to be the Italian ambassador today.'

'Then who am I?' Hannah asks.

'You're the Italian ambassador's wife.'

'I always wanted to be an Italian ambassador's wife.'

'You will be sitting with the French ambassador.'

Hannah cocks her head. 'Who's got his ticket, then?'

'No, it is the actual French ambassador. Pascal. You'll like him.' Niall holds up an apologetic finger as his mobile rings. 'Sorry, I'm going to have to take this.'

Edward turns to face the front.

While Niall talks, Hannah taps her father's shoulder. 'I've forgotten to bring the Ferrero Rochers,' she whispers. She then chews her lip in a mime of anxiety.

When Niall ends his phone call without saying good-bye, Edward turns in his seat again. 'I'm looking forward to this,' he says. 'Such a treat. Do you pay for anything?'

'God, no.'

Edward eyes his old friend, wondering if he is joking. Niall has changed, taken on the mantle of the powerful, uncaring man. The constant swearing. This business of not ending his phone calls with 'goodbye'. He has even noticed this at their regular chess games. He can appreciate that Niall felt the need to protect him when he was first released, but he has become more controlling over the past year, not less. He always seems to be checking up on him, acting as gatekeeper to old friends who simply want to meet for a drink and a catch-up. Edward isn't even sure whether he likes Niall any more. Perhaps it is that he seems to have lost the capacity for friend-ship, for conversation. He can't even remember how to cry – although, if he is being honest, since he stopped taking Prozac and Xanax a few days ago he has felt un-familiar things rise to his surface, like a first thaw of spring, that film of water on the ice.

Once he is in the stadium, thousands of milling fans seem to be blocking his path, a crush of buffeting, apologizing, laughing, inebriated rugby supporters. And when they make their way to their stand, they find themselves walking against this tide.

Though his olfactory sense has yet to return fully,

Edward thinks he can detect old familiar smells – urine emanating from lavatories; the waft of warm beery breath coming from the open bars as they walk past them; hot burger grease; salt and vinegar – but they are too fleeting to identify properly, mere pastel shades and soft hues rather than bold primaries.

The fans look different from how they were when he was last among them here at Twickenham. When would that have been? Probably 1999, the year of the Kosovan intervention. Back then the fans had all been wearing waxed jackets and flat caps; now it seems more fashionable to wear Puffa jackets, funnel necks, baseball caps. They queue up for three pints of Guinness. At least that hasn't changed.

Niall leads the way through the crowd and up through the tunnel into the watery afternoon sunshine. Their seats are three from the front, below and slightly across from the Royal Box. The Princess Royal is already in hers, having arrived a few minutes earlier by helicopter. Edward stands and stares out over an ocean of faces. The stadium seems to have doubled in size from how he remembers it.

'What do you think?' Niall shouts. He sounds pleased, as if this were his stadium.

'A new stand?'

'Yep. Seats eighty thousand now.' Niall sees the French ambassador arriving and holds out his arms in greeting. The two men kiss on each cheek. Niall introduces the ambassador to Edward with a comment that seems light but also vaguely patronizing: 'He used to be our man in Oslo.'

'I was only deputy head of mission,' Edward corrects. 'I never made it to full ambassador.'

'I know all about Monsieur Northcote,' the ambassador says. 'Welcome home. You are looking well.'

'I do feel better.'

'You are a rugby fan?'

'Yes.'

'You must have missed it.' The ambassador looks embarrassed by his comment, realizing too late how trivial it sounds.

Edward helps him out. 'I did miss it, yes.'

Soldiers in desert uniform now carry the flags of England and Scotland around the pitch, prompting a cheer as they pass each stand. As they assemble on the try line at each end, a military band marches on to the field. The players follow them out, Scotland first.

Edward cannot believe the size of them. They are like creatures from another species; some look to be about seven feet tall. Their necks and shoulders seem bigger than human necks and shoulders, thicker and more muscular, like those of bulls. And their heads seem abnormally square, perhaps because of the shape some are given by scrumcaps. They look more handsome than he remembers rugby players being. When Edward last saw England play, the forwards had paunches, socks rolled down, baggy shirts. But these men are athletes. Supermen, like some sort of experiment in eugenics. Their brows are glistening with Vaseline and pre-match warm-up sweat.

There is an announcement over the speakers. A minute's silence so that 'the world rugby family' can remember the victims of a coach crash in Wales, the seven members of a school rugby team who lost their lives. The roar of a thousand conversations falls away and the silence that follows seems charged with expectation.

A whistle blows to mark the end of the minute and then a blonde opera singer in an evening dress steps on to a podium and leads the singing of the national anthems. As 'Flower of Scotland' is sung, Niall puts his hand over his heart in the American style. Edward chews his cheek. When did his friend become like this? He seems a parody of his former self.

The whistle sounds for the kick-off and a Scotland prop gathers the ball safely. The thump of the first contact follows. A flurry of movement now as boots churn up the grass. There is blood on one of them already, a Scottish player. The referee blows his whistle and sends him off to the blood bin. He is replaced from the benches. The Scotland scrum-half finds touch. The tallest forwards in the line-out reach almost double their heights because the other players are lifting them; another practice that is new to Edward. England wins.

As the ball passes to the fly-half, time seems to slow down. It is as if space is opening up around him, that some invisible force is holding the Scotland players back. With great composure, he slows the motion down even more, assessing his target, judging the weight and balance of the kick, making a thousand tiny calibrations in a second that seems to last a minute. He is going for a drop goal. The ball leaves his boot and spirals through the air in a perfect parabola before slotting through the posts. The linesman's flag goes up. The referee blows his whistle and time resumes its normal speed.

In this moment, Edward understands something about his years in captivity that he hasn't been able to grasp until now – that time does not tick forward in a steady and predictable way. It compresses, expands, doubles back on itself, skips beats and shimmers. It is not an external river flowing past him; it is a construction of his brain, part of him.

He turns to Hannah, wanting to share this revelation, but she is cheering and jumping up and down. He tries to work out why his senses feel heightened today. Is it because chemicals are no longer holding them down? He wants to sit. He wants to stand up. He doesn't know what he wants.

The crowd starts singing 'Swing low, sweet chariot, Coming for to carry me home,' but no one knows more than that one verse. Something else that hasn't changed. In answer to this, the skirl of the bagpipes can be heard from the other side of the stadium.

As Niall shouts, 'Come on, Scotland!' he notices Edward staring at him and says: 'Everyone thinks I'm English, this is the only time I . . .'. He smiles. 'You've heard me say that before, haven't you? Hey, listen, I've got to go and say hello to HRH at half-time. Would you like to meet her?'

Edward grimaces good-naturedly. Shakes his head.

'Han, would you like to meet the Princess?'

'I'm good, thanks. I was going to get a couple of beers in. Do you want one?'

255

'No, I'm fine.'

Niall's phone vibrates and he studies its screen. 'Bollocks. Looks like the Princess won't be having the pleasure of my company either. The PM has called a Cobra meeting. I can send the car back for you if you like.'

For the first time since his release from captivity, Edward finds himself in mourning for his lost career, missing the rush he used to feel at times of international emergency. 'We'll be fine,' he says. 'Thanks again for the tickets, by the way, and the lift here. It's been great.'

People stand to let Niall through, not taking their eyes off the ball as it is passed down the line.

With play stopped while medics attend to an injury, Edward hears his name being mentioned and a murmur begins in the seats around him. Someone in the row in front has recognized him, presumably from the documentary, and is nudging the person next to him. The recognition spreads through the stand and soon people are taking photographs of him on their mobile phones. When some start applauding, a TV cameraman turns his camera away from the pitch and focuses on Edward. His face suddenly appears on the giant screens at either end of the stadium. The whole crowd seems to be cheering now. Edward is forced to acknowledge them with a wave.

He is relieved when the referee blows his whistle for a re-start scrum. Sixteen bulls snorting in unison. Edward realizes he is losing himself in the game. For the first time in a year he isn't thinking about the cave, or about Frejya, or about anything other than rugby. As he thinks this, the surrounding stadium seems to tilt away into darkness, drawing the eye to the action on the pitch.

There is a wild throw at the line-out and a Scotland pick-up. A forward makes ground, then the winger takes over and, before England can scramble its defences properly, he has put himself into touch. England wins the line-out and begins passing down the backs until Scotland intercepts and runs in a try. The kick misses the conversion, then the half-time whistle goes and the bloodied and muddied players jog off the pitch, steam rising from their shirts.

Edward sits down, only to stand up again straight away as an ironic cheer goes up from the crowd. There is a fox in the empty ground on the other side of the pitch. People are pointing at it and laughing. It must have been hiding in the stands and has now decided to make a dash for it, only to find itself penned in by a bewildering wall of noise.

The creature runs from one end of the empty pitch to the other, and every time it gets to a corner it sees more stewards and turns back into the centre with loping strides. Its tongue is out. It clearly doesn't know where to hide, scuttling into the stand and lying flat, only to trot back out on to the pitch again.

When Hannah returns carrying two pints of Guinness in plastic cups, she sees the fox and says: 'At least you're not the half-time entertainment. I saw you on the screen.'

'Why don't they leave it alone?' Edward says. 'Can't they see it's frightened?'

Hearing the tension in his voice, Hannah says: 'Hey, it's OK; it'll run off in a minute. It must be used to people. There are thousands of urban foxes around here.'

'It won't be used to eighty thousand people. It's terrified.'

It is becoming apparent that the fox isn't going to find a way off the pitch and the start of the second half will have to be delayed. A dozen stewards in high visibility jackets now come out of the tunnel and run towards the creature. It doubles back past them and, when they turn in pursuit, the crowd begin laughing at the spectacle. The fox is jogging now, not out of nonchalance but exhaustion. Its tongue is lolling again. The crowd seems to be treating it as a parody of a bullfight, their cheers increasing in volume as the fox runs towards the stewards, then veers away at the last moment. A further dozen stewards come on.

'Stop laughing at it!' Edward says loudly, to no one.

Hannah hands him his Guinness. He takes a sip. His eyes are glistening.

'Stop laughing at it,' he repeats in a lower voice.

There is another cheer now as a man in an RSPCA uniform comes on carrying a cage and a metal rod with a wire loop on the end. The stewards organize themselves into a giant circle around the fox and begin walking in, driving it into the centre. The fox is pacing from side to side, a few feet at a time. Seemingly realizing it has run out of options, it lies down, resigned to its fate. The RSPCA man walks forward and loops the wire around the fox's neck. It begins writhing and struggling, then goes still again. It looks smaller now, more the size of a cat. The RSPCA man drags it into the cage, releases the loop and closes the cage door behind it. There is another cheer.

Hannah is staring at her father. He blinks slowly and, after two plump tears wind down the contours of his cheeks, he wipes their trails with the heel of his hand.

Back at the house, Edward pours a glass of milk, opens one of the five folio-sized lined notebooks he bought on the way back from Twickenham and unscrews the top of his fountain pen. The ink bottle is already open on his desk and, when he dips the nib into it and turns the piston first anti-clockwise then clockwise, he is reminded of blood being drawn into a syringe.

Hannah has taken a train down to Brighton to go clubbing with friends and he, alone overnight in the house for the first time since his return, feels restless and galvanized. He closes his eyes and absorbs the silence. For a moment he thinks he can smell the ink, but he is not sure.

Though his fingers have hovered several times over the keyboard of his laptop, he hasn't so far been able to think of a way into the autobiography he has promised Niall, not least because his years of captivity have blurred in his memory, one into the other. Now, as he feels the pen between his finger and thumb, senses the pulse of its black blood, he finds an opening line.

When he begins to write it is in the scrolly copper-plate he spent months refining in his youth, the thin steel nib scratching as it moves across the paper. A few minutes later he blots the first page and re-reads it, corrects a spelling, crosses out a clumsy phrase, blots again and turns the page.

Five hours later, the flow of his writing has still to ebb.

II

PEOPLE ASK ME WHAT I MISSED MOST DURING THE ELEVEN YEARS
I was held captive in a cave in Afghanistan. It is not an easy question to answer. I missed my wife and daughter, of course. Missed my father. Missed my friends. Missed milk, and proper food, and soap, and toothpaste, and a bed with sheets, and books, and music, and sunlight . . .

But only now as I sit in my study in London do I recollect that the things I craved, more often than anything else, were a pen and paper, and a candle to write by. If I had only had these simple tools, I think I could have ~~held~~ retained my sanity.

I have them now, and should ~~perhaps~~ begin this memoir with an account of my capture, ~~a time~~ before time lost its definition and the years began collapsing one into the other.

Our landing in Kabul on 31 March 2001 was not smooth. The plane spiralled down abruptly; a jerky manoeuvre intended to make it harder for surface-to-air missiles to lock on to their target. To the same end, the fighter plane that escorted us in released magnesium decoy flares. It was clear we were entering a war zone, even if the war had yet to be declared.

~~There was a rest for a couple of hours and then~~ I remember thinking, as we were being driven from the airport, how strange it was that the road had no white lines or central reservations. As it shimmered in the afternoon heat, it looked as if its surface was melting. Because it had no kerbstones either, its edges looked ragged, like a lava flow that had cooled at the point where it met the desert.

I was in the third of four white UN Land-Cruisers spaced well apart in case of mines. All were clearly marked on their bonnets, roofs and doors with the large blue letters 'U' and 'N'. The lead vehicle also had a UN flag flapping from its bonnet and I had noticed, when we set off, the two UN ~~peacekeepers~~ 'Blue Helmets' sitting inside it wearing flak jackets and armed with assault rifles. They were peacekeepers. A reassuring sight.

As we sped through a basin surrounded by ochre-coloured mountains, past a train of camels carrying what looked like woolsacks, the two long radio aerials on the vehicle in front of ours bent over backwards like loose-jointed gymnasts. The only other vehicles on the road were old and overladen trucks and equally old motorbikes ridden by bearded men wearing turbans rather than helmets.

As we drove, I studied the brief I'd been handed: a manila folder with the Foreign Office crest embossed on its flap. It revealed that we would be meeting Abdul Wali, the minister for the Propagation of Virtue and the Prevention of Vice (check???). He had been the one to declare the Buddhas of Bamiyan 'idolatrous' under sharia law, another thing to be banned.

As we drove that day I remember staring at a goatherd

walking towards his flock and feeling sorry for the Afghan people. They didn't deserve the Taliban . . .

Permission had been granted for our visit with reluctance, only after a representative from ~~the US~~ the Great Satan, a Harvard professor, was replaced with an apparatchik from the Arab League, a Jordanian. The multinational UNESCO team now included an expert on Buddhist antiquities from India, a French academic and a Dutch diplomat.

My wife Frejya hadn't wanted me to go, but I had told her I had no choice. It wasn't a complete lie. I had had my arm twisted by my friend and Foreign Office colleague Niall Campbell, who can be very persuasive. He had told me that the Foreign Secretary was taking a personal interest in the visit. ~~and that my participation would not go unrewarded. I took the job out of ambition, then, more fool~~

I remember I removed my tie at some point, wound down the window and breathed in the clean, incense smell of the desert. All around us was a rocky scrubland ~~devoid of trees and plants~~. The only features were chunks of jagged stone that clinked against the bottom of the vehicle when dislodged. In the distance the mountains seemed higher now, their sharp edges fringed with what looked like pouches of snow.

I took from my wallet a photograph of myself with Frejya and Hannah, my nine-year-old daughter. We were sitting in a hollow on top of the cliffs at Doyden Point, our favourite place in Cornwall. For some reason, instead of putting it back in my wallet I slipped it into the pocket of my trousers. I was to have it with me for the duration of my captivity, though I could not see it.

As I had left the house that morning I had written 'I love

you' on a sheet of paper and folded it repeatedly until it was a tight ball. 'Don't open it until I'm gone,' I had said, handing it to Hannah. Frejya had looked almost disappointed that I hadn't given her a note too, but her love message was waiting for her on our bed, written in items of clothing three feet long across the duvet.

~~I thought too of the~~

As we began to ascend, the road became bumpier, the Land-Cruisers swerving to avoid potholes. We were spiralling again, this time upwards towards the clouds. As we came out of each bend, we met a rising wall of red dust we had created going into it below. Occasionally the vehicle bellied with a crunching metal sound.

Twenty minutes later we crested the hill, and, for a second, I thought the ball of fire I could see in front of the convoy was the sun, but a compression of the air made clear it was an explosion. As the shock wave reached me, I watched the Land Cruiser at the head of the convoy lift several feet off the ground. Time seemed to slow and, when I saw a flash from the top of a gorge, I tracked, almost in a detached way, the RPG swerving towards us, trailing white smoke. A noise louder than sound seemed to fill the world to its edges, smothering the sun.

I don't know how many hours passed before I came round, but when I did there was nothing to see. I widened my eyes until they ached in their sockets, but the blackness crowding me delivered no shapes.

I could feel the ground I was lying on. It was solid and cold and, like a blind man ~~groping~~ feeling with his hands, I groped for its contours, but there weren't many and I remained staring into the dark, feeling disorientated and nauseous. Fear was scraping its claw down my back.

Feeling helpless, the helplessness of a trapped ~~fox~~ animal, I touched my own face and realized my cheeks were wet ~~with tears~~. There was a ringing in my ears like tinnitus (sp?) and it took me some time before I noticed a dripping sound. I tried to sit up and focus on where it was coming from, but a pain in my right hip prevented me.

Remembering my watch – I thought its luminous face would give me a bearing – I felt for my wrist. But the strap was not there. I ran my right hand down over my left and felt for where my wedding ring should be. This had gone, too. I became aware of the coldness of my left foot and felt for that. I was missing a shoe. My trousers were ripped. About this time I realized I no longer had my jacket, wallet and mobile phone.

My head was burning and I felt dehydrated. Recalling the dripping sound, I concentrated on it in order to orientate myself, but it was hard to locate because of the echo. I was in some sort of light-locked chamber. A cave? I dragged myself towards the dripping and, as I did this, I realized my hip was injured, possibly dislocated.

Feeling a splash on my forehead, I held out my tongue and tasted the water. It had a metallic flavour, but it partially ~~quenched~~ relieved my thirst. I felt with my hand until I reached a vertical surface, a slimy wet rock face ~~worn smooth by the drips of water~~. I rested my back against it and, feeling breathless, filled my lungs with air.

The dripping sounded too loud now, almost sinister. And the black silence between the drips seemed claustrophobic and close, like a pressure on my inner ear. I felt panic rising inside me, my intestines becoming a string of beads counted by icy fingers. I think I might have said 'Hello?' out loud a few times, as much as anything to hear a ~~human~~ voice.

Several hours passed, possibly a day, before the screaming started. Opening my eyes, I could see only the same thick, fleshy blackness as before, and then I realized the screams were coming from me. I had been asleep and the silence that was now pouring into the hole left by my own noise terrified me.

~~It was cold and the air was salty. I could feel panic mounting again as my eyes strained to penetrate the dark.~~ Then I could hear Pashto voices. I looked up, my heart ~~thumping~~ palpitating. They were coming from above me, which meant I was underground. My own voice began tentatively again, but soon I was shouting, asking who was there.

Then came the crunch of rock against rock. About twenty feet above me I could see a shaft of fuzzy light growing bigger to reveal a ragged opening in the ceiling, twice the size of a manhole. I blinked, trying to adjust my eyes. The hole looked manmade, and didn't open out on to daylight but rather on to something that looked like another chamber. A smell of kerosene suggested the light was coming from oil lamps, though I thought I could hear a generator somewhere in the distance.

I looked around and got more of a sense, through the gloom, of the dimensions I had until now only been able to guess at. I _was_ in a cave, and it had sloping walls that met above me, where the hole was. There were ~~more~~ voices again, and a painful jab of torchlight in my face.

I said something I had learned in Pashto. 'Salam? . . . Sho Ismak?' Instead of answering, one of them directed the torch at a basket that was being lowered on a rope by the other. As my eyes adjusted again, I could see that both men were wearing black lungees (sp??) on their heads, which meant they were Taliban. The one holding the torch had a beard and a Kalashnikov hanging from his shoulder. He was wearing my watch. The other man had his face covered with a black and white keffiyeh (sp?) scarf. This, I remember thinking, might be a good sign. The man would not have bothered to cover his face if he was there to perform an execution.

I considered telling them my name, but already I was making ~~calculations~~ calibrations: perhaps they weren't the Taliban and they didn't know I was a British diplomat; perhaps I would be in less danger if it stayed that way.

I asked them what they wanted. This time there was a clinking sound followed by radio static and then some excited chatter on a walkie-talkie. I could now see a third, taller man looking down. His lank, bearded face ~~was uncovered~~ wasn't covered ~~either~~. He had calm and neutral eyes. Full lips. He was wearing a camouflage jacket.

The basket had reached the ~~cave floor~~ floor of the cave. Adopting an unthreatening posture, I edged towards it and saw it contained a chunk of unleavened bread, a bowl of rice, a spoon and a plastic bottle of water. I reached for it and, as soon as I'd taken the items out, the basket was pulled back up. The torch was shone across to the corner of the cave. 'Hammam,' one of the men said. It means ~~loo~~ lavatory. My eyes followed its beam and took in two planks across a raised rock formation. I heard the scraping sound overhead again, and, as I looked up, saw the boulder was being rolled back over the hole.

The cave seemed even darker than it did before. Colder, too, and I found myself trembling. Only after I had been swearing for a few minutes to give myself courage did I regain my nerve and realize what I was doing. ~~I stopped and ground my teeth instead.~~ I remembered from the Foreign Office 'Hostile Environment' course (check name??) ~~I had been required to attend,~~ that it was important to remain calm. I also recalled that it was essential to retain your dignity. If your captors respect you, they will find it harder to kill you. Do not grovel, beg, or become hysterical. Try to establish a rapport. Make them humanize you.

I tried to work out how long I had been down there, but there were no markers. The only way I could calculate the passage of time was through my hunger. I remembered the food and, feeling for the pitta bread, took a bite. It was stale. The fullness of my bladder also gave me an indication of how much time had passed.

I groped in the direction of the two planks they had shown me, then moved on my hands and knees. I couldn't find them at first. When I did, my hands could feel that there was a gap between them. The updraft of air meant a drop below. I stood to relieve myself and the length of time before the ~~piss~~ liquid splashed against a surface indicated that the pit was several yards deep. For a moment I wondered if this might offer a means of escape, but it seemed to be nothing more than a crack in the ground that led nowhere.

~~Feeling my stress levels beginning to rise again,~~ I tried to order my thoughts. I had been kidnapped. The Foreign Office would know I had been kidnapped. They would be having a Cobra meeting in Whitehall to consider their options. ~~Niall My friend and colleague Niall Campbell would be making a~~

~~big fuss on my behalf.~~ In all probability they would have an SAS squad on standby to helicopter themselves in. My job was to stay calm and try and keep out of the crossfire when they came.

But then doubts crept in. How were the SAS going to find me? There were caves all over Afghanistan and I could be anywhere. In the north. The south. I could even have crossed the border into ~~Waziristan~~ Pakistan. I had no idea how long I had been unconscious for; it could have been days.

My thoughts returned to Frejya. She would have received the 'next-of-kin' phone call from the ~~FCO~~ Foreign Office. This would have set off a cycle of speculation and uncertainty for her. At least I knew what was happening to me, even if I wished I didn't. Frejya would not have the same consolation. She would be wondering if I was dead, or being tortured, or if I was going to be executed. The thought of her facing these questions on her own filled me with guilt and anger.

(Should maybe have a section here about Frejya's campaign in London . . . Niall to write??? Or get him to talk me through it??)

Not long after this I remember waking to a warm rain on my face. I looked up and saw the silhouette of a man urinating on me. I got out of the way and saw that he looked more like a boy of about ~~eleven~~ ten. As I spluttered and wiped my face, he laughed and shouted: 'Haraam!' It means 'unclean'. But at least the boy had spoken to me. ~~At least I had had some human contact.~~

'My name is Edward,' I said. 'What's yours?'
The boy frowned.
'Namey shoma chiyst?' I tried instead.

269

Seeing the boy was wearing a football shirt – it looked like ~~Man U~~ *Manchester United – I said: 'David Beckham?'*

The boy laughed, threw down some food, and then, as an afterthought, ran a finger across his neck. Another guard appeared, there was an argument and then the boy was cuffed across his head. Seemingly on his own, the man ~~guard~~ *then pushed the boulder back over the hole and I had a sudden feeling of compression. Enveloped in darkness once more, I began shouting.*

The image of the boy running his finger across his neck came back to me ~~and I started crying shaking again~~. *I knew that was how they killed infidels there, slitting their throats like sheep. I had once watched a man perform such Halal butchery behind a restaurant in Algeria, binding three legs together before feeling for the carotid (sp??) artery and drawing the knife across the ewe's throat in one quick movement. As blood spurted out, the ewe took jerky breaths, eyes closed, its deflated chest trying to heave. Then it lay still for a minute before its free leg started to shudder violently.*

Despite willing myself not to, I found myself imagining what it felt like when your head was pulled back and the knife cut into your skin. Can you taste the blood in your windpipe before you die?

To distract myself I tried to picture the boulder. As I recreated its movement in my memory, I realized that it must be hollowed out, intended not to keep me in so much as to disguise the opening in the roof of the cave.I thought if I could only climb up there I could perhaps dislodge it myself.

I crawled until I reached a wall, then I stood up. As I scraped my way along it, I came to something small and round. It was cold and hard . . . Metal. There was another one a few feet ~~further~~ farther on at the same height and, at my feet now, the rattle of more metal. It was a chain. Feeling my way along it, I came to a flat, rounded surface and, when I realized it was a manacle, I dropped it. This cave had been used as a prison before. I wondered what happened to the previous incumbents, whether they had been released.

But at least this meant the guards sometimes came down there. They must have a ladder. I tried to work out whether I could hide the next time they brought food, then, when they ~~would come~~ came down to look for me ~~and~~ I could overpower them. ~~But I knew I was deluding~~

~~My lack of resolve left me feeling cowar~~

I attempted to find foot- and handholds in the wall but soon realized that its overhang made climbing impossible. I had another attempt, but succeeded only in breaking a nail.

Walking stiffly, I began to pace backwards and forwards. Three steps, turn. Three steps, turn. I kept this up for about an hour before I decided to try a circuit of the cave, to measure the circumference. Then my feet touched something. It was a toshak, one of the narrow mattresses that Afghans use instead of chairs or beds. It was hard and thin and stank of sweat and urine, but it was a mattress nonetheless. I found there was a blanket on top of it so I lay down, pulled it over myself and shivered, more from solitude than lack of warmth.

After this the days and weeks merged into each other. The dripping noise which had sounded so loud now seemed quite distant. I would try to focus on it but it would keep slipping from my attention. I was becoming deaf to its repetition.

The slightest bump from 'upstairs', as I had begun thinking of the world above me, made me jump, but it was the

271

absence of noise that frightened me more. The absence of contrast. ~~The sensory deprivation.~~ Already I was cursing the contortions of my ~~mind~~ imagination. As my eyes strained, trying to make out shapes, I fancied I was staring at my own sanity, as if it was an entity with which I was sharing the cave.

III

One year and two months after Edward's release

WHEN SHE HEARS THE DOORBELL RING, HANNAH PUTS HER glasses on and looks through the spyhole. If this is the journalist, he is ten minutes late. Whoever it is has his back to the door and is holding a mobile to his ear.

As she releases the latch, the phone in the hall rings and the man turns and smiles. He has a few days' stubble on his face and looks to be in his late twenties, early thirties. 'Have I got the right house?'

'If you're from the *Guardian* you have.'

The journalist touches an icon on the screen of his mobile and the phone in the hall stops ringing. 'Damn. I'm from *Farmers Weekly*. Wrong house.'

'What?'

'Sorry. Joke. Attempted joke. I *am* from the *Guardian*. And that was me calling to check the address.' His voice is warm, well modulated, as Irish as whiskey with an 'e'. 'Sorry I'm late.'

They shake hands. His is dry, hers, she realizes, is clammy.

273

'Hannah, right?'

'Right.' She is rubbing her palm on the seat of her jeans, wishing she could remember his name. Too late to ask now.

'Martin Cullen,' he says.

With his beige cord jacket, open-neck shirt not tucked in properly and scuffed suede shoes, he looks to Hannah more like a part-time lecturer at her college than a full-time journalist from a national.

'Come in,' Hannah says. 'Your photographer is still out in the garden with my dad. I think he's nearly finished.' She closes the door as the journalist steps in. 'They take a lot of shots, don't they?' she adds.

'Oh, they'd go on all day if you let them. Some of them even try to . . .'

Hannah doesn't hear the rest of the sentence. She is feeling dizzy as if she has just risen from a hot bath. The gaps between the objects in the hallway seem to be warping.

'What?' Cullen is wiping his mouth with the back of his hand. 'Have I got . . .'

'What?'

'You were staring at me.'

Hannah looks away. 'Sorry, I didn't mean . . .' She feels hollow and full at the same time. And in motion. As if she is standing on wet sand, sinking. 'I think I'm going to . . .'

When she comes round she is lying on the sofa and the journalist is standing over her, holding out a glass of water.

'You fainted,' he says. 'Are you OK?'

274

She sits up and takes a sip. 'I'm fine, thank you. I think I just need to . . .' She reaches for a banana from a fruit bowl on the coffee table, peels it and eats half of it. 'I haven't eaten anything today,' she says between mouthfuls. 'Completely forgot! I'm not normally like this.'

'No worries.'

Hannah looks around as if only now realizing where she is. 'Did you carry me in here?'

'Well, you sort of fell into . . . my . . .' He holds out his arms and grins.

'Thank you.' She fans her face with her hand. 'That wasn't embarrassing at all. Where would you like to do the interview? I thought maybe the kitchen or in here. You won't be disturbed in either.'

'Here, then. Thanks.'

She watches the journalist's eyes flick around the room. His hand is being drawn to a signed rugby ball on a stand. He strokes it like it's a baby seal. 'Yours, I take it?'

Hannah smiles. 'Yeah, I was tight head prop for the Quins.'

Cullen has now picked up the carved handle of an African switch and is flicking the horsehairs over each shoulder in turn, dispersing imaginary flies. 'I'm sorry about your mother,' he says. 'That must have been so hard for you.'

'You think?'

'And hard for your father to come back and find that his wife . . . I guess you have had to take on that role.'

'What do you mean?'

'Nothing. You know, just . . . hard for both of you.'

Yeah, she thinks. Funny how I almost wanted to

275

become my mother, to help my father adjust. Bring her back to life, for my benefit as well as his. 'Yeah,' she says. 'Yeah, it was hard. Can I get you a coffee?'

'Do you have any herbal tea?'

'Sure.'

Cullen studies her for a moment then asks a question which seems vague and yet to a purpose. 'Have you and your father been living together since he got back?'

'Yeah.'

'And before that?'

'Had a couple of friends living here with me.'

'How would you describe your relationship with him?'

'Good. Why? Has someone said different?' Hannah laughs falsely.

'Can I just check? This is an exclusive, right?'

'The interview? Yeah, I think so. I didn't set it up. But I'm sure Dad's not talking to anyone else. And as far as I can tell, he didn't want to do this one. My godfather had to bully him into it.'

'Sir Niall Campbell, right?'

'Right. Is there any chance we can see the piece before it goes to press?'

''Fraid we can't give copy approval. That's more *Hello!* magazine territory. Don't worry, it'll be fine.'

'You will go easy on him though, won't you?'

'Don't worry.'

'Did you see the documentary?'

'Yes. Really interesting.'

'I should warn you, Dad can seem quite cold and distant with strangers at first. It can be disconcerting when you're not used to it. Sometimes it's like throwing a brick in a lake and not only not creating a splash but not creating a single ripple. It's like he drags everything down into the depths.'

'Now you're scaring me.'

Hannah throws out a laugh, a single syllable. Her turn to reassure. 'You'll be fine.'

'I'm hoping he'll talk about his time as a hostage.'

'Well, good luck with that. I don't think he's talked about it to anyone yet. Certainly not me.'

Cullen picks up his ringbound notepad and flicks to an empty page. 'Can I quote you on that lake stuff. What was it again?'

'Um, not creating a single ripple. As if the calm surface hasn't been disturbed.'

He is scribbling. 'Oh, you're good. Can I talk to you again after we've done the interview?'

'Sure.'

'If you give me your mobile number, I'll call you once I've transcribed the tape and started writing it up.'

Hannah cocks her head to one side as she tries to get the measure of him. Is he hitting on her? Possibly. Yet he seems too . . . gentlemanly. With his drawing-room manners he even seems a little amateurish. And she likes the calm way he holds her gaze. Before she can change her mind, she snatches his pen off him, pulls his hand towards her and, with her lips pursed to stop herself from grinning, writes her number on the back of it. 'I was going to make you a herbal tea, wasn't I? Peppermint OK?'

'Thanks. And is there a toilet I can use?'

'Upstairs. First door on the right. I think I just heard your photographer go into the downstairs one.'

She makes her way through to the kitchen. As the kettle comes to the boil, she realizes the journalist is taking a long time. The house is silent. She climbs to the first landing, treading carefully to avoid spilling the tea.

He is in the master bedroom staring at the corrugated sheets on the unmade bed. Her mother's dressing gown, the one she sometimes uses, is on the pillow. There are a pair of men's boxer shorts on the floor. 'Are you lost?' she asks.

'Sorry. Big house. Lot of bedrooms.'

'Yes.'

Cullen nods at the bed. 'Which is his side?'

Hannah looks at him without answering.

'This *is* his bedroom?' he prompts.

'Why?'

His eyes fix on the boxer shorts.

Hannah can feel with her memory the cool touch of linen as she slides between these sheets. She can hear her own laughter as her father flinches when she warms her cold feet against the backs of his legs. 'Yes,' she says. 'This is where he sleeps.' Her brow puckers for a moment then clears. 'Or tries to sleep. He gets nightmares and I have to come in here to reassure him, stroke his hair, sing to him.'

Cullen gives a sympathetic nod. 'All right, so.'

'Sometimes it's me who can't sleep. When I'm frightened. Didn't you do that with your parents? Come into their bed?'

'When I was six maybe, but not . . .'

'We're both afraid of the dark.'

This seems to satisfy his curiosity. 'Well, that's under-standable.'

Hannah tries to smile. 'It is, isn't it? Anyway, here you are.' She hands over the mug. 'Peppermint.'

They go and check the progress of the photographer. He is finally packing up his equipment and Edward is waiting for them in the sitting room. Cullen smiles broadly as he goes to shake his hand and introduce himself.

'I'll let the photographer out,' Hannah says. 'Leave you two in peace.'

Cullen is looking at a photograph in a frame on the dresser. He has his back to Hannah and seems not to realize she is still in the room. 'She's very photogenic, your daughter.'

Edward rubs the bridge of his nose. 'That's my wife. My late wife.'

'Really? They look identical.' When the journalist looks up and sees Hannah, colour rises to his cheeks for a moment. 'Would you mind if I put these on?' he says, turning back to Edward and taking out two identical digital voice recorders from his laptop case. Placing them side by side on the table next to an abandoned game of Scrabble, he presses two 'record' buttons on the sides of the gadgets and a red light appears on each. He then clicks his fingers and, like the wide lines that register a lie on a polygraph test chart, sound-level meters register thick pulses on both screens.

'Let's start with your release,' he says, the gentle tone gone from his voice. 'Was a ransom paid?'

IV

Three days later

AS CUSTOM DICTATES, THE PERMANENT UNDERSECRETARY WAITS to greet the new Foreign Secretary under one of three arched and pedimented porches off King Charles Street. Although this entrance is on a side road, a conceit the architects borrowed from Somerset House, it never-theless affords the most impressive view of the building. Two Union flags are stirring gently on the poles above his head, their cords clanking.

They're giving her the full treatment, Niall thinks. But where is she? He checks his watch and rocks back on his heel. The new Foreign Secretary is late. Is this a deliberate tactic to show Niall who is boss? How tiresome, if so.

Standing a few feet behind Niall are three senior mandarins representing different departments within the Foreign Office. To his right, talking to a knot of press photographers, is the Principal Private Secretary, Linda Coleman. To his immediate left is Sir Simon Bradley, the British ambassador to the UN, a Wykehamist who always wears one red sock and one yellow sock with his bespoke suits because, he says, they help him keep things in perspective. As might be expected, he is highly skilled in the arts of negotiation, compromise and concession – no one in the diplomatic service used the word appeasement any more – but he is also a legend of ironic urbanity. 'Tonal balance,' he likes to call it. 'Cultivated vulgarity,' his colleagues teasingly prefer.

Bradley has delayed his return to New York by three days so that he can brief the incoming Foreign Secretary in person. Show willing. 'So do we hold our new boss in high regard?' he asks without turning to face Niall. His lips barely move as he talks, as if afraid of letting something slip.

'We must regard her as the oyster regards the grain of sand,' Niall says. 'An irritant that may, nevertheless, be capable of producing a pearl.'

'I've heard her special area of interest is Lithuanian prostitutes.' Bradley raises an eyebrow. 'The trafficking of.'

Niall smiles. 'I'm sure the new Secretary of State will be interested in all aspects of immigration.'

'Smart?'

'Brain so big it crosses time zones.'

'And a liberal, right?'

'Liberal as a leotard.'

'First priority?'

'Hers? A phone call from Washington, I should think. She'll want to feel loved. They all do.'

'And ours?'

'Iran going nuclear. Afghanistan. Timetable for withdrawal. Should we or should we not be negotiating with the Taliban.'

281

And mine? Niall thinks. My priorities are more opaque. Mine will be to deflect attention away from recent history, concentrate on the present, move on . . .

'So?'

Niall glances at Bradley. 'Sorry, what?'

'So should we or should we not be negotiating with the Taliban?'

Niall shakes his head as if to clear it. 'Not sure. What do you think we should tell her?'

'That we should. We have to show Downing Street that the FCO still matters; that it would be madness to even consider cutting our budgets at this delicate time; that when it comes to diplomacy, English has become the lingua franca.'

'Well, that will annoy the Francas.'

Bradley chuckles. 'Exactly. We must send them a communiqué about it.'

'And Pakistan?'

'And Pakistan is going to do everything in its power to queer our pitch with the mullahs in the peace talks, unless we give them a seat at the top table.'

'And as long as we let the Taliban keep the profits of the opium and heroin trade they will let us pull our troops out without any more humiliation than is absolutely necessary?'

Seeing a motorbike turn into the quadrangle, Niall adjusts his tie and takes the gum out of his mouth. He looks around for somewhere to throw it, then, on a second thought, puts it in a tissue in his pocket. 'Thought this lot were going to dispense with outriders,' he says out of the corner of his mouth.

When the Jaguar comes to a halt and the new Foreign Secretary waits for the car door to be opened, the two mandarins standing under the arch exchange a glance. At fifty-five, Sonia Ross is almost ten years older than Niall. She is a slightly stooped woman with wavy silver hair and a tendency to glance sideways at people through wire-rimmed glasses.

They have already met, briefly, a few weeks earlier on an 'orientation' day at King Charles Street, a tour that didn't include the Foreign Secretary's room. It was as much a hedging of bets as a gesture of civil service good will and impartiality, and the balance of power had been with Niall then. Now it has swung the other way. And Ross has a reputation for being chippy. State school then straight into local government. Her Geordie accent is not a problem as far as the FCO is concerned. Unlike Birmingham and Liverpool accents, it tests well with focus groups – 'warmth' and 'canniness' being the words most associated with it. No, of more concern to them is her Jewishness. How is that going to play in the Middle East peace talks? Appointing a Muslim junior minister to travel with her, that would be the obvious answer. Tonal balance.

'Sir Niall, good to see you again.' Ross turns towards the photographers as she shakes hands. 'I've pronounced that right, haven't I?'

'Actually it's pronounced Neil. It's Scottish.'

'You don't sound Scottish.'

'I know, I know. My father is so ashamed.' A grin. 'Welcome to the Foreign and Commonwealth Office. Congratulations on your victory.'

283

The introductions over, Niall leads the way through the black entrance door, across the echoing marble floor of the Durbar Court and towards the Grand Staircase. When the welcoming party reaches its smooth balustrade, they pose for a group photograph and then peel off. At the point where the red-carpeted stairs divide, Niall stops and looks up at the barrel vaults above and, beyond them, the painted dome. 'The best view of it is from here,' he says.

'It was all restored quite recently, wasn't it?'

'Yep, not that long ago. Did the outside too.'

'Is it true you use a hawk to keep the pigeons away?'

'Twice a week. Really works. No more shit on the statuary.' Niall wonders whether the word 'shit' is well judged. Might the new Foreign Secretary think she is being patronized as an uncouth northerner? But 'guano' or 'pigeon mess' would be too twee. Send out the wrong signal. They will need to talk tough in the coming weeks.

'Don't they use an electric current to keep the pigeons off Nelson's Column?'

'Believe they do, yes. But we try not to waste electricity here. We have energy-saving lights through-out the building. Movement-sensitive. If you sit still for long enough at your desk the lights go out.'

'All over Europe?'

Niall gives a thin laugh. The new boss has a sense of humour, it seems. 'Let me show you something.' At the top of the Grand Staircase, Niall leads the way into the Foreign Secretary's room and, as the carpets give way to oak flooring, the soles of his leather shoes clatter. It smells of polish and with its tall windows looks more like a museum gallery than a working office. Niall stops at a window case comprised of marquetry panels of mahogany, walnut and cedar. He taps his foot. 'We had this put in.'

Ross looks down at a small metal plaque that is inscribed with the words ' "The lamps are going out all over Europe; we shall not see them lit again in our lifetime." Lord Grey, Foreign Secretary, August 1914'.

'People always ask which window he was standing at,' Niall says, 'and though he doesn't specify in his memoirs, the consensus is that it must have been this one. And that,' Niall points down at a lamp-post below, 'must have been the one that inspired the quote.' He turns to face the room and, with a sweep of his arm, takes in the ornate gilding of the cornice, the red leather armchairs, the green-shaded desk lamps. 'Anyway, here we are. The largest office of any cabinet minister, far bigger than the PM's, and the one with the best views. You can see Horse Guards Parade there and,' he directs a thumb over his shoulder, 'St James's Park to the west.'

Ross steps forward and gives a large and ancient globe a spin, causing her jacket to ride up a little and show that her shirt has come untucked from her waistband. 'Imagine the foreign secretaries who have put their fingerprints on this . . .' She looks up. 'Not sure about him.' Glowering down at her is a painting of an Empire-period Nepalese prince clutching a curved sword.

'No one ever is. One of your predecessors even had it put in storage, but a painting couldn't be found that fitted the space, so our Nepalese friend was brought back.' Niall points to a document two inches thick on the desk, next to two red boxes with the letters 'ER' embossed in gold underneath a crown. 'We've prepared a report for you. It's a bit bulky but it will get you up to speed on most areas. Perhaps once you have had a chance to digest it we can have a proper brief.'

Ross sits down and, in what Niall takes to be another little power play, indicates for him to do the same. He undoes the middle button on his jacket but realizes too late that the buttons on his shirt underneath are straining against his paunch. As he eases himself into the chair and crosses his legs stiffly, he can feel the bottom button give up its struggle and pop open.

'I think my first call should be with Washington,' Ross says. It is obvious she's trying not to stare at the shirt. 'Do I phone them or do they phone me?'

'We are expecting a call shortly.'

Ross makes as if to fold her arms and then appears to change her mind halfway through the manoeuvre, resting them on her desk instead. 'I imagine they will want to talk about the withdrawal from Afghanistan. What channels do we have with the Taliban?'

Niall hesitates. 'We've been calling them "indirect talks", as opposed to "direct talks". The President of Afghanistan has been having "indirect talks" with one of the senior mullahs and he has taken an offer to the Taliban Ruling Council.'

'But no indirect talks with al-Qaeda, right?'

'Right. As you know, the British government doesn't talk to terrorists. But we will sometimes talk to insurgents. We always get mocked for our pedantry here at the FCO, but it does matter and it is useful.'

'Yes, well. We are where we are.'

Niall studies her face. Is this impatience or nervousness?

'And what other issues should I know about before I talk to Washington?'

Nervousness, then. 'I'm sure it will be a courtesy call, you won't need to go into specifics.'

'Yes, but if we do . . .'

Niall smiles. Thinks: you don't need to worry, pet, the President won't be able to penetrate your accent. 'The opium and heroin trade in southern Afghanistan is the thing that most concerns the Taliban,' he says. 'It's the equivalent of Sicily, with mafia godfathers running the drug rackets. Increasingly they see Western forces as a sideshow. As far as they are concerned they are fighting a civil war – a rebellion by the Pashtuns of the south against the Kabul regime, which is controlled by northern Tajiks, Uzbeks and Hazaras. It's essentially the Corleone family taking on the Barzinis and the Tattaglias.'

'You have to answer for Santino, Hamid. You fingered Sonny for the Uzbek people.'

Niall smiles again and speaks at the same time. 'Very good.'

Ross tries to suppress her own smile and fails. Pleased at her joke. 'And you've been working on a draft treaty?'

'Yes. We are trying to decide whether to say we have come to an "agreement" or a "decision" over the release of prisoners. Like I said, nuance matters.'

'We're keen to set up a truth and reconciliation commission.'

Not if I can help it, Niall thinks. 'That is certainly something to which our American allies will be receptive.'

'How is that friend of yours who was kidnapped?'

A chill passes through Niall's body like a path of electricity. 'Much improved.'

'Has he talked about what happened?'

'Not yet. Our psychiatrist says we shouldn't rush things. He'll tell us when he's ready.'

'His pastoral care should be our main concern. I imagine his experiences have left him pretty traumatized.'

'Yes, they have.'

'Do we know who was holding him?'

Niall hesitates again, cracks the joints in his fingers. 'We've known for some time.'

Ross studies her hands. 'Is it going to prove an embarrassment?'

'In what way?'

'Will we be negotiating the peace terms with the people who kidnapped one of our diplomats?'

'We can't rule out that possibility.'

'But there was no deal to have him released?'

'I didn't say that.'

Ross inclines her head. 'So there *was* a deal?'

'We entered into negotiations.'

'We?'

Niall misses a beat. 'I was involved.'

'The Foreign Office was talking to al-Qaeda?'

'Not directly. Our contact was with the Taliban.'

'Was a ransom paid?'

'The British government does not pay ransoms.'

'That wasn't my question.'

Niall stiffens. 'As far as our partners in Europe are concerned, no ransom was paid.'

'Well, if there was, that would get us off on the wrong foot. We can't be seen to give in to blackmail. We need to come across as firm. Peace on our terms. The families of the British servicemen who have died out there deserve that.'

'Indeed.'

Ross rises from her chair, goes to the window and stares out for a moment before turning back to face Niall with a cold smile. 'Well, congratulations . . . You got our man back. And no one can know it was thanks to you because it will weaken our position in the peace talks? Is that it?'

Niall feels relieved now. Perhaps he might survive this one after all. 'Quite.'

'And you did well out of it.'

'I don't think "well" is the right word. He was my best friend. Is my best friend.'

'Forgive me. I was given to understand that you were promoted to PUS as a consequence of your handling of it. Perhaps I have that wrong.'

'I believe there were other contributory factors.'

'And you are the youngest ever PUS?'

'Only by a year.'

'Will he be coming back to work, your friend?'

'I've said he could.'

'Perhaps he could take a holiday first. A long, long holiday. Somewhere the press won't find him. Sorry, am I keeping you?'

Realizing he must have glanced at his watch, Niall sits up. Oh, she's good, he thinks. Taking a firm hand with him. He feels a frisson of personality compulsion, what he imagines Alan Clark felt when he described his encounters with Margaret Thatcher as *Führerkontakt*. 'Actually, there is someone I am supposed to be meeting, but it's OK, I can—'

'No, no. You must go. Let us continue our conversation this afternoon when I have had a chance to get my bearings.'

The drive across Whitehall to the Mall takes two minutes. Niall would have preferred a less public meeting place than the Travellers Club, but his notice has been short and it is too late to arrange somewhere more discreet now.

'Good afternoon, Sir Niall,' the porter says as he holds open the heavy wooden door. 'Your guest has arrived. He is in the smoking room.'

Friedrich Walser, recognizable from behind by his collar-length silver hair, has his back to the door. He is resting a polished leather shoe on the fender of the fire. A monsignor in a mahogany reading chair lowers his newspaper gripper rod and watches as the two men shake hands. A club barman approaches before Niall has a chance to reach for the iron bell pull.

'G and T,' Niall says. 'Go easy on the T.'

Walser signals that he is not drinking.

Niall waits for the barman to leave before turning to his guest and saying: 'So, Friedrich, what is it that couldn't wait?'

V

WHEN HER MOBILE RINGS, HANNAH IS STANDING UNDER A bower of gleaming copper pots, shaving Parmesan from a nubbly pale-yellow block. She tilts her head to hold it against her raised shoulder.

'Hi, it's Martin Cullen from the *Guardian*.'

She puts the knife down and takes hold of the phone properly. 'How did you get this number?'

'Er, you gave it to me.'

There is a pause while she digests this. Then: 'I did, didn't I. Sorry. The press make me twitchy. We had them camped outside the house for . . . Were you wanting to speak to Dad?'

'Actually, it was you I wanted to talk to. I was wondering if you fancied meeting for a drink.'

Pause.

'A drink?'

Pause. 'Sorry. That made it sound like I was . . . There's something I want to ask you.'

'Go on then.'

Pause.

'Go on then and ask me, or go on then and meet me for a drink?'

Hannah tries to hide the amusement in her voice. 'Go on then and ask me.'

'OK. Have you heard of Friedrich Walser?'

The name grips, but Hannah cannot think why. 'Remind me.'

'He's an investment banker. A German. CEO of Rheinisch-Westfälische Bank.'

'What about him?'

'A contact of mine in the City told me something rather interesting about him. After 9/11, he was one of the bankers who helped find and freeze al-Qaeda's assets around the world.'

'What's that got to do with me?'

'Someone in the back office of Walser's bank came across a numbered account that had three million dollars sitting in it. Spare change in the financial world. It was registered in the Yemen.'

'I'm sorry, why . . . why are you telling me this?'

'I think a ransom was paid for your father. And I think I know who paid it.'

Hannah closes the kitchen door. 'Who?'

'The British government. I think they paid it into a secret account that had been set up by Walser on behalf of al-Qaeda. The one registered in the Yemen. He would have known how to channel the money to the kidnappers, you see.'

'When did this happen?'

'Just before he was released.'

'Did you tell my dad about it?'

Cullen hesitates. 'No. When I asked him if he knew whether a ransom was paid he went quiet for a while, so I thought I'd better let that one go.'

Hannah breathes out slowly. 'I think it's something he broods on a lot, the question of why he was released . . . You think Walser had something to do with it?'

'I suppose what I wanted to find out from you is whether your father has ever mentioned him.'

'Not to me. I could ask Niall if he's said anything to him.'

'Sir Niall Campbell? No, best not to bring him into this. Not yet. I need to do a bit more digging.'

'Have you tried contacting Walser directly?'

'I've left messages, but he isn't returning my calls.'

'OK, well, if I hear anything, I'll let you know.'

'That would be great. My number should have come up on your phone.'

Hannah opens the laptop on her desk, Googles 'Friedrich Walser', and reads several articles about him. Next she keys in the name Martin Cullen and sees there is a brief biography of him on the *Guardian* website. It mentions that he read history at Trinity College, Dublin, that he used to play keyboards in a band called the Hormones and that when he was twenty-four and working for the *Irish Independent* he was named Young Journalist of the Year. That was five years ago.

She checks her reflection in the kitchen window, sees the mild smile touching her lips and composes a text to him: 'Where are you taking me for this drink, then?' She changes this to 'where u taking me 4 this drink then?' and presses send.

*   *   *

293

Instead of a drink they meet a week later at the National Film Theatre to see a press screening of a digitally restored *Doctor Zhivago*, though they miss the start of it because Cullen is late, and then they leave half an hour before the end and head for the bar. There, as they drink bottled lager and share a bowl of olives, they talk about the film then move on to their favourite bands and writers. Hannah is the first to raise the subject of Walser, how he had offered her and her father the use of his château in France, either together or with other friends. Before they separate at Waterloo Underground, they joke about taking him up on the offer and then trashing the place by having a wild party there, announcing it on Facebook so there are hundreds of gatecrashers.

By the time she arrives home, Hannah has formulated a plan, and when she wakes in the morning it still seems like a good one. She takes from her drawer the card she had been given by Walser's driver and rings the number on it.

A week after this, Hannah's large rucksack sits beside her like an allegation as she waits in the kitchen sipping Diet Coke through a straw. She checks the clock on the wall for the fifth time in two minutes, then checks her mobile for a text from Martin Cullen. He is late again. Luckily Walser's driver is also running late, and it's not as if the flight is going to leave without them.

The flight. Just saying the words in her head fills her with excitement and panic. She and Cullen will be flying to Strasbourg for the weekend in a private jet. The two of them. No one else . . .

When she thinks about this now she pulls a face, then emits a snuffle of laughter. How could she have been so impulsive? And what will her friends think when she tells them? Perhaps she won't tell them, just as she didn't tell Walser's driver the name of 'the friend, or friends' who would be flying with her – because, she said, she was waiting to hear whether or not they could come. It was a white lie. She does consider Cullen a friend, even though she has only known him for a couple of weeks. And it has even crossed her mind that, given time, they might become more than friends. Besides, after a week of text traffic between them, she thinks she has the measure of him. Thinks, more to the point, that she can trust him.

She eyes the envelope she has left for her father on the table. Unlike the one he left for her all those months ago, this one doesn't contain disturbing news. It simply states she will be gone for a couple of days; that he isn't to worry about her. She will explain where she has been once she gets back.

It will take some explaining. If Walser is somehow connected to her father's release, she needs to find out how, and why, to put her father's mind at rest, as well as her own. If he isn't, she needs to know that, too. The château, she figures, might provide some answers. He must have invited them there for a reason – other than simply wanting them to take a holiday.

She has considered asking her father if he would like to come with her, but has decided against it. He doesn't need to know about Walser, for the moment. And she doesn't want to put him in a situation he might find stressful, not when he has been making so much ground lately. Since that day he allowed himself to cry over the trapped fox at Twickenham, he seems to have turned a corner, become a different person. Besides, he might appreciate some time on his own without her in the house.

As for herself, she will have Cullen with her. And he strikes her as the sort of person who can look after himself, and others.

She checks the clock again. Where is he? If they don't leave soon, her father will be back. When she hears the key turning in the front-door lock she jumps.

Edward appears in the doorway and looks at her rucksack with an expression of puzzlement on his face.

Hannah closes the door and whispers into her mobile. 'Sorry, Martin, there's been a change of plan. Dad's going to come with me. He's upstairs packing now. I'm really sorry.'

'Did he know I was coming?'

'I didn't tell him. He thinks I planned it all as a surprise.'

The doorbell rings. 'Look, I'm going to have to go. I'll ring later and explain everything. And I'll keep you updated on anything I find out about Walser. Sorry, sorry, sorry.'

As she ends the call she sees the letter she left for her father on the table, grabs it and stuffs it into her pocket. She then scoops up a couple of DVD boxes from the shelf and puts them in her rucksack. When she opens the front door she takes in the moustachioed man on the doorstep. He looks like he is more used to being in a gym vest than the suit and open-neck shirt he is wearing.

'Morning, Miss Northcote,' Mike says. 'There's been a slight hiccup. The Learjet is grounded in New York, along with my boss, so I'm going to drive you to Alsace instead.'

Hannah is momentarily thrown by this. When she regains her composure she says: 'What happened?'

'European air space has been closed again. Another eruption of ash from that Norwegian volcano.'

'Well, we've had a change of plan, too. Dad's coming with me now, instead of my friend.' As an afterthought she adds: 'And I'd be grateful if you didn't mention the bit about my friend to him.'

Mike makes a sealing gesture across his lips, picks up her rucksack and uses his key to pop open the boot of the black Mercedes parked outside the house.

As Hannah gets into the back seat, she looks over her shoulder at the house. Two minutes pass before her father appears carrying a suitcase in one hand and her guitar in the other.

As soon as the car leaves the London orbital, Hannah drops her shoulders, as if the muscles in her neck had been flexed against the capital's gravitational pull. She presses a button and, when a red light comes on, she pulls a worried face at her father. In response to her gesture he makes as if to bite his nails. While this may lack conviction, it is at least an attempt at humour, she thinks. Another sign of improvement.

She tries to recall what he had been like when she

was a child. Had he been funny? Had he played with her much? She knew he had played football with her in the park, and table tennis at home, and they had had running races on a beach somewhere, because there is family video footage of it . . .

Her thoughts are interrupted as a soft, slightly nasal voice comes through on the intercom. 'It's the speaker, Miss Northcote. That red light. Like in a taxi . . . Don't worry; there are no ejector seats. You can press anything you like. Actually, one of them buttons does operate the seats. They are fully reclinable, so if you want to get some rest, once we've got through the tunnel, feel free. It's about a five-and-a-half-hour drive the other side. There's a picnic hamper in the boot. I thought we could stop for lunch somewhere around Reims, which is about halfway. By your feet you'll find a cooler full of drinks. Wine, champagne, fruit juice. Help yourselves.'

'Are you sure you don't mind driving us?' Edward says. 'It seems an awfully long way.'

'Not at all. Be my pleasure.'

'Won't Mr Walser need the car?'

'Not while he's stuck in America. He was the one who suggested I drove you. By the way, the windows don't open. A security feature. But you can control the climate inside using the system console in the armrest. It also operates those screens in front of you. There's TV, music, internet. If you click on "movies" you'll see a list of new releases. Same with the iTunes menu. Mr Walser tends to listen to classical, but we've got pretty much everything downloaded. I prefer country myself. Willie Nelson. Patsy Cline. You're completely soundproof back there so it don't make any difference to me.'

'Life jackets?'

Mike angles his rear-view mirror and studies his passenger with an amused eye. 'Under your seats, miss. Now, if you will make sure your tray tables are in the upright position I'll point out the exits. They are here,' he raises his hand above his head and directs a thumb at Hannah's side of the car, then a finger at Edward's, 'and here.'

The red light goes off. Hannah puts on her sunglasses, presses her forehead against the window and inhales deeply. She then gives Edward a knowing, sideways glance – a tilt of the head, a dip of the chin. Up to this point she has found the driver a little intimidating – more to do with his moustache than his manner – and she suspects her father has been feeling the same because he is now studying the buttons in his door again, trying to avoid her eye. Hannah presses her intercom button and says: 'Does he go to New York a lot then, your boss?'

'Yep. New York, London, Frankfurt. Hong Kong sometimes.'

'What's the château like?' Edward asks.

'You'll love it. It's got a tennis court, gym, cinema and riding stables, though I think the horses might have gone away until the autumn. There's an indoor swimming pool, but most people prefer to swim in the river. The garden is spectacular. I believe there were more than a hundred species of butterfly recorded in it at one time . . . Here's one for you. Know how long a butterfly lives?'

'Three summer days,' Edward says. 'According to Keats.'

'Oh.' Mike sounds disappointed. 'Well, that's my nature trivia used up.'

Hannah presses the intercom: 'Mike? How long have you worked for him?'

'Coming up to five years. I was doing security before that. That's partly my job now. Personal protection officer. When the boss is over here. He has someone else to look after him when he's in the States. Don't worry, I've left my gun at home, otherwise it would take for ever to get through the tunnel . . .' He looks over the top of his sunglasses and winks. 'Joke.'

'But something tells me you know how to use a gun,' Edward says.

'Yeah, I was in the army for eighteen years.'

Edward leans forward again. 'Which regiment?'

'2 Para. Iraq. Afghanistan . . .' Remembering who his passenger is, Mike trails off.

'My father was in the army,' Edward says, trying to ease the tension that has crowded the car. 'Not the Parachute Regiment. Although I believe he did fight alongside them at one point in the Second World War.'

'Yeah? Whereabouts?'

'To be honest, I'm not sure of the details. After the war, the French awarded him the Croix de Guerre.'

'They didn't talk about it much, that generation.'

'No, it wasn't that. He was a war artist so he was sort of freelance. Went everywhere. I wish he'd kept a diary. Some of his paintings are in the Imperial War Museum.'

There is a lull in the conversation as Mike negotiates

300

a lane closed by an accident. Then he says: 'I was there not long ago. Great museum, that.'

'Dad was wounded during a bombing raid in the early 1940s and spent the next few years convalescing. Then he got assigned to cover D-Day. That's where he was with the Paras, I think.'

Mike seems distracted by something he has seen in his side mirror. ' "The Forgotten D-Day"'.

'What's "The Forgotten D-Day"?'

Mike seems to realize what he has said. 'Nothing.'

'You said, "The Forgotten D-Day". Why did you say that?'

'That's what they called the liberation of southern France, when the Allies landed on the Riviera and pushed all the way up to Nancy.'

Edward sounds confused. 'Nancy? That was where my father met my mother. She was French . . .'

The car swerves as a Porsche comes up from the slow lane and undercuts them. 'Arsehole!' Mike shouts, thumping the steering wheel with the flat of his hand. The Porsche has now crossed over into the fast lane. Mike follows it and, when it returns to the middle, over-takes it before pressing a switch which makes alternating blue lights flash in the top corners of the rear window. He signals with his hand for the Porsche to pull over. It obeys. Mike is clenching his jaw. As he parks ahead of the Porsche on the hard shoulder and un-buckles his seat belt he starts breathing quickly. 'Won't be a minute,' he says.

Edward and Hannah watch Mike from the back window as he marches up to the man – designer stubble, aviator sunglasses – who has stepped out of his Porsche and is holding up his hands in an imitation of surrender. Without saying a word, Mike grabs his arm, twists it behind his back and frogmarches him to the passenger side of his car. There he makes him place his hands apart on the roof and splay his legs. He pats him down, then forces him to the ground, making him lie on his front with his hands on the back of his head. There he leaves him.

When he gets back in the car Mike says: 'He won't do that again in a hurry.'

As they drive away, Hannah and Edward continue staring at the man lying down on the hard shoulder. They look first at each other, then at the back of Mike's head.

'Sorry about that,' Mike says in a calmer voice.

This brings their three-way conversation to a close.

Once they join the motorway out of Calais, a blur of EU-subsidized crops – a pastel-blue mist of linseed, the dazzling yellow of oilseed rape – proves soporific. Hannah yawns as she studies the music list. She knows she probably shouldn't choose albums that will remind her father of her mother: *Blood on the Tracks*, say, or *Blue*, or *Tapestry*. Nor can she go for something too contemporary that will alienate him. She will have to introduce him to Amy Winehouse and Rumer at some point, and break the news to him that Take That have reformed and split up again, but for now she needs more neutral ground. 'What do you fancy?' she asks.

Edward thinks. 'Know what I'd really like to listen to? *Test Match Special*. Would you mind?'

'Sure. Let me see if I can find it.'

'It's on Long Wave. If they still have Long Wave. We should be able to pick it up here.'

Hannah taps the screen a few times and then the distinctive sound of Henry Blofeld's voice can be heard painting a word picture of Stuart Broad running up and delivering an in-swinger that is clipped away for a single. 'That's Blowers,' Edward says with a grin. 'Can't believe he's still going. He calls everyone "my dear old thing". Don't know much about this Broad. He's one of the new generation. Probably still at school last time I listened to *TMS*.'

They both recline their seats and fall asleep to the sound of the commentator trying to decide whether a bird that is walking around next to the square leg umpire is a pigeon or a dove.

It is 5.15pm by the time the Mercedes leaves a road that winds down through a spine of pink and blue mountains and comes to what looks like an amphi-theatre of foothills. Their descent is less steep now and the road begins snaking as it levels out. They turn a corner and stop at an imposing wrought-iron gate on the outskirts of Natzwiller, a village in the fold of one of the hills. It opens electronically. Beyond it there is a gatehouse with a CCTV camera directed at the drive and, after this, an avenue of trees that continues for about a quarter of a mile. When Hannah sees the château, a white manor house with mullioned windows and a turret at one end, she catches her breath. It looks weightless, poised above a symmetrical parterre of flowerbeds, urns and statuary.

'Wow,' she says, leaning forward.

'Wow,' Edward echoes.

The air is warm and, when they open their doors, they can hear a lulling drone of insects. Noticing the granite statues either side of the entrance, Hannah grimaces and says: 'Check out the eagles.' She is the first out of the car and, after a couple of elaborate stretches, she walks over to the nearest one and pats its head. It is cold to the touch. She crouches down and studies the angry curve of its beak, the angular shape of the wings, the hooded, unseeing eyes. 'Brr,' she says. 'I just got chills. Who would have these outside their house?'

The front door is arched and the black-painted, brass-studded wood from which it is made looks old and grainy. Mike tests the doorknob and, finding it open, lifts Edward's case from the boot and drags it on wheels that tick against the marble of the entrance hall. 'You have my card. I'll come and collect you whenever you are ready, although hopefully we should have the Learjet back in action by then.'

'You're going to drive all the way back to London tonight?' Edward asks.

'Think I might go back via Paris. There's a friend I thought I might call in on.'

Something about the way he said 'friend' makes Hannah think he might have meant enemy. 'Please thank your boss for us,' she says.

'I'll write to him properly when we get back,' Edward adds.

'I'll just wait for François to show up, then I'll show you to your rooms. The fridge and the wine cellar are stocked and if there's anything you need just make a list for the housekeeper. If you would like her to come in and have a clean, write a note, otherwise she will leave you in peace. We want you to relax and have a good time. You must treat this place as your home for as long as you want it, that's what Mr Walser asked me to tell you.'

'How about exploring the area?' Hannah asks. 'Is it best to hire a car?'

'You could. Though I think the nearest car hire place would be Strasbourg. If you're feeling energetic, there are a couple of bikes in the stable.'

'*Bonjour*.' The voice is frail, barely audible, coming from behind them. 'Welcome to Le Jardin des Papillons.'

Edward and Hannah turn to see a bow-legged old man standing in the doorway. Already short, his height is further reduced by his stoop. It is as if an invisible hand is pushing down on his neck and he has to strain to look up. In his arthritically crooked hands he is carrying a rattling tray upon which three flutes and a bottle of champagne are cold-sweating in an ice bucket. He has a tanned and freckled scalp, a white moustache and pale, rheumy eyes distorted by thick glasses. The skin around his elbows is hanging in pleats. 'I am François,' the old man says in a voice that is more a croak, one that begins at the back of the throat and barely has the energy to leave his mouth. 'I live in the gatehouse.' He kisses Hannah's extended hand, says: '*Trop belle pour moi*,' then turns to Edward and says, 'You had a good journey, yes?'

'*Très bon, merci. Je suis Edward. Et c'est Hannah*.'

'Your French is good,' François says, 'but I need to practise my English.' He then shakes Edward's hand and pats Mike's back. He only comes as high as the driver's chest. 'You are staying with us tonight, Mike?'

'No thank you, sir, got to get back.'

Edward and Hannah exchange a glance, surprised by Mike's deference to the old man.

'Shame,' François says. 'Never mind. We shall talk next time.' With gentle, fussy movements he wipes condensation from the neck of the bottle, pops the cork and fills the glasses.

Hannah takes a sip from hers. She clinks glasses with Edward. '*Santé*.'

'*Santé*,' he echoes.

'You are to help yourselves to wine from the cellar,' François says. 'The Alsace region is an odd mixture of French and German. White wine mostly. Riesling and Muscat. But we have some good Burgundy down there. I recommend the Pinot Noir. There's some Italian, too. We want you to enjoy yourselves.'

Edward is intrigued by the way the old man refers to the house as if it is his own, as Mike had done. *We* want you to enjoy yourselves. 'We'll pay for anything we drink,' he says.

'That won't be necessary, *monsieur*. Herr Walser would be upset if you did. Now, let me show you to your rooms and then I will leave you in peace.'

Mike steps forward to take the bags. 'Let me do that, sir.'

'No, Mike, you have a long drive. I shall do it myself. These are very special guests.' François regards Edward for a moment, his head on a tilt. He then nods slowly to himself and smiles.

Mike strides to the car and, running a hand over its still-warm bonnet, says: 'One part Mercedes, two parts Panzer.'

As she watches the car glide back down the drive, Hannah says in a whisper to her father: 'Well, he wasn't weird at all.'

Edward nods. 'Wouldn't like to cross him.'

When François attempts to lift the suitcase, Edward prises it from his grip. François does not protest – honour has been served – and they follow him along a corridor lined with free-standing, glass-topped display cabinets full of pinned butterflies. Hannah stops to read out loud some of the labels, translating as best she can from the French – 'Green-veined White, Common Blue, Brimstone, Painted Lady, Small Tortoiseshell' – a roll call that sounds like an abstract poem. Realizing François hasn't waited for them, Edward tugs gently on her shirt.

When they come to an oak-panelled room with a vaulted ceiling they nod at one another, impressed. A carved marble fireplace dominates one end, a faded tapestry depicting medieval hunting scenes the other. Mounted along the wall opposite the windows are dozens of antlers, and the heads of a stuffed bear and a wild boar. On the wooden floor there is a faded black stain that could once have been ink, or ancient blood.

They are now at a wide spiral staircase made from white-painted stone. Following the old man up it is a slow process, as he has to pause every third step. On the landing he stares out of an armorial window for almost a minute then, at the top, his pace quickens as he shows them to their adjoining rooms. They are at the end of a long hallway which has four identical white bedroom doors either side.

François opens one of them and steps back. Hannah goes in first. 'I bagsy this one,' she says putting her rucksack on the bed. She moves to the window and opens it with a clatter. Below is a courtyard and, beyond that, the garden. 'Wow,' she says again. 'What is that smell? Sweet alyssum?' She inhales deeply. 'And lavender?'

'No good asking me,' Edward says, touching his nose.

Hannah is now studying a series of six small erotic pastels hanging on the wall. She doesn't need to check the signature to know they are by Gustav Klimt. One shows a semi-nude woman in a chair examining her foot. The drawing seems to throb steadily with life and she feels an urge to step inside it, inhabit its space, lose herself in its planes of shimmering, shifting colour.

'*Monsieur,*' François says, opening the door to the adjoining room and stepping to one side to allow Edward past. When Hannah comes through she sees he is staring at a dark mahogany four-poster bed; its tapering spiral posts are swagged with faded red velvet tied back with gold tassels. The canopy has an embroidered serpent winding across it and on the headboard there is a carved crest.

'Want this one instead!' Hannah says.

'Too late,' Edward says.

'This is the bed in which Lord Byron slept,' François says, pointing to a hand-painted plaque which reads:

'*Lord Byron a dormi ici 1817*'. Then he gives an amused shrug as if to say 'it takes all kinds'.

'This place is breathtaking,' Edward says. 'How long has Mr Walser lived here?'

'He bought it in, let me think, 1998 . . . The year France won the World Cup.'

Once they have done a little unpacking, father and daughter head back downstairs together and find François sipping champagne on the terrace.

'Before I leave you there is something I would like you to see,' he says, getting to his feet with the aid of a stick. The old man leads the way along an avenue of cypress, flowering cherry and magnolia, to a small stone bridge. 'This was built by the Romans,' he says. 'Because it feeds down from the Vosges mountains, the river water is very pure. I recommend a swim in it, but not now perhaps. In the heat of the day.'

Beneath the sunbeams glancing off the surface of the river they can see fat trout poised motionless against the current. And on the far bank, near an elegantly rotting Doric temple, there is what looks like the darting shadow of a water vole. Scrambling for footholds in a ruined archway on the other side of the bridge are wild roses and bougainvillea tangled with ivy. Beyond these is a grove of petrified oak timbers, stripped and faded to the colour of old bone.

'Beautiful,' Hannah says in a wistful voice, momentarily forgetting her reason for coming here.

'Beautiful,' Edward echoes.

François looks pleased. He is staring at Edward again.

*   *   *

After a light supper of aubergine rolls with spinach and ricotta left for them by the housekeeper, Edward blows out the candles, leaving a smell of snuffed-out wax in the air. 'Think I might get an early night,' he says with a yawn. 'We can explore properly tomorrow.'

'I might watch a DVD. I saw a machine in there.'

'Or you could try the cinema.'

'Another night. I want to watch this.' She holds up a DVD of *The Railway Children*. 'It came free with a Sunday paper.'

'You brought it with you?'

'Yep. Do you remember when we watched it together before you went away?'

Edward nods. 'Put it on.'

After opening a bottle of red, pouring two glasses and slotting the DVD in the machine, Hannah presses play on the remote. When nothing happens she unclips its back, rolls the batteries from side to side and tries again. This time it works and, when she sits next to her father on the sofa, he places his arm around her shoulders. An hour and three quarters later, as it comes to the final scene in which the elder daughter looks down the platform as the steam clears, then runs into her father's arms crying, 'Daddy, my daddy!' they look at one another, see they are both wet-eyed and splutter with laughter.

When Hannah sits up, little beads of sweat appear on her arms where their skin has been touching. She replaces the DVD with an old home movie that she has also brought with her and the two of them trade glances once more as they watch a two- or three-year-old

Hannah riding her father like a pony as he crawls around on all fours. It then cuts to a Hannah who must be about six years old having a race across a lawn with him, before they are next seen playing rounders together on a beach. These clips are followed by Hannah at a school swimming gala, in a school play, and taking part in the long jump on sports day. There is also some footage of her that was taken after Edward disappeared. When Frejya's voice can be heard giving a commentary, Hannah looks sideways at Edward again. 'This is for you to watch when you get back, Ed,' Frejya says. 'I know you're going to come back one day. Your little girl is growing up. She needs you.'

When the film has ended, Edward wanders into the kitchen and opens the double doors that lead out to the garden. He stands in the doorway, listening to the cicadas and staring up at the stars.

'I haven't been much of a father to you, have I?' he says without turning round when he hears Hannah approaching from behind.

At which a laugh bubbles up in Hannah's throat. 'No, you've been bloody useless!'

Edward laughs too, moving over as his daughter joins him in the doorway. He puts an arm around her shoulders again as they watch a big-bellied formation of cloud momentarily obscure the moon.

'I came back to a daughter I didn't recognize,' he says. 'You should have been nine. I used to keep sane by thinking of you and then you were taken from me and replaced by a stranger.'

'Then get to know me.'

'Where do I start?'

'Well, you could ask me what I like doing.'

'What do you like doing?'

She takes hold of the hand that is draped over her shoulder and begins stroking it. 'Um, playing pool. Drinking with my mates. And I like lie-ins, and cooking and watching *X-Factor*. And I go to Glastonbury, though I think it has become too commercial.' Her brow furrows. 'What else? Oh yeah, and surfing. I like to surf.'

'I used to think about surfing when I was in the cave. Memories of being with you and Mummy in Cornwall . . .' Edward trails off.

Hannah wants to keep him talking. 'Were you any good?'

'Don't you remember?'

'No.'

'Then I was brilliant.' He removes his arm, crosses the terrace to the lawn and lies down. Hannah joins him. With the top of her head to his, the two of them form one line.

'How many constellations can you name, Han?'

'Well, that's Orion's Belt. That's easy.' She points. 'You taught me that. And that must be the Seven Sisters. And that one is Mummy.'

She points at a bright star in the north. Edward raises his arm and their fingers entwine.

PART FIVE

I

London. Early summer, 1944

THOUGH THE LONDON SKY IS NO LONGER BLACK WITH Luftwaffe crows, the capital is still bombed at regular intervals and, through his taxi window, Charles surveys the latest damage: rubble moved to the side of the road to clear a space for traffic, cracked windows in smoke-blackened buildings that are held together by their crosses of tape, a crater out of which is protruding the boot of a Morris Oxford. It looks like a torpedoed ship that is rearing up defiantly before sliding below the surface. The firemen have been at work here, too, judging by the dimpled pool of water that surrounds a collapsed wall. Steam as white as papal smoke is snaking across the still-hot bricks.

When the taxi draws into Carlton Gardens he sees the sandbagged entrance to a public air-raid shelter where once a café had stood. The iron railings outside the Forces Françaises Libres headquarters are all missing, cut down to two-inch-high stumps of teeth. No attempt has been made to disguise the five-storey house itself.

There is a tricolour flapping on a pole outside it and a uniformed guard standing to the right of its black entrance door.

Having handed over two shillings for the taxi, Charles listens to the noise of its engine as it fades away. He then becomes enveloped in silence. The air smells of petrol and brick dust. There is a haze of it, clinging to his jacket. As he approaches the door, he brushes the shoulders of his uniform – unworn for three years, it smells of mould – and gives a half-salute. The guard salutes back. As Charles enters, he is immediately struck by an acrid smell of smoke and cleaning fluid. There are four buckets of sand, two either side of the entrance. Painted in red on a wall opposite the door is the Cross of Lorraine, the official symbol of the FFL. Alongside this is a photograph of General Charles de Gaulle, the unofficial symbol.

When the guard sitting at the reception desk sees Charles, he stares rudely at the scar tissue on his face, then says in heavily accented English: 'Can I help you?'

'I have an appointment with . . .' he checks the piece of paper upon which Sir Kenneth Clark has written a name, 'Major Lehague.'

The guard leads the way to a back room, stepping around a hole in the floor. 'You can wait in here. He shouldn't be long.' The room has burnt timbers in the ceiling and a view over St James's Park to the Foreign Office. Below the tethered barrage balloons across the park there are tulips. On the cherry trees there is blossom. It is an incongruous sight. Nature keeping calm and carrying on.

There is an oak desk and, behind this on the wall, a map of France marked with blue, green and red pins, swastikas and curving black arrows. The country is divided in two. There is cross-hatching in the north. The south has not been drawn upon.

That an Allied invasion of northern France is imminent is not exactly news. The south of England has become a giant sprawling army camp, with more than a million troops counting down the weeks to . . . when? That is the secret. And where? Where exactly? Calais? Probably. As for the build-up, the Germans do not need spies to monitor what is going on. They can probably hear it from France, a continuous rumble of trucks, jeeps and tanks, blocking the back roads as they make their way to Portsmouth, Southampton and Dartmouth. It is as if the whole landscape is moving. Operation Overlord.

There are also whispers that Charles has heard about Operation Anvil, an invasion of southern France, possibly at the same time as the invasion of northern France. Sir Kenneth had heard them too.

When Major Lehague enters and sees Charles studying the map on the wall he makes a point of standing in front of it, blocking his view. He is a short and wiry man with a neat moustache cut in the style of Clark Gable. In the corner of his mouth is a roll-up. He is wearing the uniform of the Free French Army.

'*Bonjour, monsieur. Je m'appelle Captain Charles Northcote.*'

The Frenchman removes his kepi and stubs out the cigarette as he pretends not to notice the Englishman's scars. 'I am a guest in your country, Captain Northcote, we should speak English here. I am Major Lehague, London liaison for the Zone Libre.' The Frenchman sits down and points at a chair for Charles. 'How may I be of assistance to you?'

'I was given your name by Sir Kenneth Clark.'

'Yes, he has been in touch with General de Gaulle. You have friends in high places, it seems. You are a war artist? Into battle armed only with an easel and canvas?'

Charles has heard the tease before and has a ready response. 'The paintbrush is mightier than the sword.'

'Your accent is good, by the way.'

'I have an uncle and aunt in Avignon. I used to spend holidays there, before the war.'

Lehague studies him. 'You are fluent?'

Charles shrugs. 'My spoken French is better than my written.'

Lehague opens his hands. 'So . . .'

'I was wondering if you knew anything about the Natzweiler-Struthof concentration camp in Alsace.'

Lehague studies the Englishman again, cocking his head. 'A little. It is a work camp. Most of the captured Resistance are being held there.' He turns and contemplates the map for a moment before tapping a pin. 'It is here, in the Vosges mountains between the Alsatian village of Natzwiller and the town of Schirmeck. The only such German camp on French soil, as far as we know.'

'I imagine the liberation of Natzweiler-Struthof will be a priority for you, if the Resistance are held there.'

'May I ask why you want to know about it?'

'I have a friend who is a prisoner.'

'I could find out from the local partisans what they know about individual inmates. I know they have contacts there.'

'That would be kind.'

'He is French, your friend?'

Charles looks at the floor. There is a time for truth and a time for lies. 'Yes. He was studying over here before the war. At the Slade. He's an artist, too.'

'And he was Resistance?'

'Yes.'

Lehague eyes him narrowly. 'Have you seen any action?'

'In a manner of speaking. Dunkirk. RAF bases. That was where I got this.' Charles touches his cheek.

Lehague looks puzzled. 'You were a pilot?'

'No, no. I was working at an airfield when it was bombed. I'd been commissioned to do some paintings there.' Charles studies the floor again. 'I was hoping to volunteer for Operation Anvil.'

'What do you know about it?' The Frenchman sounds defensive.

Charles responds with an attempt at nonchalance. 'An invasion of France from the Mediterranean.'

'Well, I am not at liberty to discuss the details with you.'

'Of course.'

'All you need to know is that it's going to be a French show with the Americans making up the numbers. The British will have a token presence only. A few ships. Handful of Paras.' A grin. 'And you.'

'So I can come?'

'Well, I'm not sure we will need a war artist, but perhaps it would be useful to have a British officer with us as a liaison, one who speaks French. It might help us overcome a little diplomatic obstacle we are facing. I will talk to de Gaulle about it.' Lehague stands up and proffers his hand. 'We have to do these things by the book. Relations between our countries are sensitive at the moment. Do you have any other languages?'

'Some German.'

'It is always useful to have a translator.'

'So what happens next?'

'Have you ever been to Naples?'

Charles shakes his head.

'That is where we will be assembling. We will be attached to the Free French Army, working alongside the Forces Françaises de l'Intérieur. They will be involved in a campaign of sabotage before the landings take place, attacking railway lines, roads, telephone exchanges and so on. I am to act as liaison between them and the Allies when we reach Nancy. That is where I come from.' Lehague looks thoughtful. 'By the way, how do I know you are not a spy?'

Charles thinks about this for a moment then runs the backs of his fingers down his neck. 'Spies are supposed to be inconspicuous,' he says.

As Charles walks back on to Pall Mall, he shakes his head and smiles as he hails a cab. Once he is in the back seat, he takes Anselm's letter from his wallet and touches it to his lips.

*　*　*

The Valkyrie is now used to the routine of escorting Anselm across to the Commandant's house. The guards on the gate are used to it too, waving them through. She always waits for him on her chair by the front door and sometimes takes some knitting with her to pass the time.

The Commandant and his prisoner have also fallen into a routine. As one paints and the other sits, they talk about philosophy and art. They drink wine. They listen to Bach and Schubert.

Anselm may still be a victim but now he is an alacritous one, and this is allowing him to find a vestige of his former humanity, his identity as a man, as an artist. He willingly confuses the Commandant's lack of abuse for an act of kindness. In truth he has come to regard him as a kind of god who gives him life every day, simply by not taking it away. And perhaps this relationship suits both men well.

Back in the camp, the brutality continues – the gratuitous beatings, the experiments, the deaths from exhaustion, starvation and disease. There are still executions every few weeks – hangings and shootings, sometimes carried out summarily by the Commandant himself.

But Anselm no longer allows himself to be affected by these barbarities. He occupies his own space, a purgatory somewhere between salvation and damnation. None of the other prisoners talks to him, partly out of fear, partly out of resentment at the preferential treatment he receives. With his proper diet, his strength has returned. Even his striped uniform is cleaner than that of other prisoners.

And then, several weeks after he began work on the figure of the Commandant, Anselm realizes it is nearly finished, though the oil has yet to dry. It is time to begin on the horse. This is done in the stableyard. There are butterflies here that come in through a Gothic, ivy-covered doorway. Their dithering flight entrances him, and, one afternoon, he follows some of them out as they make their way back through the door. Finding himself in a tumbling formal garden, he stands and stares in wonder, enchanted by the colours, by the smells of damask rose, jasmine and thyme, by the throbbing life of the place.

It is crossed by a river that, with a mist undulating on its surface, looks as if it is breathing. A Doric temple stands by the water's edge and, beyond it, a row of marble nymphs, and beyond these a pleached alley where fruit trees, privet and hawthorn are wrought into arches to provide shade.

Glimpsing a movement in his peripheral vision, Anselm turns and sees a small group of men and women in striped uniforms weeding the flowerbeds.

A fortnight later, the horse is also finished and Anselm realizes the moment he has been dreading has arrived, or rather it cannot be postponed any longer. Though the Commandant clearly likes him, and even seems to treat him as an equal, Anselm knows how compromising their strange relationship must be to him. He will have to be silenced, sooner or later.

But the Commandant does not appear to share this view yet. He is in a buoyant mood and so pleased with his portrait that he hangs it over his fireplace. 'I might take it back to Berlin when I next go there,' he says. 'You might get some commissions from those in high places.'

'Thank you.'

'What will you paint now, Anselm?' he asks as he stands back to admire it.

'I don't know.'

'Well, I'm sure we can find something.'

Anselm smiles. He has been given another hour, he thinks, another day, another week of life.

Without fans, the air below deck is as heavy as liquid. Having clung on to a notion of British decorum for as long as he can – perhaps to prove some esoteric point to his American shipmates – Charles relents and peels off his khaki shirt. It is so wet it clings like a second skin.

They have been anchored in the Bay of Naples for three days now and even the ship seems to be sweating. There is a layer of tar on the turret deck that bubbles and spits in the heat of the day. At night, with the steel of the hold retaining the fever as efficiently as a radiator, the bulkheads steam with moisture.

'This heat,' Charles says to himself.

A sleepy voice in the semi-darkness: 'You got that right, Buddy.'

At least the water is becalmed. Charles checks the luminous hands on his watch. How much longer? Why don't we get on with it? It is as if time is mocking him, slowing down so that minutes stretch to occupy space that properly belongs to hours. Though he has only been here for three days, he feels as if he hasn't slept for three months. Hurry up and wait: the army paradox. Men can be bored and nervous at the same time; this is another paradox.

Even without the heat, Charles would feel unsettled. His hammock is hard to sleep in; its hairy rope cuts into the skin and bends the spine. And the sound of thousands of men sleeping keeps him awake. It is as if they are trying not to breathe too loudly. Charles has pointed out that, as an officer – technically speaking – he should have been given his own quarters, but he has been told that this US destroyer was not built to accommodate two thousand men, so until a cabin can be found he will have to muck in with the ranks.

Major Lehague has managed to get a cabin and has told Charles he will have to fend for himself because he is too busy to nursemaid him. Charles suspects his testy mood is because the invasion of southern France, now called Operation Dragoon, has been postponed until mid-August, after endless bickering between Churchill on one side and de Gaulle and Roosevelt on the other. It had originally been planned to coincide with D-Day in June. The other reason is that it isn't a 'French show', as Lehague had grandly described it to Charles in London. It is very much an American show. The French won't even be landing on the first day.

Charles has done some sketches of the troops sleeping in their hammocks and pinned these to the wall, alongside a poster of Betty Grable. And he finds the rankers good company, especially the ones from the Deep South with their musical drawls. Quite a few seem to be from Alabama, and they talk of home nostalgically. But at least they are used to this humidity. Charles, by contrast, feels as if his marrow is melting.

And the land of the night reminds him of Anselm. It was their time together. Their intimate space. At night they felt safe from accusation, from the narrowed glances of strangers. Though Anselm was the taller man, it was always his head that lay on Charles's chest, in the crook of his arm, gathered and protected like a child. They were almost the same age, yet Charles always assumed the role of the senior partner, the responsible one, the worrier. Anselm was carefree. A child acting on his whims. A seeker of instant gratification. Charles envied that.

Anselm. Now that he is moving closer to seeing him again, he finds he is thinking about him constantly. Yet the name has become an abstraction. Anselm. Anselm. Anselm. His incantation. His craving. His madness.

He can barely even hear Anselm's voice in his head any more. It has been washed from his memory through overuse, just as the single photograph he has of him has been somehow worn away from staring. It hasn't faded but it no longer seems vital. He must draw Anselm. That is the answer. And as soon as he has the chance, he will do a painting. From memory. That will bring his friend back to life.

Back to life.

Charles closes his eyes as if hiding from the words.

As he has thought far too many times in recent weeks: what if Anselm is dead?

His eyes open. He cannot allow that possibility to creep up on him. Not now. Not here when he is so close. Anselm cannot be dead because Charles would know, would he not? Anselm's death would have been felt in his heart.

Alive, then. But what will Anselm make of his disfigurement? Will he be disgusted by it? And what will prison have done to him? Will his friend look the same? Five years have passed since they stood together at that hotel window overlooking Piccadilly. All that really remains is a nebulous ache of longing.

Does he believe he is going to be able to rescue Anselm? Even if his friend is still alive and in that camp, the Germans will destroy it before the Allies get within fifty miles.

Lying in the shirtless dark, eyes open, Charles becomes aware of pressure building against his eardrums. It is the sense too of noise being deliberately stifled. An armada should make more sound. You should be able to hear more than the water lapping against the bows and the rats scratching the steel decks with their claws. Some run across men as they sleep. Charles has seen them. Though he feels safe down here – the shadows mean men don't stare at his scars – he decides to go for a walk. A man cries out in his sleep: 'Not no . . .'

Of what is he dreaming? Not. No. A double negative. It sounds ominous and Charles feels spooked by it. He retrieves the boots he has tied to a stanchion and negotiates the rows of bulking hammocks, heading towards the next cabin. There will be gambling in there. Sure enough, crowding around a flickering blue light-bulb that swirls with cigarette smoke are half a dozen men playing blackjack. Some are in vests, others wearing only their dogtags. Charles can smell their sweat as he feels his way along the wall towards the hatch. One soldier, wearing his cap on back to front, has accumulated a pile of dollars, quarters and cents. Behind their whispers can be heard swing music on a distant wireless.

Outside, stars. As the humidity has grown more oppressive, some men have taken to sleeping on deck. But even here, the air is steaming, and there are also mosquitoes to contend with. The showers below deck are unpopular because they use salt water that leaves the skin itchy. Men prefer to use the improvised fresh-water ones on deck. There is a man soaping himself under one now. The mosquitoes do not trouble him.

The catches of fear and excitement about the looming battle are palpable. Everyone seems to feel pride at being part of a mighty invasion fleet, including Charles who hears the historical echoes lost on most. They are overlooking the Tyrrhenian shore above Naples where once the entire Roman fleet had foundered. Bad omens were seen everywhere that day – lightning, comets, the birth of two-headed animals.

Are there any bad omens here? Not. No. That double negative. Charles studies the night sky, thick with planets. Is Anselm looking up at the same sky, he wonders? The same quarter? The night is clear and, as he stares across at Mount Vesuvius, he fancies he sees wisps of smoke. The volcano had erupted in March, destroying dozens of USAAF B-25 bombers on a nearby airfield. Is it going to erupt again? Is that sulphur he can smell?

Glancing left and right he sees the hulking silhouettes of more than fifty battleships, cruisers and destroyers, dangerous islands of steel. The vessel nearest them is a submarine, its curved shoulders like a whale, blue in the moonlight. The German forces left to defend southern France are surely doomed. But even though the south coast couldn't possibly be as well defended as the north, Charles has heard there is to be a heavy bombardment from the Allied battleships and bombers before the landings begin. No chances are being taken. It is mid-August now, a little over two months since D-Day, but Omaha Beach is still fresh in the collective memory. Soldiers still chill each other's blood with what they have heard about the massacre there, thousands of GIs washed up in the surf like flotsam. At least there is no danger of a surprise attack from Japanese zero fighters here. Naples is no Pearl Harbor. America rules the skies as well as the waves. The Mustangs and Thunderbolts that patrol overhead in pairs during the day fly unopposed.

Charles checks his watch for the fourth time in an hour, as if it will tell him the date of the invasion. When will the order to weigh anchor come? Will this second D-Day happen at all? Perhaps Eisenhower has finally given in to Churchill's lobbying and called it off. After all, with the Allies nearly in Paris, the Germans ought to retreat back over the Rhine now.

But they are fanatical. Charles knows that. They fight to the last man and the last bullet. And they are vengeful. Reports have reached them of an atrocity in June: Oradour-sur-Glane, a village in the Limousin region of central France, was razed to the ground by the Waffen-SS, with hundreds of villagers murdered in two or three hours. The men were machine-gunned. The women and children were herded into a church, which was then burned to the ground. If the bastards could do that to civilians, what could they do to prisoners in a concentration camp? Charles shivers, takes Anselm's letter from his wallet and whispers to it: 'Are you still alive, Dopey?'

If the invasion goes to plan, Charles calculates he can be in Alsace within a month. 'Stay alive,' he adds under his breath. 'Stay alive.'

And then Charles feels a coldness in his spine, a dry mouth, an emptiness in his gut. Without any fuss – no shouted instructions, no whistles that might alert German spies in the town – the anchors are being slipped and, with a gentle churning sound on the surface, the great propellers below have come to life. The fleet is moving.

As Anselm waits to find out what his next painting assignment is to be, he inspects – without touching – a leather-bound translation of *The Tempest* that is open on the Commandant's desk. It is printed on vellum and has deckle edges that are magnified beneath a pair of half-glasses. Also on the desk is a framed photograph of an SS general playing a violin. He picks it up and tries to read what is handwritten across the bottom. When he realizes it is a signature – 'Reinhard Heydrich' – he puts it back down quickly, as if afraid it will burn through his fingers. He wanders over to the gramophone and tilts his head so that he can see what the Commandant has been listening to lately: *Die Fledermaus*.

'Do you like Strauss?'

Anselm turns to see the Commandant standing in the doorway dressed in full SS cavalry uniform. He has spurs on his riding boots and is carrying a silver cavalry sword with two golden silk tassels on its hilt. He makes a little play of conducting with the sword and says: 'Actually, Strauss is not a bad idea. One of the Viennese waltzes, perhaps.'

He places his sword on the desk, and runs his fingers along his record collection until he comes to a section devoted to Strauss. He eases a vinyl record from its sleeve and marches out of the room with it.

In his absence, Anselm stares at the sword and then watches in horrified fascination as his own hands pick it up. Its grip is wrapped in leather and gold braid. There is an inlaid swastika and the SS *Totenkopf* on its forward-swept guard. What if he were to charge at the Commandant when he comes back? Run him through? He realizes at this moment how confused he feels about his captor. He hates him and yet he doesn't. And the thought of running at him with a sword now seems grotesquely symbolic, a sexual act.

When the Commandant returns he says: 'Heavier than you imagine, isn't it? Solid silver.'

Its cutting edge, as Anselm discovers from testing it with gentle side-to-side pads of his thumb, is as sharp as a guillotine. He rests its blade on his forearm and hands it to the Commandant, handle first.

'I've laid on an entertainment for the camp,' the

Commandant says, returning his sword to its scabbard. 'And Strauss would be the perfect accompaniment for it.' He clicks his heels together and holds out his arm in the direction of the door. 'Come and join us, Anselm. You might enjoy it.'

In the courtyard, there is a strong smell of polished leather and fresh horse manure. A groom is waiting with the black stallion already saddled up. As the Commandant strokes the horse's downy nose it paws the ground with its hoof. 'Such an impatient brute,' he says with affection as he works his hands into his riding gloves and tugs down the stirrups, making the leather slap loudly. 'Would you give me a leg-up, please.'

When Anselm bends down and joins his hands to form a cradle, the Commandant places the point of his boot in it before hopping twice on his other leg to get momentum. He then mounts his horse with a sound of creaking leather. 'Remember your Nietzsche, Anselm,' he says over his shoulder as he gives a nudge of his spurs. 'Without cruelty there is no festival.'

As Anselm and Hilde the Alsatian follow the horse and rider out of the courtyard, keeping a discreet distance as they navigate the avenue of trees and turn towards the entrance gate, he wonders what the Commandant's comment means. When he hears a crackly Strauss waltz start up through the camp's loudspeakers he begins to suspect. A dozen or more rooks explode from the trees above, their raucous cackling making him flinch.

The entire camp of several thousand prisoners is lined up in two blocks facing each other across the square, with a long, empty space about twenty feet wide dividing them. They are all giving the Nazi salute, and, in the fervour of Anselm's mind, their arms seem to form a shifting sea of erections. This has been carefully choreographed, then, he thinks. A film camera has been set up on a tripod and there is a cameraman turning a handle and panning the lens along the line.

In the middle of the space, about fifty yards from the entrance gate, is a prisoner tied to a post with thick rope, from his ankles to his chest. The top of the post reaches just below his shoulders, leaving his neck exposed. He is struggling to free himself, but his binding is too tight – and his attempts to turn his head and see what is going on behind him are similarly futile. Anselm doesn't wonder for what the man is being punished. In this bubbling pit of fear and despair, such questions are irrelevant.

Because his back is to the Commandant, the prisoner cannot see him framed by the cast-iron 'Arbeit Macht Frei' sign that arches across the entrance to the camp. Nor can he see the Commandant now trying to steady his horse as he waits for the waltz, which Anselm recognizes as 'The Blue Danube', to build to a particular moment. When this comes – the furious major chords of the coda punctuated by cymbal crashes – the Commandant takes his sword from its scabbard and, pointing it in front of him, spurs the horse into first a trot, then from a slow canter to a fast one, and then, after twenty yards, to a swinging gallop that makes the camp echo to the rising drum of hooves. The horse's mane and tail are streaming out in undulating horizontals. Spits of dirt are blurring its fetlocks. After forty yards the Commandant sits forward in the saddle and accelerates into a full charge. Then, as he closes in on the prisoner, he raises his sword above his head. As it catches the sunlight, it looks like an ocean roller frozen in the act of breaking. He then loops it around in a deft windmill and brings its blade down against the neck, decapitating the man with a single stroke.

He reins his beast back almost on its haunches before wheeling it about. On a second pass, he leans down low over the right side of his saddle to scoop up the severed head with the point of his sword. This he now raises, splashing his own face with blood. Tendons and muscles are bunching out of the neck in a thick white cluster, like the congested petals of a sea anemone. The horse rears up and boxes the air, its nostrils flaring. The Commandant is laughing now, intoxicated by the smell and taste of blood, and, as the waltz comes to its gentle end, he tries to catch his breath. Prompted by the guards, the prisoners begin applauding, as if the brightness of the blood is a welcome splash of colour in the greyness of their lives. The Commandant stands up in his stirrups, sticks his chin out and acknowledges their applause with curt nods of his turning head.

The crossing, through the Sardinia–Corsica straits, has been calm. Now, as day breaks, the Riviera is in sight. As Charles looks out across the bay of Saint-Tropez with his binoculars, he finds the palm trees incongruous. This is 'Delta Beach' and convoys of ships with anti-aircraft balloons tethered to their sterns are converging on it from all directions, taking up their allocated positions.

The assault, he has been told, will be made up of three American divisions of VI Corps, reinforced with the French 5th Armoured Division. They will follow tomorrow. Major Lehague has arranged to go in with the US 45th Infantry a day ahead of his fellow country-men. The Resistance are already there, divided into two factions, the non-communist Mouvements Unis de la Résistance and the communist Francs-Tireurs et Partisans. Lehague has said that he is needed as go-between, which is why he is going in early. But Charles knows it is more a matter of him wanting a pair of French boots to be among the American ones landing on the beach.

The dawn is silver-edged, heavy with incense and cordite. As the sun crests the horizon, the sea glitters and gulls hang suspended above it, as if waiting as well, sensing that something of great import is afoot.

At 0600 hours, the naval guns begin bombarding the coastline, juddering the boat with each salvo. At the same time, two hundred and fifty Flying Fortresses begin their unopposed bombing raids on coastal defences and radar stations, sending up jagged flames and leaving glowing embers. The noise is numbing and the entire coast soon disappears in a pall of smoke and dust.

On board, Charles sketches men as they strip and oil their rifles. Some are yawning, an ironic effect of nerves. While a few shave their hair off to make it easier for medics to deal with head wounds, others slip condoms over the ends of their gun barrels to protect them from salt water. Charles smiles grimly to himself, thinks this symbolism apt.

He watches a young GI, no more than nineteen, tape a photograph of a loved one to the inside of his helmet. As a chaplain holds an impromptu service on the upper deck, administering bread, wine and absolution for future sins, a Pathé Newsreel crew sets up and films him. They then turn the camera 180 degrees and film men slinging bandoliers across chests, filling canteens to the brim, sharpening bayonets on whetstones.

Rubbing the back of his neck, Charles wanders over the slippery deck and listens in as the newsreel director questions a Doughboy about his training. 'We've been taught how to kill a man silently by slicing through the jugular and the voicebox,' he says in a Texan monotone, demonstrating with a mime. 'And we had to crawl through the fresh entrails of pigs. I guess it was to toughen us up. Get us used to blood and all.'

Some men have their eyes closed, though they are clearly wide awake, while others write last letters or attach kits of bandages, sulfa tablets and syrettes of morphine – 'one for pain, three for eternity' – to the backs of their camouflage-netted helmets. Most are behaving like schoolboys on a trip, chattering excitedly, trying out French phrases on their tongues, experimenting with the shape of them, preparing for their oral examination. Charles can hear one of them talking in a southern accent about 'gittin' me some French pussy'.

As the rum ration is passed around in a stoneware flagon, the convulsion caused by the naval bombardment all but stops, with only what sounds like a few shunting freight trains still audible in the distance. In the relative silence, a colonel with liquid brown eyes gives his men a pep talk.

'I will not lie to you about what it will be like at the beachhead,' he says. 'It'll be ugly. Look to the man to your left and right. By the end of this day, it might be that only one of you is still alive. Your chances of being that one will depend on you keeping going forward across the beach. If you stop, you are either a dead man or a man who is going to die.'

Signals are being silently flashed between the ships. The tannoy comes to life. 'Now hear this! Crews report to their assault craft!'

It is time.

Charles is carrying his art equipment – rolls of paper, pencils, charcoal sticks, inks, pens – in a leather map tube that looks like a small mortar. With a strap buckle at either end he can sling it over his shoulder, and he has been assured the container is watertight. His fold-up easel isn't as easy to carry, but he thinks he has found a way to secure it to the backpack he now shrugs higher on to his shoulders. As an official war artist he is not supposed to carry a gun, but he has decided to anyway. He has read in the papers that Ernest Hemingway, who is working as a war correspondent attached to the American forces converging on Paris, carries an automatic, and so Charles has a gun, too, a standard-issue British Army Webley break-top service revolver. It is in a holster attached to his Sam Browne belt.

When he sees the short, moustachioed Lehague making his way to the assembly point, trying to keep his

French dignity as he is almost carried along by a crowd of jostling infantrymen, he shouts: 'You go on ahead. I'll catch up in a minute.'

Feeling jittery, Charles has decided he needs to make his third visit to the head in an hour; the sound of water sloshing around must be contributing to his urge to go. The latrines smell of wet metal and rust and he finds himself wrinkling his nose at them. A minute later, as he emerges carrying his pack in front of him, he loses his footing and holds out his hands to break his fall. As he does this, his thumb is caught between the wood of the easel and the metal of the doorframe, pulping under his own weight.

At first he stares in puzzlement at his thumbnail. It is in the wrong place, half an inch to the right of where it should be. Then the blood appears and with it comes a rolling wave of pain. Numbly, he watches the blood splash on the floor at his feet. The pain has bubbled up to his throat now and black spots are dancing before his eyes. Realizing he is about to faint, he sits down.

His brow is damp with sweat, but he does not curse. Instead he remains rooted to the spot, transfixed by the sight of his own blood. Think. Think. He needs to staunch the bleeding. Pressed tight, his hanky serves as a tourniquet.

The medical room. It is near here.

As he makes his way to it, Charles holds his hand up to reduce the flow of blood and simultaneously let the men coming the other way know he is there. But their eyes are down, their helmets on. They are too distracted to notice him walking against their tide. He stands to one side. When he reaches the medical room he stumbles again in his rush to get out of the way of the advancing men. He takes off the handkerchief and worries that, if he touches it, the nail will come off altogether. He looks around for some morphine, but the shelves, full an hour ago, are now empty. He sits on the bed. The blood is on his trousers. Think. He cannot let this stupid accident prevent him reaching Anselm.

'You bin hit?'

'It's my nail. I . . .' He feels embarrassed to say it. 'I tripped.'

'Let me see.'

Charles takes in the man's Red Cross armband. The medic is perhaps fifty, with weathered features, freckles and horn-rimmed glasses.

'Can you patch it up quickly, I'm supposed to be in the first wave.'

'You're not going anywhere with that, buddy. You're going to have to sit this invasion out. Consider yourself lucky.'

'But I want to go. I need to.'

'Look,' the medic is preparing a syringe, 'you can whistle "Dixie" if you think I'm letting you down those nets with that. You would be a danger to the other men.'

The medic presses a swab around it. Charles winces. 'You're a Limey, ain't you?'

Charles nods, his face now wet with sweat. He thinks he is going to be sick.

The medic can smell whiskey fumes on Charles's breath. 'Dutch courage, eh? Don't blame ya.' He opens the compress. 'Good. It's clotting. The nail should stay on, but the end of your thumb looks broken. I'll give you an anaesthetic into the thumb then I'll try and reattach the nail.' He pushes the needle of a syringe into the base of the thumb. 'This will take twenty minutes, then you won't feel a thing . . .' He checks his watch. 'Shit. I gotta go.'

'Don't wait for the anaesthetic, Doc. Just do it now.'

'You don't want that kind of pain, I'm telling you. The nerve endings in the cuticles are . . .'

'I'll be fine.'

The medic looks at the skin graft on Charles's face and nods. 'Well, I guess you know about pain.'

'Yes.'

The medic takes the patient's hand in his and turns his back on him so that he is shielded from view. As he pushes the nail back into place, embedding it and ignoring the blood, Charles breathes deeply and scrunches the blanket tight in his other hand.

'All done,' the medic says. 'You're a brave guy. That's how the Gestapo torture prisoners.'

Charles manages a smile, relieved he hasn't fainted. His thumb is still throbbing with pain, but already the pressure is ebbing. 'Well, thank goodness I didn't talk.'

The medic laughs. 'It should seal itself, but you gotta keep it dry.' He pours iodine on to gauze and presses it on to the nail, then wraps a bandage tight around it. 'Why you so desperate to be in the first wave?'

'Long story.' They listen to the dull, muffled thunder of artillery as the bandage is taped up. A French frigate somewhere is playing the Marseillaise over its tannoy.

'On a mission, huh?'

'Something like that.'

'Well, good luck. If you get yourself on one of the craft they're lowering over the sides, you won't need to use the nets. But keep that bandage out of the water, otherwise it will go septic. And take these antibiotics.' He tosses over a small bottle rattling with pills. 'Three a day. If you remember. Gotta go.'

Ten minutes later, Charles manages to negotiate a space on one of the flat-bottomed landing craft about to be lowered from davits. It is as ungainly as a hippopotamus and, as it slips unevenly on its chains, its blunt bows clank against the side of the ship. It lands with a splash that nearly pitches Charles over the side, and then, with a snort, it goes to join two others from its herd. All three circle each other, their great jaws closed tight against the water.

As they set course for the beach, waves slap against the forward ramp sending up cascades of spray that drench and shock in like measure. Soon their feet are wet too as a pool of water sloshes from one end of the craft to the other. Charles can feel the salty wind in his face. He can taste it, too.

Heavy shells have started screaming overhead again, creating a vacuum in their wake. The men in the troop-well watch open-mouthed as the water rises up and follows their course before dropping back into the sea. As the craft pitches and rolls, one soldier, his face as grey as the boat, vomits. There is a geyser of water not far away as a German shell explodes; either that or it is an Allied shell landing short.

Charles's bandaged hand is shaking as he tries

unsuccessfully to keep it dry. With his other hand he fumbles for the hip flask in his pocket. He stares at the initials engraved in flowery lettering on the side – 'HR' – and then takes three big gulps. He offers it around and, when there are no takers, screws the lid back on before taking a grip of the rope that runs along the side of the craft. Every slap of every wave jars his bones.

Not long now, he thinks. Stay alive, Anselm. Stay alive.

II

WHEN THE VALKYRIE FAILS TO COLLECT ANSELM AFTER THE morning roll call, he goes in search of her. 'He has gone,' she says brusquely when he finds her smoking behind the administration block.

Anselm is taken aback. 'I had an appointment with him. A sitting. Do you know when he will return?'

'No.' Her tone does not soften. 'And if I were you, I would lie low.' She draws a finger across her throat and gives a thin smile.

An hour later, Anselm is in the square for the roll call when he hears an order he has not heard before.

'All prisoners with the pink triangle will remain standing at attention.'

As the other prisoners disperse, the pink triangles look at one another, their throats dry. The guardhouse door of the command tower opens and two SS doctors stride forward. They are accompanied by a senior SS officer Anselm hasn't seen before. All three are talking earnestly as they walk. The detail sergeant barks: 'One hundred and seventeen deviants present as ordered.'

Anselm looks around in vain for the Commandant, but he cannot see him. Where has he gone?

A mattress is brought out and placed on the scaffold. A woman with long brown hair and a rounded figure is escorted over from the camp brothel, the one used by the guards. She removes her dress in a resigned way, revealing large, tubular breasts and a dark, curly pelt of pubic hair. Once on the mattress she opens her legs wide. Anselm finds himself filled with curiosity about her. What would it be like to have sex with a woman? He has never entertained such thoughts before.

A prisoner Anselm recognizes from the experiments is escorted over from the infirmary. He too is made to undress.

'This homosexual has been cured,' the doctor announces, indicating the man, who is now covering his genitals with his hands. 'And he is about to take the renunciation test.'

The guards give an ironic cheer.

'You may mount her now,' the doctor says to the man, making impatient circular motions with his hand.

The guards form a semicircle around the scaffold as if it were an amphitheatre. They stand legs akimbo, watching expectantly. The Valkyrie is one of them. Though it is not yet dark, a guard in a nearby watchtower directs his spotlight at the couple, making them look eerie and two-dimensional.

The prisoner lies on top of the prostitute, his thin physique barely making an impression on hers. He does not move.

The Valkyrie climbs up the scaffold steps and holds the handle of her whip to the prisoner's chin. 'Come on then,' she says. 'Don't be shy.'

The man makes thrusts with his hips but it is obvious that his member is not co-operating. The doctors talk among themselves before shaking their heads and walking away. The guards are laughing now and also walking away. The woman does not look at the prisoner as she pushes him off and gathers her clothes. She waits until she is off the scaffold before she gets dressed and walks with a side-to-side gait back to the brothel.

With the matter-of-fact air of one who is carrying out a dull, domestic chore, the Valkyrie spools out her whip and then brings it down hard on the man's back. Half a dozen lashes later, she signals the Ukrainian over to finish the job. He strides up to the prisoner and beats him unconscious with the butt of his rifle, delivering three smart blows to the back of his skull.

As the Valkyrie is making her way back down the steps and catching her breath she sees Anselm and shouts: 'Hey, Artist! You next, eh?'

He remains standing to attention as she marches up to him and brings her whip across his face. As he staggers back clutching the welt he looks up to see the Ukrainian approaching. There is blood on Anselm's hands now and, as he stares at them as if they are not his own, he feels the barrel of a rifle being pressed into his chest. The Ukrainian holds it there for a few seconds as if considering whether to pull the trigger, then he withdraws it and turns the rifle around so that the barrel is in his hand. Anselm can still feel the sharp pressure made by the muzzle. It lingers on his skin like hot wax. Then the butt of the rifle slams into his solar plexus, driving the breath from his lungs. As he doubles up, he feels the butt hit the skin over the bone on his shoulder. Between waves of pain, he is aware of the Valkyrie speaking again, saying through her laughter: 'No Commandant to protect you now, Artist.'

The landing craft hits the beach with a bang that causes Charles to lose his footing. A crunching sound follows, shingle against metal. But as the door cranks down and he braces himself for a whip of bullets, he sees instead a smiling Frenchman with reddish hair holding out a tray of champagne. The others scramble past him, their boots heavy in the wet sand, but it is soon obvious that there are no targets for them, only wisps of smoke in the treeline, a grove of lolling palms. Apart from an occasional crackle of small-arms fire in the distance, a sound like a dry log on a campfire, it seems the Germans are not putting up a fight.

Sections of the beach are blocked by double rows of barbed wire. Flail tanks are clearing minefields. An old woman, the shape of a bell, now appears with a tray of crepes and omelette. Bewildered, the soldiers take off their heavy packs and bandoliers and throw them on the beach along with their rifles and entrenching tools. Some laugh in relief as they sprawl in the sand and signal the old woman over. Others look around for the red-haired man with the champagne. Charles clenches and unclenches his good hand. His fingertips are remembering the hairy texture of the rope that served as a rail around the side of the landing craft. He had been clinging to it so hard his knuckles still ache.

He takes off the US M1 helmet he has borrowed, tugs

the beret from his shoulder strap and puts that on instead, positioning it two fingers above his left eye. He wants the Americans to know he is British.

A command post is being set up on the beach, a folding desk, a radio transmitter and a chair. An officer is pointing and shouting and, at his command, some men begin unreeling telephone wire while others dig foxholes. A line of about a dozen men are on their knees prodding their bayonets in the sand to check for mines.

Charles looks back out towards the Mediterranean and sees, about fifty yards away, what looks like a single uniformed body washing ashore. The ships are shimmering several miles out, firing occasional volleys that are signalled not by a bang but by a puff of smoke. The noise comes moments before the shell arches overhead, its destination a couple of miles inland.

Along the entire length of the Riviera, tens of thousands of men are now pouring ashore unopposed. Charles overhears from a radio operator that the only resistance encountered in this sector has been from two anti-aircraft coastal batteries supported by a German garrison of a couple of hundred men, but they have now surrendered.

He looks around for Major Lehague but, unable to see him, he gets out his sketchpad. Holding his pencil awkwardly because of the bulging wet bandage on his thumb, he sketches a group of GIs who are clearly spoiling for a fight and feeling disappointed not to find one. Behind them a jeep is stuck in the sand. As it grinds its gears, two fighters patrolling low over the beach drown out its noise.

* * *

As he is backing down the steps of the scaffold, helping another prisoner carry the body of the homosexual who failed the renunciation test, Anselm slips. For a moment he thinks he has sprained his ankle, but, to his relief, he finds he can still put weight on it. A sprained angle is a death warrant in this place. He turns to see if the Ukrainian has noticed. It's fine. He takes hold of the wrists again and lifts, but not high enough to prevent the bony buttocks from being grazed as they descend.

The body is light and, as they carry it in the direction of the crematorium, it swings between them like a hammock. There are already two corpses stacked outside it, in differing stages of decomposition, so they add this one to the pile. They are walking away when they hear someone shout at them.

'You there.'

They turn and see an SS doctor standing next to a handcart stacked with crates that are about two feet square. He is signalling them over with impatient hand gestures.

'You are to take these to the Commandant's house,' he says.

Anselm and the other prisoner take one shaft each and, as they pull, the iron-tyred wooden-spoked wheels make a crunching sound against the small rocks hidden in the dirt.

Half a dozen prisoners are shuffling in and out of the château as they load more of these crates into the back of a three-ton truck. A guard sees Anselm and barks an order for him to take his crates inside.

Coming from the kitchen there is a distinct smell of meat being boiled. Anselm is directed through to the drawing room. All the paintings, records and Persian rugs have gone. The only evidence that the Commandant was ever here is one of the photographs of a Fräulein holding a baby. It is lying flat, the glass in its frame broken.

'Bring them here!' Anselm follows the voice. It belongs to another SS doctor. He places the two crates he is carrying on the desk as instructed. The doctor takes two handfuls of sawdust from a bag on the floor and uses them to line one of the crates.

When Anselm returns with the next two crates he sees the doctor carefully placing something that looks like a large egg in the crate packed with sawdust. As he moves closer he sees it is a skull. The doctor is now removing odd small chunks of flesh and gristle from it with tweezers.

By the time Anselm has returned with his last two crates, another skull is being delivered from the kitchen. Steam is rising from it and he realizes it has been boiled, presumably to remove its skin and hair. The first crate has now been nailed shut and the doctor is writing a number across its lid.

Anselm lowers his eyes, as if to persuade the doctor he has not witnessed this scene. He notices the ink stain on the wooden floor.

The residents of Saint-Tropez have come out on their balconies to stare. Chairs have been arranged and parasols opened so that the events below can be followed by entire families, from children in striped swimming costumes to elderly men resting their chins on walking canes.

To Charles, as he sits sketching them from a café on the promenade, it is as if they dare not take their eyes off the thousands of American troops occupying their boulevards and squares, for fear that, if they do, these invaders will slip away to their landing craft and head back out to sea.

Some of the soldiers, leather-faced men from the 45th Infantry Division, are marching, to where and what purpose it is not obvious. Others have stripped off their shirts to enjoy the sunshine, sitting on low walls, dangling their legs like bored teenagers. Others still are shaving, smoking, listening to bebop on their radios, chewing gum, or dealing cards as they lounge in doorways. Most are milling in a directionless way, unsure what to do next, now that they are here.

The soporific clank of halyards against masts, audible even above the noise of engines, seems especially inappropriate to Charles.

As his gaze shifts to the chaos of the beach, he has a sense of déjà vu. A bulldozer is churning out blueyblack smoke as its driver, an engineer stripped to his waist, tries to rescue a tank abandoned in the sand. German prisoners are being herded on to the beach for removal by ships. They have pieces of card tied around their necks as if they are items of luggage. Two cranes on caterpillar tracks are gathering jeeps and artillery equipment in their nets and unloading them from a barge docked in the bay. Not far away from this there are yachts moored, and, an even stranger sight, fishermen selling their catches to American soldiers, while herring gulls circle, mewling as they wheel.

In front of them, a hundred-foot pontoon causeway is being dragged on to the beach. Further out, a second one is being lowered into the water. They remind Charles of the makeshift jetty he saw at Dunkirk. Two events five years apart, one at the top of France, the other at the bottom. The main difference between them, he thinks, between an evacuation and an invasion, is the expressions on the faces. The Thunderbirds, as the US veterans of Sicily, Salerno and Anzio are known, look relaxed. Relieved.

Having had a decent night's sleep in a hotel, Charles, too, is feeling calm. He smiles to himself, takes a sip of black coffee that tastes of chlorine and then frowns. The caffeine has made his thumb start throbbing again. He searches for the bottle of antibiotics the doctor had given him, but cannot find it.

As his thoughts return to Dunkirk, his positive mood changes and he feels a tug of melancholy. This war has been grinding on for too long, he thinks. All those years of hoping, of convalescing, of painting, of running to stand still, of pretending to be things he isn't, of making promises to himself, of waiting to get here, gun in hand, within touching distance of Anselm . . . all these things have left him feeling exhausted and frustrated.

'We'll meet again, Don't know where, don't know when . . .'

Vera Lynn's words are drifting up from a radio somewhere and they seem to be directed at him. The sensuous memories they evoke flow unresisting through him, teasing him, weakening his resolve. All he has had to keep himself going is a photograph, and a couple of letters, and a few memories. And now all of these things have worn thin, to the point of irritation.

He is not irritated with Anselm but with himself, with his own company, with the crushing pointlessness of his personal crusade. He takes out Anselm's letters and starts to re-read them, only to be distracted by the sound of someone running. He looks up. A soldier has a jerrycan in each hand and, with an awkward, rocking motion like that of a penguin, is hurrying away, as best he can, from the scene of his crime. Two GIs notice what he is doing and sidle over to the fuel depot, apparently to do the same. An MP sees them and blows a whistle.

The rumours are true, then. The large German garrison at Marseille is putting up a token fight only. And because the Allied invasion plan assumed that German resistance would be tougher at the ports, lasting weeks rather than days, the immediate need for transport and fuel has been woefully underestimated. Already VI Corps has secured a beachhead twenty miles long and nine miles deep. And Charles has overheard two American officers talking about an advance on Grenoble by 'Arrowhead', the 36th Infantry Division. It has been so rapid that they have run out of fuel and have had to halt. The ships carrying new supplies, meanwhile, are not expected for several days.

At midday the American uniforms in the port are joined by Free French ones, a steady stream from the French First Army, which is only now, on D-Day plus one, coming ashore. Charles keeps scanning the faces to see if he can see Lehague.

Half an hour later he does see him, but coming from the opposite direction to the troops arriving from the azure water. He is wearing tank goggles over his kepi and is behind the steering wheel of a green, open-top jeep, one that has a large white encircled star on its bonnet. When he sees Charles he waves and, with a crunch of gears and a brake squeal, comes to a halt.

'*Bonjour*, Artist!' Lehague says. 'Had your fill of champagne yet?'

'The locals do seem pleased to see us.'

'Get in. *Vite!*' He taps the steering wheel. 'I have liberated this in the name of the French Republic.'

The two men look conspicuous as they join a convoy of ten-ton trucks, amphibious craft, ambulances and Sherman tanks leaving the town past the hanging baskets filled with Mediterranean flowers, past the blur of terracotta roofs, past the cannons that line the crumbling mellow stone of the Citadelle.

A French uniform. A British uniform. A stolen American jeep.

The chinstrap on Lehague's kepi is dangling and, when they swerve for potholes, it whips up like a spaniel's ear, making him look, for the first time since Charles met him, frivolous.

'So what's the plan?' Charles asks.

'I've done all I needed to do here. My priority as liaison now is to get to Nancy as quickly as I can. Try and keep up with the advance. You will join me for the ride, won't you?'

The pastel-coloured shutters on the tall seafront houses are being closed and the tricolours that were flapping lazily below the balconies are being gathered in. Siesta time. Charles breathes in deeply, enjoying the blue skies and the briny smell of the sea. His pleasure is short-lived. The bumps in the road jar and aggravate his thumb, making him curse under his breath each time they mount one.

As they head north-west towards Digne, they see evidence of the airborne assault that preceded the amphibious one: parachutes and gliders abandoned in meadows. And pushed to the sides of a lane lined with cypresses there are the parachute-borne dummies that were dropped by Allied planes, as well as tons of radar-obscuring chaff.

As they drive, Lehague points out with pride the sabotage work done by the partisans in the hours before the invasion: destroyed bridges and rail lines, telegraph poles blown in half, their wires tangled on the ground. There are also the vehicles which the retreating Germans abandoned as they ran out of fuel, their tyres shot or engines burned so that they cannot be used by the Americans. Some have careened over on their sides, or been tipped that way.

About thirty miles out of Saint-Tropez they see a column of hundreds of German prisoners, some wounded. They look old and tired: veterans, *Volksdeutsche*, relieved that the war for them is over.

Moving through agricultural land now, Charles takes in the threshing machines working in fields of wheat, and the dozens of dust-covered labourers stooking sheaves of straw. It strikes him as an incongruously bucolic sight in the middle of a war.

By the late afternoon, the convoy has slowed to a crawl as it negotiates narrow lanes flanked by high hedges. By nightfall it comes to a stop. Seeing the lights of a farmhouse, Lehague heads for it, cutting across a small vineyard. Charles waits in the jeep as Lehague strides up to the front door, knocks, enters. Five minutes later, he comes outside to inform Charles that they have beds for the night.

As they dine on bread and vegetable broth, and drink vinegary table wine, Charles enjoys listening to Lehague regale the farmer and his wife with stories of London. His French, he realizes with satisfaction, is just about good enough for him to keep up with the conversation.

The next morning they are woken at dawn by the sound of the convoy trundling past. While the farmer's wife changes the dressing on his thumb, Charles hears Lehague outside trying to get a signal on his wireless transceiver.

By the time Charles joins him, Lehague has packed the radio set away and is sharpening a double-edged commando dagger on a stone as he waits in the shade of an avocado tree. The dagger is twelve inches long and has a serrated edge and a black foil grip. Charles eyes it apprehensively as he lowers himself into the passenger side of the jeep. 'Any luck?' he asks.

'I could hear them,' Lehague says, slipping the dagger into a sheath strapped to his belt and thigh, 'but I'm not sure they could hear me. From what I could make out, the Germans are planning to withdraw as far as Lyon,

354

then make a stand there. They are calling in reinforcements from Strasbourg to the east. The Resistance are going to try and blow up the bridges to stop them.'

By driving at speed they catch up with the tail of the convoy within ten minutes, but feeling frustrated by its lumbering pace they decide to make their own way to Grenoble. Though all the signposts have been taken down, Charles tries to work out from their map which towns they bypass over the next five hours – Sisteron, Veynes, La Mure. He is starting to suspect that they are lost.

As they move up the Rhône valley they contemplate the rippling fields and huge skies. They also witness the damage caused by the roaming American fighters that have strafed the roads and bridges. Long German convoys have been destroyed and the entire zone is covered with a mass of burned vehicles, trains and the bloated corpses of cattle and horses. Lehague slows down when he sees a civilian dangling from a roadside tree like a piece of rotting fruit. 'Vichy,' he says with a shrug, before speeding away.

When next they stop for a break, an hour later, Charles records the sights he has seen in his sketchbook. While he does this, Lehague crumbles oatmeal blocks into water and cooks them over a biscuit tin filled with earth and soaked in petrol. When the porridge is ready he serves it with hardtack biscuits, powdered egg and margarine. They eat in silence using their hands and afterwards Lehague lights up a cigarette and slips some headphones on as he tunes in his transceiver. 'The Germans are in full retreat,' he announces excitedly, speaking too loudly. 'We're chasing them in a great arc. If we don't hurry up, the war will be over and we won't have fired a single damn bullet!'

About ten miles from Grenoble, the jeep begins to make a crunching noise, as if trying to clear its throat. 'Don't like the sound of that,' Lehague says. He pulls to the side of the road as the jeep lurches to a halt. He taps the fuel gauge. 'Empty.'

Charles lights a cigarette. 'What do we do?'

'We could wait here for the next convoy. See if anyone has any spare cans; which they won't have.' Lehague studies a map and takes a compass bearing. 'Do you fancy a walk? Grenoble isn't far.'

Charles looks up as he hears bombers droning high overhead. He shields his eyes and sees they are American B-24s leaving a trail of white vapour. 'Well, it looks like the war is that way,' he says, slinging the map tube containing his art materials over his shoulder.

A mile down the road they come to a fork. As Charles watches Lehague consult their map again and take a sighting on his compass, he feels a sense of camaraderie with him that he hasn't felt before. The diminutive Lehague seems to have grown in stature since returning to his homeland. His eagerness to fight the enemy is infectious.

'This way,' the Frenchman says, marching towards a hillside olive grove.

After about six miles, the conversation lulls as they fold into their own ruminations. Charles realizes he is getting blisters on his feet. His face feels sunburnt and he can see white lines of salt streaking his shirt. 'Can we stop for a moment,' he says. 'I think I have something in my boot.'

He sits on the verge, unlaces his boot and massages his toes.

'Why are you here?' Lehague says, with a quizzical tilt of his head. 'I mean, why really?'

'I told you, my friend is in the work camp in Alsace.'

'He must be a very dear friend.'

'He is.' Charles wants to change the subject. 'Sounds like they are having fun up in Paris. You must wish you were up there with them for the liberation.'

'I would rather be here in the south.'

'Are your family still in Nancy? Wife? Children?'

'My wife is dead. The Germans killed her. We didn't have any children.'

'I'm sorry.'

Lehague raises and lowers his hands. A few minutes later, as they are walking side by side, he adds: 'They tortured her.'

Charles cannot think of an appropriate response. 'I'm sorry,' he repeats.

After a further mile they see two old bicycles parked outside a house and look at one another. Five minutes later, as they are cycling along a narrow lane flanked by high hedges, the two look at each other again and start laughing. 'Is this how you imagined the invasion would be?' Charles asks.

'I feel like a naughty schoolboy,' Lehague says.

Charles hasn't heard his companion laugh before and the sound takes his mind off the purpose of his mission.

A mile further on, the hedges are replaced with fences. They are now cycling through rolling hills and lush pastureland dotted with grazing sheep, but there is still no sign of the convoy. Charles squints into the sun. He then notices up ahead what look like two giant grizzly bears standing on their hind legs in a frozen clinch.

As they get closer they see it is two French half-tracks that have reared up in an explosion and, with each supporting the weight of the other, they have been welded together as they burned. The rubber in their caterpillar tracks has melted. Wisps of smoke are still rising from it.

Charles and Lehague look at one another again as they dismount their bikes.

Lehague takes the safety catch off his Sten gun as he treads carefully around the side of the vehicles. He stops and, as Charles catches up with him, he sees why. The carbonized corpses of the crew are hanging down, their skulls black, their grins grotesque.

The stench of scorched metal is oppressive, but it is the smell of burnt hair and fat that makes Charles gag. He touches the scar tissue on his cheek as he looks down at what appears to be a beanbag lying on the running board. It is another body, this one with its head crushed from ear to jaw. One of his legs has been rammed through the shattered glass of the windshield; the other has been lopped off at the thigh and has come to rest at a right angle to his torso, as if placed there meticulously. He has a fat-lipped wound in his side and his intestines are spilling from it like twisted water balloons.

Lehague taps Charles on the shoulder and says: 'Binoculars.'

Charles removes the binoculars he has around his neck and hands them over. Lehague trains them on something he has seen in a nearby field. He starts walking carefully in that direction, assuming a crouching position and raising his hand as an instruction to Charles not to follow him. He does anyway and soon sees what Lehague has seen. About two hundred yards away there are three men, French soldiers, kneeling on the grass in a semicircle, their heads bowed as if in prayer. When they are fifty yards away, it becomes clear that they are dead and have been propped up in that position on their rifles.

Lehague comes to within five yards of them before stopping and paling in horror. Once he is alongside him, Charles follows his gaze. The dead men have had their genitals sawn off and placed on their own tongues like communion wafers. Flies are crawling over their papery cheeks.

'Waffen-SS,' Lehague says.

Charles cannot find his voice for a moment. Eventually he asks hoarsely: 'How do you know?'

'It's what they do. They want everyone to know it was them.' Lehague rolls the nearest body on to its side and attempts to straighten out its legs. Rigor mortis prevents him. Instead he removes as delicately as he can the genitals from the mouth of the dead soldier and places them back where they belong before tugging up his trousers and attempting to wipe the dark caked-on blood from his mouth. Charles does the same for

359

the second one while Lehague moves on to the third.

'We should bury them,' Charles says.

'With what?' Lehague heads back to the road. 'Come on. Let's try and find a farmhouse before it gets dark.'

Charles takes off his backpack, unstraps his easel and throws it away. He picks up one of the French clip-fed MAS-36 carbine rifles instead and, slinging it over his shoulder, removes the magazines from the other two rifles, stuffing them in his pocket. He buckles his pack again and hefts it on to his shoulders before breaking into a jog to catch up with Lehague.

For the next half-hour, as they cycle down the road in silence, they do not encounter any traffic, though Lehague keeps looking over his shoulder as if he has heard vehicles approaching. Eventually he stops and raises his hand. 'Listen,' he whispers.

Unable to hear anything, Charles pulls a puzzled face. He is conscious of the rifle strap chafing his shoulder.

'Singing,' Lehague says, leading the way off the road again and heading for a nearby hill. By the time he has reached the top of it, the singing has stopped. He raises the binoculars to his eyes and studies the landscape in a 360-degree sweep. He stops, adjusts the focus and, handing the binoculars to Charles, says: 'There.'

Rising from a copse about a quarter of a mile away is a thin trail of smoke.

'You think it's them?'

'Let's take a closer look.'

They move in a crouching position at first and, when they are on a knoll halfway to the wood, they get down and crawl. They can hear the singing again and can make out that the voices are German. 'I can see four of them,' Lehague says. 'And no sentry.'

Once he has adjusted the focus on his binoculars, Charles sees them, four figures drinking from the necks of bottles as they sit around a campfire. Three are wearing camouflage, one a leather trench coat. All four have their tunics unbuttoned. One is wearing a black field cap with what looks like the *Totenkopf* above the scalloped front on the turn-up. But he cannot be sure. Another is wearing a French kepi. A trophy. 'Are they SS?'

'Tank crew is my guess. SS Panzer Division. I think they might be deserters.'

'I think they might be drunk.'

Lehague cocks his Sten gun and, nodding at the rifle in Charles's hand, whispers: 'Do you know how to use that?'

Charles nods.

Lehague mouths the words 'cover me'. As he crawls forward, Charles pulls back the bolt on his rifle as quietly as he can and aims it at the nearest of the Germans. They are close enough to smell the woodsmoke.

By the time Lehague has taken cover – behind a tall tree with knotty roots on the edge of the wood – it is dusk and the four Germans are almost silhouetted against the flames of their campfire. They are still singing and taking swigs from the bottles they are passing between themselves. Three of their rifles are arranged in a tripod, their muzzles together. There are

361

four empty bottles on their sides, one of them broken. The fire is crackling and sparking as they stir it with sticks. Though they are unshaven, they look young, teenagers. Their heads are shaved at the sides.

One stands and walks towards the tree behind which Lehague is concealed. Wondering whether the Frenchman has seen him, Charles adjusts the sights on his rifle by a couple of clicks and takes a bead on the German. Though he did some rifle training in the RAF, he has never killed a man before, and the gun feels heavy and dull in his hands. A trickle of sweat stings his eyes and he rubs them with his sleeve. He can feel the knots in his back and taste the hot bile in his throat, the sour tumult of his gut. A mosquito is singing around his ears and neck and, as he waits for it to bite, he feels his awareness of his surroundings intensifying: the snapping of twigs, the rustle of leaves. He tries to remember if he has pulled back the bolt on his rifle. Does it have a safety catch? He looks up and, for a panicked moment, realizes he can no longer see the German.

Then a man's shape looms up. His steps are faltering, as if he is unsure where the ground is. When he reaches the tree he unbuttons his flies and, swaying slightly, starts to urinate. Charles watches as Lehague slips his commando dagger from its sheath, stands and, in a single fluid movement, lunges at the German, covering his mouth with one hand while stabbing the blade firmly into his gut with the other. He twists it as he withdraws it before stabbing him twice more in quick succession.

As if helping an elderly patient, Lehague supports the

362

man as he sinks to his knees. He then dips back behind the tree. Charles watches as the German remains poised, encircling his wounds with his hands, as if wanting to draw attention to them. His eyes then roll back in his head and he falls forward with a groan. When the others hear the dull slap of his face hitting the tree root, they look up and, no doubt thinking he has passed out from drinking, cheer.

When the remaining three start singing again, Lehague emerges from behind the tree and, crunching pine cones underfoot, advances at walking pace towards them, his Sten gun cocked at his hip. One looks up with confusion in his eyes and stops singing. A second later, as he fumbles for his rifle, Lehague shoots him with a sustained burst that produces flame-licks from the muzzle of his gun. In their shock, the other two raise their hands.

Charles gets to his feet and runs into the wood. He then stands guard over the prisoners while Lehague rummages in his haversack. When he produces a length of rope, Charles wonders for a moment if he intends to lynch the men, and is relieved when he cuts off two lengths instead and uses them to tie the prisoners' hands behind their backs.

Lehague makes them kneel and studies them for a moment before kicking the nearest on the shoulder, forcing him to roll over on his side and knock the other one off balance too. He lifts them up again by their hair and circles them.

'Parlez-vous français?'

The men do not answer. With their heads bowed they

look like errant schoolboys awaiting a caning outside a headmaster's office. One of them spits to the side.

'Charles, ask them if they attacked the French convoy.'

'*Habt ihn den Französichen Konvoi angegriffen?*'

When the men still do not answer, the major picks up the kepi one of them had been wearing and, with his other hand, grabs the nearest German by the hair, raising his head so he is forced to stare at the cap. He then tosses it on the ground, unbuckles his revolver from its holster and, as he walks behind the two men, slowly and deliberately loads its chamber with six metallic clicks. He cocks it and presses the barrel to the back of the first prisoner's head.

'No!' Charles says, levelling his rifle at Lehague.

Without looking over at Charles, Lehague says: 'This does not concern you, Artist.'

When Charles does not lower his gun, Lehague looks at him. The prisoner kneeling nearest them turns his head towards Charles and looks up as well. His eyes are cold and feral. There is no fear in them. Instead his expression is serious and thoughtful, as if in deep concentration. He then snaps his head so that he is facing forward again, composing himself for what is to come.

Without taking his eyes off Charles, Lehague squeezes the trigger. A shot leaves deafness in its wake and the young German slumps forward, his body in brief convulsion. There is a neat hole in the back of his head. Smoke wisps out of it followed by blood that pulses softly into his hair. The other prisoner does not look at his fallen comrade, but he is shivering now. Lehague takes a step towards him and, still staring at

Charles, pulls the trigger again. The second German falls sideways on top of the first and the two look like they are children cuddling up to one another in their sleep.

Lehague walks up to Charles and puts a hand on his shoulder. He then crouches down and stokes the fire. A smell of blood cloys the damp night air for a moment. Charles is still staring at the bodies, awed at how lives can end so politely, with so little fuss.

Rumours are beginning to swirl around the Natzweiler-Struthof concentration camp like lampshades and chairs in a tornado. The Americans have invaded southern France. They are about to meet the Allied forces advancing down from the north. They will be here soon, to liberate the camp and punish the hated enemy.

But, for Anselm at least, there are worrying signs and portents also. Something has happened to the Commandant. He hasn't been seen for weeks. Summoned to Berlin? Sent to the Eastern Front? Arrested? Promoted? Who knows? Perhaps he is *kaput*. The Commandant had intrigued him and chilled him in equal measure. He had grown used to his fearful presence, had come to admire his strength, his Teutonic dignity. Without him he has no protector.

His replacement is about to arrive and he has orders to oversee the evacuation of the entire camp. There is to be a forced march across the German border to Dachau. Only the sick will be left behind.

Anselm tries to summon Charles's face, but it has hardened and dried. Cracks have begun to appear across its surface. The sensual lips are turned downward. The glitter in the eyes has faded and the wide brow now suggests the skull beneath. It has become a stranger's face.

Yet he still feels in his gut that Charles will come for him, as if it is ordained.

He also feels that the resentment that has been building up among his fellow inmates over the past few months – at his preferential treatment, at his collaboration with the enemy – will surely erupt soon. The camp feels a colder and darker place. He knows revenge from the other prisoners is coming because of the space they leave around him. No one will meet his eye. He is toxic. Contaminated. He has never felt more vulnerable.

It happens at night. They come out of the gloom without a word, and as he feels something heavy – an iron bar perhaps – across his back, he sags to his knees with a grunt. The heavy object is smashing into his mouth now, breaking his teeth and splitting his lips like cooked sausages. Kicks and punches follow. A clog drives hard into his stomach, draws back and strikes again in the same place, pushing the breath from his lungs and causing a purple-pink bloom of pain to open up around his heart. He hears his own nose break with a pop. Then the clean snap of bone.

There must be a dozen of them. Fleetingly, he can see the prisoner's stripes on their arms as he curls up into a ball. As he cannot will the pain away, he absorbs it. A fist hits hard into the bone below his eye. The toe of a boot tears the cartilage in his knee. There is a taste of iron in his mouth. He knows they will not stop now until he is dead, and he prays that this release will come sooner rather than later.

III

FOR NINE DAYS, THE PANZERKORPS, UNDER THE COMMAND OF the monocle-wearing General Heinrich von Lüttwitz, have been tenacious in their defence of Nancy. Though they are outnumbered, they still hold all the approaches to the Moselle, the river dividing the city, and, thanks to this advantage, they have managed to repel two crossing attempts by the US XII Corps, one in daylight, the other at night.

The Americans are under the command of Manton S. Eddy, a major general who favours round, metal-framed glasses and a pistol worn in a shoulder holster on the outside of his bomber jacket. He has ordered a change of tactic. There is to be an encircling manoeuvre with simultaneous attacks on the north and south of the city. The Battle of Nancy, he has predicted, will be over by the end of the day and leaflets are now being dropped by the USAAF over the town. They invite the Germans to agree to an honourable surrender.

It had been hoped that, for symbolic purposes once more, the 1st Free French Division could liberate the town, as they did Lyon a fortnight earlier in the balmy end days of August. It had, after all, been two French officers who, for the benefit of the news cameras, met thirteen miles west of Dijon three days earlier on 11 September: one representing Operation Overlord, the campaign in the north, the other representing Operation Dragoon, the south. Their handshake, as their jeeps met and they leaned over their bonnets, closed the last escape route for the Germans in the south and west of France.

But the Free French soldiers, along with the Forces Françaises de l'Intérieur, as the Resistance has now officially been renamed, are pinned down on a mist-shrouded hillside overlooking one of Nancy's main bridges. And the sun has gone down.

For the past three weeks Major Lehague and Charles have been attached to them. And as the American artillery bombardment of the past hour is answered by a salvo from the German self-propelled guns positioned either side of the bridge under camouflage nets, Charles wishes he were anywhere else on earth.

The fury of the shelling is cold and mechanized, and he can feel in his bones the intense shock waves it is causing in the ground around him. As the barrage creeps closer, he finds himself instinctively hardening his muscles in an attempt to defy the jagged, burning teeth of the shrapnel. The shells are like molten furies screaming through the night air, turning it liquid, sucking away their very oxygen. When he finds himself covered in half an inch of soil and branches, he crawls to the twisted body of a nearby French soldier and takes his helmet from him. Half the man's face is flapping off the bone.

After crawling back to his foxhole, Charles takes off his beret, stuffs it in his tunic and puts the helmet on, leaving the chinstrap dangling loose. The wet, splintered smell of fir bark is being diluted by the less sharp smell of blood.

Some of the French militia around them who have practised combat only with blank ammunition are now learning something which Charles has already learned: that you cannot train for the noise on a battlefield; that it paralyses thought. They are finding it impossible to communicate, even with sign language. One man in a trench about five yards away is curled into a foetal position and is sobbing.

During the bombing raid on Biggin Hill, Charles had wondered why strangers were trying to kill him. Why they hated him. Why it felt so personal. But now, as he hears an explosion so loud and tumescent it seems to fill every atom of his body, he feels more composed. Either the next salvo will leave me vaporized, he thinks, in which case I won't know anything about it, or it will leave me injured. And if you are going to get hit, it is best to be hit by hot mortar fragments, because they sear the wound shut.

The next sound gets inside him, making his teeth ache and carrying down to the balls of his feet. It is a screech of metal tearing through metal: a tank exploding. Realizing from the pungent smell that the man in the foetal position has emptied his bowels, Charles looks up to see that a shard of shrapnel has torn his skull in half. He is dead but is still holding his brains in with his hand, in a gesture that looks almost apologetic.

After five minutes, the German bombardment ends and, from behind his position, Charles hears the hollow, answering crump of a French howitzer. Feels its fearful concussion. He watches the soaring plunge of the shell through the night sky and listens to its downward whistle. As he thinks about the Germans it has landed on, a strange primordial ecstasy stirs his limbs for a moment before leaving numbness in its wake.

The smoke clears and he looks down at Nancy once again as it burns. In the fields directly below him he can see the silhouettes of cattle stampeding ahead of the flames now engulfing two Panther tanks. Charles watches as a bomb bursts, a yellow tongue leaps and a third Panther is flipped over on its back like a turtle.

Another bombing run is under way and the planes are being caught in the sweeping arcs of searchlights. Charles sees the bombs oscillate as they fall. A building shudders and looks as if it is about to collapse but then settles back into place. Another does fall and Charles watches as it blocks the narrow street below, sending up a cloud of brick dust. The masonry produces swirling patterns that are like abstractions. German stretcher-bearers emerge covered in a pale grey film. An impression of rain is given by the molten lead dripping from the roofs, and then the city disappears once more behind black smoke.

Charles fingers the magazine on his carbine, removes it, clicks it into position again, and points the muzzle in the direction of the bridge. As sweat trickles down his back, he scans the German lines for signs of white flags. Why aren't the mad bastards surrendering?

On the contrary, when a flare goes up, the Germans counter-attack, their bodies seemingly frozen as though in a stroboscope. The French soldiers around him send them back with rapid volleys, their red tracer bullets like luminous blood in the darkness. Once more Charles's gun feels too heavy in his hand. He isn't sure he can persuade his muscles to pull the trigger.

He becomes conscious of Lehague's short frame further along their foxhole. As he listens to the Frenchman shouting out orders, he recalls his words in the wood. This does not concern you, Artist. Had he been right? No. He now realizes he has to make this his concern, his fight. He has to earn the right to get Anselm back. If he can help win this battle, he tells himself, hasten its end even by a minute, he will be entitled to see Anselm again. And if he dies, he will ask that his heart be cut out and sent to Anselm. Who should he tell? Lehague? No, he can't do that. Lehague would despise him if he knew his secret.

He recalls a line in the marriage service of the *Book of Common Prayer* which speaks of 'the dreadful day of judgment when the secrets of all hearts shall be disclosed'. Realizing there is no one he can give this last instruction to, he curses. Society demands that he take his secret to the grave.

He hears in his head now the voice of the group captain at his court martial. 'Consider yourself lucky to get away with a dishonourable discharge. A hundred years ago a man found guilty of gross indecency would have been hanged.'

The thought sends electric wakening shudders

through his body and he now feels indignation mount-ing. Finally a cold anger tightens the muscles in his neck and jaw. As a German machine gun shrieks and spits out a vindictive white light like a blowtorch he thinks: why are these bastards preventing me from reaching Anselm? I have come too far; survived too many injuries to allow them to get in my way now. He winces as dirt snaps at his skin. He then becomes aware of a dull ache in his thumb. Has he been hit? No, he realizes the ache has been building insidiously for days.

Charles now sees a human torch emerge from the flames below and stagger across the bridge. A German. The Resistance fighters to Charles's left laugh when they see him. Charles puts the stock of his rifle to his shoulder, takes aim and, squeezing his trigger, feels the rifle buck. He then sees his bullet ricochet off the iron bridge about five feet behind the burning man. Charles adjusts his sight by two clicks and fires again. This time the man falls to the ground.

As daylight breaks, there is an order to fix bayonets. The Free French are about to attack. Charles can hear the scrape of metal as the bayonets are attached in fox-holes along the line. He looks around him and sees that, in the night, the trees they have been sheltering under have been stripped of their leaves and their trunks are blackened. Most of them have had their branches sheared away.

The act of fixing bayonets will, he knows, send a signal to the Germans that the French are willing to kill at close quarters to get their country back, and with any luck it will sap their morale.

He watches how Lehague attaches his. The MAS-36 carries a seventeen-inch spike bayonet reversed in a tube below the barrel. A spring plunger is pressed to release it. It is then free to be pulled out, turned round, and fitted back into its receptacle. Charles attaches his.

A whistle blows and three or four hundred men rise from their foxholes and charge down the cratered hill. Charles is up and on his feet without thinking. He shouts as he runs, stopping every few yards to work the bolt action of his rifle. His movements are reflexive, his knuckles white. As the smell of gunpowder, oil and hot metal eddies through his senses, he is no longer conscious of where he ends and the weapon begins. Its heat is his heat.

PART SIX

I

Alsace. Present day. Summer. A year and a quarter after Edward's release

FOR A FEW SECONDS, AS SHE RISES LIKE A BUBBLE TO HER OWN surface, Hannah does not know where she is. She has been dreaming about her mother; that they were walking together on a beach talking about . . . something. She cannot now recall what, but this ritual is familiar. For these confused moments, her mother is alive, then sentience returns and reality enters her bloodstream like a trickle of ice water. Without any fuss, her mother dies again. Alive one second, then, with a hiss of steel being tempered, dead the next.

Through the bowed curve of the window, milky light is now slanting in. She had forgotten to close the curtain and it is this, the rising sun, that has woken her. Wrapping a sheet around herself, she crosses the room and opens the window wider. Though the courtyard is immediately below, she nevertheless has a good view of the garden from here. Or at least she will as soon as she puts her contacts in. She finds them

377

in her wash bag and tips back her head to fit them.

Below her she now sees small sections of lawn covered in a mosaic of cobwebs beaded with dew. A marzipan smell of meadowsweet is rising in the air. She pulls on some shorts and a blue T-shirt with a large peace sign on it, and creeps down the stairs so as not to disturb her father. His door is ajar and she can hear the shallow breaths of sleep coming from within.

In the kitchen, she flicks on the lights, only to fuse that part of the house. On top of the fridge, she notices, is a torch and, after testing it, she steps tentatively down the stairs to the wine cellar. The fuse box is mounted on the wall here and, after tripping the only switch that is down, the lights come back on. She tries the brass bulb of the door handle at the far end of the room, thinking it might be an alternative way of getting to the garden, but it is locked.

Back in the kitchen, she dustily snaps a breadstick, pours herself an orange juice and takes it out into the garden to drink. As she walks barefoot towards the river, her hair loose down her back, her eye is caught by the shapeless, wavering flight of some swallows. As they spiral and stall, their tails fine-tuning their balance, they look like windblown paper.

There is a fork in the river where the water becomes shallower and the mud on the edges is turning pale grey as it dries and cracks in the early morning sun. The swallows are skimming the surface here like flat stones thrown by children. As she sits down to watch them, she feels at peace.

Later, when she sees her father limping towards her,

his suede shoes wet with dew, she realizes she has lost track of time. He is unshaven. The cuffs of his shirt are undone. This is good, she thinks. He is relaxing, too.

She pats the ground next to her. 'Look at these swallows.'

'Are they after the dragonflies?'

'Midges, I think. Watch.' They move their heads as the swallows jink back and forth over the river, grazing both air and water. When they touch the surface they cause explosions of shifting colour. Hannah's attention is transferred to the heavily veined pouches of an orchid a few feet away. She crawls over to it and examines its downy smooth petals. They seem to pout in the direction of its own tautly curved stem. When she looks up, her father is staring at her. There is something in his eyes, an energy and vitality she hasn't seen before.

She points at some nearby vegetation. 'Know what that is?'

Edward shrugs.

'Honeysuckle and bindweed. See how the bindweed grows anti-clockwise and the honeysuckle clockwise, so the two entwine, weed and flower.'

'Poetic.'

Hannah nods. 'Yeah, poetic.'

After a couple of minutes, she gets to her feet and crooks her arm so that her father can link it with his. They walk slowly, out of step, and come to some wild thyme over-canopied with sweet musk roses. She takes a deep breath. 'Can you believe this place?' she says.

'It's quite something.'

'Some people live such privileged lives, don't they?'

Hannah says. 'Private jets. Houses in different countries. He lives like a pharaoh, this guy.'

'I found a framed cover of the *Economist* in my bedroom, put away at the back of a cupboard, face down. It's got this picture of a man with long white hair and fine features. Serious-looking. The coverline reads: "Meet Germany's answer to George Soros." I guess it must be him.' Edward stops walking and pulls Hannah to a stop, too. 'Look!'

A few yards in front of them is a buddleia that appears to be floating. A cloud of butterflies is moving slowly and silently around it, like confetti on a breeze.

After contemplating them for a moment, Hannah says, 'I was thinking of doing some painting. Will you sit for me?'

'Sure.'

Edward follows his daughter back to the house, walking a few paces behind her, and when he sees her struggling with a large bag he takes it from her, shouldering its strap so that he can carry a kitchen chair with both hands. He sets the chair down under the bough of a chestnut tree and hands over the bag. Hannah unzips it and pulls out some brushes, a palette and what looks like a fold-up music stand. She opens it and takes some paper from a tube. Once she has pinned this to a board, she half fills a jar with water from the river. 'Did you ever talk to Grandpa about art?'

'Not really,' Edward says. 'Wish I had.'

Hannah pulls back her hair, twists it into a casual knot and begins sketching. A minute later she cocks her head and, with the side of her thumb, smudges a pencil line she has drawn. 'I never get bored with observing faces,' she says. 'Each one is a unique and complex pattern of planes, shapes and colours. It's, like, such an intimate thing. Studying the subject's face tells you so much about their experiences and character.'

'What do you see with me, Frejya?'

'You called me Frejya.'

Edward massages the sides of his head. 'Sorry.'

'It's OK.' She thinks for a moment. 'I see someone who is haunted.'

Edward sighs and runs his hand through his hair.

Hannah sketches for a few minutes then looks up. 'Do you want to talk about it?'

'Talk about what? Your mother?'

'Yeah.'

'Not really. Do you?'

'Not really. Tell me about the cave instead. What did you miss most?'

A look of puzzlement clouds Edward's face. 'Why do you suppose I was released after so long? Niall gave me his theory but . . .'

'No idea. Perhaps we'll never know.' Hannah becomes distracted by the whooshing sound of a coach passing on the road beyond the garden wall, its blue roof blurring for an instant between the trees. 'That's the third this morning.'

'You hold your pencil in your fist, like Grandpa used to. When you draw.'

'Do I?' She looks at her hand. 'Yes, I suppose I do.'

Beyond the wall another coach drives past. 'That's the fourth,' Hannah says. She turns the board round. 'There.'

'That was quick.' Edward walks over. His eyebrows lift and he nods judiciously as he takes the sketch in. 'It's good. Very good. I recognize myself, which is more than I do when I look in the mirror. Can I keep it?'

'Only if you make lunch. I think I might use it as a preliminary study for an oil painting. And hey . . .'

'What?'

'Good talking.'

Edward ruffles Hannah's hair, a fatherly gesture that seems to take them both by surprise.

Having drunk one bottle of wine with lunch they feel frivolous and open a second which they drink as they explore the house, opening doors and cupboards. 'Look at this,' Edward says, pulling out a drawer. Headlines about the Taliban attack on his convoy are yellowing on the newspaper lining. 'I guess our host really was following my story.'

Hannah studies them with unfocused eyes, as though looking at a space a few feet beyond the paper.

Edward is now flicking through some old album covers. '*Cabaret*. He's a Liza Minnelli fan. Oh and look, he's got *Revolver*.'

'Germans like the Beatles?'

'Hamburg was where they properly came together as a band. And have you seen this?' Edward is peering at a red-leather hand-stitched football in a glass case. 'Looks like the 1966 World Cup football. A replica, I presume.'

At one end of the bookcase there is a lamp with a shade made from bruised, almost transparent leather and at the other is a chessboard. Edward examines one of the pieces, a bishop, holding it up to the light.

'Look what I've found,' Hannah calls from an adjoining room.

Edward follows the sound of her voice and finds her standing in the cinema with its dozen deep and comfortable-looking seats. On the back wall are metal containers of film. 'Interesting film library, don't you think?' She trails her finger along the titles. '*Schindler's List. The Pianist. Downfall. Escape from Sobibor. The Night Porter. Triumph of the Will.* Don't you think it odd?'

'What?'

'The films. And the books that have been left lying around for us to find.'

'You think it's deliberate?' Edward picks up a book. '*Das Rosa Hakenkreuz.* The Pink Swastika . . . See if I have any German left.' As he reads the blurb on the back, his lips move. 'According to this, one of the administrators at Treblinka was gay. He had a harem of Jewish boys dressed like little princes.' He arches an eyebrow. 'There were quite a few gay men in the SS, it says here. It was to do with the Spartan way they trained. All that bonding and male nudity got to them. But any who were caught were automatically condemned to death.'

'Those Nazis,' Hannah says with a shake of her head as she drains her glass of wine. 'They were such . . . Nazis.'

Edward taps the spines of the books on the shelf. Half of them are in German. There is a collection, in English, of Byron's poetry, along with anthologies of Coleridge, Keats and Shelley. Edward opens the Keats. 'I always liked the Romantic poets.'

'Weren't they all obsessed with suicide?'

'Obsessed with *memento mori*,' he corrects. He reads from the page. '"She dwells with beauty – Beauty that must die; / And Joy, whose hand is ever at his lips / Bidding adieu; and aching Pleasure nigh." I seduced your mother with Keats . . . Think I'm going to take this out into the garden to read . . . I might try writing something as well. By the way, I couldn't find the notebook I was using in London. You didn't see it lying around the house anywhere, did you?'

'Where did you see it last?'

'I think it was in the bathroom.'

Hannah's brow creases.

'What?'

'Oh nothing,' she says. 'I'm sure it will turn up.'

'Why did you frown?'

'It was just that that journalist was up there. Was there anything compromising in it?'

Edward chews his lip. 'It was a draft of . . . It's not important. I have a spare notebook.'

While Hannah goes up for a siesta, Edward heads outside wearing a straw fedora with a red and yellow MCC band. A hosepipe, demented by the pressure of water, is snaking across the lawn. It must be part of the sprinkler system, he figures, come unattached. He follows it to a tap on the wall, switches it off, then heads for an oak tree by the riverbank and sits under its boughs, finding a comfortable position with his back to its trunk and his legs dangling over one of several coiling roots. He opens his new notebook, unscrews his fountain pen and, savouring the warmth infusing his bones, writes down a line of poetry that has been on the edge of his mind all day.

He looks at it and sighs. If he is going to write he must write properly, at a table. There is one in the ruined temple, he recalls. That will be a better location.

That evening, while he looks around the house for the volume of poetry he is reading, Edward leaves the brass taps running on a claw-footed bath made from a single piece of granite. When he returns, he sees Hannah has climbed into it. She has her back to him and, with her hair coiled up, she looks more like her mother than ever – more Nordic, like a vein of sunlight refracted through snow. When he eventually moves, Hannah hears him, turns her head and smiles. Her slightly gapped teeth are bone white.

'Beat you to it,' she says.

'Leave the water in when you're finished.' As he walks back downstairs he recalls that that was what he used to say to Frejya. He recalls too how much he used to enjoy the thought that it was her water he would be slipping into.

He realizes now that his memories of Frejya have not receded with time, but somehow grown more vivid. He surprises himself by also realizing that he feels closer to his wife now than at any time since they parted. It is as if, through Hannah, she is coming back to life. He is falling in love again, with a ghost.

A few minutes later, Edward is carrying empty wine bottles to the recycling bin in the kitchen. Finding Hannah's iPad, he looks at the BBC news website. There is still no sign of an end to the Norwegian volcano's eruption. A photograph shows a mushroom cloud of ash. The Romantic poets would have approved, he thinks. Man humbled by the violence of nature.

He clicks on a report about the President of the United States announcing a phased withdrawal of troops from Afghanistan. The tide of war is ebbing, the President says, and it is time to focus on nation-building. Edward finds himself wondering once more why he was released. Niall's explanation seems too neat. Too easy. He reads on. 'Taliban rules out UN talks.' A statement from them declares that they believe they have the 'upper hand' and are certain that they are 'winning'.

'Anything interesting?' Hannah asks as she saunters barefoot down the stairs wearing her mother's dressing gown and towelling her hair.

'The Taliban are winning in Afghanistan, apparently. Did you leave the water in?'

'All yours.'

With a shiver, Edward realizes that this is what Frejya used to say when she vacated the bath. All yours.

Hannah slumps into a chair by the fireplace, puffs out her cheeks, exhales loudly. She can feel the tiny pin-points of sweat on the sides of her nose and on her upper lip. Wiping them away with a finger and thumb she sits up again, reaches forward to the coffee table in front of her and picks up a German interiors magazine from a pile. She flicks through it distractedly before using it to fan herself. After a few seconds she tosses it on to the cushion beside her and sighs again, a throatier noise. Remembering an electric fan she has seen in the kitchen, she fetches it and plugs it in, directing it at the sofa. She feels restless. There is a sensation like butterflies in her belly, yet she doesn't feel nervous. It is more . . . excitement. Sensitivity.

She picks up her lighter and, as she taps it on the armrest, her eyes flit around the room before fixing on the ornate clock on the chimneypiece. How long has it been stopped? She rises to her feet. Behind it she finds a key, but it is obviously not the one for winding the clock.

She walks from room to room, trying to locate Walser's office. Unable to find it she returns to the drawing room and looks under cabinets and behind paintings and tapestries, unsure what for. A wall safe perhaps. By pressing with her foot she tests the floorboards. Taps oak panels to see if they are hollow. Nothing.

Her mobile pings and she returns to the sofa. A text from Martin Cullen. She smiles as she types a reply: 'Nothing to report so far. Over and out x'. When she puts the phone back on the table she sees the magazine she had been flicking through earlier was covering a notebook. She opens it. Written in a sloping hand so neat it looks like calligraphy are lines from a poem.

' "*Of peace and pity fell like dew / On flowers half dead – thy lips did meet / Mine tremblingly; thy dark eyes threw / Their soft persuasion on my brain.*" – *Shelley*'

She wonders if this is her father's handwriting. It seems so elegant and Victorian. How strange, she thinks, that she doesn't even know what her own father's handwriting looks like. She turns the page and finds more writing, prose this time. Realizing this is his memoir, she looks towards the stairs and listens. Satisfied that he is still in the bath, she begins to read.

Sometimes a song would enter my head and not leave. 'What's The Story Morning Glory?' was one. It would ~~grown~~ grow louder and louder. As I lurched around the cave like a drunk, shouting at the dark and jumping at imagined shapes, I tried to rid myself of the song, and then it would disappear to be replaced with a nothingness so dense it left me questioning whether I could get through the next five minutes, whether there would be enough left in my head.

Hannah feels a chill pass up her nape to the base of her skull. She looks at the stairs again, not wanting to disturb the air by breathing. Her eyes fall on the page again, hungrily now.

I would have vivid fever dreams about Frejya that would leave me confused about the difference between being asleep and awake. They were not erotic in content – I had long since been rendered impotent, even in my dreams – but sometimes, when I woke from them, I would recall how she used to touch my shoulder in the night. Even there in that cave I would sometimes wake to the sound of her voice saying: 'You were dreaming, Ed.'

I craved conversation. The monotonous repetition of my own ~~thinking~~ thoughts exhausted me. But the darkness offered no stimulation, nothing to feed my imagination. I no longer worried that the world outside the cave might have forgotten me, because I ~~had forgotten~~ was forgetting myself. I could spend hours trying to remember details about my life: my age, my phone number, even my own name.

As the solitary confinement ate into me I would talk to myself and fixate on the things I missed. A chair. If only I had a chair to sit on I could feel like a man again. A candle and a box of matches. A book. If only I had a book.

Concentrating on one thing at a time ~~sometimes~~ helped me push away the emptiness and silence of the cave. But half-remembered lines of poetry left me frustrated and ~~I couldn't~~ often I couldn't work out whether some poem circulating in my head was one I had made up or one I had learned. I would fantasize about having a pen and paper to write it down.

At one point I attempted a hunger strike, but the stomach cries out to be fed and this, I sometimes thought, was what I had been reduced to: a stomach without a brain. An empty stomach and an open mouth. (MORE ON THIS??? TOO UPSETTING FOR H TO READ???)

~~When weakened by lack of food I sometimes hallucinated and imagined that I was sharing the cave with . . . some-thing, a presence. Not malign necessarily. Sometimes I can hear it purring throatily, like~~

At other times, when I thought I might have managed a new idea, I would find myself turning to tell someone, only to be reminded of my solitude. My memory was growing slack, my emotions loose. I realized familiar faces were turn-ing blank. I could no longer remember ~~properly~~ what Hannah looked like, not properly. I could see her hair but not the details of her face. Even Frejya was becoming a ghost.

Slowly closing the notebook, as if fearing to disturb the words any more than she already has, Hannah shakes her head. Having often tried to imagine how her father had coped in that cave, without light, without conversation, without love, she now realizes that he barely had. She is about to place the notebook back under the magazine when she hesitates. Listens. Her father is still in the bath. She opens it again.

The daily arrival of food created a brief pool of fuzzy light in which I was able to mark off the weeks on the ground, six vertical lines crossed with one diagonal, scratched into the ~~ground~~ stone. After a few months of doing that I ran out of space, but it didn't matter because I had other ways of measuring time, such as the length of my nails and my beard. It was so long it reached below my ribs.

Night-time was detectable by a slight drop in temperature. The mornings, ~~meanwhile~~, I could sometimes work out from the sound of a cockerel crowing, or a muffled call to prayers ~~somewhere~~ in the distance. Allahu Akbar. This was usually followed by the bubble of a kettle 'upstairs', walkie-talkies being tested, blankets being rolled up and, finally, a campfire being stamped out.

I could even work out the seasons. In the summer the dripping water stopped. In the winter it froze. One ~~year~~ winter I worked out how I might get some warm clothes. There was a guard ~~nicknamed~~ I had nicknamed Brains, because he had a dull, bovine look about him. As well as being ~~a moron~~ stupid, Brains was also sadistic. He liked to spit on me and sometimes he would amuse himself by pulling the trigger on an empty gun, laughing to himself when it clicked. It was Brains I ~~had~~ decided to trick.

Knowing that Muslims were offended by nudity, I removed my tattered clothes and, when the boulder was rolled back and I saw Brains ~~on guard duty~~, I stood directly in the light

390

spilling through the hole. It had the desired effect. After curs-
ing at me to put ~~the~~ my clothes back on, and making a show
of clicking fresh bullets into the magazines of his AK-47,
Brains threw down a shalwar kaneez (sp??), a sheepskin
jerkin and a pakul (sp?) for my head. A small victory. As I
put them on, I found myself laughing ~~for the first time since~~
~~my arrival in Afghanistan~~.

(MORE DETAILS ABOUT THE GUARDS HERE???)

While thinking of Frejya gave me strength, thinking of
Hannah weakened me, making me slip into self-pity and sen-
timentality – emotions I knew were dangerous in that place.
I pitied myself for not being there to look after my little girl.
I would think of her performing in school plays ~~without me~~
~~being there to watch~~; how she would be playing in hockey
matches; singing in the choir; growing up . . .

I longed to read her one more bedtime story before she left
her childhood behind. What did she use to call them?
'Bednight stories'. By the time I had left, she had been able
to read books for herself, but she liked me to do it. What were
her favourites? Little Babaji . . . The Tiger Who Came to
Tea . . . The Twits. *Afterwards I would kiss her goodnight,*
on her brow. I missed her so much . . .

Hannah stops reading to blot a tear that has fallen on
to the page. It has made the ink run and she blows on
the paper to dry it. She sniffs and dabs at her eyes with
the sleeve of her dressing gown before closing the notebook and hugging it to her chest. Realizing she hasn't
heard her father in the bath for a while, she wonders if
he is OK. Then she hears the sound of a tap running for
a few seconds and opens the notebook again.

Sometimes when I woke to find the darkness hissing about

my ears, I would wonder whether I had been talking to myself again, whether that was what had woken me. I would widen my eyes, searching for something to focus on. But ~~there was nothing. The~~ the blackness was complete. There was almost a purity to it.

The sound of my voice would seem muffled. At other times I would force myself not to speak, feeling that I must not disturb the darkness with my words because I would awaken it, and I would rather it was asleep.

Feeling concussed, I would close my eyes ~~once more~~ and points of light would blotch behind my eyelids. I could no longer be sure when I was hearing my voice in my head or when the words were being spoken out loud. Questions were coming from somewhere. 'How does Frejya know I am alive?' 'How do I know I am here?' I would pinch my skin or tug at my beard and say out loud: 'If I can hurt myself, does that mean I am alive? That I exist?'

~~I would sometimes think of Sartre's idea that~~

As a coping strategy I began thinking of myself in the third person, to stand outside my body. This was not happening to me, the inner man, but to Edward Northcote, the outer man. In this way I would allow ~~myself~~ my self-awareness to be swallowed up in the black incubus around me. I meant the white, for that was another coping strategy: the darkness was, in fact, lightness. I was merely living in a negative world where white was black. In this parallel world, the tarry blackness was not palpable. You could not touch it with your fingers like something liquid, something heavier than air, something that seeps into your blood like ice water. In this world the blackness was my friend, not my enemy.

~~Sometimes when the food basket was lowered and pulled~~

back up again, I would resist the urge to plead with my guards not to roll the boulder back into place. It did no good anyway and they seemed to enjoy my fear. On these occasions, as the last blur of light disappeared, I would think of it as the light being dimmed before a performance at the theatre. This was good, I told myself. I could be alone with

Sometimes the guards couldn't be bothered to lower my food and just threw it down to me, like scraps to a dog. I found the potato peelings hardest to eat, but I ate them nonetheless.

Sometimes I would bend down to pick something up and stay in that position for hours, saliva dripping from my open mouth, as if I was catatonic.

The guards sometimes stood around the opening staring down at me, like gods looking down on the world, determining the fate of mortals. They seemed to change fairly regularly, presumably to prevent me building up a bond with them, but there were two who kept coming back: Brains and the boy, who was now a teenager with a line of dark, downy hair above his top lip.

The boy, who I had nicknamed Becks, was kinder than the others. He gave me a candle one day and I stared at my reflection in a spoon for the first time in years. It was distorted, but that was not the reason I did not recognize myself. My skin was waxy, almost translucent. There were black pools under my eyes. All animation had gone from them. My cheekbones were raised and I had a straggly beard. Every minute of my confinement seemed to be graven into my face. With my Afghan clothes and beard, I looked like one of them.

Another small mercy was that after a few years the guards

no longer bothered to roll the boulder back over the hole. I would spend hours ~~passively~~ staring up at it, imagining myself at the bottom of a well ~~looking up at the stars~~. I would contemplate spiders' webs, awed by their delicacy, by the way they caught the silky light.

The boredom was like a physical pain, raw and scratchy. It was the enemy, along with time. I tried to kill it, but could not. No strategy worked. I felt weightless. Hollow. Unanchored, as if asleep. Asleep and awake at the same time. I longed to see the stars and feel the sun on my face. But I'd forgotten what the sky looked like~~, at night and during the day~~.

Most days I would wake to the lonely, soundless dark only to find, after my initial disorientation, that it was not silent, after all, that it was loud with the pulse of my blood, my breathing, the tiny clicks my eyes made as I blinked.

Feeling as if I was being drowned by the darkness, that it was inside me, pouring into my lungs, I would put my hands over my mouth and nose and ears. It didn't work. It was soon seeping in behind my eyeballs. If my veins were cut, I became convinced, my blood would be ~~black,~~ as black as ink.

My days did not separate in any meaningful way. There was nothing to distinguish them, nothing with which to measure their silent, monotonous drag. My mind had nothing to hang on to, nothing upon which to concentrate. I could no longer find a direction for my thinking, or even recall my dreams in the first few seconds after waking up.

~~And I could no longer bear to think of Frejya's warmth. For so long she had seemed the opposite of that cold, colourless place, but now my memories of her were too painful. In place of memory, a thick and heavy loneliness poured into me.~~

394

It was as sluggish as wet concrete and it left me feeling as if I was being drowned from the insi

Often I was driven so deep into myself, the daily arrival of my food came as an unwelcome intrusion, one that frightened and unnerved me, making me scuttle backwards into the shadows. In moments of insanity I no longer even wanted to be rescued. The thought of being freed filled me with as much panic as the thought of being held hostage had once done.

(Mention here ???? how random cricket statistics kept passing through my head and driving me mad because I couldn't work out what the numbers meant . . . Sir Donald Bradman – average of 99.94. Geoffrey Boycott – 8,114 runs. Top score 246 not out. All abstract, all out of context. I knew I used to love cricket but by then I couldn't remember how the game worked.)

In the early days, my emotions had been closer to the surface. Now my feelings had been buried so deeply they no longer affected me. My my eyes had dried up. In this I had finally found a way to deal with the painful, crushing boredom. I had decided to go mad on my own terms; allow myself to sink into it. Light-headed from hunger, I sometimes felt as if every thought I had ever had was passing through my mind all at once. The cave was full of my thoughts, my memories, and my theories. They were all competing for space. I was drowning in my own thoughts; they were too heavy, too liquid, wave after crushing wave.

One day, in what might have been the morning, I thought I heard footsteps 'upstairs', first coming closer, then farther away, then coming back again. A guard I hadn't seen before appeared. He was in his mid-twenties, at a guess, wearing

395

glasses and a black waistcoat and ~~he appeared to be~~ he was holding a small video camera. He filmed me staring up at him and then said something gently in Urdu to someone hidden from view. A ladder was lowered. I stared at it in confusion. Then another guard appeared, this one with a gun, and he shone a torch in my face as the guard with the glasses began to climb down, carrying a torch in his mouth. He had a bag over his shoulder. When he reached the floor of the cave he covered his nose and made a wafting gesture with his hand.

I backed away, shielding my eyes. There was the crackle of a walkie-talkie. As the guard approached me, he reached into his bag and pulled out a newspaper. He handed it to me, and then rummaged in his bag for the video camera. He pressed a button and held it to his eye. A recording light came on. He directed me to hold the newspaper up as he filmed. Then he said, and I can hear it now: 'Go on then, say summat.'

I thought I could recognize these words. They were English. The accent was familiar. Was it Yorkshire?

'Say summat for the folks back home then. Talk to your wife and kiddy. Go on.'

It _was_ Yorkshire, I was sure of it. South Yorkshire. Bradford or Leeds.

Thoughts were tumbling ~~in my brain~~ but I could not give them shape. I could not deliver them. I had forgotten how to speak.

'You've got a daughter, yeah?' the man said. 'Say hello to her.'

I remained silent. I recalled that there was something I had planned to do if ever one of the guards came down there, but I could not remember what it was.

He then said something like: 'We need to show the people back home that you are still alive. They need proof, otherwise they won't pay up.'

And he added something I had forgotten until this moment. At least I think he said this, but I cannot be sure because my mind was delirious ~~and weak~~ from hunger ~~at the time~~.

'We've been asking your people in the Foreign Office for years, but they keep ignoring us.'

Have I imagined this? The words have been so long buried they have decomposed in my memory, become worm-filled and barely recognizable.

After a minute, the guard lowered the camera and, when he pressed a button again, it made a two-tone pinging sound. When he gestured for the newspaper to be handed back, I hugged it to my chest like a petulant child.

'You want to read it? OK, mate.' The guard smiled and handed me his torch and then he climbed back up the ladder, pulling it up after him.

I shone the torch on the newspaper and read the words 'Daily' and 'Telegraph'. They had some traction. The Daily Telegraph. I remembered this newspaper. There was a photograph of a woman on the front page. She was in tears and was trying to cover her face from the intrusion of the camera lens. There was a man next to her. He was wearing a pinstripe suit and a tie and he was consoling the woman, ~~with~~ putting an arm around her shoulders. He looked familiar. They both did. It took me a long time to realize it was Niall and Frejya, they had both changed.

My eyes slid down to the words below the photograph, and, after a moment's confusion, the ability to read returned to me. 'Ten years after his UN convoy was attacked in Afghanistan, the British diplomat Edward Northcote was yesterday declared officially dead.' According to the article, Frejya was said by friends to be 'devastated'. She had asked that the media and the public give her and her family space to grieve in private. 'For Edward Northcote's obituary see page 28.'

I looked at the date at the top of the page – 31 March 2011 – and realized it meant I had been there for ten years. As I tried to take this in, I found myself edging backwards from the precipice of my silent ~~madness~~ hysteria. I shone the torch around my cave and saw dozens of cobwebs~~, each an intricate piece of engineering~~. I also saw my attempt at art, how I had once used my own excrement as paint ~~to daub the wall~~.

As my eyes roamed the walls, I saw for the first time that there were Arabic words scratched there. It no longer felt like my cave~~, my home. It was much smaller than I had imagined it~~. I realized that for all those years of not seeing the walls I hadn't appreciated how limited my space was. The yards had sometimes seemed like miles.

I ~~numbly~~ turned the pages of the newspaper until I came to the obituaries. There I saw another face I recognized. My own. It seemed to be guiding me gently out of madness, showing me where to place my feet. My lips moved as I read about my own life, and death.

II

THE FOLLOWING MORNING, EDWARD IS SITTING UNDER A TREE again, unshaven, listening to *TMS* on the radio. Hannah approaches with something hidden behind her back. 'Guess what I found in the garage,' she says. Before he can answer, she produces a cricket bat. It looks old; dark with linseed oil. In her other hand she has a tennis ball. 'Fancy a game?'

He takes the bat and shakes his head. 'I don't believe it. A Gunn and Moore. Dad bought me one exactly like this for my tenth birthday. It was his favourite make.' He runs his hand over the face of the bat. 'This has hardly been used. I wonder what it's doing here? Germans don't play cricket.'

'Are you going to bat to me or what?'

'Bowl to you. OK. We can use the tree as the stumps. Go and stand in front of it and take your guard.'

When Hannah starts tapping the ground with the bat, as if tamping down bumps, Edward laughs. 'OK, Michael Atherton,' he says, 'I'm going to teach you what a googly is. Ready?'

They play for a few minutes, until Hannah loses

the ball by hitting it over the wall. 'Four!' she shouts.

'Actually, six,' Edward corrects.

Later, while Hannah works on her painting, sitting on a wicker chair in an alcove of the Doric temple, Edward sits nearby trying to read the book of poetry on his lap, but he cannot concentrate on the words. His gaze keeps rising from the page to his daughter's face. He feels mesmerized. It is Frejya. Her tangible double. Without looking up from her easel, Hannah loosens her hair before gathering it into a band and says: 'You're staring at me again.'

To divert himself, he points at her tattoo. 'It's Sanskrit, isn't it?'

'Yes, it means Father.'

Edward wishes he hadn't asked. Her answer seems to be charged with meaning. 'I thought we could have mozzarella and beef tomatoes for lunch,' he says, looking down at his book. 'There's some pesto and vinaigrette that could go with it. Something simple.'

'I don't mind, you know,' Hannah says. 'You can stare at me if you want.' With a creak from the chair, she leans forward to pat his head. As she stands up and walks past him, he notices the marks left by the wicker chair on the backs of her legs. His arm rises up involuntarily and his fingers lightly trail her hip as she passes. The hand remains suspended in the air for a few seconds after she has gone.

Resisting the urge to follow her back to the house, Edward wanders towards a barn he has noticed on the east side of the garden, along a path scythed through nettles. Stacked against its gabled end he finds a pile of seasoned but unchopped logs. Inside, there are dead

400

leaves on the wooden floorboards and house martins fluttering under the cobwebbed eaves. Stacked randomly against the walls are harnesses, pitchforks, rakes and spades, and weighing down some musty sacks in the corner, an axe.

He practises swinging it above his head, narrowly missing the low beams of crankled oak. Its shaft has been worn smooth and shiny from use, the sweat of several generations ingrained in its wood, and as his own hand slips down from its shoulder, and over the gentle bow of its belly, he feels a chemical pulse pass through his muscles.

The logs all appear to be from the same tree, a beech, and, judging by their circumference of about five feet, it had been an old and tall one. Edward selects the biggest and knottiest as his chopping block, dragging it sideways into position, and then he lifts a smaller one on top of it. Working from the outside in, following the grain, he is able to split one log every four or five minutes. When the heel of the axe becomes too firmly embedded, he picks it up with the log still attached and rotates it in the air. Then, in an underarm action, he uses the heft of the log against itself by bringing the blunt side of the axe down against the block. It makes a satisfying noise, a clean and brittle crack. It also seems to be giving off a smell. A red smell. Is that resin? Yes. A red, sappy smell of beech resin. His sense of smell seems to be returning in glimpses, and it is bringing back memories of chopping logs in Norway, at his in-laws' cabin near the fjords, with Frejya bringing him out a cold beer.

Drawn by the noise coming from behind the barn, a repeated sound that is sometimes an echoey crack, sometimes a thud, Hannah collects from the fridge a bottle of cold French lager and walks towards it. At the corner of the barn she stops. She has seen her father, but he hasn't seen her. Even from a distance of twenty yards the sweat on his brow is visible, glistening in the sun. She watches as he swings the axe in an arc above his head and then brings its blade down on the log, splitting it cleanly in two. How contented he seems as he bends to pick up the pieces, tosses them on a pile beside him, places another log on the block. The swing again, the muscles working in harmony, the unself-conscious grunt. She has never seen her father in this way before, fine-looking and fervent in the bright sunlight. The dark and disturbing world he described in his notebook seems a million miles away.

His chest still heaving, Edward takes a break to pull a splinter from his palm. He takes in the pile of logs and feels a deep and unfamiliar sense of communion with nature, as if an entangled part of him is coming loose. More than that he feels masculated again, no longer the impotent captive. His brow feels gritty with dried sweat and dust, and his hands are tingling from the vibration, and this makes him feel not tired but exalted. Oddly transcendent, too, as if the monkey chatter in his head has been stilled and he is being led to his own calm centre.

'Feeling better now?'

He turns. Hannah is watching him from the corner of the barn, a lit cigarette between her lips. As he studies her he feels a tenderness in his fingertips, like an erogenous ache. 'Yes, surprisingly so,' he says.

She takes a drag and eyes him as she gives a long out-breath. 'Let's see those muscles, then.'

Edward flexes a bicep and grins.

As she walks towards him she flips the porcelain cap on the bottle of beer and holds it out by the neck. 'Brought you this.'

'Thanks.'

After handing it over she drops to her knees slowly and, as if preparing for execution, lowers herself until the side of her head is flat against the chopping block. 'Look at these rings,' she says, running her finger over the clammy surface of the log as she tries to count them. 'Each one a year. This tree must have been here for a century.' Her voice seems distant, as if she is talking in her sleep.

That night, when her father has gone to bed, Hannah looks under the magazine again for his notebook. It has gone. She rests her hands on the chimneypiece. The key she had found the night before catches her eye. She passes it from one hand to the other, back and forth several times as she thinks, then she heads downstairs and tries it in the locked door she had found on her first morning here. It turns easily.

She feels for a light switch but when she finds one and flicks it no bulb comes on. Recalling the torch on top of the fridge she collects it and, casting its beam around the room, sees it is a gallery of some kind: half a dozen framed charcoal drawings of scenes from what looks like a concentration camp. There are identical skeletal prisoners in striped uniforms. A gallows. Some sort of a roll call. One shows a prisoner being crucified upside down. Her hand rises to her mouth as she takes in another sketch, this one depicting a naked man being hanged. Another two prisoners are apparently copulating on a gallows while a soldier points a rifle at them.

Her grip loosened by shock, she drops the torch and backs out of the room.

After breathing deeply for a few seconds she nods to herself in determination and walks back in. She now notices the dustsheet over a cabinet at the end of the room. Removing it, she sees a glass-topped display case similar to the ones containing butterflies upstairs in the entrance hall. Inside it is an SS ceremonial sword with two gold tassels on its handle, a silver cigar holder with the SS initials engraved on it, some white fencing gloves embroidered with the letters SS in gold thread and three bowls with gold-plated rims and small swastikas in the centre.

This time she runs out and slams the door behind her.

Back in the kitchen she puts the torch back on top of the fridge with trembling fingers before moving to the sink and splashing cold water on her face.

III

THE NEXT MORNING, HANNAH EATS HER BREAKFAST IN A thought-filled silence. She has not slept well, feeling unsettled by her discovery that their host appears to be a neo-Nazi. As she lay awake she weighed up whether she should tell her father what she had found, before insisting that they both pack their bags and leave. But she has decided it would be best not to. Not yet. He seems happy here, happier than she has seen him since his release, and she doesn't want to introduce anything that will change his mood. Besides, he has finally started coming to terms with his years of captivity, enough to write about what happened. She is sure he must be finding that process therapeutic, so much so that he might soon be able to talk about it too, if not to her or Uncle Niall then to a professional.

She must look distracted because when her father comes down to breakfast he asks: 'Everything all right?'

'I was thinking I would quite like to get out of the house for a while,' she answers too airily. 'I found those bikes that Mike mentioned. They were in the stable propped up against a wooden horse. Do you fancy exploring?'

'You go. I think I might stay here and do some more writing.'

'Writing?'

'Oh, it's nothing. Some ideas I wanted to get down on paper.'

'Your memoir?'

He falters. 'Yeah. A draft of sorts.'

'Can I read it?'

'Not yet.'

'Why not?'

'It's incomplete. There's something missing, but I haven't worked out what yet.'

'A resolution?'

'Yes, maybe.'

Having arrived at the house from the right, Hannah decides to turn left at the main entrance gate. Seeing the tennis ball she had hit over the wall, she stops to pick it up, dropping it into the bike's basket. Five hundred yards further on she comes to a sign which points to '*Camp du Struthof*' in one direction and '*La chambre à gaz*' in the other. Puzzled, she continues cycling and comes to a structure made from wooden scaffolding, a gateway. It is partly concealed behind a line of trees and hanging from its central beam is a wooden sign reading: '*Konzentrationslager Natzweiler-Struthof.*' There is a middle-aged woman in a baseball cap posing for a photograph beneath it. Grey tendrils of hair are spiralling out from under the cap, as if trying to escape.

Behind her Hannah now sees three parked coaches in a semicircular area with a public lavatory and a hot-dog stand. Two boys are playing with a football there, bouncing it against a wall. She parks her bike and walks to the entrance gate. Here she finds herself looking down on a perimeter of concrete fence posts covering an area about three-quarters of a mile square. Wire is suspended between them, some barbed, some, judging by the plastic insulators, electric. The camp is constructed as an amphitheatre with a series of terraced platforms linked by steps. The wooden barracks are painted blue-grey and are separated by grassy slopes.

At the highest point of the valley there is a white stone monument the size of a three-storey house. It coils around itself in the shape of a spinnaker. Carved into its side is the outline of a man.

There are perhaps fifty tourists wandering around inside the perimeter and coming from one of the buildings is the sound of a young child having a tantrum. The other visitors are silent. Hannah steps forward so that she can read a small sign. 'This camp where so many martyrs died for their homeland is more than a cemetery. A most absolute dignity is requested. Decent clothing and behaviour are required. Smoking and pets are not allowed.'

'Hello, Hannah.'

She turns to see the diminutive, stooping figure of François emerging from what looks like a ticket office. He is walking with the aid of a crooked stick that seems to have been chosen to mirror his posture, two twisted roots rising from the earth.

'Oh, hello,' Hannah says, trying to hide the confusion in her voice. 'I was exploring. We didn't even know this place was here.'

'I wondered when you would find it,' François says. 'I helped liberate it during the war. Now I help out as a guide.'

'Was this a concentration camp? Here, in France?'

'It was, yes. One of the smallest. It was a work camp. What they called an *Arbeitserziehungslager*, a labour-education camp. But many thousands of people died here from starvation and exhaustion.'

'Did you say you helped liberate it?'

'I was a major in the Free French Army, in charge of co-ordinating the Resistance from London. There were some Jews and gypsies in this camp – the *Untermenschen* as they called them, the subhuman races – but most of the inmates were political prisoners. Frenchmen. Resistance. Communists. Homosexuals. Come, let me show you around.'

They follow a tarmac path curving down the slope and come to a square where the dust is red. 'This was where they had the roll call,' the old man continues. 'They had to assemble here at five o'clock every morning, then again at noon and in the evening.'

Hannah, thinking back to what she has seen in the hidden room, points at a raised platform. 'What's that?'

'The gallows. The original rope is in the museum. Whenever there was an escape attempt the prisoners would be forced to watch the executions.'

He raises his stick and prods with it in the direction of a building made of brick. 'And that is where the kapos slept, the prisoners who saved their own skins by working as guards. The inmates hated them. They were sadists. Some of them were worse than the SS. Let me show you something.' He comes to three rows of sturdy red-brick barracks. 'This is the thing about which I am most proud. The Museum to the Resistance. I helped set it up.'

Inside they watch grainy black and white footage of the liberation of the camp by American soldiers, as well as images of prisoners marching to a quarry. A framed photograph shows de Gaulle inaugurating the camp as a French national monument in 1968. Alongside this are other black and white photographs of executions and beatings.

'Their efficient prison system required that log books be kept,' François says, tapping a thick ledger with his walking stick. 'In here are listed the prisoners' names, nationalities, political status, date of entry, and also dates of death and cause of death.'

Once outside again, François says: 'See this building here? Come. This was the medical pathology room.' He leads the way, making a sharp tapping sound on the stone with the stick. 'In here SS doctors performed experiments on live patients. The homosexuals usually. The Nazis would try to "cure" them. Sometimes the patients would be given the opportunity to undergo "renunciation tests". If they succeeded in being aroused by the prostitutes provided for them, they passed.'

'François, I have to ask you something,' Hannah says, raising her sunglasses up on to her forehead. 'I probably shouldn't have, but I went into the locked room at the house last night.'

'Ah yes,' the old man says. 'The house was where the camp commandant lived, you see. It was his official residence. Those sketches were found behind a false wall,

409

along with the sword.' François studies her with rheumy eyes. 'You are wondering about your host, I think.' He looks around. 'Yes, Herr Walser is German, but he is a good German. I know this in my bones. Besides, he was born after the war. And he has been most generous. The Nazis abandoned this camp more or less intact but there has been a lot of pressure to develop the site over the years. The locals don't like it because a lot of collaborators were held here after the war and they don't want to be reminded of the fact. And in the 1970s Nazi sympathizers burned down some of the buildings. Herr Walser paid for its restoration. In fact it would not have been preserved at all were it not for him. He does not tell people, but much of the funding for this camp comes from him. I think it is his way of atoning for the crimes of his people.'

François shakes his head as he points to a tray laden with syringes, scalpels and clamps. In the middle of the room is a porcelain dissection table with grooves for draining blood. 'In their efficient way, the Nazis built the crematoria next door. Follow me.'

Hannah follows a few paces behind as the old man leads her into a building with a smokestack made of brick rising above it. Inside is a room with peeling walls and three ovens with their heavy steel doors open. There is an arrangement of long pokers hung on the wall next to these, and flowers and candles spitting hot wax placed inside them on the sliding trays. 'This was where they burned the bodies.'

Hannah covers her mouth.

'I said earlier that this was not officially an

extermination camp but there was a small gas chamber . . .' François points out of the window to a white building with a ventilation chimney in the middle of its roof, 'in that old farmhouse over there. After the war they found eighty-six skulls preserved in alcohol at the University of Strasbourg's Institute of Anatomy. They were Jews who had been gassed here so that their skulls could be sent for analysis. It was said that that inn over there continued to serve guests as they watched the naked Jews being led into the gas chamber across the street.'

'What monsters,' Hannah says in a small voice.

'Have you heard of Adolf Eichmann?'

'We did him in GCSE history.'

'Well, that incident came up at Eichmann's trial in 1962. He had arranged the transport of the skulls, you see. The artist who did those sketches you found also did a sketch of the Jews being led to the gas chamber, and that was used as evidence in the trial. And the prosecutors were able to produce a document written by the project contractors which made specific mention of a gas chamber at Natzweiler-Struthof. That was unusual because the Nazis were careful about destroying such things and when they did put anything down on paper they normally used coded terminology.'

Hannah sniffs. 'Thank you for showing me all this, François.'

'I am going to have my ashes scattered here,' he says with a cheerful, stained-tooth grin.

Hannah rubs the back of her neck. 'So this camp was discovered at the end of the war?'

'No, the Americans officially liberated it in November

411

1944, but it was empty by then. The inmates had been evacuated to Dachau in September. One of the so-called death marches. All the Americans found were a few corpses in the infirmary. They had been left to die in their beds when the rest of the camp was evacuated.'

'Didn't you say the French liberated the camp?'

'It's complicated. Your grandfather never mentioned it?'

Hannah starts. She studies the old man's face. 'My grandfather? How do you know about my grandfather?'

'We were comrades in arms.' The old man turns and leads the way back to the entrance gate.

Hannah remains standing where she is for a moment, then she jogs to catch up with the old man. 'What's going on? How do you know about us? How do you know about my grandfather?'

François waves the questions away with his stick. 'I told you, we served together. The invasion of southern France. How is he?'

'He's in a nursing home.'

'Well, tell him Lehague sends his regards.' He checks his watch. 'Now, I must go. I have a tour waiting.'

'Wait. Tell me about my grandfather. Did he help liberate this camp, too?'

'It was his idea. He never spoke about what happened?'

'Not to me.'

'Then I am afraid I cannot speak of it either. It is his wish. What about your grandmother? Did she tell you?'

'I never knew her. She died when my father was one.'

'I'm sorry. I didn't know that. She can't have been very old.'

'Lung cancer.'

François shakes his head sadly. 'Ah yes, she had a fondness for cigars that one. It makes me sad that we lost touch after the war, after all we had been through together.'

'I'm confused. You knew my grandmother, too?'

François studies the ground, nods to himself. 'I am sorry, Hannah, I'm a foolish old man who talks too much. I can't say any more.' With this he turns and gives a wave of his stick before disappearing back into the ticket office.

Feeling as if she is about to faint, Hannah sits down on a step and puts her head between her legs. A couple of minutes later the camp no longer seems blotchy before her eyes and she makes her way back towards her bike, lost in contemplation.

Back at the château she pours herself a cognac to steady her nerves and goes to find her father to tell him about her strange encounter with François. But when she finds him writing contentedly in the Doric temple she hesitates.

'How was your bike ride?' he says, looking up and smiling.

'Fine.'

'Did you go far?'

'Not really. It was too hot. Get much writing done?'

'A lot actually. There's something about this place. I just feel . . .' He trails off. 'I like it here. Do you?'

Hannah purses her lips.

Over dinner that night – a salad niçoise – they drink two bottles of wine followed by armagnac. Edward wonders

413

why his daughter is drinking more than usual, and why she seems so quiet, but he doesn't say anything, assuming this is how she is when she is feeling mellow. Once they have washed up, he suggests a walk in the garden to clear their heads.

As they stroll in step, fireflies signal their path, and Edward trails his hand in the sticky, cool fuchsias, savouring their texture against his skin. Away from the floodlights around the house, his eyes try to adjust to the steaming dusk but are tricked by the phosphenes, the fleeting mirages of fading light. And then come the electric flicker of bats and a clatter of wings as half a dozen wood pigeons rise from a seedbed and melt into the trees. A hidden sprinkler comes on and they have to hurry forward out of its range. Hannah lights up a cigarette and as she smokes it they fall into step again.

The garden seems to have expanded, offering up new paths to explore. Though neither speaks, Edward senses that his daughter is enjoying the feeling of being lost, the blotchy, hallucinatory sights of nightfall. He squeezes her hand. They cross the river not by the stone bridge but the smaller wooden one. They then find themselves circling back by a row of marble nymphs, eerie sentries that appear to be wavering in the light of a three-quarter moon. The churring of a nightjar can be heard now, a watery staccato that seems to exist only in their imaginations.

When they reach the hump of the Roman bridge, Hannah flicks away her cigarette. As it makes a hiss, Edward pulls her back towards him, looping his arms around her neck. When her hands meet around the small of his back in answer to this, he realizes how long it has been since he felt this aware of another person's body, of another person's texture and heat and substance. With the darkness listening as it closes in around them, he begins shifting his weight from one foot to the other, swaying in time to the unheard music of the garden. She follows his lead.

Later, when they say goodnight and head to their bed-rooms, Edward takes his notebook from the drawer in the bedside table and re-reads what he has written that day. Feeling drowsy after a few pages, he switches the light off and rolls over, only to be awoken, he knows not when, by a turn of the door handle and a creak of the floorboard. There is a movement in the shadows then Hannah is lying on the bed the wrong way round, her feet level with his head.

'Are you awake?' she whispers into the darkness.

'Yes.'

'Do you mind if I sleep in here? I was feeling frightened.'

'By what?'

Hannah hesitates before answering. 'Had a bad dream.'

'Sure.' Edward turns on his side, props his head up on his hand and feels his daughter's proximity so acutely it is as if she is occupying every molecule in the room. How easy it would be to gather you in my arms, he thinks, for me to hold you.

'Did Grandpa ever tell you about what he did in the war?'

'Not in any detail. Wish he had. I used to think about him sometimes in the cave, wondering if he was still alive. Then I would start to wonder if I was still alive. Because that's all death is, isn't it? Darkness. Silence. Nothingness. What I was experiencing every day.'

'Do you want me to put the light on?'

'No, it's all right.' In the semi-darkness he can make out her profile at the end of the bed, see the rise and fall of her chest. 'Weeks would go by without a noise, then I would realize a sound had crept up on me and I wouldn't be able to place it. Footsteps? A distant motorbike? A helicopter? Then it was gone.'

In the bedroom now there seems to be white noise buzzing around the edge of the silence. The air around them has become so dense he can barely breathe. He wants to reach down the bed and touch his daughter's hair.

'Night-time is when I miss Mummy the most.' Hannah puts her arms above her head and stares up at the canopy. 'I never used to be afraid of the dark but then . . . I still have dreams about her, you know.'

Edward sighs. 'So do I. In the cave I wore my memories of her down, slicing them so thinly they were virtually transparent. I had replayed them so often in my mind that I no longer knew whether they were based on real events, or whether I had imagined them and given them solidity through repetition.'

'What about me? Did you remember me?'

'Of course.' Edward extends his arm to touch her feet, but hesitates. 'I remembered the way you used to come into our bed when you were frightened. I would go and sleep in the spare room, leaving you with Mummy.'

Hannah now turns on her side to face him and props

herself up on one elbow, mirroring his position. 'So I was afraid of the dark even then?'

'We used to have to leave a night light on for you.'

'I'd forgotten that. Do you remember reading me bednight stories?'

'I do, yes . . . Bednight stories.'

There is a thickening of the darkness now. They lie back in it mutely. Edward can feel his heart thumping in the silence, his whole body rocking to its tempo. He feels acutely alive. Tensed.

'Dad?'

'Mm?' He tries to disguise the shallowness of his breathing.

'I feel safe here with you.'

'And I with you . . . Night.'

'Night.'

There is another long silence. Edward rolls over and takes deeper and slower breaths, to make Hannah think he has fallen asleep.

His stillness gives him away.

'Dad?'

'Yeah?'

'I can't sleep.'

He props his head up again.

'I know Mummy's dead,' she says. 'But I don't, like, feel it in my blood.'

'I know what you mean. Perhaps she lives on in your dreams, and mine.'

'And our memories.'

'Yes. And in our memories. And she lives on in you, Han. In your mouth, and your eyes, and your hair.'

Edward grinds his teeth. 'You're very like her, you know.'

'Really?' She gives a hollow laugh. 'No one's ever pointed that out before.'

Edward smiles; he is finding it easier to talk to his daughter in the gloom than in the daylight. 'Obviously you look like her, but I mean in terms of personality.'

'In what way?'

'She was a free spirit.'

'Mummy was? Really?'

'I guess you never saw that side of her while I was away. She could be very funny. Reduce a whole room to weeping laughter. At restaurants she would do daft things like slipping a piece of cheese in someone's handbag, knowing they wouldn't find it until later. When the bill came once she wrote a rude message on the signature strip of someone's credit card.'

'What was the message?'

'I can't say.'

'And she would always sing when she had had a few drinks. Get others to sing, too. Once, when we were on holiday in Bali, she persuaded all the diners in a restaurant to start dancing, and then jump into the pool fully clothed. It was one of those restaurants on stilts and the pool was below it. Off to one side. It was unbelievable. I can still hear her laughter.' He sighs again. 'When I was away, what was she like?'

'What do you mean?'

'How did she seem?'

Hannah thinks for a moment. 'Uptight. I used to get angry with her because all she could talk about was you. In some ways I felt I had lost her even before she died.

She had her bad days . . . You know, on the day
Uncle Niall told her that you had to be declared dead she
went and burned all your clothes in the garden. Didn't
ask me if I wanted to keep any of them . . . Then she
came in and blew out the candle on the hall table.
She had kept one burning almost continuously for ten
years. After that . . . Is there anything you want to ask me,
Dad?'

Edward nods.

'Do I think she killed herself?'

Edward nods again.

'Yes.'

Pause.

'Thank you for being honest.'

'She'd tried to do it before,' Hannah says. 'Her wrists. I
stayed with Grandpa while she was in hospital.'

Edward reaches across the bed now and squeezes her
foot. 'She was a good person.'

'I know.'

'Poor Han. My poor baby. Larkin was right; they fuck
you up, your mum and dad. They may not mean to, but
they do.'

'I'm not fucked up.'

'You're not, are you?' Edward laughs affectionately. 'I
don't know how you managed it, but you're not.'

'You don't have to feel guilty about this, you know,
about being with me. It's not a betrayal.'

'What?' Edward sounds guilty. He is grateful for the
darkness again. 'What are you talking about?'

'If you enjoy my company like you used to enjoy hers,
that's OK.'

He leans over and kisses her foot. 'I'm glad we've had this conversation.'

'So am I.'

'I miss her, Han, that's all. I miss her so much.'

'You don't have to.' Hannah sits up, takes his hand and places it over her heart. 'She's here in this bed, under these ribs.'

Edward jerks his hand back, as if removing it from a flame. 'Night,' he says, rolling over again.

'Night.'

Half an hour later, she is asleep. Feeling relieved, Edward slips out of his side of the bed and goes round to hers. In the moonlight her skin looks like marble and, for one frozen moment, he wonders if she is dead. No, her mouth is closed and she is breathing silently through her nose, like her mother. Feeling suddenly lonely, he wonders if she is feigning sleep as he had tried to do. No, again. He studies her eyelids. They are trembling to the turns of an unknown dream. Once or twice her breathing turns into a mild snore.

There is a scent of evening jasmine and lilies drifting in from the garden, through the open window. The breeze is welcome after the stillness of the previous night and he knows he will now forever associate the fragrance it carries with Hannah. It is the smell of the natural world. Of summer. Of love. The sheets seem to be undulating slowly around her, like waves in slow motion.

IV

THE LUNCH OVER, THEY OPEN A SECOND BOTTLE OF WINE, refill their glasses and stand side by side at the sink, one washing, one drying. 'Quite tart,' Hannah says, taking a sip. 'But it should broaden out.'

'What should?'

'The wine. I'm getting gooseberries.' She is grinning. 'Possibly a hint of melon. What are you getting?'

Edward swirls his glass and holds it to his nose before taking a sip. 'Pissed.'

'A joke! Oh my God, my old man has cracked a joke!'

She flicks him with her tea-towel, then wanders outside with a sarong draped around her neck, a bottle of suncream in one hand, a Zadie Smith paperback in the other. Her sunglasses are pushed up to rest on her hairline.

'See you out there,' she says over her shoulder, turning from the waist in one supple movement. The hand holding the book is resting on her hip. For a minute after she has gone Edward continues staring at where she has been. His mouth has gone dry.

A quarter of an hour later, he steps out of a cooling

shower, towels his still-tingling skin, and has a shave. The hissing sound made by the foam as he squirts it into his palm, the slap as he pats it on his jaw and the bristly scrape as he takes it off again induce in him a sense of satisfaction, similar to that he felt when chopping logs. He dabs his face with aftershave and savours its cold contracting bite as he stands sideways on to the bathroom mirror, a towel around his neck.

Wearing a navy polo shirt, cream chinos and flip-flops, he heads back down to the kitchen, picks up an orange and begins peeling it. He is still hungry. When he reaches the terrace he wanders over to the easel to have a look at the portrait Hannah is painting of him. It is in oil and is still wet, but he cannot make out its colours.

As he maunders out into the garden, he tears off a segment of orange and places it on his tongue. The juice is sharp and fragrant and, feeling suddenly delirious with hunger, he devours the rest of it quickly before tossing the peel into a bush. With the return of his sense of taste, he realizes he is feeling something he hasn't felt for years, a thing so long buried in his memory he cannot place it at first. It's not happiness quite, it is more that he is not unhappy, a double negative that equals a positive.

These past couple of days he has felt himself taking tentative steps across an ice sheet, listening to the creaks, and expecting it to give at any moment. Now that it suddenly has, he is finding he is in over his head, not in cold water but warm. And the warmth is carrying through to his bones, melting a core that has been frozen for a decade.

When he doesn't find Hannah under the ivy-covered bough of the tree they used as cricket stumps, he continues walking, listening to the dried-out stag's horn lichens crunch under his feet as he follows the worn path that leads to the Roman bridge. Here, in the honeyed afternoon light, he stands and contemplates the reeds that fringe the riverbank. They seem to be shimmering in a haze of heat, and a sheen, like white satin, seems to be lying over the idly flowing water. As his gaze follows the jerky puppet movements of two monarch butterflies in flight, he fancies he sees flecks of amber, but cannot be certain. Are they male and female? As they perform a hovering tarantella, they seem as weightless as paper, their wings rising and falling so quickly they look like orbs of mist. He takes a deep breath and exhales slowly. Where is Hannah? He wants to share this with her.

He strolls on a few yards and sees her on the other side of the river, unaware of him. She is wearing the sarong and it seems to melt around her as she walks. When she slips it off, he sees she is wearing a bikini underneath. He feels mesmerized by her loose and careless beauty and realizes, with a jolt of guilt, that her body is proving a source of aesthetic pleasure to him. It is to do with her narrow waist and wider hips, the inflection where the pelvic crests meet the upper abdomen to form two opposing triangles.

She runs towards the river and, as she dives, the golden light in the garden seems to waver and roll across the surface of the water.

He walks on, feeling excited and charged. When he

reaches the bridge, the blue, electric bolt of a kingfisher in his peripheral vision interrupts his thoughts. He watches it pierce the river.

Blue? He takes off his sunglasses and looks up. Is his colour vision returning? No. The cloudless sky is still grey. He stands still, closes his eyes and breathes deeply again. The air is heavy with pollen, dandelion seeds, summer.

Something blue again. A blue smell. Is that lavender? Mint? Something clean and antiseptic. And now something yellow. Burnt mushroom? A hint of mown hay? The smells are weaving a gauze of colour around him and it feels like being in love.

He takes another breath as deep as his lungs will allow and holds it in until he sees blotches. Then he exhales.

I am alive, he thinks. I am here.

There is something about this garden, its delightful corrupting power over him, that makes him feel more awake than he has ever felt before, more in contact with the world. He continues walking and finds himself deep within its tangled heart, trailing his fingers through the long pampas grass as if each stem is a string on a harp.

As he walks he wonders how long they have been here. He is no longer sure. A couple of days? Three or four? The flowers no longer seem tight in their buds. He has reached the fruit cage. Here he leans forward so that the nearest raspberry is no more than a few inches from his eyes. Each of its drupelets seems to be bursting out of its satiny skin, eager to spill its pulp. Yesterday the raspberry was a little too hard. Tomorrow it will lose its elasticity. But today it is poised and tender and a powdery sheen is giving it a gradation of tone, the deeper colour roiling below the pale surface. He watches as his hand rises and plucks the berry, careful not to bruise it, and, as he examines the delicate hollow where the white bud of its stem had been, he feels his gums tingle in anticipation.

Relaxing his eyes as if contemplating a pointillist canvas, he notices a blurred pattern behind the raspberries. He adjusts his focal length again and sees that on a mound about fifteen yards away, Hannah is lying on the sarong, sunbathing topless, her head resting on her arm, her back half turned to him.

As he approaches her he sees the bottle of suncream has tipped over. The cap is open and the liquid glooping out on to the rug is attracting a mosquito. Next to this is her mobile and the paperback she is a quarter of the way through, lying face down, its spine broken.

He is about eight yards away from her now and, realizing that she is asleep, he stops so as not to disturb her. As he traces with his eyes the curving ridge of her backbone, the dip of her waist and the swell of her hip, he feels dizzy and short of breath, as if the sight is straining his heart and making him ill with her.

A light gust passes over them, and Edward marvels at the fleeting, goosebumped roughness of her skin. There is something else he notices for the first time: there are downy hairs where the sun catches the backs of her legs, and, above these, two dimples on the low parabola of her back. Another genetic signature.

'She looks just like you,' he says under his breath.

Hannah stirs and rolls over on to her other side, so that she is now facing him, but with her eyes still closed. She murmurs, a fragment of conversation rising up from a dream. There are tiny beads of perspiration on her forehead. As he notices that her hairline forms the top of a heart, his vision blurs momentarily, a blur of tenderness against which reason can find no grip. His blood is singing.

She is shifting to get comfortable now, tucking her knees up into a foetal position, laying one arm the length of her flank, following its contours. The palm of her other hand is near her face, warming in the sun. He can make out the pale pink hue of her skin.

Pink. The word has traction. Edward is seeing in colour properly now. Hannah's lips are pale pink too. Realizing that he can also see the barley colour of his daughter's hair, Edward blinks and looks down at his hands. They are still grey. He glances around the garden. Everything else is still in shades of black and white. His gaze returns to Hannah, and there it is again. The pink pigmentation of her skin, the pale gold of her hair. It seems miraculous. She is shimmering with colour.

He feels a swollen, tingling sensation in his belly now and a sweet, euphoric chill at the back of his neck. He is inhabiting the limbic region of his brain, the melting edges of his sanity. Signals travelling up his spine connect with nerve fibres. Involuntary muscle contractions in his lower pelvis release peptide hormones. With puzzlement, then horror, he realizes he has an erection, his first in years. Shocked by the mechanical fact of it, the lack of ambiguity it represents,

426

he makes a guttural noise. Hannah must hear it because she sits up and stares evenly at him, an arm covering herself.

'Do you mind?' she says. It takes him a moment to realize this is not an accusation but a genuine question. She must realize the ambiguity, too, because, to make her meaning clearer, she adds: 'I didn't think anyone would see me here.'

For a moment Edward is incapable of speech, then he says: 'The gardeners.'

Hannah looks around and reaches for her bikini top but does not rush to put it on, making fussy adjustments instead.

Edward finds himself willing her hands to move more slowly, to give his eyes more time.

'It was the garden,' he says.

'What was?'

Has his feverish face betrayed him, he wonders? Has she seen the hunger in his eyes and heard the animal howl below the calm timbre of his voice? Still on his feet, he sways slightly, feeling too light-headed and off centre to walk away.

When Hannah returns to the house, drying her hair after another plunge in the river, she hovers at the entrance to the kitchen. Her father is sitting at the table. His eyes are downcast and he has not noticed her. Scratching at a mosquito bite on her arm, she studies him as she tries to work out what just happened in the garden by the fruit cage. He had worn an expression she had never seen on him before.

Becoming aware of her presence, he raises his head and says: 'She looked so like you.'

Hannah averts her eyes, smiling tightly, holding back a careless remark. 'Who did?' she says eventually, looking over at him again. 'Who were you talking to?'

Edward does not answer but instead places his hands flat on the table, as if trying to steady himself on a tilting sea.

'Do you fancy a game of chess?' she asks. 'Uncle Niall taught me to play.'

He looks confused for a moment, then says, 'Why do you call him Uncle Niall?'

'That's what Mummy used to call him, for my benefit.' She thinks about this. Folds her arms. 'I think she just thought it would make things seem more normal for me.'

They set up the chessboard on the terrace, the pieces casting shadows that lengthen as the sun sets. Hannah is about to check using a rook and knight combination when she hesitates. 'Can you hear that?'

'What?'

'That humming sound . . . Look.' She points at a hummingbird beating the air as it dips its needle-fine beak into a hanging blossom. She creeps on the tips of her toes around to Edward's side of the table so that she can see it better. 'Wow. I've never seen one before.' Without taking her eyes off the bird she perches on his knee, realizing too late that her bikini bottom is still damp.

Her quiddity, the soft heft of her, seems to catch him by surprise. Sensing his tension, she turns her gaze from the hummingbird. Their eyes meet for a beat too long and something seems to pass between them, a pulse that signals a new and deeper intimacy.

When he moves a hand up and down her back, she shivers and rolls her shoulders. As he begins to knead them, she says: 'That's nice. Keep doing that.' She can feel the pentameter of his heartbeat, pitching through his whole body like tiny electrical shocks. *Lub-dub, lub-dub*. 'You OK?' she asks.

He covers his eyes with the back of his hand, so that they no longer have to meet hers. 'Stop me,' he whispers. 'Please stop me.'

V

IN HIS ROOM IN THE NURSING HOME, CHARLES STARES AT THE
newspaper cutting in his old and desiccated hand. It is
a grainy picture of a bearded man looking up from a
hole. Who is he? He blinks. The caption reads: 'Hostage
Edward Northcote'. Northcote? That name sounds
familiar. Charles puts his Beatles record on and, as he
sits down again, feels an unbearable pressure on his
lungs. Several tons bearing down on him.

Now he is on his back on the floor staring at the
ceiling and George Harrison is singing about being
the taxman.

Charles cannot feel his arms or his legs any more.
Before his eyes, motes of dust are churning lazily in the
sunlight. It is turning cloudy inside. What is happening?
He has a clear notion that Anselm must be told of this.
He will be at home worrying about him.

On the edge of consciousness, Charles pictures that
gentle face looking down at him as he pillows his head
on his lap. They are young men again, twenty and
twenty-two, in the hotel overlooking Piccadilly Circus.
Anselm is giving one of his slow, knowing grins.

In these final moments of his life, Charles realizes how much he loves his friend; how much he wants to hold his hand, kiss the parting in his hair, touch his brow with the tips of his fingers. Anselm. His crime, his need, his dying thought.

VI

BY THE TIME THEY GO TO BED, THE TEMPERATURE IN ALSACE IS rising again. Edward, his mind full of Hannah, is too hot to sleep. Even the walls seem to be sweating, as if in fever. Though he has opened his bedroom window, no air is circulating, and, as he lies awake staring into the semi-darkness, he considers running his bedsheet under the shower so that it will be cool and damp against his skin.

Hearing his daughter pacing in the room next to his, he sits up and stares at the handle of the adjoining door, willing it to move, dreading that it might. As he listens to her uneven footfalls, his eyes follow the noise of creaking floorboards, back and forth.

His throat is dry now, his fists clenched against his longing, but this leaves him feeling not stronger but weaker, as if his muscles are fatigued from a long fight. In the moonlight he sees his skin is glistening.

He crosses the room with a heavy-footed walk and, picking up his swimming trunks and a towel, opens the main door. He goes down the stairs barefoot and heads out into the garden. The air is cooler here and as he lowers himself into the river he finds the water affords him some relief. There is a raw, loamy, rotting smell of vegetation coming from the reeds along the bank. Below him his feet are sinking into the velvety silt of the riverbed and, when he lifts them to regain his footing, clouds of mud rise to the surface, swirling hypnotically. He can now feel weeds tangling and slithering around his feet, like eels trying to pull him down into the depths. He is motionless. An immense silence follows, as empty as space, as if all nature senses he is afraid to move.

By the time he returns to the bedroom, he is feeling feverish again. As he lies on his bed he pictures Hannah lying on hers. The temperature rises once more and, as if in self-accusation, his priapic state returns.

Ten minutes pass before he hears the door handle being tested. He listens as Hannah crosses her room, opens her main door and treads lightly along the hall until she comes to his. This time the door opens with tiny complaints of unoiled hinges against wood. It is followed by the feathery sound of a hand feeling its way along the wall. When Hannah's features ghost out of the shadows, he can see she is blinking slowly, hardly stirring the air around her. He notices again the way her hairline dips in the centre of her brow; how her face seems to form a perfect heart.

With a crackle of static she slides under the sheet and lies on her back, arms by her sides. Edward is in the same position and is trying to control the sound of his breathing. As he holds his breath he realizes his daughter is doing the same. It merely draws attention to the slight rocking of the mattress underneath them. He cannot move, paralysed with tenderness.

'Couldn't sleep again,' she whispers.

'I don't know how to stop this,' he whispers back.

She lights up a cigarette, its burning tip a single orange eye in the dark.

'I love you,' he says, and the shadows around him seem to absorb the words so quickly there is doubt that they have even left his mouth. She takes a drag, and then she exhales loudly, the smoke pluming, pushing the words away.

When he finally summons the will to sit up, blotches appear before his eyes. He swings his legs over the side of the bed and walks unsteadily towards the door. Supporting himself with his hand against the wall, he descends the stairs. When he passes the barometer in the kitchen he sees it is dropping and, as a gritty breeze begins to stir the shutters outside, he wonders if the sirocco reaches this far north. A windchime that has been silent for their stay now ripples.

He runs a teacloth under the tap and fills it with ice before pressing it to the back of his neck and continuing down another flight of stairs to the cellar where he hopes the air will be cooler. Here he sees a key in the door of a room he had previously found locked. He takes it out, enters, finds the light switch and, when no light comes on, he closes the door behind him, locks it from the inside and pushes the key back under the door. As he lies on the cool marble floor, with the ice pack pressed against his brow, his breathing returns to normal. Saved from temptation by the locked door, he feels his composure returning. The hot night has cooled around him. Within minutes, he feels as if he is afloat on a gentle river, drifting towards the sanctuary of sleep.

When Edward awakes, everything is black and he doesn't know where he is. There is a distant howling in his ears, one that might have been building for minutes, perhaps hours. At first he cannot even tell whether it is coming from outside or inside and he wonders if it isn't so much a sound as an insidious pressure on his inner ear. A repetitive clatter becomes discernible within the cacophony – shutters flapping against a wall – and then he hears Hannah's voice calling him.

'Dad? Where are you?'

'In here.' He hears the door handle move up and down as Hannah tests it.

'I can't open it,' she says.

'The key is on the floor by your feet.'

There is a pause as she looks for it then he hears a rattle as the key turns. 'Why did you do that?' she asks as she opens the door. 'Come upstairs. You need to see this. It's like the end of the world.'

By the time they reach the bedroom, the curtains are billowing in like sails and Edward has to dip his shoulder and plant his feet solidly on the floor to reach the open window. As he peers outside, a bolt of lightning illuminates the garden for a second, revealing a stormy sea of twisted boughs and dark foliage. Tiles are being ripped from the roof and are smashing on the terrace as if hurled there by some vengeful demon.

Without pausing to put on any more clothes, Edward runs downstairs, opens the front door and marches out into the garden. Rain is lashing against his face and chest, making him gasp at its ferocity. But instead of sheltering from it, he opens his arms wide and throws back his head. The hard clay under his feet is churning to mud. Cataracts are appearing all around him, creating an obscene dark foam that covers the lawns. As he runs towards the river, Edward sees the cause of this. It has burst its banks and its surface appears to be boiling. At this moment, a tree comes crashing down in front of him, blocking his path.

Becoming aware of a torch being shone in his face, he shields his eyes.

'You OK?' It is Hannah.

There appears to be white ash in the air now, caught in the beam of the torch like eddying snowflakes. Wondering if this storm is something to do with the volcanic eruptions on Jan Mayen island, Edward begins laughing loosely. This is nature in all its untempered violence, and he feels intoxicated by it. He scoops up a handful of mud and rubs it into his chest before running deeper into the garden. Here he finds the ground is like a sponge under his bare feet, with beads of black blood squeezing out. In a thicket of hazel, he grabs at a clump of young fir that is budding with soft paws, wanting to feel them against his skin, saturate himself with their texture, savour their sharp needles. He is bleeding now and, as he lies down, he longs for the blood to mingle with the mud and smuts of ash. The night, the undergrowth, is in his veins.

He looks back to see Hannah catching up with him, her shoulders hunched. Everything around her seems to be in movement, the whipping branches, the spiralling leaves, but she is the still centre of the storm. Even her hair, clinging in wet snakes to her forehead, is not moving.

'The gods are angry!' Edward shouts. Lightning and thunder crackle and, with every bolt on the horizon, he can see the surrounding mountains looming claustro-phobically, crowding in on him. He feels a delicious terror at his own scale beside them, a small human figure in a vast landscape – man lost in the immensity of nature, without horizons, without confinement. The rain is black ink now, bouncing as it hits the ground. Hannah was right; it is like the last day on earth.

He runs over to her and takes her by the hands. Blood is beating visibly at her temples. She is trembling.

'Come back inside,' she shouts, her tears mixing in-visibly with the rain. 'Please! You're frightening me.'

'You can't fight nature, Han!' he shouts back.

He is exhausted now. Releasing her from his grip, he lies down in the mud again and allows himself to be flayed by the rain. Its whip is hard and emphatic against his skin, an invading force that cannot be resisted. He feels as if the earth is rising up beneath him, a presence, a living creature that wants to flood his senses. It is prevented only by a fragile membrane of skin.

When Hannah wakes next morning she feels momentarily confused by the silence. The storm has passed. In the dawning light, she treads tentatively down the stairs to survey the damage. The drawing room is all but impassable, blocked by a tree that has come through the window, taking with it a part of the wall. It has brought with it the soily, peppery smell of freshly fallen timber and she has to climb over its muscular limbs to reach the kitchen. Here she picks her way around a broken wine glass with a rust of purple sediment in its bottom. Leather-bound books are scattered around. Paintings, tapestries and antlers have been blown from the walls and the base of the lamp is smashed, leaving the shade intact.

Outside, fragments of terracotta tiles are strewn all over the terrace, along with broken pots, upturned garden chairs, fragments of a bird table, a ripped canvas parasol and a wheelbarrow.

Her father is on the riverbank, and she wonders if he ever came back in last night. He is standing with his back to her, mist rising off the ground around him. In his hand there is a book. When he hears her he turns, a mild smile touching his colourless lips. 'I found this,' he says, holding out the volume. There is Arabic writing on its cover. 'It's the Koran. It was wrapped inside a prayer mat. It must have been on top of one of the cupboards knocked over by the tree.'

Seeing the query in her father's raised eyebrow, Hannah says: 'Perhaps they belong to the housekeeper.' But she doesn't believe it. Martin Cullen had told her that Walser helped freeze al-Qaeda assets. What if his link with the Muslim world went further than that? What if he was implicated in some way in her father's kidnapping? Her mind is racing now and she is feeling guilty for having brought her father to this disturbing place, putting him in harm's way again. She wants to leave as soon as possible. Their summer is over.

PART SEVEN

I

Nancy. Late summer, 1944

ONE MONTH AFTER THE ALLIED INVASION OF SOUTHERN FRANCE begins, the US 'Blue Ridge' Division rolls into Nancy, effectively marking its end. The psychological impact of seeing an old-fashioned bayonet charge had proved too much even for the most hardened German veterans, and the white strips of cloth they waved in surrender have now been tied to railings and doors, making it look as if there is a carnival about to start.

The liberators enter through the city gate, bulky twin towers that date back to the fifteenth century. The arch between them displays the Cross of Lorraine, the symbol of Nancy, and as Charles cranes his neck to take this in, he realizes the hour of his own personal liberation may now be close.

Yet the realization makes him uneasy. For five years, barely a day has passed in which he hasn't thought of ways to reach Anselm. Now that there is a more realistic chance of it happening, he finds his resolve slipping from underneath him like a shelf of sand. He tries to picture his friend. In his memory he always wears a sleeveless sweater and a loosened tie. His hair falls forward over an angular face. Now? God knows. Will they even recognize one another?

'We will have to be careful here,' a tired and dusty-looking Lehague says, snapping Charles out of his reverie. 'The Germans will have left booby traps. Wire strung taut at neck height across roads. And Bouncing Betties. Do you know what a Bouncing Betty is?'

Charles takes a drink from his canteen. Shakes his head.

'Castration mine. They explode shrapnel at crotch height.'

On the outskirts of the town, they pass the carcasses of cattle swollen in the heat. Humans too: the legs and buttocks of one German lying face down in the earth have ballooned to such a degree they have stretched his grey breeches to ripping point. In his now skin-tight trousers he looks like a Regency fop in pantaloons.

They pass the charred corpse of the burning German soldier Charles had dispatched with merciful marksmanship. His fingers are tiny stumps. The cloth of his uniform has burned away, exposing his scorched torso. His pubic hair is reduced to a clump of steel wool. When Charles covers his body with a ground cape it makes a crispy sound.

The civilians on the now-open bridge do not acknowledge them. They are mostly elderly women wearing shawls over their heads. Some are pulling handcarts stacked high with bundles, boxes and pans. Their town has been under siege and they have been cut off

442

from the outside world; now they are free to come and go as they please, visit their families, conduct business.

As they enter the town proper, French soldiers receive an enthusiastic welcome from the locals. German prisoners are greeted with cold stares. There is a steady metallic clanking sound as they throw their bayonets on to one pile, their guns on another. As they are marched past the crowds, some are spat at and punched. The German bodies that litter the street are not being given a burial. Instead locals are pulling their boots off – a reminder that the Wehrmacht has been commandeering their leather for years.

A gang of half a dozen men are looting a hardware shop.

One bare-headed German emerges from a cellar after the others have been marched away. His grey field tunic is unbuttoned and torn. Though he waves a white flag this is ignored. He is dragged down a side street and moments later a shot is heard.

Anselm's entreaties have been answered, but not in the way he had hoped. His release from pain has been to lose consciousness. When he comes round, trying to locate through his blurred vision the shadowy world he has re-entered, it takes him a long time to realize he is in a single bed, not the shelves of bunk beds to which he is accustomed. The pain he feels in his back, his legs and his chest is so sharp he begins panting. At alternate instants he feels feverish and cold.

He tries to sit up but cannot. Instead he turns his head to one side and winces. His ribs feel broken. The

443

side of his face is pulp. His blood-matted hair sticks to the pillow. A pillow? What luxury is this? He must be in the infirmary. There are no other single beds for prisoners in the camp. It is dark outside. Who brought him in here? Has he been left to die?

The door opens and, recognizing the swaying silhouette of the Valkyrie, a whip in one hand, a bottle in the other, Anselm closes his eyes and listens to the sound of her pacing up and down the ward. Every few yards there is a whip crack as she checks that the bodies in the beds are dead. This is followed by the gulping sound of her having a drink.

She is standing at the end of his bed now. Without moving he mentally braces himself, knowing that his only chance of life is to feign death. When the whip lashes against his leg, he does not flinch. 'Raus!' She screams. 'Raus! Raus!' Another lash, this time across the fulcrum of his ribcage. Again he does not react. He can hear her laboured breathing and, for half a minute, he waits for another lash. It does not come. Instead he feels her hands tugging down his trousers and lifting up his jacket. He can sense her eyes studying his penis. Still he does not move. A minute later he hears her take another drink and then walk away unsteadily, muttering to herself.

And then, unable to stand the pain any longer, Anselm blacks out.

When he comes round again, it is daytime. The swelling in his eye has reduced enough for him to see that the beds closest to him are empty, but there are dark shapes in the ones nearest the door. They appear to be covered in black paint. Have they been shot? The

444

putrid, almost unbreathably heavy stench confirms it. As do the flies. Anselm sees movement now. There are rats feasting on the bodies.

Realizing he is hungry, too, he tries to shift his position, but his legs do not respond. One of them feels as if it might be fractured. His eyes roll back and he clenches his teeth.

Why is the camp so quiet? No whistles. No barks. The rattle of his breath scatters the rats for a moment, but they soon return. He realizes now that he is lying in faeces. He must get to the window. Open it. See what is happening outside. As he is sure he cannot put any weight on his leg, he must lower his upper body to the floor first. He rolls over on his belly and gasps at the stabbing sensation in his ribs. With his hands out-stretched, he can touch the floor. Now he must bend his arms to lower his head, but the action makes him lose his balance and he screams as his broken leg flops down. There is a bone sticking out. Sweat on his fore-head now. He drags himself towards the window, reaching for a broom as he does so. The effort to raise himself up on it leaves him shaking.

He looks out on to a desolate square. Everything is deserted, silent and flattened by the heavy sky. It is rain-ing steadily, oily drops churning the red dust. There are some discarded petrol cans, as well as boots and rags. There are also half a dozen skeletal corpses that have been dragged to the side of the infirmary and piled up. The guard towers are empty. All that remains is the sweetish smell of decomposition, like rotting potato peelings.

He understands now. The camp has been evacuated; all the other tormented souls have gone. All the SS demons have gone, too, apart, perhaps, from the hated Valkyrie with her whip. And he has been abandoned. Left for dead in a world of darkness, excrement and mud.

But with the collapse of the hated old order has gone all his structure, all his certainty. This has been a place of work, of exhaustion, of death, but food was provided every day. Barely enough to keep a man alive, it was true. But barely enough is still enough.

Anselm feels another stab of hunger, of thirst, of self-pity. How long has he been unconscious? It must be days judging by the corpses on the beds by the door. He feels as if he is the last man alive in the world. Now he must walk this alien planet alone. Except he cannot walk.

How is he to survive until . . . Until what? Until Charles gets here? He knows that he must not pretend, even to himself, that Charles will be coming for him. But he cannot help it. Charles *will* come. He knows it, if only he can stay alive long enough. Can he do that? As if in answer to this he feels pins in his leg. Teeth. A rat has bitten him. He chases it away with the stick, but it doesn't go far. It senses his vulnerability, the delicious whiteness of his bones.

Anselm stares at it. A stillness holds. He realizes what he must do before the Valkyrie returns, where he must wait for Charles. He moves his improvised crutch and, neither fully living nor dead, takes his first excruciating step towards the door.

446

* * *

Charles and Lehague try to keep their balance as they stand in the back of a half-track rumbling through the mist into a square near Nancy cathedral. The Cross of Lorraine has been freshly painted on its side and dust is sticking to its wet coat. An eerie muffled sound can be heard above the noise of the engines, even above the pealing church bells. It is a soft clapping, rising from the blurred forms of women and children lining the road. They have emerged after days of hiding in their cellars to applaud their liberators.

Charles wonders where they have got their flags from, because they are waving not only tricolours but also Stars and Stripes. As he focuses on them he sees they are made from rags, cut-up shirts and curtains.

Closer to the square, the crowds swell and women in their best summer dresses surge forward, blowing kisses, waving their hats and holding their fingers up in victory signs. After four years of occupation, the sense of relief and joy for some is being expressed through tears.

An impromptu exchange of goods is going on between the crowd and the tank crews, flowers for chocolates and cigarettes, each being tossed in the air like ticker tape. The advance is slow, bumper-to-bumper through narrow streets littered with abandoned gas masks, defaced portraits of Hitler and the burnt remnants of swastika flags.

Standing on a mangled nest of black metal and still-smoking rubble, a boy is playing an accordion. One woman appears from behind an armoured personnel carrier, half on its side in a ditch, its tyres taken, and

447

raises her arms to be dragged on to a passing Sherman. As she is lifted, her shawl snags on the tank track and she has to jump down, divesting herself of the garment. She laughs as she watches it being chewed up. An elderly man whose toothless mouth has folded in on itself is standing above the crowd on a wrought-iron balustrade. He is giving a salute. Charles salutes back and smiles, but the smile is false. Because of the now-permanent ache of his thumb, he is feeling feverish. There is sweat on his chin and brow.

And now he sees that a mademoiselle has clambered on to his half-track. If she senses how distracted Charles is, she doesn't show it. Instead she presses her lips firmly to his. He is surprised by the wetness of her kiss, by the taste of tobacco and smell of alcohol on her breath.

'Merci!' the girl says, finally breaking off. 'Vive l'Amérique! Merci!'

Charles smiles as the girl moves to kiss Lehague, smearing his cheeks with lipstick. She gets a better re-action from him, a squeeze of the buttocks as he tips her backwards. When her hat falls off, she reaches down to pick it up and almost loses her footing as the half-track swerves. And now the girl is jumping off without her hat, running to the next vehicle behind theirs. Doughboys are holding out their arms to drag her up. She grabs an officer's cap and puts it on. It is too big for her.

An old man by the side of the road is holding out a bottle of wine and the driver grabs it, takes a swig and passes it back to Charles. He takes a gulp too, feeling parched. When he wipes his mouth, he smears oil across his cheek. There is a pungent smell of sewage in the air.

Come nightfall, the Americans in their bivouacs and tents enjoy the generosity of the young women of Nancy. Lehague joins them, but Charles finds a hotel overlooking the cathedral and sits there sketching. Holding the charcoal loosely, he records from memory the sights of the past few weeks: the body hanging from the tree, the young men executed by Lehague, the charred remains of the French half-track crew. That they were like the piece of charcoal he is drawing them with occurs to him only when he has finished.

He is too tired to sleep well and passes the hours of darkness shivering under a blanket. The ache in his thumb seems to be increasing and, in the morning, he notices a smell. Something sickly. Realizing it is coming from his bandage, he unravels it and sniffs. The thumb has turned pasty with black blood. Has it gone septic? He searches again for his antibiotics. When he fails to find them, he rebandages it and wanders outside. As he makes his way across a park of tussocky grass wet with dew, he sees tank hatches opening to allow the lovers of the night to return to their homes.

Later that morning, Charles sees a dozen, sad-faced French women being rounded up and led into the town square. Here he watches as a crowd gathers, two men produce scissors and the women are held down in chairs as they have their hair shorn. Some have a swastika daubed in tar on their foreheads.

Charles taps a man on the shoulder and shrugs to ask what is going on.

'*Collaboration horizontale,*' the man says.

When the cut hair is piled up and burned, the sulphurous smell carries to Charles's nostrils and lingers there. He has to look away. Sleeping with the enemy is a crime to which he can relate.

As the crowd disperses, another young woman is dragged by her hair into the square. A latecomer. It soon becomes apparent her treatment is going to be different. She is wearing a nurse's uniform and, as its front is ripped, her brassiere becomes visible. Instead of cutting her hair the men look at each other and then haul her off down an alley. Judging by their lurching gait, most of them are drunk.

Charles follows. When he catches up with them the nurse has had half of her clothes torn from her and one hand is covering her chest, the other the join of her legs. One of the men, unshaven and heavily built, takes his jacket off and slips his braces from his shoulders. He then unbuttons his flies, tugs his trousers down and positions himself on top of the girl, forcing her legs apart. When she tries to resist, he slaps her face and, running a greedy hand over her hips, kisses her. She is hysterical now. Her whole body seems to convulse as she sobs.

Charles takes out his Webley and fires a shot in the air. As the crowd turn round as one, he shouts in English: 'Leave her alone! Everyone back! *Tout de suite!*' He pushes his way through them to get to the nurse. Still pointing his gun at the crowd, he puts an arm

450

around her waist and lifts her up. When the man who had been about to rape her grabs her arm and pulls her back, Charles shoots him in the foot. The rest of the crowd back away and, as the man falls to the ground cursing, Charles leads the nurse back down the alley. Seeing an open door, he moves a stiff yard broom out of the way and ushers her inside. There is a man's coat hanging up in the hall. He takes it off its peg and hands it to her.

'*Merci*,' she says, her voice clotting with tears. 'Sank you.'

She turns to the wall as she slips the coat on.

Charles checks the alley. 'I think they've gone. *Ils sont partis*.'

'I speak some English.'

While the nurse sits down at a table stacked with casserole dishes, pans and soup tureens, Charles fills a carafe of water from the tap. He then sees a bottle of cognac on a shelf and, reaching for that instead, pulls out its cork with his teeth, pours a glass and hands it to her. She cups it in trembling fingers, takes a sip and notices her lip is bleeding. 'Here,' Charles says, dabbing at it with a hanky. He pours himself a glass and then lights two cigarettes, handing one to her.

'I prefer cigars,' she says, taking it from him. 'But right now I will smoke anything.'

They sit down and, as they face each other across the table, Charles takes in her high-planed cheeks and her wide, dark eyes. Still wet with tears, they look like melting chocolate. Her upper lip protrudes more than her lower, as if bruised and pushed out by her teeth. It

451

makes her look sulky and hot-tempered. With her olive skin and her curly brown hair, tousled from her ordeal, she has the wild and exotic look of a gypsy.

'You are American?' she says.

Charles shakes his head. 'English. How are you feeling?'

'I'll be OK.'

The nurse notices the scars on Charles's cheek. 'What happened?' she says, without sounding the 'h'.

'A fire. Aviation fuel.'

'You are a pilot?'

'I was. Once. What's your name?'

'Inis. Yours?'

'Charles. We'd better go. Find some proper clothes for you. I have a friend who can protect you.'

When Charles and Inis find Lehague, he is stripped to the waist, with a towel around his neck. He has his back to them as he trims his moustache in the side mirror of an ammunition truck. 'Ah, Charles,' he says when he sees their reflection behind him. 'I was looking for you.' He turns and kicks over an upturned helmet filled with boiling water. The small fire it had been resting on is extinguished with a hiss and a feathery column of smoke rises up.

'I have word from the Resistance in Alsace that the Natzweiler-Struthof camp has been evacuated,' he says, dabbing his clean-shaven cheeks with the towel. 'They are taking them across the border to Dachau. Force-marching them. Those too sick to march are being left behind.' He takes a drag from his cigarette. Exhales slowly. 'Your friend is German, yes?'

Charles misses a beat. 'How did you know?'

'They think he might have been one of those left behind.'

'How do they know it's him?'

'They don't, but there were only a handful of German prisoners in the camp and one was known as "the artist". He was left in the sanatorium.'

'Have they got him out?'

'No one is going near the camp. Typhus.'

'So what's the plan?'

'There is no plan. We will have to wait until the Allies reach that region. It could be weeks.'

Charles looks at Lehague. 'I cannot wait.'

'I'm sorry, Charles.'

'I'm going to see if I can borrow a jeep. We could be there in a couple of hours. What about this?' He pats the door of the truck. 'Would anyone miss this?'

'The Americans won't let you.'

'Then I won't ask them.'

The major studies Charles for a moment, then nods and pats him on the shoulder. 'Maybe you should ask them. Go to the top. I'll come with you, for the sake of the Entente Cordiale.' Lehague notices the nurse who seems to be wearing nothing but a man's overcoat. 'We haven't been introduced . . .'

'This is Inis,' Charles says.

Lehague kisses her hand. '*Enchanté*. And I am François.'

Charles stares at his comrade. He had never thought to ask his first name and it seems somehow strange that he has one. He looks up at the sky and, shielding his eyes against the gritty gust of wind, wonders if this is the mistral arriving.

Under tumbling clouds, Charles, Lehague and Inis – now changed into a spare nurse's uniform from the hospital – come to a perimeter of barbed wire that is guarded by two machine-gun emplacements. They show their papers to a sentry whose eyes linger hungrily on the nurse and are then directed to the end of a long row of jeeps and fly tents. Here they come across an arrangement of bigger tents, some with kitbags piled up outside them like sandbags. The hessian smell of the guy ropes pricks the air. A field shower, mess tent, three latrines and two field kitchens suggest this is head-quarters for the Nancy campaign. A chalk sign a few yards further on confirms this: 'XII Corps/ 35 & 80 Inf Div HQ (Group Planning)'.

'We're here to see General Eddy,' Lehague says. 'I am Major Lehague, liaison officer to the FFI. This is Captain Northcote. He's with the British Army.' He does not introduce Inis.

'Take a seat,' an NCO says with a chewy Bostonian accent, 'I'll let him know you're here.' He balances on one leg as he pops his head around a flap and says something Charles cannot hear. He is smiling at him when he returns, then, when he sees Charles's scarred face in full profile his smile drops. He looks flustered and pretends to search for something on his desk. 'Five minutes,' he says.

As he waits, Charles takes out his sketchbook and begins sketching Anselm's face. Inis winds her watch.

Lehague removes his kepi and massages his temples with small rotations of his fingers.

The NCO turns to a portable typewriter on his desk, feeds in a sheet of paper and begins typing using one finger only, each time circling the key for a moment before touching it. Exactly five minutes later he looks up and says: 'You'd better just go in.'

The General, whose narrow lips seem to contradict his jowly face, is staring at the field telephone in his hand. He cranks it twice, listens to its earpiece and mutters: 'Goddamn.' He does not look up as the three enter but instead signals them in with impatient rotations of his mottled wrists. He studies a file on his desk next to a helmet with two stars on it then looks up and, seeing the discoloured skin across the side of Charles's face, frowns, his round-rimmed spectacles making his eyes look smaller than they are. Then his expression softens. 'How'd you get that?'

'Bombing raid.'

'I see. Well, they can do wonders these days. Skin grafts and so on.'

'Yes, sir.'

The General seems distracted again. 'So, gentlemen, ma'am, what can I do for you?'

Charles's fingertips are chattering in his lap. 'We need to get to Alsace,' he says abruptly. 'There's a concentration camp there which the Germans have evacuated, leaving the sick behind to die.'

The General raises his eyebrows in surprise. 'A concentration camp? In France?'

Lehague leans forward. 'Natzweiler-Struthof. It's

455

where the Nazis sent captured members of the Resistance. We were wondering if you could spare any men. A few jeeps. It would be a recon mission.'

'You're kidding me, right? That whole area is crawling with Krauts. Look.' He turns and taps the large, laminated wall map behind his chair. 'Here, here, here.'

Charles notices the General's fingernails have been chewed down to the quick.

'The 11th Panzer Division is conducting a fighting retreat to Alsace,' the General continues. 'We believe it is their intention to make a stand right here,' he jabs the map again, 'at this pass between the Jura and the Vosges mountains. The Krauts know that if they lose control of this area, Strasbourg and all of Württemberg to the east will be exposed.'

'But this is an emergency,' Charles says.

'I'm not risking the lives of American soldiers on a recon mission,' the General says without bothering to mask his irritation. 'The 7th Army will get there soon enough, in strength. Then we can do the job properly.'

'How soon?'

'Three weeks. A month.'

'That'll be too late,' Lehague says.

'Well look, if it's so goddamn important to you, why don't you risk the lives of some of your own men? You're with the FFI, aren't you?'

'Could we at least borrow a couple of jeeps?'

'No.'

A dirty fog is descending and, as they walk back to the Hôtel de Ville, they feel disorientated by its glow. All three are lost in their own considerations. Eventually Charles says: 'So now what?'

'Now we get ready to go,' Lehague says.

'We?'

'I have comrades at that camp, too, remember. They could be in the sanatorium along with your friend.'

'Didn't you just hear the General?'

'I needed to know exactly where the Germans are. Now I do. Besides, it will be safer if we go there disguised as civilians. I can find some papers for you, Charles. And I'll see if I can borrow something less conspicuous than a US Army jeep. There will be roadblocks, I imagine, but an army in retreat is not going to be interested in two French civilians.'

'Three,' Inis says.

Lehague looks at her and grins. 'Three. *Bon. Bon.* We will need a nurse. I heard what happened today, by the way. Why were they after you?'

Inis stops walking as she lights up a cigar. She takes a couple of drags to get it going. Then: 'Why do you think?'

'Well, I want you to know you are safe now. No one will harm you.'

'*Merci.* I am in your debt.'

That night Charles and Inis arrange to meet Lehague in a bar in the main square. It is full of drunken revellers and Charles is jostled as he waits to be served, ordering his first whisky in days. Not Irish, but he is not complaining. The intermittent waves of pain coming from his thumb are so acute he has been feeling faint and nauseous. The whisky, he feels sure, will help.

A piano is playing. A couple of American war correspondents, one balding, the other overweight, both identifiable by their armbands, are trying to chat up Inis. Charles signals for four glasses, pays for a bottle and carries it over to the table. 'Where are you chaps from?'

'*Stars and Stripes*,' one says with a shrug, looking slightly put out that someone might be ruining their chances with the nurse. 'You a Limey?'

Charles nods as he places the four glasses on the table, tucks the bottle under his arm and holds out his hand.

'*Baltimore Sun*,' the other says, looking at the 'Official War Artist' armband on Charles's sleeve as he shakes hands without standing, an awkward, high-elbowed gesture. He then pats Inis's knee without looking at her. 'I was just about to buy Rita Hayworth here a drink.'

'I've got her one,' Charles says, pulling the cork from the bottle and pouring generous measures into the glasses. 'Do you gentlemen have any transportation?'

The reporter tries not to stare at the scar on Charles's face. 'Why?'

'I've got a story for you.'

'Yeah?'

'There's a Nazi concentration camp a couple of hours' drive from here. The only one on French soil. They've evacuated it. Fancy a look?'

'Where exactly?'

'In the Vosges mountains. Alsace.'

'Are you nuts?' the *Stars and Stripes* reporter says. 'That's where the Krauts have withdrawn to.'

'Did you say evacuated?' the other reporter asks.

'They are force-marching the inmates across the border to Germany. Resistance mostly. Political prisoners. They are leaving the sick and dying behind. I'm going over there tomorrow for a look. See if I can help. Will you join me?'

'Count me out, pal.'

'Yeah, me too. I've been sent to cover the liberation of Nancy. I have to stay with the troops.'

Lehague arrives and pulls up a chair. 'We have transport,' he says. 'A butcher's van. I have managed to get hold of a couple of cans of petrol and some compo rations.' When Lehague opens a map and points to Natzweiler-Struthof, the two reporters look at one another sulkily then drain their glasses.

'Well, good luck, fellas,' the *Stars and Stripes* reporter says. 'You're going to need it. You too, sister.' They move to a table where there are half a dozen young French women singing as they sit on the knees of GIs.

The butcher's van is parked outside. All three get in the front, Inis in the middle. Lehague pats her knee. 'Now all we need are some civilian clothes.'

'I can help with those,' Inis says. 'At my apartment.'

The apartment is small and Inis looks a little embarrassed by it.

'You can both sleep here, if you like. I'm afraid it will be the floor but I can find some blankets.' She sizes up the major and the captain and nods to herself. 'My father's clothes are in there.' She points at a cupboard. 'Help yourselves. When you have found something we should go to the hospital. We will need bandages, morphine, saline solution and penicillin. Have you been inoculated against typhus?'

Charles and Lehague shake their heads.

'Then I will arrange it.' She turns to Charles. 'And I think someone needs to look at your thumb. I can smell it.'

'I'll be OK.'

'No, Mr Charles, you will not be OK. If you get gangrene from it you could die.'

At the hospital, the nurse unwraps Charles's thumb and recoils, partly from the fetid smell of ripe cheese, partly from the sight. It is black and is oozing putrid matter. As she dresses it with sulfa powder, a doctor comes over to inspect the wound and speaks in French without realizing Charles can understand him. *'Faut amputer ça.'*

'Alors faites-le,' Charles says, holding out his hand and making a cutting gesture.

The doctor shrugs and indicates that the patient should lie down on the operating table behind him. As Charles does so, he takes off his shirt. It is damp from pain-sweat. Inis prepares the wound with iodine and Charles watches with strange detachment as the doctor inserts a needle into his arm. Then he feels himself on a spiral towards sleep.

II

WHEN CHARLES OPENS HIS EYES IT IS MORNING AND, FOR A moment, he does not know where he is. Then an ache in his hand brings back a memory. He had an operation. He raises the hand and studies the shape of the bandage: four fingers and a stump. He is in a hospital, still in uniform trousers and boots. How long has he been here? He swings his legs over the side of the bed and, feeling dizzy, steadies himself for a moment. He is in a ward full of beds, of the groaning injured, civilians mostly, but some American soldiers, too.

A knife of pain twists in his hand now and he finds himself laughing. He knows about pain. Knows he can cope with it. Knows how to cope with it, too. Morphine and whiskey. He slips his shirt over his shoulders as he walks down the ward and sees a bed being wheeled towards him. They are too busy to bother with him. At the end of the ward there is a room with medicine. Recognizing the word 'morphine' on a bottle, he grabs it and steps outside into the ravaged city.

Though there is still a smell of shattered masonry in the air, the sun is shining hazily. He realizes he does not

461

know the way back to Inis's apartment. Stepping over rubble, he tries to get his bearings. The German bodies left out in the street seem to have gone now. There is a stray dog. A woman with a pram. A horse and cart. A shopkeeper is sweeping up broken glass from under his awning. A café is opening for business. The city is trying to return to a semblance of normality, washed by the pale sun.

Seeing the two ornate towers of the cathedral, Charles heads towards them and finds himself in the Place Stanislas, the main square with its fountains, statues and gilded ironwork. He remembers the nurse's apartment was somewhere off here.

A few minutes later he knocks on her door. There is no answer but, as it is open, he walks in and checks the rooms. Inis is in bed. Lehague is by her side, asleep. Charles stares at him in disbelief, wondering if there is a French word for collaboration with a collaborator.

When she opens her eyes and sees him, Inis smiles and sits up without attempting to cover herself. Her breasts are slightly asymmetrical, as Maggie's were: two gently convex slopes. As she leans over to nudge the major awake, they lose their rounded shape a little, but not their hypnotic draw.

'How is your hand?' she asks as she stifles a yawn.

'Lighter,' Charles says.

Inis reaches for her uniform, part of which is draped on the bedhead, part on the bedside table next to an empty wine bottle and two glasses. She slips it on before crawling down the bed to inspect the bandage on Charles's hand. 'Did they give you painkillers?'

Charles retrieves the small bottle of morphine from his pocket and, holding it between finger and thumb, gives it a little shake.

Lehague is sitting up now, eyeing Inis. When she rolls on a pair of stockings, he whistles and says: *'Trop belle pour moi.'*

'Come on,' Inis says, slapping his leg. 'Get dressed.'

Moving carefully to protect his hand, Charles changes into a collarless shirt and a jacket that has a musty, damp odour. Lehague wears a trilby and a suit with a pistol tucked behind his belt.

Under noonday clouds that are low and heavy, they leave for Natzweiler-Struthof on a narrow potholed road that winds steadily upwards and forces them to negotiate overhanging boughs that whip at the wind-screen. Lehague is driving, Charles map-reading. Inis sits between them again. About five miles out of the town they pass a sign in English which reads:

YOU ARE NOW ENTERING ENEMY TERRITORY:
KEEP ON THE ALERT

When they reach a more open stretch lined by the tall spires of Lombardy poplars, Lehague breaks his silence. 'It is said that the poplar leaf shakes because of shame.' He takes his hands off the steering wheel to point at the trees. 'Because it was the wood used to make the cross. But actually it shakes because its leaves are long.'

'At least it has an excuse,' Charles says, holding out his bandaged hand. Inis steadies it gently in her own hand.

There is sweat on his brow again and his eyes close tight against the pain.

As they stick to back roads, the wooded crests of the Vosges rise above them and the incline becomes more noticeable. They watch a mist eddy about the peaks. Though an American plane buzzes them, they do not pass a single German checkpoint. For reassurance, Charles nevertheless feels with his boot for the French rifle concealed in the footwell. It is still there.

'I need to make a stop,' Inis announces.

Lehague pulls over. When Inis disappears behind some bushes, Lehague says: 'Do you think we can trust her?'

'What do you mean?'

'She's a collaborator. How do we know she hasn't tipped off her German friends that we're coming?'

Charles stares at him. 'You know your trouble, Lehague? You're too romantic.'

Lehague laughs. 'The thought hasn't crossed your mind that she could make the Gestapo very happy by presenting them with a senior member of the Resistance?'

'No. We can trust her.'

'How do you know?'

'I know people.'

'Why didn't you sleep with her?' he says. 'It is you she wants, you know, I can tell.'

'Her bed looked rather full to me.'

'Do you think me a hypocrite?'

'Why?'

'For sleeping with a collaborator.'

'I prefer not to judge others.'

Lehague laughs. 'You are a tolerant man, Charles. That is a good quality. It's a pity you are not French. We could do with men like you to help rebuild this country.'

'You don't want men like me.'

Lehague narrows his lips and nods. 'This German friend of yours, why are you prepared to risk your life for him?'

'What do you mean?'

'I saw your file. Back in London.'

'I have a file?'

'It said that you were court-martialled for gross indecency in 1939 for "conduct unbecoming an officer".'

Charles puts his head in his hands. He cannot look at Lehague as he mutters: 'You knew all this time?'

'You didn't expect me to not check up on you, did you?' He touches his moustache. 'It also said you were awarded the George Cross, the highest civilian medal for bravery.'

As he is speaking, Inis slips back into the van. 'You were awarded a medal, Mr Charles?' she asks. 'What did you do?'

'It was nothing. Anyone would have done the same.'

'He tried to rescue a pilot from a burning Spitfire. That was how he got the injuries to his face.'

'I failed.' Charles stares out of the window at a high spine of mountains. It seems to hold an answer to something he wants.

'And now you are trying to rescue your friend,' Inis says. 'You are a good man, Mr Charles.' She takes hold of his hand and kisses it. 'I feel safe with you.'

Slate clouds are washing the eastern sky and mounting thunderheads in the north and south. As they set off again, the road becomes narrower and a branch sweeps along the entire length of the van. The road is meandering through a pine forest now. When they crest the next hill they see a column of Germans trudging across the road ahead of them where another hill starts. It is too late to turn back, so they slow down and come to a stop about ten yards from them. Charles feels for his rifle again with his foot. The back of his neck is numb and he is grinding his teeth. His missing thumb begins to throb. Finding it hard to breathe, he gives a sideways glance at Lehague. Inis takes hold of his good hand. The major tilts his head slightly as if to say, it will be OK.

The faces of the Germans are dirty, their uniforms tattered and unbuttoned. They look defeated and broken. Some have bandages on their heads or their arms in slings. Others barely have the energy to lift their boots. They look either too young or too old, but nothing in between. Their rifles are clanking against their helmets, their bayonets against their mess tins. Their packs give them a humped, misshapen appearance and Charles once more recalls the sight of the British Army retreating to Dunkirk. There are perhaps two hundred of them and those that notice the van as they tramp past look up with dead eyes.

They can now hear the gentle percussion of rain on leaves, but Lehague does not put the wipers on. And he does not start the engine again until the last of the

Germans is out of sight – but even then he doesn't put the van in gear straight away. His hands are shaking and he grips the steering wheel to steady them. Inis retches emptily and lights up a cigar to settle her nerves.

The road where the Germans have crossed is now churned up and their tyres make spinning and sucking sounds as they sink into the mud. One of the Germans has thrown away his helmet, and, once they are clear of the mud, Lehague has to swerve to avoid it.

It is nightfall when, following the contour of a hillside, they reach, or think they reach, the right village, but there are no road signs to confirm this. There is instead the sound of singing around a piano coming from an *estaminet* – melancholy German songs about lost love. The air is leaden and moist.

'Wait here,' Charles says firmly when Lehague opens his door.

The inn is crowded with Frenchmen, in one half of the bar at least. In the other, half a dozen drunken Germans in grey field uniforms are singing around a piano. The barman's forehead has a sheen on it, as if he has been running. His hair is pushed back over a monkish tonsure.

Charles orders a Pernod.

'Haven't seen you in here before,' the barman says.

'This is Natzweiler-Struthof, yes?' Charles asks out of the side of his mouth, keeping his eyes on the Germans.

'Yes.'

'I thought they had gone.'

The barman pours the shot. 'They left a few guards.'

'What are they guarding?'

'Nothing. They get drunk all day.'

'They are not guarding the camp?'

'Most of them won't go near the camp. Typhus.'

'But there are still prisoners in there?'

The barman shrugs.

Charles drains his glass. '*Santé.*'

The barman smiles sourly and gives a sideways glance at the grey uniforms before saying in a low voice: '*Santé.*'

When Charles returns to the van to collect his rifle he says: 'Six guards. Drunk. There doesn't seem to be anyone up at the camp.'

'Let's take a look, then,' Lehague says.

The sound of the singing fades into the night air as the three leave the inn and head up into the main part of the village. It is so quiet as they walk through it that they become conscious of the clatter of their boots and shoes on the cobbles.

When a dog barks in the distance they stop.

They then see Gothic lettering on a sign: 'Halt!' Behind this there are the black and white chicane stripes of a sentry box and a wire fence inset with photoelectric cells. On this is painted a sign with a skull and crossbones and the single word '*Typhus*'. Above this is a '*verboten*' sign. Lining the fence are white rags.

'Are they expecting visitors?' Inis says in a whisper.

The burning smell of a coke brazier becomes noticeable but in the dim moonlight it is not obvious where it is coming from. Charles throws pebbles into the darkness of the camp to see if the sound will draw out any hidden sentries. Nothing stirs. He feels uneasy, though, and presses the spring plunger that releases the built-in

468

spike bayonet on his rifle. He pulls it out, turns it round and, with a click, fits it back into the receptacle before advancing to the sentry box.

Inside he sees a guard sleeping, his head on the table, his back to the door. He is wearing a cape that conceals his shape. There is an empty bottle to his side, next to a whip. Charles is standing over him when he opens his eyes and, in panic, reaches for a snub-nosed pistol. Mechanically, Charles thrusts the spike as hard as he can, stabbing the guard between his shoulder girdle and neck. In the same moment, the man pulls the trigger and a parachute flare hisses out of the sentry box and illuminates the night sky. With a grunt, Charles withdraws the spike and, cupping the butt of the rifle, plunges it in again, this time stabbing the guard between the ribs as he rolls forward. He makes an answering gurgle as his punctured lung projects blood out of his mouth. A jet of it soaks Charles's trouser leg and he finds himself staring at the man without anger or pity. This is his enemy. An obstacle. Only now, as the man's body jerks and he slides down the door like a drunkard, his legs spreading out from under him in a V-shape, does Charles see he is wearing a skirt. Her head lolls back. A red bubble forms on her lips, blown by a final breath, and then it pops. Her dying eyes glaze, but do not blink.

As he backs away from the box, Charles realizes the butt of his rifle is wet with blood. He wipes his hands on his jacket and replays the sound of the struggle, as if it is a recording he has been listening to, a wireless play involving two actors. Lehague and Inis are standing frozen and spectral in the potassium light of the flare as it slowly descends. All around them sinister shapes are emerging: smouldering heaps of rags, abandoned boxes and vehicles.

'Come on,' Lehague hisses. 'The flare will have alerted the whole village. We have to hurry.'

Charles shakes his head, coming out of his trance. He sees the camp is not so much a prison as a set of municipal buildings. The wooden watchtowers are empty. As they tread carefully behind the checkpoint, he notices a flat, sour smell like curdled milk and reaches for his hanky, holding it to his mouth.

The flare goes out and the returning darkness seems more absolute than before.

Not only has the camp been abandoned, it seems to have been closed down. Lehague, who is also holding a hanky to his nose, tries a tap. No water. Charles flips a light switch in the entrance of a tall building draped with swastikas. No electricity. A sign here reads: 'Kommandantur'. It is dark inside. He shines a torch in and sees an unfinished game of dominoes. A portrait of Hitler. Plates of bread. The Germans have left in a hurry.

A loose iron sheet from the roof creaks.

Charles rejoins Lehague outside and shrugs. 'Anything?'

'Nothing.'

The camp falls silent again. The perfume of death is everywhere. Charles has come to recognize it. He directs his torch at a long building ahead of them and takes in a pile of green and purple corpses that have been left against the wall, stacked like sandbags, six of them awaiting burial. The lumps on their faces look swollen and putrefactive. They have grown obese in death: heat-swollen legs, bellies and buttocks. A few ribs are protruding from the cadaverous chest balanced on top of the pile and, as the torchlight passes over them, they appear to have a silvery sheen. Charles sees the maggots now as they lust after the corpse, a train of them filing into the gaping chest wound.

When Charles points at himself, then at the building, Lehague gives him a thumbs-up sign. As he enters he realizes this is the infirmary – a red cross behind camouflage netting. He flicks his torch around again. More bones in rags, but nothing living. There is a dead body on the nearest bed. It is moving with lice. Charles scratches his arms, suddenly aware of their itchiness.

Death, the unmentionable odour, is overwhelming in here, searing the lungs and twisting the stomach. There is no language for it. Realizing he has entered the world of a nightmare, Charles fears even to breathe the polluted air. He presses his handkerchief hard to his face. 'Anselm?' The voice is hesitant, as if disturbing the silence will bring out demons. There is a scurry of move-ment in his peripheral vision. Rats on yet another body inflated with decomposition, half the head missing. He doesn't make it to the door before vomiting.

The three walk back to the entrance of the camp in silence. Their journey has been futile.

'What should we do?' Inis asks when they are beyond the perimeter fence.

'There is nothing else we can do,' Lehague says. 'When we get back to Nancy we tell the Americans that the

471

Germans have gone. They can then get over here and round up the last of them, force them to clean up the camp and dig the graves. That's the . . . What is it, Charles?'

Charles is staring at a large, pale building with a turret that seems to disappear into the night. He feels drawn to it by a gravitational tug, as if an electronic magnet has been switched on in his abdomen. That is the place, he thinks. After travelling nearly four thousand miles, and across five years, I have reached my destination. 'Give me ten minutes,' he says. 'I want to take a look in there.'

'Forget it,' Lehague says. 'We've been lucky so far. If we leave now we might be able to avoid the guards.'

'Please.'

Lehague ends the discussion by turning and walking back in the direction of the van.

'François.'

The Frenchman stops. Rubs the back of his neck. Turns. The two men hold each other's glare for several seconds that are broken into smaller units, slower frames of time in which cold calculations are being made. Charles can feel his sinews tightening. He squares his shoulders.

Lehague seems to see an energy in his eyes he hasn't seen before. He holds his hands up in mock surrender. 'OK, OK. But if you're not back in ten minutes, we're leaving without you.'

Two stone eagles either side of the front door seem to narrow their gazes at Charles as he approaches the house. He becomes intensely aware of his surroundings,

hearing every murmur of every leaf in the tall trees swaying overhead. He tests the door. It groans open. Inside,
the darkness is thick.

He hears the snap of a chain before he sees the
animal attached to it. When he shines his torch,
the Alsatian's eyes glow eerily. It bares its teeth but is too
weak to bark. Clearly it hasn't been fed for weeks. On a
nearby table there is half a loaf of mouldy bread. He
places it at the dog's feet and, as it sniffs it, he
unbuckles its collar.

His torch now finds dry, unswept leaves, pigeon
feathers and a display cabinet. As he takes a couple of
steps closer, he sees that it contains butterfly specimens
pinned to corkboards. He tries a light switch but, again,
there is no electricity. Ghost-footing now, he enters a
long room lined with tapestries and antlers mounted as
trophies. It looks as if there has been a fight in here.
Curtains have been torn down, chairs tipped over. There
is broken glass and piles of papers scattered on the
floor, some singed. Someone has been in a hurry to
burn boxes of papers in the fireplace, but they have
piled them on so heavily they have put the flames out.

A door in the far corner of this room leads on to a
wide spiralling staircase. Charles looks behind him,
thinking he has heard a noise. He then takes the steps
two at a time.

There are eight doors in the passage at the top. One is
open. He raises his rifle to his hip, pointing it in the
same direction as his torch beam.

A four-poster bed dominates the room. There is
someone lying on it, his face moving with flies. Were it

not for his occasional blinks, he might be stone.

The man attempts to shield his eyes, but is too weak. Realizing what he is doing, Charles lays the torch down, takes a step closer and sits on the bed cautiously, as if expecting it to collapse under his weight.

Bony fingers feel for his. They are dry and cold. When the wraith tries to speak, his breath is sordid and faecal. Charles edges closer and, brushing away the flies, leans over so that their lips can touch.

He can feel his heart blooming within his chest.

'Anselm.'

PART EIGHT

I

London. Present day. Summer. One year, three months and eighteen days after Edward's release

THOUGH THE TEARS HAVE DRIED ON HANNAH'S CHEEKS, INSIDE she still feels saturated and heavy with grief. First her father's symbolic 'funeral', then her mother's real one, and now this. When her mother died, her grandfather became her family, her only surviving relative in England, as far as she knew. And though he hadn't been able to communicate with her in any meaningful way in his final years, she had, nevertheless, found his company reassuring.

Now she is on her way to his funeral and the London sky is grey, sagging with the prospect of rain. Her clothes feel like lead on her shoulders, their blackness adding to their weight – black coat, black beret, black leather gloves.

Her father is in the seat beside her, holding her hand.

With a ticking sound, the first drops of rain appear on the sunroof. They form fat pools on the glass. The funeral procession, which consists of the black limousine they are in and the hearse ahead of them, has come to a halt. When they start moving again, the big sloppy drops drag into new patterns. Some of the pools are an inch across, ovals with one side lined black, catching the dark cloud.

'Do you think there will be many people there?' Hannah asks.

'Doubt it. Don't think Dad had many friends. A few cousins maybe. Perhaps there will be some people coming along out of curiosity after reading his obituaries.'

As her father lets go of her hand now, Hannah feels as if she might sink into the car seat, pulled down as if in quicksand, as exhausted as her tear ducts. She draws her arm back, rubs it and, laying her head back on the rest, thinks about her grandfather's last request, as conveyed to them by a nervous-sounding probate lawyer. Apparently, he wanted to have his heart cut out before he was buried. The solicitor's reassurances that there are precedents for this have not convinced either of them. He is not at liberty to say what her grandfather wanted done with the heart. It is to be removed and handed over to the law firm, and that will be that. She shivers at the thought. It seems such a macabre thing to do.

'Still can't believe all the broadsheets ran obituaries,' she says. 'I had no idea he was considered that influential.'

'Neither had I, to be honest. I imagine the *Guardian* and the *Telegraph* felt they had to run something after *The Times* gave him so much space.'

The hearse ahead of them draws up to the church. Cars outside churches, Hannah thinks. What harbingers of news: some carry babies, some carry corpses, some carry brides. She wonders if Edward will be reminded of his wedding day. A remembered smile. A mental picture of his bride walking down the aisle.

When their car pulls in behind the hearse, Edward steps out and goes around to open the door for Hannah. As she emerges, she notices how many cars are parked in the roads around the church. Among them is a black Mercedes-Benz.

'Hey, isn't that the car we went to France in?'

Edward looks over.

So attuned to his moods has Hannah become, she can sense his brow pricking.

'That's strange . . .' he says.

Litter from an overturned bin is spiralling, giving shape to the breeze. Women mourners arriving late have to hold their hats on with their hands. Men hug their coats around them as if about to open them suddenly. There are half a dozen press photographers checking their flash units and battery packs as they wait by the church's porch.

Martin Cullen arrives. Hannah is about to go over and say hello when she sees he is with a woman walking a few paces behind him. When he stops to wait for her she stops too and rubs the expectant swell of her abdomen. Its compressed weight and rounded line is bellied like a fig. She is out of breath and, as she tries to catch it, she holds up a finger to say 'one minute'. Martin looks over and, seeing Hannah, walks in her direction and greets her with a single kiss on the cheek.

Hannah looks across at the pregnant woman, an eyebrow rising.

'My colleague Helen. She wrote the *Guardian*'s obituary of your grandfather and wanted to come along to pay her respects. As did I.'

The funeral director approaches. Behind him is Niall, along with two other men wearing black suits and coats: 'Whenever you are ready, Mr Northcote. The trick is to form a bridge with your arm under the coffin and put your hand on the shoulder of the bearer next to you. I'll be walking in front.'

Edward stands behind the hearse as the back is opened and the arrangement of lilies taken from the top of the coffin. The first two pallbearers pull the coffin out, moving along its length as Edward and the third bearer step in. Its lightness seems to take all four men by surprise, as if its contents are already dust.

Hannah follows the coffin. As they march slowly in step along the church path, she notices the flag bearers lining the route, three on each side. They appear to be army cadets and the flags they are struggling to keep upright in the wind seem to be regimental ones, faded and threadbare. When the pallbearers reach the porch, electronic flashes turn Edward bluey-white.

As soon as the cadets are inside, the door is closed behind them, blocking out the rustle of the wind in the leaves. The stillness seems to be exaggerated. Though it is mid-afternoon, darkness has crept into the church already. Dozens of candles are guttering.

Only now does Hannah become aware of how many

mourners there are. The church is full. There are a couple of old-timers in RAF ties whose faces are unnaturally smooth. Burn victims, perhaps. But many seem to be young, in their twenties. Few are wearing ties. Art students? Did her grandfather have some kind of cult following? There is one man who looks familiar. In his sixties or seventies but with his round glasses and a white side parting he has a boyish appearance. Where has she seen him before? Is it Alan Bennett? No, he is dressed too flamboyantly, a maroon jacket over a black shirt and tie – in fact he looks as if he has stopped off at this funeral on his way to a regatta. It isn't David Hockney, is it? Surely he lives in California? She nods at the man and he acknowledges her with a firm little smile.

Once the coffin has been laid on the bench, Edward bows at the altar and then takes his place alongside Hannah in the warped and creaky front pew. As they stand for the first hymn, 'I Vow To Thee, My Country', she looks around and sees that the regimental flags are those of the Association of War Artists.

As they come to the penultimate petition of the Lord's Prayer – lead us not into temptation – she feels her father's hand squeeze hers and wonders if this is a coincidence. He is an Anglican atheist, after all. It is the source of his moral strength and courage.

How perfect the Church of England funeral service is, Edward thinks. Not too mawkish. Not too detached. A form of words that has evolved over centuries to strike exactly the right tone, even if it does lie as lifeless on his

481

tongue as the small print on an insurance document.

As his daughter edges past, pressing against him in negotiation of the narrow pew, he feels a frisson, the twitch on the line. His eyes follow her as she makes her way to the front of the church to do a reading. Shakespeare. *Cymbeline*, Act IV, Scene 2.

Her strides lengthen as she nears the lectern and, as she reads in a clear voice – '. . . Fear not slander, censure rash; / Thou hast finish'd joy and moan; / All lovers young, all lovers must / Consign to thee, and come to dust . . .' – Edward gazes up at her in wonder and feels weak. I love you more than life, he thinks. More than life.

Before she has finished the reading, her face, already pale, turns paler. Her eyes roll up in their sockets and then her knees give and she falls neatly and quietly to the floor of the chancel. Edward is the first to her side. He gathers her up and, by the time he has carried her the few yards to the north transept, she has come round. The organist hands her a glass of water. She puts her head to her knees for a moment, then sits stiffly upright, as though guarding a secret. Edward repeats the words in his head: I love you more than life.

Once she has reassured him that she is fine, he returns to his pew and the vicar indicates with a discreet nod that it is Edward's turn to walk to the lectern. When he reaches it he coughs to clear his throat. 'Thank you all for coming. I know my father would have appreciated it.' He studies the faces for a moment and, when he sees in the front row a small, stooping old man who looks weighed down by the Légion d'Honneur he is wearing, he acknowledges him with a nod. 'I thought I would mention some of the milestones in my father's life,' he begins, taking out some notes from his jacket. 'After graduating from the Slade School of Fine Art in 1938, he joined the RAF. I'm not sure where he was stationed, but I think he was medically discharged before he saw any action. Certainly he never mentioned having taken part in the Battle of Britain. Like many of his generation he didn't talk much about his war service; in fact I learned quite a lot from reading the obituaries.' There are murmurs of laughter at this. 'Apparently he took part in the evacuation of Dunkirk. I knew he had done some paintings of it and that they were reproduced in the *Picture Post*, but I'd always assumed he had painted them from news photographs. On the strength of those he was asked to become an official war artist and, some time in the early years of the war, he was commissioned to paint front-line RAF bases in the south of England. While doing that, he was caught up in a bombing raid. After attempting to rescue a pilot from a burning Spitfire, he was left with disfiguring burns on his face. For these heroics, as I discovered from his obituaries, he was awarded the George Cross. He spent the next three years convalescing and became a member of the legendary Guinea Pig Club. Then, in 1944, he took part in . . .' Edward holds up two fingers and punctuates the air with them as if pitching a title to a Hollywood producer, ' "The Forgotten D-Day", the Allied invasion of southern France, again documenting the action. For this he was awarded a second medal, the Croix de Guerre. Again, he never dwelt on the details of this, not with me anyway. At some point he managed to get himself injured for a second time, losing a thumb.'

Edward looks across at Hannah, mouths 'You OK?' and when she gives a thumbs-up he continues: 'After the war, my father was made a Royal Academician and had exhibitions at Tate Modern and the Imperial War Museum.' Edward pauses. 'This is what we know about him, anyway. But I suspect he has taken a lot of history with him. Not secrets exactly but . . .' He searches for the right word. 'He was quite a bohemian in his way. A restless spirit who never settled down. And he had a colourful circle of friends who included, at various times, Francis Bacon and Lucian Freud. And,' he looks at another elderly man he has recognized in the congregation, 'if I'm not mistaken, David Hockney.' When the congregation turns to follow Edward's gaze, the ageing artist raises his hand in acknowledgement.

'I didn't know him when he was younger, of course, but I got the impression that he became more at ease with himself when he joined the beat generation of poets, artists and musicians. He had digs in Paris for a while in the 1950s. He also, I believe, spent time in Amsterdam and New York. And Germany. I know that for a fact, because that's where I was born!'

He turns the page of his notes. 'Whether he was an easy man to live with, I don't know. I don't think he was perfect. He probably drank too much. Experimented with drugs. And he could be self-absorbed, always putting his art first. But he did have a sense of responsibility. He raised me on his own.'

484

Edward glances up at the stained glass window. 'What else can I tell you? When he spoke you could watch him thinking because he would leave long, searching gaps between sentences, and instead of raising his voice in an argument he would speak more quietly. He was an intrepid traveller, a witty guest, a man women fell in love with.'

Edward narrows his eyes. At the back of the church he has seen a tall, moustachioed man he recognizes. He is holding a wreath of leaves. Next to him is a slightly shorter man whose face is expressionless; his thick silver hair is cresting his grey-jacketed back. He has dark alert eyes and his gaze now and then shifts – from mourner to mourner – like an automatic course correction, and then it settles down. Nothing else moves.

'My father didn't believe in life after death,' Edward continues, 'but he did believe that we live on in the memories of our children, for a generation at least. And he did believe in art and beauty. Aesthetics was his religion. I wish I had been around for his final years. I saw him not long ago and all he would say was "answer". I don't know what the answer was, but I hope he has found it now.'

After the service, Edward helps carry the coffin out again. The wind is stronger, lashing with rain. It is bending the trees and the vicar is having to hold his cassock down. A woman clinging on to a black umbrella staggers as it snaps inside out, a broken-backed crow in her hands. The hearse is going back to the morgue, where the heart is to be removed. The rest of the body is to be buried in the coffin tomorrow.

Edward is searching for Walser but as he edges his way through the mourners he is stopped by a small, white-haired old man he hadn't seen in the church. He has a hearing aid, a broken nose and a DSO on his barrel chest. He must be almost a hundred.

'Your father was indeed at Dunkirk,' the old man says in a surprisingly strong voice. 'I know because he helped crew my little boat, *The Painted Lady*. The two of us went over and picked up a dozen or so soldiers as part of the evacuation. That's when he did his sketches.'

'You were friends?'

'Yes, before the war. I thought it was outrageous what they did to him.'

'His burns, you mean?'

'No, the court martial.'

'What? What court martial?'

'That was no way to treat an officer. But that was how things were in those days.'

'What court martial?'

The old man looks blank. 'What?'

'You said something about a court martial.'

'I didn't see him much after the war, though I gather he had a child.'

'Me, I'm his child.'

'What? He was a good man was old Charlie. A good man . . . Funf. That was what he called me. I thought it was a disgrace what they did to him after the war. I think it was that more than anything that killed her, you know.'

'Killed who?'

'Your mother.'

486

'My mother died of cancer.'

'Yes, but she never quite recovered after the shock of the trial.'

'What trial? The court martial?'

'No, the other one.'

The old man looks at him with confusion in his eyes. 'Who are you?'

'Edward. Charles was my father.'

'Charles, that's right. I remember now . . .'

With a shake of his head he walks away looking distracted, as if he is late for something but cannot remember what.

Edward watches him for a moment then looks around for Walser, but his car has gone.

II

Three weeks later

IT ISN'T THE SMELL THAT EDWARD NOTICES FIRST AS HE TURNS the front-door key and pushes against a weight of piled letters and magazines, it's the silence. Frown lines appear on his forehead as he listens. There is no bleeping, which means the alarm isn't set. Hannah must be at home. Her bike in the hall confirms it.

'Han?'

The silence deepens and becomes more alert, as if the whole house is holding its breath to listen. He picks up the post and flicks through some bills, pizza leaflets and circulars before coming to a handwritten cream-coloured envelope. A card from Walser, three lines long. It extends his condolences for the death of his father, thanks him for his letter and the wine, trusts that his stay at the house in France wasn't too marred by the storm.

That's it? Edward thinks, looking on the back of the card to see if he has missed something. After the funeral he had written to Walser to thank him for inviting them to stay at the château and to commiserate about the storm damage. He had sent a case of burgundy as a gesture of his appreciation: expensive bottles recommended by Berry Bros & Rudd.

He is at the foot of the stairs now, the card still in his hand. 'Hannah? You here?'

Again, silence.

She has been staying with friends in Brighton for a few days – something about her band having reformed, though Edward hadn't been aware that they had split. They have a new drummer, apparently, and she has a friend who has booked some studio time for them so that they can put together a demo.

Edward had taken the opportunity to visit some friends of his own: a couple with a farm in the Peak District. He had known them since university and, over the past year, they had written several times to insist he visit them, and suggested other old friends who could come along at the same time, but Niall had advised against it on the grounds that he wasn't ready for social contact as demanding as that.

As it turned out, Edward had enjoyed the trip. They had gone on long walks, drunk too much, used long wooden spoons as microphones as they sang out of tune to old hits. And in the mornings, before the others were up, he had gone for walks on his own.

He had hoped that the break would clear his head of the chatter curdling there: unresolved questions about his father, about what was said about him by the old man at the funeral; but also questions about the circumstances of his release by the Taliban, why, seventeen months on, Niall's version of events was ringing false in his ears.

The unease was to do with the way Niall had gone from being merely controlling to paranoid, insisting he should be the first to read the memoir; that he should be the one Edward turned to, about anything that was worrying him, 'anything at all'.

But what was worrying him, what was making him increasingly angry, was the thought that if Niall hadn't had him declared dead, Frejya would still be alive, and he wouldn't be having these dreadful, crippling thoughts about his own daughter.

In France, he had experienced an emotion so long buried he hadn't recognized it at first. Love. It had approached in disguise, as stealthily as an assassin, and then it had shifted in his imagination from noun to verb. What would it feel like? It? The act itself? His mind shied from the questions, yet, as he pictured himself with her, he felt intoxicated as well as repelled.

He had even persuaded himself that she might be complicit in these dangerous thoughts, that his feelings for her could be reciprocated. But as he listened again to the echo of her words – 'I will do whatever it takes to make you happy', 'You don't have to feel guilty about being with me' – they seemed ambiguous.

The funeral had reduced his fever, helped take his mind off the gnaw he felt. But as soon as they were alone together in Parsons Green again, his tension, as well as his confusion, had returned. He had found himself lost once more in a dark and steaming jungle. And, what was worse, Hannah seemed to sense his appalled fascination with her: the glances, the unexplained frowns, the tight, self-conscious smiles.

His meditative early-morning walks in the Peak District had provided him with only one resolution. That he must not discuss his predicament with anyone else – not her, not his friends in the Peak District, not even Niall. Of these dark thoughts he must remain silent.

He is in the sitting room now. On top of the piano is a full ashtray: roaches from joints as well as cigarette butts. There are five empty wine bottles here, too, some on their sides, but no glasses. He wanders around the house, checking rooms. The heavy, colourless smell is permeating the whole house.

Hannah does not respond when Edward knocks lightly on her bedroom door. He pushes it ajar and sees her suitcase open on the bed. He also sees the door to her bathroom is open. With a chill in his heart, he walks towards it and looks in. There is no sign of her. Back in the bedroom he sees a large canvas stretched on a wooden frame, facing the wall. He pulls it back. It is the portrait she did of him in France. Finished now.

Striding to the window he sees his daughter on the floor by the bed, partly covered by a duvet. He is about to check her pulse when she turns on her side, adjusting her pillow. There is a damp patch where her mouth has been.

He hardly recognizes her. Her face looks thinner and she has not only had a pixie crop but she has dyed her hair black.

It looks like the dye has run down her face, but then

491

he realizes this is smeared mascara. She has been crying. Drinking, too. Even from a few feet away he can smell the alcohol coming through her pores. There are three empty wine bottles on the floor and another on the bedside table.

'Han?'

She opens her eyes and shields them against the light. 'Oh it's you. Hi. When did you get back?'

'Just now. You OK?'

She yawns, pulls back the duvet and reveals that she has been sleeping in her clothes, a baggy sweatshirt and jeans ripped at the knees. A wipe of her mouth now. A feel on the bedside table for the glasses she has taken to wearing instead of contacts. 'Yeah, fine, I must have . . .' She glances at her alarm clock and sits up. 'I'll go and put the kettle on.'

'I like your new look.'

'Thanks. It's one of the requirements for the witness protection scheme they've put me on.' Seeing his look of confusion she adds in a flat voice: 'That's a joke.'

When Edward sees that she is unsteady on her feet he asks again if she is OK.

'Don't worry, I'm not about to faint again.'

'Your mother used to faint, you know.'

Hannah knits her brow. 'I'd forgotten that . . . But she did, didn't she? . . . She fainted when Uncle Niall told her you had been declared dead . . . Is it hereditary?'

'I don't know.' He follows her down the stairs. 'Can you smell something?'

Hannah now has a roll-up dangling from her lip, a half-smoked one taken from an ashtray. She lights it, tests the air and wrinkles her nose. 'It's coming from the kitchen.'

She seems quieter, he thinks. Withdrawn and distracted. They walk into the kitchen together and Hannah opens the pantry door. Winces. It smells like putrefaction. 'There's something decomposing in there.'

Edward opens the window and retrieves some sheets of newspaper from the recycling bin. 'What is it?'

'I think it might have been a tuna steak. I, like, vaguely recall putting one out to defrost the night before I left.' She hooks her thumbs in the belt straps of her jeans and shrugs apologetically.

Edward opens the back door, scrapes the rotting fish into the bin and sprays the dead air with a can of something intended to evoke the freshness of mountains. It makes it worse, merely adding a chemical smell to the noxious mix. 'I'm going to take a shower,' he says.

Ten minutes later, wrapped in a towel, Edward gathers up his clothes and makes his way along the cool corridor to his bedroom, savouring the air on his tightening pores. Instead of dressing, he looks out of the window and sees Hannah in the garden, her face now washed and clean. She is sitting at the table listening to her iPod through headphones while applying fresh mascara to her lashes. He continues staring as she dips a brush in and out of a tube, then, with delicate little upward flicks, moves down the length of a lash, then across to the other eye, then back to the first, brushing again and again, as if in a trance.

Now she is holding a compact mirror up to her face, her eyes wide, brushing off stray lashes. A crimping device comes next, and all the while she is studying her reflection – her hardened, hopeless face – as if trying to come to a decision.

He hears himself asking: what have I done to you? What have I become? You look so self-possessed as you sit there in the sunlight, so deep within yourself.

In moments such as this, when the fog lifts, when he is feeling morally strong, he understands that he is being selfish, and that there is a sacrifice he can make which will improve things, for both of them. He must leave. And when he does, he cannot tell her the reason.

She looks up. Puts her glasses on and sees him looking down. Neither looks away.

Early the next morning, when he is more awake than asleep, Edward tries to slip back into his dream. As it drifts away from him, losing its shape and colour, he remains lying on his front in an erotic stupor. After half a minute, he tenses his buttocks and shifts his position in the bed, savouring the prickling sensation in the backs of his thighs. 'I love you,' he mumbles into his pillow, and the articulation of the words brings him closer to the surface of consciousness.

He now opens his eyes and gasps for breath, as though he has been breathing underwater only to realize in panic that this is impossible.

He rolls over and, feeling evidence of nocturnal emission against his back, sits up and looks around the bedroom, dazed and heavy-limbed. The stillness in the house intensifies and is then broken by a knock at the front door. He blinks. There are three more taps, evenly spaced.

He reaches for his dressing gown and, as he descends the stairs unsteadily, his knees still watery, he curses to himself. Bloody journalists. Why won't they leave me alone? Niall had promised he would make them stop.

When he looks through the spyhole he sees it is a woman with a grey fringe and glasses, middle-aged. It takes a moment before he recognizes her as Hannah's therapist. Instead of letting her in, he watches as she knocks again and paces for a couple of minutes before walking away.

More awake now, he draws his dressing gown around himself and knots the cord before heading back up the stairs to his bedroom, pulling his sheet and duvet cover off and carrying them in a loose bundle down to the washroom. He stops. Thinks: What am I doing? This is crazy. Hannah isn't going to inspect my sheets. He continues anyway and, as he slams the door of the washing machine and clicks the dial to the correct cycle, he hears someone entering the room behind him and flinches guiltily.

'Who was that at the door?' Hannah says with a yawn.

'No one.'

'What are you doing?'

He doesn't look up, hiding the colour rising in his cheeks by studying the temperature settings. 'Putting a wash on.'

'I can see that. Why are you doing it now? You're not even dressed.'

As he searches for a way out of this conversation, a

diversionary tactic of some sort, Edward looks up at her and says with a tight laugh: '*Carpe diem*, Frejya.' He knows it has been a long time since he has mistaken his daughter for his wife, and he wonders if she will hear the falseness in his tone, recognize the deception for what it is.

'You called me Frejya again, Dad.' She says it wearily. Exhausted by all this now.

'I'm sorry. I . . .' He knows her question about the sheets has already been forgotten, that he is in the clear. He also wonders whether his pretence might help their situation. If he can convince Hannah that the love he has started feeling for her is not the same as that which he felt for her mother they might yet avoid the fate that seems ordained. 'How did you sleep?' he asks.

'Not great. You?'

'I had a dream about Frejya, that was why I said her name just now.'

'Do you ever dream about me?' Her question sounds like an accusation. She is studying him with furrowed interest.

'Not that I'm aware,' he says. Every night, he thinks. Last night. But I cannot tell you that.

'Mummy never really loved me, you know.'

'Of course she did.'

'She didn't. Not in the way she loved you. She thought of me as a rival. She couldn't bear it when I made you laugh.'

'She loved you.'

Hannah raises her hands in an open gesture. 'She used to cut me out of photographs. I found them.

Photographs where the three of us had been together. That's why I always made sure I was in between you two, so she couldn't get the scissors out.'

Edward shakes his head. Looks away.

'Didn't you ever wonder why you didn't have more children after me?'

He meets her eye now. 'We weren't able to.'

'She wanted you to herself.'

'Stop it, Han.'

'It's OK, I can live with it.'

Edward freezes. He sees for the first time a truth that had been glaring at him for years. The way Frejya had looked at him whenever he was playing with Hannah . . . 'She loved you with all her heart,' he says.

'How could she kill herself, then?'

Edward stares at the floor as he takes two steps towards his daughter and gathers her in his arms. My darling girl, he thinks. How we have failed you as parents, one loving you too much, the other not enough. 'She did love you, and so do I.' More than I should, he adds in his thoughts. More than is right. 'But I don't know how to be the father you need.'

Hannah finishes the thought as she pushes him away. 'But I know how to be the daughter you need. If you'll let me.'

Ambiguity again? The phone rings in the hall. Neither moves to answer it.

Hannah checks the time on her mobile. 'I'm expecting someone.'

'That therapist?'

'Yeah.'

'You don't need to see her,' he says. 'You can talk to me.'

'What if it's you I want to talk about?'

Edward feels as if he has been punched.

'Sorry, Dad, I didn't mean anything by that. Perhaps you need to see her.'

'Waste of time.'

'Is it?' Hannah tents her fingers and presses them to her chin in a parody of a psychoanalyst. 'Is it really?'

He stares at her. 'You know I love you, don't you?' he says. 'That's all that matters. That I love you.'

Hannah replies with a silence that once again seems like an accusation. She then says: 'Do you love me more than her?'

'That's not a fair question.'

'I have my answer.'

Edward sees something in her eyes, like a cold wind passing over a Northumbrian beach. Good, he thinks. This is for the best.

'I thought I wanted to *be* her, you know,' she says. 'So that you would love me, but I can't do it any more. I can't compete with a ghost.'

'There's no competition. No, that sounds wrong. I mean, it's not a competition.'

'Oh, but it is.' Hannah's voice is tightening. 'And the funny thing is, Mummy knew it, too.'

The doorbell rings. *Why won't those bastards leave me alone?* Edward looks through the spyhole and sees that it is not another press photographer but a delivery man, shrunken and distorted. He jumps when the bell rings again. A note is pushed through the letterbox, informing him that a trip to the post office is required. What will it be? There is nothing he wants, nothing he expects. Besides, contact with the outside world seems unwelcome lately.

He opens the door, signs for a large parcel and carries it through to his study. Here he sits down cross-legged on the floor and opens it to find it is from the nursing home.

At the top of the box is a pair of slippers. Underneath these is a leather motorcycle helmet. Placing this carefully on the floor he reaches for his father's kimono. Next he comes to a tightly folded newspaper cutting. It shows the photograph that his Taliban guards had taken of him holding up a copy of the *Daily Telegraph*. Scrawled across it, in his father's hand, are the words 'Call F', followed by a number.

He continues searching, for what he does not know. Here is a cigar box full of letters tied with ribbon. The writing on the envelopes is Gothic. Here an RAF tie, a khaki armband with the words 'Official War Artist', a collar stud, a cravat, an exhibition catalogue, a cap badge depicting a guinea pig with wings, an old and scratched pair of binoculars, and a silver hip flask engraved with the letters 'HR'. He opens it and sniffs. Whiskey. Of course. And here is a collection of paint-brushes tied with an elastic band, some pencils and a carrier bag full of paint tubes, mostly used, carefully rolled, solidified. Paint had been his father's lifeblood, he thinks. Now it is dry and hard.

Though his father's possessions are spread out

around him on the floor, the box is still not empty. He lifts out a copy of the 'Wolfenden Report' on homosexual offences, 155 pages long and published in 1957. It is stained with coffee-cup rings. There is a bookmark halfway through: a newspaper cutting about an inquest into the death of Alan Turing, the Bletchley Park codebreaker. It reports how a verdict of suicide had been recorded after he bit into a poisoned apple in imitation of Snow White.

Paperclipped to this is a sepia photograph. It shows two men bending slightly to kiss the same woman on what looks like VE Day, judging by the flags and the crowds doing a conga behind them in Trafalgar Square. All three look to be in their mid-twenties. The men are in profile, as one kisses the woman's right cheek, the other her left. Because the faces of the men are at exactly the same height it gives the illusion that they were about to kiss each other when the woman popped up between them. She is staring straight at the camera, laughing. There is a cigar in the corner of her mouth and she is wearing an army officer's cap that is too big for her and seems to belong to the uniformed man on her left. Edward recognizes her, and him. They are his mother and father. He doesn't recognize the other man, a civilian in a suit whose face is partly obscured by the trilby he is wearing.

He puts it on the floor and takes out a picture frame from the box. It contains a black and white photograph of the same man holding a baby. Next to him is his father aged about fifty, judging by his thinning hair and paunch. His sideburns date the photograph to the

500

Swinging Sixties, as does his striped jacket, open-neck shirt and the silk scarf he is wearing instead of a tie. He has his arm around the shoulder of a boy holding a football. Edward guesses that the boy is about ten and wonders for a moment if it is him. No, he is sure it isn't.

Wondering when the photograph was taken, he opens up the back and feels a skid of pain as he pushes at the rusting clips with his fingernail. He presses with both thumbs to ease the glass out of the frame. There is a tourist postcard of Eros in Piccadilly Circus. It is in colour and looks as if it dates back to the 1950s. There is nothing written on the back of this except the small type of the caption across the bottom: 'Eros came to symbolise the cult of beauty for the Aesthetic Movement of Oscar Wilde, William Morris and Aubrey Beardsley.'

Under this is what looks like the back of the photograph, and handwritten on it is the word 'Anselm'. What does it mean? Is it a name? He peels it out of the frame and realizes it is written on the back of a second photograph tucked behind the first. He turns the second photograph over and sees it is of two young men laughing and raising their glasses in a toast. One of them is in RAF uniform. It is his father again. How handsome he looks. Who is he with? Whoever it is, he is handsome, too. They look about the same age.

Is this Anselm?

The sound of the word has purchase. Where has he heard it before? Anselm . . . Answer . . . Anselm . . . Answer. Was this what his father had been saying? He studies Anselm's face in the photograph. It looks familiar. He then compares it to the man holding the baby in the other photograph and the man with his arm around the woman in Trafalgar Square on VE Day.

The same.

Edward continues sifting through the contents of the box. Here is his father's Croix de Guerre and the thin silver flower of the George Cross stuffed carelessly into the same presentation box. And here in a random pile is a dog-eared copy of *The Waste Land*, a polished Sam Browne belt, motorcycle goggles, a pack of Horniman's Quick Brew Tea, a Comet typewriter ribbon, a bar of Sunlight soap in a sun-faded packet, a receipt for dinner from the Chelsea Arts Club (10s. 6d.) . . . And this . . . a yellowing cutting from the *Baltimore Sun* about the liberation of a Nazi concentration camp. It is little more than a photograph and caption.

He holds it up to the light and realizes the photograph is of his father again and that he is carrying what looks like a concentration camp victim into a hospital. He looks at the face of the victim. Then he looks at the photograph marked 'Anselm' and then at the photograph of the three people in Trafalgar Square. The same. The same. The same.

His thoughts are interrupted by the sound of keys turning in the front door. He looks up distractedly and, realizing it is Hannah coming home, lowers his gaze once more to the photograph in his hand.

Who are you, Anselm? What were you to my father? And what kind of a name is Anselm? Is it German? Why didn't my father talk about you?

He fans the photographs out on the desk and stares at them in frustration. What use are they without captions? Without names? Without dates? Photographs are only meaningful when they come with memories.

The doorbell rings again. He can feel his neck muscles tightening. Why won't they all go away? Leave me alone?

Hannah must be upstairs with her headphones on. He feels too tired to answer it himself, to find out what the world wants from him today. Perhaps it is the police, he thinks. Perhaps they have worked out the secret of my heart and given it a label. That cold and clinical word.

He can hear the letterbox flap being opened. 'It's Niall. Northy, are you there?'

He doesn't want to talk to Niall. He doesn't want to talk to anyone.

His chest expands with inhaled breath. Of what had he been thinking just now, before the doorbell rang? He is finding it hard to concentrate, as if silt in his mind has been stirred with a stick and is now swirling chaotically.

The old man at the funeral had mentioned a second trial after the war.

He thinks he knows who Anselm is now. Thinks he understands why his father never mentioned him.

III

THE PERMANENT UNDERSECRETARY DOES NOT LOOK UP WHEN he hears the knock at the door. Instead he continues chewing his gum, wincing at the ulcer that seems to be burning a hole in his stomach. There is another knock and this time a mandarin enters tentatively without waiting to be asked in.

'Something you should be aware of, Sir Niall: the *Guardian* are running a story tomorrow about Friedrich Walser, the German financier. They've been trying to reach you for a comment.'

He has the PUS's attention now.

'Why me?'

'Your name has come up on Wikileaks. I don't know the details.'

'Bad?'

'I didn't get the impression that it was good.'

'Can we take out an injunction?'

'Too late. The Twitter monkeys are all over it.'

Niall's hair has flopped over his forehead, and he now presses it back using the tips of his fingers, his hand as stiff as that of a tailor's dummy. 'Where is the Foreign Secretary?'

'Out of reach until later.'

'Thank you. Did the *Guardian* leave a number?'

The mandarin hands over a Post-it note.

When the door closes, Niall remains motionless as he weighs his options. Plausible deniability? Damage limitation? After a minute, the movement-sensitive, energy-saving light above his head clicks off. A further minute passes as he sits in the gloom, then the phone rings several times before he reaches for it, and the recessed ceiling lights come back on.

The caller has hung up. Niall pushes back his chair and walks over to a filing cabinet, taps in a security code and removes a slim dossier marked 'confidential'.

It contains his own handwritten minutes of a one-on-one meeting he had held with Walser in this very building. They are more contemporaneous notes than minutes. At Walser's request, there had been no one else present, no secretaries, no civil servants. Walser had said that day that he knew about Niall's friendship with Edward. He had heard from a reliable contact of his at Al Jazeera that the group behind the kidnap had issued a ransom demand of three million dollars and provided 'proof of life'. Walser knew the British government couldn't be seen to pay it, but there was nothing stopping him paying it, he said. Indeed he was prepared to go to Waziristan – if it was true that that was where the group was based – to oversee the transaction personally.

To this day, Niall wonders why he declined Walser's offer. After all, he had been right. Officially, the Foreign Office could not condone the payment of ransoms.

Unofficially, it condoned them all the time, so long as the hostage's family raised the money.

Niall turns to the only other sheet in the dossier, a handwritten letter from Walser dated shortly after Edward's release. 'I'm glad our mutual friend is back safely,' it reads. 'Please make no mention of our discussions. Yours, FW.'

Niall stares at the letter with his head cocked and asks himself why he had taken the credit for Walser's good deed. He considers his options again, more calmly this time. It might be possible to argue that he took 'ownership' of this issue in order to set a precedent for future FCO negotiations with the Taliban. Or he could say he did it to preserve Walser's anonymity. Yes, that might work better. Walser couldn't risk being seen as a go-between, or a Taliban sympathizer, especially as he was a Muslim convert.

For now though . . . Niall purses his lips as he holds the letter over the shredder. He turns it on and watches almost with curiosity as his hand feeds the paper in, followed by the minutes. After watching them disappear he returns to his desk, moves his mouse to bring his computer out of sleep and does a search of the dropbox he and Walser used to leave emails for one another, in draft form only so that they didn't leave an electronic trail once sent. When a dozen come up with the letters FW in the subject field, he highlights them all and presses the delete button.

He now takes a sheet of Foreign Office headed notepaper and hand-writes a letter of resignation. If he times things well, the Foreign Secretary won't accept it.

He seals the letter and places it in a drawer on top of a black folio-sized notebook. Edward's memoir. He takes it out and, as he smooths his hand over its cover, he curses himself for having worried needlessly about its contents. Perhaps it is not too late to slip it back where he found it, in Edward's bathroom.

He now stares in an unfocused way at his 'me wall' – framed photographs of himself shaking hands with foreign dignitaries including the Dalai Lama, Nelson Mandela and Hillary Clinton. The phone rings again.

'Hi, it's Martin Cullen from the *Guardian*. You helped set up my interview with Edward Northcote.'

'Oh yes, hi, did you get what you needed?'

'Yes, that's all subbed and ready to go to press. I was ringing about another story I'm working on. Are you aware that your name has come up on the Wikileaks website?'

Niall feels his stomach knotting. Remains silent.

'According to US diplomatic cables, the CIA were listening in on your negotiations with the Taliban. It seems you knew Edward Northcote was alive and being held hostage as far back as 2006, which was when a ransom was first demanded . . .'

'We absolutely did not know he was alive at that time. We had no proof. None whatsoever.'

'But you were given proof in 2011, when the kidnappers sent you a video in response to your official declaration that he was dead . . . And that was when Friedrich Walser approached you and offered to pay the ransom anonymously.'

Niall's throat has gone dry.

507

'And you turned him down.'

'It is the policy of the British government . . .' Niall coughs. His voice is as thin as a reed. 'It is the policy of the British government never to pay ransom money to kidnappers.'

'When Mr Walser threatened to go public about your unwillingness to save Mr Northcote you relented and paid the ransom with his money, through an offshore account he had set up.'

Niall swallows.

'You then took the credit for Mr Northcote's release and, as a reward, you were given the job of Permanent Undersecretary . . . Do you have any comment?'

Niall puts the phone down and stares at it until the light in the ceiling goes off again. As he opens the drawer once more, the light comes back on and he reaches for a brandy bottle, pours himself a large glass, drinks it down in two gulps and pours a second. He presses his fingertips to the hollows of his temples, then he touches his intercom button.

'Can you cancel my appointments for the rest of the day. I'm going to see Edward Northcote. And can you ask my driver to be ready in five minutes.'

Hannah opens a bottle of Verdicchio, sniffs the cork and pours herself a glass. She then roasts some peppers under the grill. When they are blistered she takes them out and, after peeling them, slices them lengthways before adding capers, garlic and parsley. She cracks an egg on the rim of a bowl next, reaches for a second one and stops in mid-air.

The doorbell is ringing. She looks up at the kitchen clock and sighs. So much for her quiet night in, she thinks. Just her, a bottle of wine, an omelette and a box set of the second series of *The Killing*. She puts the wine back in the fridge and wipes her hands on her apron as she walks to the front door. The bell rings again. As she reaches for the latch she hesitates. Takes off the apron. Looks down at the grey-marl, cable-knit stockings she had been trying on before she started cooking. They are held up above her knees by black bows and they still have the price tag attached. Too late to change out of them now. As she reaches for the latch she holds back a sigh.

Uncle Niall.

As she looks him up and down, her mild annoyance at being disturbed turns to concern. His collar is un-buttoned, his tie loosened and a vein in his neck is standing proud, like a blue pencil under his skin. He is swaying and, even across the porch, she can smell the alcohol on his breath. There is the top of a half bottle of something sticking out of his jacket pocket. It looks empty. 'Hello, Sir Niall,' she says with friendly sarcasm in her voice. 'Have we been drinking?'

'Where's Northy?'

'Out.'

As he leans in to kiss her cheeks in greeting, she tightens.

'Did he say when he'd be home?'

'Nope.'

'I brought this back for him.' Niall hands over the black folio-sized notebook in which Edward had written the first part of his memoir. 'I was vetting it on behalf of . . .' He runs his hand through his hair as he lets himself in. 'I'm not a bad man,' he says.

As Hannah follows him into the sitting room she flicks through the notebook. 'Why do you say that?'

'I've always done what I thought was best.'

Hannah is confused. 'What's up?'

Niall turns and stares at her with eyes that are red-rimmed.

'Your dad was always better than me, you see. Always a better man. More honourable. More tolerant. He had a moral compass whereas I . . .' His face crumples and a low keening starts. 'I always loved him, you know. You believe that, don't you?'

Hannah is shocked. 'What are you talking about, Niall? What's happened? Has something happened at work?'

He turns and buries his face in his hands. 'It's all over. The game's up. They're going to have to sack me.'

'I'm sure you'll be fine, Uncle Niall, whatever this is about.'

He seems to rally a little at this. 'Thanks, Han. You've always been a good friend to me.'

'And you've always been a good friend to me.' She smiles. 'And a good godfather.'

Niall sniffs again as he turns to face her. 'Even with your hair like that, you still look just like your mother.'

She rolls her eyes. 'Wish I didn't sometimes.'

He touches her hair. 'So beautiful . . .' Niall shakes his head, trying to clear it. He then smiles his joyless, pinched smile again. His mobile pings in his pocket but he ignores it. 'Have you got anything to drink? I need a drink.'

'Sure. Wine? There's some white in the fridge.'

Niall swallows deeply and stares at her. 'Thank you,' he says. He looks to Hannah as if he is on the verge of tears.

Moments later, when she closes the fridge door with a nudge of her hip, Niall is standing behind it. She twists the cork out of the bottle that is already open, pours a glass and hands it to him. Setting the bottle down on the table she finds herself covering her chest with her forearm, as though she is naked.

Edward has been parked outside Rheinisch-Westfälische Bank for half an hour when the black Mercedes appears from the building's underground car park. He follows it to Mile End station. When it pulls over, a silver-haired man climbs out of the back seat carrying a sports bag. Edward recognizes him from the funeral. Since that day he has been trying to work out why Walser attended. He had overheard Hannah talking on the phone to someone about him and was pretty sure he had heard her say the words 'ransom payment'. His thoughts had also been returning to the Koran he had found at the château. Another jarring note.

The Mercedes drives on a few yards and parks at a pay and display. Edward parks on a double yellow. In his haste to follow Walser into the Underground, he doesn't lock his car or feed a parking meter. When he sees where Walser is heading, he buys a ticket and follows him on to the escalator, keeping his distance. At the bottom, he breaks into a half-jog. When he sees the silver-haired man step on a tube, he does the same, in the next carriage. Walser gets off at the next stop.

Seeing him heading down Whitechapel Road, Edward follows, only to lose him again. He stands outside a pub, cursing under his breath. Then he notices the sports bag he had seen earlier. The man carrying it is wearing a flowing brown cloak made of wool. On his head is a white headdress tied with a black rope-like cord. It is Walser. He must have slipped the outfit on in the pub. As he watches him enter the East London Mosque, Edward feels a sudden coldness in his gut.

'Small world.'

Edward recoils as he turns to see Mike. The driver is wearing a suit and open-neck shirt.

'Always wondered where he went. Guess I must be lacking in curiosity . . . Actually, it was you I was following. I clocked your Volvo outside RWB. Little tip: it's best to put one car between you and the car you are tailing.'

They are both now staring at a half-moon illuminated on top of one of the prayer towers. 'You didn't know he was a Muslim?' Edward asks.

'No, I knew. I just didn't know he came here. His mother is a Muslim . . . Turkish. A lot of Turks came to live in Germany after the war. They would marry anyone they could to get citizenship. From what I gather, Walser was raised a Christian in Germany then converted to Islam.'

'Hasn't he ever mentioned it?'

'You wouldn't ask that if you'd met him.'

'Why didn't he come over and introduce himself at my father's funeral?'

'He had to rush off. I'm glad we've bumped into each other today though. He was a bit concerned when you left Le Jardin in such a hurry. Wanted to know why I hadn't been to collect you.'

'There was a storm.'

'Yes, we heard all about it from François. I'm sorry if it ruined your break.'

Both men turn to look at the mosque again. 'Muslims make me nervous,' Edward says. He turns to face Mike and adds: 'I don't want you to feel you are being compromised but I think your boss is . . . I think there are things about him you need to know.'

Mike doesn't seem interested. 'Your friend Sir Niall Campbell came to ask me about him once,' he says.

Edward tries to weigh where Mike might stand on what he is about to tell him. 'I think he might be involved in . . .' But he can't find the right words. 'This Muslim thing . . . I think he might have had something to do with my kidnapping.'

Mike grins. 'You think right. He paid your ransom.'

'Who? Niall?'

'No, Walser.'

'I was told it was Niall.'

'By who?'

Edward rubs his neck. 'I need to talk to . . . How do you know that about Mr Walser? Why would he do that for me?'

'That, I think, you should ask him yourself. It's time you two met properly. Let's go and wait in the car for him to come back. He won't be long.'

'OK, excuse me a moment.' Edward takes out his

mobile and dials. When Niall's mobile goes straight to voicemail, Edward leaves a message: 'Call me. We need to talk.' He dials Niall's direct line at the Foreign Office next. 'Can I speak to Sir Niall please? . . . Edward Northcote . . . Did he say where he was going? . . . Thank you.'

As they walk back to the entrance of the Underground, Edward takes a backward glance at the mosque. Rubs his neck again.

'You OK?' Mike asks.

'Yeah. Let's go.'

They emerge from Mile End station in time to see the Volvo being taken away on the back of a Parking Services lorry. Edward is still trying to get through to the car pound when Walser, wearing his suit again and carrying his sports bag, surfaces from the Underground entrance. When he sees Edward he stops walking. After a beat, he nods in acknowledgement. Edward ends his call.

As Mike takes the bag from Walser he says: 'I'd like you to meet Edward Northcote, sir. I thought we could give him a ride home.'

Edward holds out his hand and says: 'You don't seem surprised to see me.'

Walser gives a pursed smile as they shake, covering Edward's hand with his other hand. He then holds the car door open and indicates with a deferential gesture that Edward should get in.

Forty minutes later, Edward steps out of the Mercedes, gestures goodbye and, as he stands on the pavement and watches the tail lights getting closer and closer together, tries Niall's number again. When he hears a door opening, he turns to the house and hangs up.

Niall steps out, buttoning up his jacket. When Hannah comes up behind him from the hallway he turns and gives her a hug. Edward can see her hand reaching around to rub his back. The door closes behind her.

Instead of walking away, Niall stands on the step as if confused about his location. He runs his hands down his face then rests his chin on the steeple he has formed with his fingers. His eyes are raised to the heavens like a Renaissance painting of an anguished disciple. In the yellow light cast by the sodium vapour of the street lamp, Edward can see that he has tear tracks on his cheeks. The speech he has been planning no longer seems necessary.

Niall, still unaware that he is being observed, clears his throat, straightens his shoulders and treads the path towards the road. When he sees Edward standing half in shadow he freezes. The two men regard one another for a few seconds. Niall's mouth opens and closes, a still-wet grayling on a riverbank, then he raises his hand to shield his eyes.

Edward walks past him, turns a key in the lock and enters the house. Without looking back, he shuts the door. The metallic crack of its latch lingers in the night air like the sound of glass shattering.

IV

One month later

FATHER AND DAUGHTER WATCH FROM THE FRONT DOOR AS THE estate agent levers the 'For Sale' sign out of the front lawn, carries it to his van, waves and drives away. The house has gone for the asking price, after only one week on the market, and it is time for its occupants to leave too.

They both have steaming mugs of coffee in their hands and these they now clink together. 'To a fresh start,' Edward says.

'A fresh start,' Hannah echoes. 'And no more press.'

'And no more press.'

'Might just have one last look around. Make sure we haven't left anything. What time are the cleaners coming?'

Edward checks his watch. 'They should be here in about a quarter of an hour.'

They wander from room to room in silence, turning on lightbulbs that seem naked without their shades, staring at curtainless windows, trailing their fingers over the ghost outlines that indicate where pictures have been hung. The house has an unfamiliar smell: damp and dusty. And familiar noises – the creak of the floorboard outside the spare room, the ping of the top-bathroom light switch – seem too loud and echoey today.

Each room seems to trigger a different memory: Christmas mornings, birthdays, the drunken laughter of dinner parties. But emptied of possessions it already feels as if the house is no longer their home.

The two crates that Hannah wanted to keep out of storage were delivered to her halls of residence at the Slade that morning. Edward has managed to pack the things he wants kept out into one suitcase. When they reach the master bedroom and see it on the bare floorboards, next to the pewter urn containing Frejya's ashes, Hannah says: 'Are you going to tell me why Walser paid your ransom?'

'At some point, perhaps. Not yet. There are some more details I need to establish, some information about your grandfather. I'll write it all down for you when I get to Norway, that will be the easiest thing.'

'But it's given you some closure, right?'

Edward looks down, smiles and looks up again.

'Do you know why Uncle . . .' Her mouth puckers as she hesitates. 'Why Niall tried to prevent Walser making the payment?'

'I imagine because it was Foreign Office policy.' His words lack conviction, as if his throat has constricted in an attempt to prevent them escaping.

'Really? I think it suited him to have you out of the

picture. He always, like, felt threatened by you. Always envied you. Envied your talent, your family, your wife.'

'Actually, I think it was Frejya he envied.'

'What do you mean?'

'It doesn't matter,' Edward says, turning to pick up the suitcase and end the conversation.

'When he came to the house drunk that night he said something about . . .' She looks up at the ceiling as she tries to recall exactly. 'That he always loved you.'

Edward, still with his back to her, draws in breath, holds it and then exhales slowly. 'I think he did, in his way. He told me so once, when we were students, in a drunken moment after a Varsity match. I forgot all about it, but I guess he never did.'

Hannah thinks she understands now. 'When you were posted to Norway he could forget about it, too, but as soon as you came back to London . . . Is that why he and Sally never had children?'

'That's not for . . . That's between them.'

'Now that he's resigned, do you think you can forgive him?'

'It's more a question of whether he can forgive himself.'

'Have you spoken to him?'

Edward sighs again. Shakes his head. 'Not yet.'

'He keeps ringing.'

'I know.'

Hannah drops her shoulders. A lock of hair is trembling across her pale grey eyes. 'Don't go.'

'You're better off without me.'

'I'm not.' She rubs her arms. They have had this

518

conversation before and she is no longer sure she believes the lines she has assigned to herself. 'Dad?'

'Yes.'

'How long do you think it will take to finish your memoir?'

'Not sure, six months maybe. A year.'

'I was thinking of taking Mum's ashes down to Cornwall later this month.'

'Good idea.'

'Are you sure you don't want to do it with me?'

'Sure. But I will if you want me to . . .'

Hannah pats his arm. 'No, I'll be fine. Actually, I think I need to do it on my own.'

'I understand.'

Hannah wonders if he does. She barely understands herself. It is something to do with the anger she feels about being neglected throughout her teens, about being abandoned in the middle of her A levels. Mother and daughter need to make their peace.

As Hannah gathers up the urn, Edward picks up his suitcase and they walk down the stairs together.

'I'll wait to let the cleaners in,' Edward says as he opens the front door. 'I've got a cab coming soon. Are you sure I can't give you a lift to your halls?'

'Thanks, but I fancy a walk to the tube. Clear my head.'

'I couldn't be more proud of you, you know. You are going to be a great artist one day.'

Her cheeks colour a little. 'Thanks.'

'Bye then. I'll ring when I get to Oslo.'

'Bye. Oh, almost forgot.' Hannah sets down the urn

on the pavement and rummages in her bag. 'Here, take this. Don't open it until I've gone.'

Edward takes the rolled-up piece of paper and slips it in his pocket as they hug goodbye. Something about the tension with which he clings to her, a rigidity of his muscles, gives her the impression that he is pushing her away as part of the same gesture.

As they step back from each other, she crouches down to pick up the urn. Straightening her back again, she hears her father mumble something and, raising her head to listen as he lowers his, their lips touch by accident. It is so glancing a contact, Hannah almost doubts it even happened. Only her father's embarrassment as he backs away again confirms that it did.

As she walks down the street she can feel his eyes on her, and she half expects him to call her back. When she reaches the end, she turns and sees he is unrolling the paper. She wonders if he will recognize his own writing. Wonders if he will remember giving her the same piece of paper on the day he went to Afghanistan. Three short words.

V

London. Winter 1956

AFTER SHAKING HANDS WITH THE WARDEN AND STEPPING OVER the lip of the door into the outside world, Charles stands for a moment, feeling disorientated. Tucked under his arm is a cardboard box tied with white string. The 'civilian' clothes he is wearing are now, after a year of prison food, baggy on him. His collar, loose by two inches, is nipped together by his tie.

He turns and leans back as he takes in the Gothic gatehouse towering behind him. The sky above it is slate grey and seems to be bulging petulantly. As he contemplates it, the first drops of rain arrive and he turns up the collar of his overcoat. He feels beaten by his year in prison. It has robbed him of his humour and optimism. But he nevertheless feels relieved to be on his way back to Anselm, his home.

When the door closes behind him and its bolt clatters into place, he regains his focus and notices the short, hoary-haired man who is standing under an umbrella next to a Humber Pullman with white wall tyres. He raises a gloved hand.

As Charles walks towards the man, he transfers the box to his left arm and holds out his right. 'Funf,' he says as they shake. 'Merry Syphilis.'

'And a Happy Gonorrhoea.'

Eric Secrest holds the door open as Charles gets in and acknowledges a man wearing a trilby and scarf sitting rigidly in a shadowed area on the far side. He has pouchy cheeks and an unused smile. Eric pumps his umbrella a couple of times before getting into the driver's seat.

'This is Mr Barnard,' Eric says over his shoulder as he starts the engine. 'The gentleman I mentioned in my letter.'

'How do you do?' Barnard says.

The two shake.

'Thank you for the lift,' Charles says to Eric.

'You are heading to Germany, I gather,' Barnard says. 'Yes.'

'Would you like us to stop off at your house en route?' Eric asks as he flicks a switch on the dashboard and pulls out into the traffic. As the indicating finger slides out from the side of the car, he adds, 'To collect anything?'

'No. I don't have a home in London any more.'

Barnard takes out a pipe and begins filling its bowl from a pouch. 'I'm sorry,' he says to Charles, tamping the tobacco with his thumb. 'Do you mind if I . . . ?' He holds up the pipe.

Charles is examining the walnut fillets in the door panel. 'Not at all.'

Barnard strikes a match and sucks wetly on the pipe a couple of times before winding down the window and throwing the spent match on to the road. 'I don't know how much Dr Secrest has told you already,' he says, blowing smoke out of the corner of his mouth, 'but I'm part of a committee investigating the current law on homosexuality. We are being chaired by Sir John Wolfenden.'

'Yes, I've read about it.'

'We've been hearing evidence from a range of men who have been affected by the law as it stands and your case was of particular interest to us.' He takes a small notebook and pen from his pocket. 'May I?'

Charles notices the crisp white handkerchief in the man's breast pocket. Realizes he hasn't seen anything so elegant in a year. 'By all means,' he says.

'May I enquire why you are going to Germany?'

'Because that is where Anselm lives.'

Barnard makes a note of this. 'Anselm was your . . . ?'

'Is.'

'And he was the one you were living with in Chelsea at the time of your arrest?'

'Yes, him and Inis.'

'There were three of you sharing the house?'

'Yes. When I was arrested, Anselm was deported to Germany. Inis followed him a few weeks later, after she had had the baby. She was pregnant, you see. Anselm was the father.'

'I see. And you, meanwhile, were charged with gross indecency and given a custodial sentence?'

Charles catches Eric's eye. 'Yes. One year. That's the

maximum sentence allowable for my . . . crime. I was given the choice of that or a course of hormonal treatment.' He runs his hand over the cardboard box between them on the seat. 'Designed to reduce the libido. Chemical castration, in other words.'

Barnard looks up from the notes he is making. 'Why did you not take that option?'

'Didn't exactly work for Alan Turing, did it?'

'Yes, an unfortunate business, that.' Barnard taps his notebook. 'Tell me about Inis. Did you have a relationship with her as well?'

'Yes.'

'When did you discover you were bisexual?'

'When I was twenty-four.'

'So before that time you assumed you were heterosexual?'

'No, I assumed I was homosexual.'

'Are you planning on sharing a house with Anselm again in Germany?'

'No. We have learned our lesson. I will take an apartment nearby. Anselm and Inis are living together as man and wife.'

'But they are not married?'

'No. And can you make sure not to identify them by name in your report, please?'

'Of course. May I ask, were you blackmailed in any way, before your arrest, I mean?'

Charles ponders this. 'No.'

'Do you know who reported you to the police? What their motive was?'

'No.' Pause. 'Perhaps they were jealous of what we had. Me, Anselm and Inis.'

'What did you have?'

'We loved each other, all three of us. It was love.'

When Charles sees a sign for the airport, visible briefly between beats of the windscreen wiper, he smiles. Barnard notices this, tightens his lips and nods.

VI

Cornwall. Present day. Late autumn

FOR A FEW MINUTES AFTER TURNING OFF THE VOLVO'S ENGINE, Hannah stares at the rainwater on the windscreen. She opens the window and a salty gulp of Cornish air jolts her from her reverie. Mingled with it is the resinous smell of bladderwrack, an evocation of childhood summers. She turns the key enough for the windscreen wipers to come back on and the rubber drags and squeaks in protest. She can make out the misty sealine now and the narrow, slate inlet where the cliffs fall sharply into the tide. It is nearly dawn.

There is a pile of newspaper cuttings on the seat next to her, dozens of items she has collected over the years – from her father's kidnapping to Niall's resignation. Her therapist has suggested she put them in chronological order, maybe even make a scrapbook of them as a way of coming to terms with events. But when she looks at them now she sees only layers of sediment at the bottom of a clear river, layers it would be best not to disturb.

Instead she picks up a copy of the *Guardian* which she bought a few hours earlier from a service station near Exeter, turns to page 17 and re-reads the 'correction and apology' printed there, complete with the misspelling of the victim's name.

On 17 September this year we reported that Frederick Walser, an investment banker, was the son of a senior SS officer who had been the commandant of a concentration camp during the Second World War. We now accept that this damaging allegation is unfounded and should not have been published. We apologise unreservedly for any distress and embarrassment our report may have caused Mr Walser and his family. A significant donation has been made to a charity of his choice.

She feels partly to blame for the mistake, having told Martin Cullen about the Nazi memorabilia she found in Walser's château in France. When she texted him to apologize he texted back to say that it was OK, but that she must make amends by being his date for the *Guardian* Christmas party. She agreed. That is three weeks away. For now she carefully tears the apology out and, placing it on top of the cuttings pile, tries to work out its significance. It seems connected in some way to the letter that arrived from Norway the previous day, but she has yet to figure out how. She retrieves this from her rucksack, which is jammed in the footwell on the passenger side, and, though she has already memorized it, reads the final page of it again.

As you know, I was born in Aachen in 1964 and then returned to London with my father a year later, when my mother died. What I didn't know until quite recently is that he hadn't been living in the same house as my mother in Germany. She had been living with a German, Anselm, who was the father of another child of hers. It's complicated, but the three of them were in some kind of relationship. Anselm was a convicted homosexual and, fearing arrest by the German authorities after my mother died, he and my father decided it would be best if they went their separate ways. A few months after my father returned to London with me, Anselm came to an arrangement with a Turkish woman seeking German citizenship. A marriage of convenience.

I'm telling you all this because I think it important that you understand. Anselm and Charles clearly loved each other, but they separated for the sake of their children. If my father had been arrested in Germany, I would have been taken into care. He sacrificed his own happiness for the sake of mine. He left Anselm out of love for me.

I hope you are closer now to understanding why I have had to cut myself off from you. I hope too that you will one day be able to forgive my act of surgery. I know it must be difficult for you, but it means you will have the chance of a relatively normal life. My time in Afghanistan has put that permanently out of reach for me.

It is beautiful here in the snow. And I now know that this place is as close as I will ever come to finding peace, and privacy. The cabin is like a monastery to me. I'm growing a beard! You may not believe me, but I am actually feeling sane again here.

Sometimes we have to make sacrifices and trade-offs. I have had to trade a lesser freedom for a greater one: a life free from guilt, from moral responsibility, from choices – free from that capricious organ, the heart.

Thank you for keeping that note all these years. I sleep with it under my pillow. I meant it, by the way. And still do.
Dad

Hannah touches the letter to her lips before slipping it back into the rucksack. From the same pocket she takes out a torch, turns it on and, against a gathering breeze, pushes open the door. When she walks round the car and opens the passenger side to collect the rucksack, the newspaper cuttings spiral up, carried on a gust. She tries to grab the nearest, but the sight of them caught in the torch beam, rising like untaken souls, is strangely liberating. They belly like small white sails against the dark sky, before plunging limply and then drifting off again.

As she walks away from the car she shrugs the ruck-sack on to her back, over her cagoule. It feels lighter than it ought to, as if the things that are weighing her down are left planing and circling around the car – the newspapers, the rest of the world with its morality, with its value system, with its bourgeois judgements about what is right and what is wrong.

The short walk up the road is steep and winding and, once she reaches the crest, she catches her breath. There are no cars. Cornwall is empty. She shines her torch at the familiar sign marking the way to Doyden and notices that the silver National Trust oak leaves are the same as those worn by Nazi officers on their collars. It gives her a sense of being connected; of how the world reveals its own connections, in its own time.

She follows the muddy path through the kissing gate and has to negotiate what looks like frozen smoke, a tunnel of blackthorn that reminds her of the coils of barbed wire surrounding the concentration camp in Alsace. The castellated folly on the promontory looks lonely as it takes shape in the gloom. She can hear the cannonades of breaking waves, the ocean's roar as it thunders into the narrow sea-caves below, before rearing back against itself.

A few minutes later, at Doyden Point, she sets down the rucksack and looks out to sea, to where the first hints of dirty light are marking the horizon. She feels exhausted yet content, as if after a lifetime of running over mountains, ice fields and deserts, she has finally reached the coast and can rest. Her mother used to say that Cornwall reminded her of home, of Norway. The coastline at least. The deep fjords inhabited by trolls, creatures of shadow and darkness. Any troll who was exposed to direct sunlight would be turned to stone.

The horizon is clearly visible now, grey and baggy.

Feeling vertiginous, she gets to her knees and crawls over ground that is slithery with white lichen. The entire cliff seems to sway. To anchor herself she fixes on the barren volcanic shelves of slate. The rocks below them are black, but white with spray and foam and jets erupting through blowholes. Where it has had the chance to pool, the water seems to boil up then ebb away – black and white bubbles swirling, swelling, bulging. She sits in the hollow, draws her knees up under her chin and, as she stares at the veined sea-campion buds around her, she wills herself not to faint.

She looks up again. The clouds are black and low, heavy with rain. A gannet appears from under the ledge on which she is lying. It swoops up close to her face, riding the thermals, wings outspread, brilliant white. It continues soaring high above her before disappearing, spiralling upwards into the clouds, a sliver of rolling light between two immensities of shade.

There is a shower now, carried on a raw easterly wind. It leaves her hair wet and clinging to her cheeks, but she does not notice. Sensing the hulking cliff face below her, and knowing its scale, she closes her eyes. The patter on her cagoule seems too loud and intrusive, its rhythm too dangerous. She pulls it off over her head without unzipping it, and when her fleece comes with it she takes that off, too. She feels calmer now and, as her mind clears, she realizes what the connection is between her father and Friedrich Walser. It is as if she has had to stop thinking about it in order to find it and, now that it has come to her, it seems obvious.

As abruptly as it started, the rain stops and the clouds

scud away to reveal the first salmon-pink bruises of a new day. She clicks the torch off. The rock that juts out before her is solid, shaped by millions of years of slow collision. She walks firm-footed to its edge, takes the urn containing her mother's ashes out of the rucksack, unscrews its lid and angles it towards a humpback of land rising out of the sea.

As she begins to empty it with jolts of her wrists, she finds herself smiling. A wisp of ash is spiralling up on the breeze, impatient to escape.

VII

Norway

EDWARD'S VISIT TO FREJYA'S PARENTS IN OSLO HAD PROVED cathartic. They talked politely about Hannah at first: how she stayed in touch with them via Skype and email. Then, as the vodka shots were refilled, their feelings about their shared loss came out of the penumbral world and stood shivering in the daylight. All three started crying, tears that alternated with embarrassed laughter.

Edward had been touched by their insistence that he accept the keys, and the deeds, to their log cabin near the fjords. It had been promised to Frejya, they said, and she would have wanted it to go to him. They had also insisted that he accept as a gift their old Land Rover Discovery. As it was equipped with snow tyres, he could not deny that it was useful.

On his drive across country, as he followed the rows of spectral pine like sombre guides in the white land-scape, everything had reminded him of his time there with Frejya. From the clapboard houses painted oxblood red, to the stave churches black with pitch. And the memories had left him feeling oddly elated.

When he arrived at the cabin he found it had been stocked with the things he would need to see out the winter: fishing rods, wood-and-leather snowshoes and a hunting rifle. Frejya's parents had arranged for both the larder and the wine rack to be filled. One thing he decided he wouldn't need until the spring was a razor.

That was two weeks ago and already his beard is looking full. He strokes it now as he gazes out of the window. It is getting dark. He puts on an old matching fur coat and hat he has found in the bedroom and walks around the side of the cabin, the snow squeaking as it compacts under his boots. Here he finds the axe in its old place and, beside it, a pile of unchopped logs. As he gets to work it begins to snow again, huge discs of white fluttering to the ground, softening the world. With his breath pluming, he carries an armful of logs back indoors and stamps the snow off his boots before tipping them in the basket by the fire.

Seeing that the snow has stopped falling now, he stands in the open doorway to watch the pale green curtains of light wafting hypnotically in the night sky.

Ten minutes later, as he closes the door and takes off the coat, he senses the woods closing in around him, feels the companionship of the glacier-topped mountains and the dark lakes.

He has a prickly awareness of Frejya, as if she is filling the room with her presence – not composed of matter, molecules and shape, but part of every element.

For the past few nights it has been she, rather than

Hannah, who has haunted his dreams. She will be standing at the end of the bed, her hair tumbling down over her shoulders, and she will be saying something, but he cannot hear her words. They won't carry the short distance. When he talks to her he tries to sound as if he is not surprised that she is here with him, alive and normal. Anything out of the ordinary might frighten her away.

He places his five notebooks on the table, and separates the two he has already filled with his memories. He opens the first one, the one Niall had returned to him, and sees the photograph and the letter he slipped behind its cover for safekeeping. The photograph is of himself with Frejya and Hannah, the one he had with him all the time he was in Afghanistan, but which he had no light to see. It had been taken on a timer at Doyden Point and, as he contemplates it, he thinks he can hear once more the crickets of summer. Frejya looked beautiful that day in a backless dress, laughing as she kept her hair from her eyes. There were fleecy white clouds behind them. Dandelion and thistledown were blowing on the breeze. He had five days' holiday stubble and sunglasses pushed up on his forehead. Hannah was standing between them, as if they were her wings. She was nine years old, the age he remembered her as being in all his years of captivity, and she had dimples in the corners of her mouth as she smiled.

He props the photograph up on the desk and then picks up the letter, unfolds it and flattens it out in front of him. It is written in a Gothic script and addressed to his father, sent from Berlin in the summer of 1939 by his friend Anselm. Its once-black ink has now faded to a rust colour, and, as Edward studies it, he has a revelation about how joined together the world is – something about the way ink on the page is like blood in the veins, a living thing that is never the same from one year to the next. While blood comes out red and turns black as it ages, ink comes out black and fades to reddy brown.

The letter helps him understand what it means to be linked by blood, to his father, to his daughter, how it ties a man to a genetic fate greater than his own. What Walser had told him as he gave him a lift back to his house that day had been a revelation, too. It meant a distance he had always felt between himself and his father had finally closed.

He feels he can complete his book now, the missing passages having made themselves known to him. But it will not be a memoir written in the first person, past tense. It will be a novel, written in the third person, present tense. The form will suit his story better, its truth will be more believable, its immoralities easier to forgive. It will have two time frames, one for his father, one for him.

He pours himself a glass of milk, sits down at his desk and, as he unscrews the lid of his fountain pen, realizes that it is the final chapter he must write first. Once that is complete he will be able to navigate his way back through the narrative to the start, to that small hotel room overlooking Piccadilly.

VIII

Aachen, Germany. Summer 1966

FRIEDRICH IS READING A COMIC IN HIS BEDROOM WHEN HIS father calls up the stairs.

'Can you come down, son? Your godfather is here.'

The boy doesn't appear immediately, but waits until he has finished his page: a protest. He is sulking; his plans to go and meet his friends in the park to play football have been ruined. To rub his protest in, he is still wearing his football strip, the white and black of the German World Cup team. They may have just lost to England, but Friedrich remains loyal to them. There will be other World Cups. Also, he isn't sure what a godfather is. Some kind of priest? His parents have never taken him to church and, as far as he knows, he wasn't even baptized, so why this godfather now, when he is eleven?

'You remember Charles?' his father says in English as he appears on the stairs. 'He's all the way over from England come to see us.'

'*Guten Tag*, Friedrich,' the Englishman says, holding out a hand with a missing thumb.

537

Though Friedrich remembers him well enough, as someone who always seemed to be in the background when he was growing up, dropping in for tea, waiting in the car, passing by, he only touches the ends of his fingers, and then tentatively.

The Englishman's belly pushes out the silk scarf he wears wrapped around like a cravat. His long sideburns and collar-length hair are silvery. He seems ancient. And the skin on one side of his face looks strange and smooth. And it is a different colour. But his smile is friendly.

'*Sprechen Sie Deutsch?*' Friedrich asks suspiciously.

'*Ja*,' the Englishman says, holding his hand out and waggling it from side to side to suggest his German is shaky.

'That's OK,' Friedrich says. 'I am English learning in school. My middle name is Charles, like your name. Friedrich Charles Walser.'

The Englishman looks at the boy's father and says: 'Is that right, Anselm?'

'Yes. Friedrich Charles Walser.'

The Englishman turns back to the boy and says: 'I hear you're mad about football.'

Friedrich feels shy. His new mother appears, wearing a half-veil around her head, in the Muslim tradition. Friedrich thinks of her as his mother, but he knows she is not. His real mother died last year. She was French.

'This is my wife Shaiba,' his father says to the Englishman. 'It means woman with patience. She is from Turkey. This is Charles. He is from England. He saved my life during the war.'

'How?' Friedrich says with widening eyes, suddenly interested in the Englishman. He has vague recollections of his father having told this story before.

'I will tell you properly one day, when you are older.'

'Were you a soldier?'

'When you are older.'

'I didn't really save him,' the Englishman says. 'I merely found him.' He raises his stump. 'And in the process I lost this. What a *Dummkopf*, eh? Twenty-two years it's been gone and still it aches.'

Friedrich blinks. 'How did you lose it?'

'I was being careless.'

'My father has a wound from the war also,' Friedrich says.

The Englishman turns towards the boy's father, his eyebrows raised. The father touches the mark on his cheek left by a whip and shrugs. It looks like a duelling scar.

The Englishman shrugs back. 'Now, young Friedrich,' he says. 'I've brought some presents for you.' He points to three wrapped shapes by the door, one long, one square, one flat. 'Open the long one first.'

Friedrich tears off the paper and stares at a piece of wood, shaped like a paddle. 'What is it?' he asks.

'That's a cricket bat,' the Englishman says, laughing. 'I know you don't play cricket here but I thought you might be interested to see one.'

His father nudges him. 'What do you say, Friedrich?'

'*Danke*,' the boy says, trying to hide the disappointment in his voice. 'Thank you.' He opens the flat present next.

'And that's the new LP by the Beatles,' the Englishman says. 'It's called *Revolver*. Do you like the Beatles?'

'They're OK.' Friedrich studies the cover, a strange swirling ink drawing of John, Paul, George and Ringo. '*Danke*.' He now takes the box shape, tears off the wrapping paper and, as he holds it up, his eyes widen again and he smiles broadly. It is a red-leather, hand-stitched football.

'A replica of the Slazenger 25 Challenge they used in the World Cup,' the Englishman says, ruffling the boy's hair. 'For what it's worth, I don't think Geoff Hurst should have been allowed that goal.'

Friedrich rips open the box, sniffs the new leathery smell and then bounces the ball noisily on the floor. 'I don't really mind that we lost to you,' Friedrich says. 'I was born in London.'

'I know you were,' the Englishman says with a grin. 'I have a son, too. His name is Edward and he was born in Germany! So you are a German born in England and Edward is an Englishman born in Germany, how about that?'

Friedrich has a clear memory of his mother holding a crying baby before she died. He was sure it had been hers because she had had a big belly for a long time, and then she hadn't. No one ever talked about it, then the baby disappeared and his new mother arrived.

'He is much younger than you,' the Englishman continues. 'Not even two yet. He is having a sleep in his pram. I will introduce you to him when he wakes up. I'm hoping he will be a footballer one day, like you.'

There is excitement in Friedrich's voice now. 'By the

time of the 1974 World Cup, I am eighteen. I am play for Germany by then.'

'Then we'd better get some practice in. Should we go and try it out? I see you have a net in your garden. I'll be Gordon Banks.'

'And I'll be Wolfgang Weber.'

The boy's father watches from the front door as they play penalties, with the Englishman in goal. After a few minutes his new mother joins him. She is holding a crying child.

'I'm afraid your son has woken up, Mr Charles,' she shouts.

Half running, half walking, the Englishman returns to the house. 'He'll be hungry. Is there somewhere I can heat his milk? I know he's a little old for it, but he still likes to have milk.'

'Me do,' Friedrich's new mother says as she hands the child to the Englishman, who then shifts his weight from side to side. The rocking motion soothes the crying and a small dimpled hand reaches to touch the scar tissue running down the Englishman's cheek.

When his new mother returns with the bottle, the Englishman hands the child to Friedrich's father, takes the bottle and tests the temperature of the milk on his wrist. He smiles as he then also hands over the bottle. His new mother goes back indoors and returns with a camera. She calls Friedrich over and ushers the two men together for a picture with their sons. Friedrich picks up his ball and stands next to the Englishman, who puts his arm around him.

Afterwards, Friedrich continues playing with the new

red ball while his father and his godfather go inside. After five minutes he follows them in and puts on his new LP. While it is playing he goes to look for the adults in the studio. The two men look old to Friedrich's eyes, with their paunches and their grey hair. They are discussing art and do not notice him standing by the door listening. The Englishman is talking about an exhibition he is working on. He mentions something called 'abstract expressionism'. In New York it is giving way to 'pop art'. Friedrich prefers the sound of pop art. His father shows the Englishman his framed painting of the German soldier on a black horse, propping it up on an easel and pointing out the signature and date.

'Anselm Walser, 1944,' the Englishman says, reading out loud. 'Who was your subject?'

'His name was Manfred. Manfred Hahn. He was the commandant of the camp. No one knows what became of him. He was a brutal man but also a cultivated one. Before the war he had been a professor of philosophy. He was good to me.'

'In what way?'

'He let me live.'

As they stand with their backs to him, studying the painting, Friedrich becomes distracted by the Beatles' singing in the other room. He looks over his shoulder. They are singing about someone called Eleanor Rigby who picks up the rice in a church where a wedding has been. When his gaze returns to the room, he sees his father's hand reach for the Englishman's.

He then shrugs and runs back outside to kick his new football against the wall.

Acknowledgements

Above all, I would like to thank Marianne Velmans, my editor at Doubleday, David Miller, my agent at Rogers, Coleridge & White, and Mary, my wife, for all their patience, encouragement and wisdom. I am also grateful to Emma Howard, Chris Lang, Gillian Stern and Suzanne Bridson for their close reading and perceptive comments, and to Ben Lyster-Binns, the British Ambassador to Uruguay, for his steer on Foreign Office protocol.

The Blasphemer

Nigel Farndale

Shortlisted for the 2010 Costa Novel Award

He had always been scared of flying. Now, the fear is real. A plane crash. The water is rising over his mouth. In his nostrils. Lungs. As Daniel gasps, he swallows; and punches at his seat-belt. Nancy, the woman he loves, is trapped in her seat. He clambers over her, pushing her face into the headrest.

It is a reflex, visceral action made without rational thought . . .

But Daniel Kennedy did it. And already we have judged him from the comfort of our own lives.

Almost a hundred years earlier, Daniel's great-grandfather goes over the top at Passchendaele. A shell explodes, and he wakes up alone and lost in the hell of no-man's-land. Where are the others? Has he been left behind?

And if he doesn't find his unit, is he a deserter?

Love; cowardice; trust; forgiveness. How will any of us behave when we are pushed to extremes?

'A great achievement . . . To take on the First World War as so very many have done and make it fresh is remarkable'
MELVYN BRAGG

'Does suspense exceptionally well, and it's a book that won't leave your fingernails intact . . . a terrifically exciting and thought-provoking must-read' JOHN HARDING, *DAILY MAIL*

'A fine novel; strange and unforgettable'
KATE SAUNDERS, *THE TIMES*